"We're here. My front door. Goodbye."

"Goodbye? J⸺ ⸺⸺ ⸺⸺ ⸺⸺ ⸺ a law-abiding citizen ⸺⸺ ⸺⸺ ⸺⸺ ⸺duled task of squirrel-h⸺⸺ ⸺⸺ ⸺dbye?"

Gwen put he⸺ ⸺⸺ ⸺⸺ ⸺⸺ up to her full five-foot⸺ ⸺⸺ ⸺⸺ said I'm sorry about the phone call. What else do you want from me?"

"Just this."

The assault was not what she expected. Instead of a hard, bruising kiss, Ransom's attack was soft, yet deliberate. He rubbed his lips against hers, ever so slightly, as he made circular motions at the nape of her neck, massaging her into submission. Before Gwen realized it, she'd opened her mouth to welcome him and Ransom instantly took full advantage. His thrusting tongue was hot and purposeful against the insides of her mouth, devouring her with a gentleness that belied his strength. He dug his hands into her hair and deepened the kiss. His other hand caressed her back, even as he outlined her lips with the tip of his tongue before plunging in again.

"Please," she said, placing a hand on his chest and putting as much distance between them as she could still wrapped in his arms. She didn't know that his desire-filled eyes mirrored her own. "I can't," she stuttered.

"Baby, you taste so good. I can only imagine . . ."

"Well, don't be imagining anything. You said a kiss was the other . . . payment . . . you wanted for my calling law enforcement and you . . . well . . . we've done that. Now if you'll excuse me, I have a busy day tomorrow."

"The kiss was just the beginning," Ransom said, undeterred by her stern manner. He liked his women feisty, and loved a challenge.

Raquel Hargrove 2010

Also by Zuri Day

Lies Lovers Tell

Body By Night

Lessons From a Younger Lover

ZURI DAY

Dafina
BOOKS

Kensington Publishing Corp.

http://www.kensingtonbooks.com

DAFINA BOOKS are published by

Kensington Publishing Corp.
119 West 40th Street
New York, NY 10018

All Kensington Titles, Imprints, and Distributed Lines are available at special quantity discounts for bulk purchases for sales promotions, premiums, fund-raising, and educational or institutional use. Special book excerpts or customized printings can also be created to fit specific needs. For details, write or phone the office of the Kensington special sales manager: Kensington Publishing Corp., 119 West 40th Street, New York, NY 10018, attn: Special Sales Department, Phone: 1-800-221-2647.

Dafina and the Dafina logo Reg. U.S. Pat. & TM Off.

ISBN-13: 978-0-7582-3871-9
ISBN-10: 0-7582-3871-1

First mass market printing: March 2010

10 9 8 7 6 5 4 3 2

Printed in the United States of America

For the little goddess . . .

Acknowledgments

This book was birthed and written while penning a chapter in my own life that spanned several states and a few countries. Many thanks to Selena James and Natasha Kern, who embraced my kinda crazy and encouraged the journey, and to Jumoke, Daniela, Claude, Grethe, Filipa, Leah, Laila, Daniel, Jesus (whose real name is Orlando, long story), Aunt Ernie, Mom and Dad Rich, Sharat, Valarie, Jody, Kai, Rolanda, Eden, Andrews, and JP, who so graciously hosted, toasted, and/or simply coasted with me during these travels. . . . *La Chaim!* Also, a very special thank you to Susie Hardaway, Yvonne Turner and Elizabeth Sanderson of Oak Hill Elementary, for your valuable input during my research for this novel.

I

There were two things Gwen Smith never thought she'd do. She never thought she'd move back to her rinky-dink hometown of Sienna, California, and she never thought she'd come back as a forty-year-old divorcée. Yet here she sat in the middle seat of a crowded plane, at the age where some said life began, trying to figure out how the boring and predictable one she'd known sixty short days ago had changed so quickly.

The first hitch in the giddyup wasn't a total surprise. Her mother's dementia had become increasingly worse following the death of Gwen's father, Harold, two years ago. Her parents had been married forty-four years. It was a tough adjustment. At the funeral, Gwen told her husband that she knew the time would come when her mother's welfare would become her responsibility. That she thought Joe would be by her side at this crucial time, and wasn't, was the fact she hadn't seen coming.

But it was true nonetheless. Joe had announced his desire to divorce and packed his bags the same evening. Two months later she was still reeling from that okeydoke. But she couldn't think about that now. Gwen had to focus on one crisis at a time, and at the moment, her mother was the priority.

"Ladies and gentlemen, the captain has turned on the seat belt sign indicating our final descent into Los Angeles. Please make sure your seat belts are securely fastened and your seats and tray tables are in their up-right and locked . . ."

Gwen stretched as well as she could between two stout men and tried to remove the crook from her neck. Still, she was grateful she'd fallen asleep. Shut-eye had been all too elusive these past few weeks, when ongoing worries and raging thoughts had kept true rest at bay. Fragments of a dream flitted across her wakened mind as they landed and she reached into the overhead bin for her carry-on luggage. Gwen didn't know if she wanted to remember it or not. Lately, her dreams had been replaced by nightmares that happened when her eyes were wide open.

"Gwen! Over here, girl! Gwen!"

Gwen smiled as a familiar voice pierced the crowd roaming the LAX Airport baggage claim area. She turned and waved so that the short, buxom woman, wearing fuchsia cutoffs and a yellow halter top straining for control, would know that she, God, and everyone within a five-mile radius had heard her.

"Gwendolyn!" Chantay exclaimed, enunciating each syllable for full effect as she reached up and hugged her childhood friend. "Girl, let me look at you!"

"You just saw me last year, Tay."

"That visit went by in a fog. You know the deal."

Gwen did, and wished she didn't. Her last time home was not a fond memory.

Chantay stepped back, put her hands on her hips, and began shaking her head so hard her waist-length braids sprayed the waiting passengers surrounding them. "What are we going to do with your rail thin behind? You couldn't find enough deep-dish pizzas to eat in Chicago? No barbeque or chicken and waffle joints to put some meat on your bones?"

Gwen took the jab good-naturedly. Her five-foot-seven, size-six body had caused her heftier friend chagrin for years. No matter that Gwen had never mastered how to show off her physique, put on makeup, or fix her hair. The fact that she could eat everything, including the kitchen sink, and still not gain a pound was a stick in Chantay's craw.

Chantay enveloped her friend in a big bear hug. "You look good, girl. A day late and a dollar short on style with that curlicue hair straight out of *A Different World,* but overall . . . you look good!"

Gwen's laugh was genuine for the first time in weeks. "You don't look half bad yourself. And opinionated as always, I see."

"Honey, if you want a feel-good moment, watch *Oprah.* I'm going to tell you the truth even if it's ugly. And speaking of the *u* word, those *Leave It To Beaver* pedal pushers—"

"Forget you, Tay! C'mon, that's my luggage coming around."

A half hour later, Gwen settled back in Chantay's Ford Explorer as they merged into highway traffic for the two-hour drive to Sienna. The air conditioner was a welcome change to the ninety-degree July heat.

"I still can't believe you're here."

"Me either."

"You know you've got to give me the full scoop. First, I never thought you'd ever get married, and if you did, you'd never, *ever* get divorced!"

"Obviously life wasn't following your script," Gwen muttered sarcastically.

"Oh, don't get your panties in a bunch, sistah, you know what I'm saying. And I'm not the only one. Who did everyone vote the least likely to, uh, get married?"

"I believe the exact description in the high school yearbook read 'would die an old maid.'"

"Well, I was trying to save you the embarrassment of quoting it verbatim but . . . who was it?"

They both knew the answer was Gwen. But rather than help make the point, Gwen answered the question with one of her own. "Who did they say would probably have ten kids?"

"Hmph. That's because those nuckas didn't know that fornicate does not equal procreate. After being stuck with raising one *accident* and another *oops* by myself, I had my tubes tied. I told the doctor who did the procedure that if a "baby I pulled out" number three showed up in my pee sample, his would be the name in the father line. So believe me, if there's a sperm bad enough to get past the Boy Scout knot he tied, then that's a baby who deserves to be born."

Gwen looked out the window, thought about Chantay's two daughters, and watched the world whirl by while Chantay pushed past seventy and flew down the surprisingly light 405 Freeway. While Chantay had often said she didn't want kids, Gwen had always looked forward to motherhood. She was still looking, but couldn't see any bassinet or baby bed because a divorce petition was blocking the view.

Chantay scanned for various stations on the radio before turning it off altogether. "Why are you making me drag the details out of you?" she whined, exasperation evident in her voice. "What happened between you and Joe?"

The name of Gwen's soon-to-be former husband elicited a frown. "You mean *Joey*?"

"Who the hell is that?"

"That's what he calls himself now."

"I call him 'bastard,' but I digress. What happened?"

Gwen sighed, sat up, and spoke truth straight out. "He met somebody else."

"You have got to be kidding. Corny-ass Joe Smith, the computer nerd who could barely pull the garter off at y'alls' wedding?"

"That would be him."

"What fool did he find to listen to his tired lines?"

"You mean besides me?"

"Girl, I didn't mean that personally. Joe has some good points. He seems to know his way around a computer better than anybody."

"That's one."

"We've got ninety minutes of driving left. I'll think of something else."

Gwen laughed, appreciative of the levity Chantay brought to a sad situation.

"So . . . who is she?"

"Her name is Mitzi, she's twenty-two and works in his office. They both like motorcycles, Miller Lite, and poker. He tattooed her name on his arm and moved into her studio apartment last month. But I don't want to talk about him right now."

"Whoa, chick! You're sure going to have to talk about him later . . . *and* her. That was way too much information to leave me hanging. But I can wait a minute, and in the meantime change the subject to somebody you can talk about . . . Adam 'oh, oh, oh, oh' Johnson!"

"Chantay, you are too silly! I haven't thought about that line since we left high school." Gwen, Chantay, and a couple other misfits used to substitute his first name in Ready for the World's hit, "Oh Sheila." Chantay would hum it as he passed in the halls and the other girls would break into hysterical laughter, making them all look like fools.

"That is the single welcome surprise I've had these past few weeks—that Adam is the principal at Sienna. Can you believe it?" Gwen said.

"No, because I never thought a brothah with that much weight in his lower head would have any brains in his upper one."

"Well, there's that, but even more the fact that he's back living in our hometown. After being such a standout at Texas A&M and going on to play for the Cowboys? I guess a lot happened to him since he was sidelined with an injury and forced to retire early."

"I can't believe his wife would agree to move back to such a podunk town. She looks too hoity-toity for Smallville, but I only saw her one time on TV," Chantay said.

"They're divorced."

"What? Girl, stop!"

"Yep, he told me that when we talked. He was nice actually, not the cocky, arrogant Adam I remember.

He wouldn't admit it, but I know he's the reason why my getting this post is, to use his words, 'in the bag.'"

"Don't give him too much credit, Gwen. You're a first-rate teacher, and it's not like our town has to beat off qualified educators with sticks."

"Maybe, but the way everything happened . . . I'm just happy to know I have a job secured, or at least I will after my interview next week. Mama has some money saved up but that's all going into her assisted living expenses. I still need to support myself, and pay half the mortgage on the condo until it's sold."

"How's Miss Lorraine doing?"

Gwen shrugged. "Mama's about the same, I guess."

"Isn't she a bit young for what the doctors say is happening to her?"

"From what I've learned, not really. The disease usually comes with aging, but can actually occur at any time, from a variety of causes. It's usually given a different name when it occurs in someone, say, under fifty-five. But whatever the title, the results are the same—a long-term decline in cognitive function."

"Just be glad she's still here," Chantay replied. "You can always hug her, whether she knows you or not."

"Oh, she recognizes everybody, and remembers more than she lets on, I'm thinking. But I hear what you're saying, Chantay, and I'm grateful."

They were silent a moment before Chantay changed the subject. "Joe's a lowlife. He could have stayed in the condo and split the rent with the fool he's sleeping with until somebody bought it. He's just an asshole."

"That would have been too much like right. But it is what it is. Don't get me re-pissed about it."

Chantay started humming "Oh Sheila." "Wouldn't

it be ironic if you moved back to town and snagged its star player after all these years? Now, we'll have to give your dated butt a makeover, but by the time I'm done with you . . . you'll move over all those other silicone-stuffed heifas in town."

"I wonder who else from our class still lives there."

"Girl, it don't even matter. Keep your eye on the prize." Chantay shot another sideways look at her friend. "Um-hmm. If it's Adam Johnson you want— trust, I can help you get him."

Gwen had thought about Adam, and what a nice balm he might be for the hurt Joe had caused her. Not that she'd get into anything serious right away. It would be months before the divorce came up on the back-logged Illinois court docket and was finalized. But since speaking to Adam, she'd fantasized a time or two about the heartthrob she remembered: tall, lanky, chocolate, strong, with bedroom eyes and a Jheri curl that brushed his shoulders. She never dreamed she'd get another chance with someone like Adam. But as she'd learned all too painfully in the past few months— life was full of surprises.

2

Ransom Noel Blake stretched six feet and three inches of caramel sweetness out on a canvas lounge chair, covered only by a loose-fitting pair of white swim trunks. His coal black hair, which unbound neared his waist, was pulled back in a loose ponytail, providing an unobstructed view of his thick, naturally arched eyebrows, Iroquoian cheekbones, tapered nose, and cupid-shaped lips. He reached up to flick an annoying insect away from his face, and his perfectly cut abdomen rippled with the movement. It was ninety-five degrees and climbing in the desert, but not only did Ransom have a high tolerance level for the sun's baking rays, he was also, quite simply, too tired to care.

But he was pleased. His firm, Blake Construction, had come in on time and under budget on their latest project. This fact was all the more satisfying because of how his half brother, Adam, had tried to thwart his bid and when that failed, to throw wrenches in their progress at every turn. But Ransom's crew was smart and their boss was smarter. When the first recess bell rang for the children of Sienna Elementary School's new school year, they'd run out and play on a brand new, state-of-the-art playground or in an equally impressive indoor gym and game center, courtesy of Ransom and company.

The melodic tone from his iPhone interrupted Ransom's musings. He reached for it lazily. "Blake."

"You're probably not expecting congratulations from me."

"Adam."

"I know I was a pain in the ass sometimes, but the job looks great."

Ransom opened his eyes and sat up in the chair. "Okay, brother, what do you want?"

Adam chuckled. "Why does it have to be like that?"

"It doesn't, but that's how it is."

Adam couldn't deny that his half brother was right. Fifteen years his junior, Ransom had attributes Adam no longer possessed, if he ever did. He'd left for college when Ransom was a toddler, and they'd never developed a close relationship. Add to that what Adam viewed as preferential treatment of Ransom by their mother, Ransom's small yet successful business and easy way with women, and Adam's competitiveness— and there was little room left for brotherly love.

"Okay, little brother, I was calling for a favor," Adam admitted.

"Uh-huh."

"I was wondering if I could handle the Porsche for a couple of days."

"What's wrong with your car?"

"Nothing. I'm just, you know, wanting to impress a certain female."

Ransom suppressed a sigh as he eased off the

lounge chair and down the steps of his backyard pool. He immersed himself to the waist before answering.

"And what are you going to do when this certain female finds out it's not your car?"

"I'm trying to fuck the girl, Ransom, not marry her!"

"I hope you're as clear about that with her as you are with me."

"Look, don't try to school me in lessons of love. I could teach an advanced study course on the subject, know what I'm sayin'?"

No, and probably neither does your ex-wife.

"Daddy, Daddy!"

Ransom looked up as his daughter ran toward him. His heart burst with joy, as it always did at the sight of his princess. "Look, man, I gotta go."

"Okay, then. But can I use the ride?"

"Sure, Adam. You can keep it until I get back from Vegas. I'm leaving in a few days and will be gone about a week."

"Perfect! Thanks, bro."

Ransom's daughter, Isis, ran to the edge of the pool. "Look, Daddy. Miss Carol bought us all bracelets. Aren't they cute, Daddy?" She showed off a colorful plastic bangle jangling on her tiny wrist.

"Beautiful, baby girl. Almost as beautiful as you."

Isis beamed, even as she covered her face. "Daddy!"

"I hope you don't mind, Ransom. They were on sale so I bought one for all the girls. Umm, that looks inviting."

Ransom looked up at his daughter's playmate's

mom, Carol Connors, and wondered if she were talking about the pool or the person in it.

"I don't have my swimsuit but if you don't mind
skinny-dipping . . ."

He had his answer. "Thanks again, Carol," he said
as he eased himself out of the water and reached for
the towel that was draped on the lounge chair. "I
really appreciate your help with Isis, especially with
me going out of town."

"It's no problem. She and Kari are like sisters."
Carol dropped her voice an octave. "Now there's an
idea."

Ransom thought Carol couldn't be more obvious
if she tattooed "available" on her forehead. But he
couldn't blame her for trying: an educated, single
mother, in a town where women outnumbered men.
A woman had to do what she had to do.

"I'll call you in a couple days when I need to drop
off Isis."

"Hey, I've got steaks if you want to fire up the—"

"Thanks, Carol, but I'm going to pass tonight. It's
been a long day and I'm beat." Ransom reached for
Isis's hand and they headed for the back door of his
three-bedroom, contemporized ranch-style home.
"I'll see you in a few days."

It was a couple hours before Ransom stretched out
again, this time across his king-sized, four-poster ma-
hogany bed. But first he'd fixed Isis a simple supper
of fish sticks, fries, and cole slaw; washed her long,
curly hair; cleaned the kitchen; put in a load of
clothes; and read her a bedtime story. Being the
single father of a rambunctious, energetic six-year-old
was hard work, but it was worth it. .

Ransom turned on his back and stared at the ceiling.

This is not how he imagined his life looking at twenty-six. He thought he'd be running the streets of LA, nursing his dreams of modeling, and living in the fast lane. But those thoughts and that life came to an abrupt halt three years ago, when Isis's mother dropped off their daughter and called a week later saying she had moved to New York. That she couldn't make it as a model with a child in tow, and at twenty-two, was too young to be a mother anyway.

Ransom had been furious. He'd flown out to New York to try and make Brea see reason. But there was no getting through to her—partly because a strapping six-foot-tall, blond-haired, blue-eyed Viking was in the way.

"He's just my roommate," she'd said.

Her roommate's eyes and protective stance had said otherwise. Ransom flew back to California and, at his father's suggestion, hired a lawyer and had papers drawn up the following month. Brea gave him full custody. That's when his life changed.

He got serious about school and, having already received an associate's degree, graduated eighteen months later with a bachelor of science degree in Construction Engineering Management from Cal State. He dropped his partying friends and moved back to the small town he felt was better suited to raising a child. Promiscuous sex was out: he loved Isis but had learned the hard way where irresponsibility could lead. A chance conversation with a teacher and mentor, the one who'd nurtured his desire to build things, had given him a place to invest some of the money he'd gotten from an automobile accident with a grocery chain semi. A year later he'd become sole owner of the then fledgling construction company.

That's how the security of his daughter's future was born, and life had been good ever since.

Ransom was a man who didn't hide or deny his sensitive side. So he didn't try and stop the tears that formed as he thought about the immense joy his daughter had brought to his life. He'd do anything in the world for the little girl in the next room. But he couldn't help thinking too, as he drifted off to sleep, that his wonderful life wouldn't be quite complete until there was a queen in the castle along with him and his princess.

3

Gwen cast a critical eye at the full-length mirror. *No matter what Chantay said, this skirt is too tight!* But she had to admit, it did give definition to her slender booty, while the suit's flared jacket added the illusion of curves to her boyish frame. As for the rest of the makeover that had taken place the previous Saturday, Gwen was pleased. She'd never plucked her brows, but liked the depth the thick yet curved arches gave her almond-shaped eyes. Having worn her hair in its naturally curly state most of her life, she felt the straightened bob that rested just beneath her shoulders was not only a welcome change that drew attention to her pouty lips, but also gave her a more sophisticated look. The hairstylist's suggestion to lighten her black tresses was also spot on: the dark auburn highlights complemented her mocha complexion, and brought out the red tones in her skin.

Gwen's eyes widened as she looked at her watch. Where had the time gone? Had she really spent forty-five minutes getting dressed, an act that usually took fifteen minutes at most? Remembering the objective, however, she forgave herself right away. She'd easily aced the online application process and Adam had assured her that because of an effort to increase minority teachers in the district, and his power of persuasion, her position was assured. Still, she wanted her education, experience, and merits to be what impressed the personnel committee at Sienna Elementary. Her mother's savings would cover expenses for the assisted living facility, but Gwen still needed to support herself. And if the conversation with Joe she had last night was any indication, she couldn't count on big bucks from the condo sale. She wanted to wait until the housing market stabilized and make a higher profit. Joe wanted to sell to the first buyer who bid. He'd made it clear that all he wanted was for their life together to be in his rearview mirror.

Gwen exited her bedroom and was taken aback at the sight of her mother sitting on the living room sofa reading a magazine. Lorraine Andrews's appearance had changed drastically in the year since Gwen had last seen her. Her hair was almost white now, and the faint lines around her eyes had deepened, joining new ones on her forehead and cheeks. She'd lost weight, which gave her a frail appearance. Once bright brown eyes were now watery and dim. She was only sixty-six, but looked older. Gwen took a deep breath, pasted a smile on her face, and walked into the room.

Lorraine looked up and smiled. "Baby, your hair looks nice. When did you do that?"

"On Saturday, Mama, remember?"

Lorraine frowned. "Was I there when you got it done?"

"No, Mama. I borrowed your car and drove into

LA. I met Chantay and she helped me with a makeover."

"How's Margaret?"

Gwen's shoulders slumped and it became harder to hold on to her happy facade. "Chantay's mother died last year, Mama. I flew home and we went to her funeral together."

Lorraine frowned slightly, placed the magazine on the seat beside her, and folded her arms. "Margaret sure loved going to bingo. Maybe I'll call her and go this weekend." She looked up as if Gwen had just walked in the room. "I like your hairstyle. Is that new?"

Gwen fought back tears as she walked over and hugged her mother. The conversation had been similar to several she'd had since arriving the past Friday afternoon: repeated questions, mention of people either dead or long since moved away, and the behavior that had scared her brother on his last visit enough for him to call and ask for her intervention. *Strongly suggested* may have been a more accurate description. Even *begged* wouldn't have been too exaggerated a verb. Both her brothers were married with children, one living in Seattle, the other in North Carolina. It made sense that Gwen was the one best able to step in and help their mother transition to another way of living.

Gwen reached for the phone, called her mother's neighbor, Mary Walker, told her she was leaving for the interview and asked that she keep an eye out for any potential wanderings of the Lorraine kind. After making sure the gas line to the stove was turned off, she felt the home safe enough to leave her mother alone.

"Here, baby, wear this." Lorraine unpinned a brightly jeweled brooch in the shape of a butterfly from her blouse and held it up to Gwen.

"It's pretty, Mama, but you know I'm not much of a sparkly jewelry wearer. I like simple stuff."

Lorraine's eyes misted over. She rose from the couch and headed toward her bedroom. "You used to like wearing my jewelry," she mumbled.

"I'll wear it, Mama," Gwen called out. She didn't bother to remind her mother that while Gwen had played dress-up with her mother's hats as a child, it was Chantay who always coveted her mom's jewelry, and to this day wore big gaudy earrings and enough bracelets and necklaces at the same time to open a pawn shop.

Lorraine turned and brought back the brooch, smiling as she pinned it to her daughter's lapel. "There, you're all set. Your hair is usually curly. I like it straight."

"Thanks, Mama."

Twenty minutes later, Gwen pulled into the neat and pristine parking lot of Sienna Elementary. She was immediately impressed with the playground, which sat to the right of the L-shaped building. Brightly colored swings moved in the breeze. Sandboxes and hopscotch imprints dotted the asphalt landscape. Several jungle gyms sat between a half basketball court on one side and soccer field on the other. A jogging track surrounded the playground, and a colorful mural of playing children painted on the school's wall lent a spirit of whimsy to the scene. *Whoever designed this area really knows children,* she thought, as she mounted the four steps to the school's front doors. If what she saw on the outside was any indication of the attention to detail on the inside, Gwen knew she'd like teaching here.

The first person she saw was a young, perky woman with fiery red hair and a bright, white smile. Joanna Roxbury, who also taught first grade, welcomed her to Sienna Elementary and pointed her toward the executive offices.

"Mr. Johnson is gonna love you," she chuckled, as she took in Gwen's stylish suit and modern haircut. "Be careful to keep your wits about you, or from what I hear, he'll talk you out of your pan—I mean . . . cast his amorous spell."

Gwen laughed. She felt she'd found her first ally at Sienna. "Oh, don't worry. Adam, rather Mr. Johnson and I, go way back. We graduated from the same class over twenty years ago."

"You're kidding! I mean, it's just that you don't look that old."

"Forty is old to you? You must be twenty-something."

"Twenty-six," Joanna replied sheepishly. "And it's not that forty is old, it's just that, well, you look my age."

Gwen cut her a sideways glance.

"Well, maybe a few years older, but midthirties, max. I hope I still look as good when I'm . . ."

"Old?" Gwen finished the sentence with a laugh.

"Boy, I sure know how to make a first impression, huh?"

"No worries. I accept what I'm sure is a compliment in the manner it was given."

"You know," Joanna whispered, moving closer to Gwen. "I bet you've got all kinds of juicy stories about the teenaged Adam Johnson. I hear he was quite a character, though no one wants to give specifics."

They reached the end of the corridor. Joanna stopped. "My classroom is this way. Hey, let's get together once your position is official. I'll be pulling for you, although seriously, your competition is slim to none." She reached inside her purse and pulled out a business card. "Here's my cell number. Call me when you get settled in. Lunch is on me." Then, with a wink and a smile, she was gone.

Gwen walked down the colorfully painted hall and made a right at the end of the corridor. She entered an office with posters covering almost every inch of wall. A white-haired lady sat behind a counter. Clearing her throat as she reached the barrier that separated guest from employee, Gwen straightened an already perfectly fitting suit coat.

"Yes, may I help you?" the elderly lady asked.

"My name is Gwen Smith. I have an appointment with Mr. Johnson."

"Ah, the first-grade teacher," the woman said as her blue eyes brightened. "My name is Mrs. Summers. Come right this way."

Gwen walked behind the counter to a short hall with doors on both sides. She stopped as her escort knocked on the first one. A familiar voice rang out from within. "Yes?"

Mrs. Summers cracked open the door and stuck her head inside. "Mr. Johnson, the first-grade teacher, uh, rather the candidate is here." Without waiting for an answer she nodded her head, extended her hand, and motioned Gwen inside.

Gwen tried to still her rapidly beating heart. It had been a long time since she'd seen Adam Johnson, the man she'd fantasized about, along with half the school's female population. She felt fifteen again, her hands clammy and throat dry. She swallowed, trying to calm the nervousness, but her feet remained planted to the floor and it wasn't until Mrs. Summers spoke that she was propelled out of immobility.

"Mrs. Smith, ahem, Gwen? Right this way?"

"Oh, yes," Gwen finally responded. "Thank you so much, Mrs. Summers."

Mrs. Summers stepped back. Gwen closed her eyes and swallowed once more before stepping through the door. She could barely contain herself as every image of the chocolate-drop jock Adam Johnson came rushing to the forefront of her mind. She placed a smile on her face, entered the lion's den . . . and saw a grizzly sitting behind the desk. In spite of her shock, she called upon every ounce of professionalism that she possessed, kept the smile in place, and approached Adam with hand outstretched.

"Aw, girl, what's with the handshake?" Adam asked as he walked over, brushed aside her hand, and enveloped her in a big hug. "We're friends from back in the day." He hugged her again, in a way that questioned propriety, and then stepped back to roam greedy eyes from head to toe before crushing her to him yet again. "You're a sight for sore eyes, girl. And better-looking than I remember!"

Gwen tried to catch her breath and process his words at the same time. Where was the fine bar of Hershey's chocolate, Adam Johnson, and who was this bowl of Jell-O pudding with the beer gut and receding hairline standing in his stead? She searched the face and found remnants of familiarity: yes, those were the same lips, and the mole was still on the right side just under his nose . . . as she'd remembered. But where was his hair? A flash of memory went back to the long, beautiful Jheri curl Adam sported in the late eighties. *And where did his waist go?* she wondered, as she discreetly scanned the huge belly that lounged between them.

She forced herself to look back into his eyes. They were the same dark brown orbs that had separated many a woman from her virginity, but the deep bags under them took away from their mysticism and therefore their magnetism. And again, Gwen wondered, *where is his hair?*

"It's, uh, it's so nice to see you, Adam," she managed finally.

"Yeah, that feeling's mutual for sure, for sure," Adam said, unapologetically undressing Gwen with his eyes. "Baby girl, you've sure changed since the days of the Sienna Spartans. I'd give you the game ball now!"

The memories of how dismissive Adam used to be of her settled the shock of his unexpected appearance. She stepped back, putting more distance between them. "Time surely changes things, huh?"

Adam's eyes narrowed a bit as he pondered whether her comment was a jab or simply an observation. He didn't want to start a fight and decided on the latter. After all, even with a few more pounds and a few less strands of hair, his was still the "rod with the longest prod" in Sienna.

"Have a seat, make yourself comfortable." Adam gestured to one of two seats sitting in front of his massive, paper-strewn desk, as he made his way behind it. He sat in a large, black leather chair and instantly assumed the position of one who held an applicant's future in his hands. He moved a few papers and picked up a folder, leaned back in his chair as he studied the contents, and occasionally glanced at Gwen to make sure she recognized his importance.

Gwen forced herself not to fidget. She knew that one, she was qualified for the job; two, she was probably only one of a handful who'd applied; and three, she was probably the only African-American. She'd done her homework, and knew that aside from three Hispanics and one Asian, there were no other minorities besides Adam on the staff at Sienna Elementary. That, along with her credentials, would have to heavily favor her getting the job. The only potential obstacle, at this point, seemed to be sitting in front of her.

"So tell me," Adam drawled, "why do you think we should hire you over all the other qualified candidate's résumés we've received in the past few months?"

Later, Gwen would congratulate herself on not rolling her eyes. She sat straighter in her chair and answered in a professional and confident voice. "I believe my credentials and references speak for themselves. I formulated lesson plans for the Chicago School District that were not only adopted by our city, but instituted in other states as well. I've received commendations each of the past four years, and have a dedication to the improvement of education within the inner cities that rivals that of Marva Collins and other groundbreakers in the educational institution. Additionally, as you know, I am a product of this town, with a personal as well as professional stake in its future success. I know what it's like to be counted out, to be considered a loser before the race begins, to wonder if big success can come out of a small town. I want to make a difference in these children's lives. And I believe I can."

"Well, well," Adam said, leaning forward in his chair and placing a chubby chin on the steeple shape of his fingers. "It looks like you've brought some other things back to Sienna from the windy city of Chicago . . . like passion." He licked his lips, so as to leave no doubt what type of passion he meant.

"It's true. I'm not the same quiet girl who graduated years ago. And I'm not that naive girl either. I'm here for two reasons: to take care of my mother and to provide an excellent educational foundation for the students of Sienna Elementary. Those are the only things I plan to focus on in the near future."

Adam chuckled. "Gwendolyn Andrews. Oops, my bad. Gwendolyn *Smith*. I can't imagine who would have been fool enough to let you go. Are you sure there's no chance for a reconciliation?" Adam asked this question as a formality; he had no plans of letting ex-anybody come between him and what he was sure was his next sexual conquest.

"My divorce plans are final," Gwen said, now wondering if telling him this part of her personal life during their phone conversation had been a mistake. "But, Adam, regardless of our shared childhood, I'd like to keep my personal life personal, and have this conversation stay focused on what matters. As I said the first time we talked about my coming here, I need this job. My mother is moving into an assisted living complex at the end of the month. And while I'm sure if push came to shove I could find a job in Lancaster, or even LA, and make the commute, that is obviously not what I'd prefer. I appreciate anything you can do to help me get hired here locally."

Adam licked his lips again. *I have her just where I want her . . . needing me.* "You know there's nothing I wouldn't do for a former classmate," he said as he rose from his seat.

"Where are you going?" Gwen asked, confused by Adam's sudden rising.

"Not where I'm going . . . where *we're* going. I'm getting ready to make those high school dreams of yours come true, girl. I'm taking you out."

4

Gwen settled into the soft leather of the fiery red Porsche 911 Carrera. His choice of cars did not surprise her—Adam had always liked living life in the fast lane. She pulled the seat belt over her midsection and brushed the straight auburn locks away from her face. Adam's middle-aged transformation had surprised her, but maybe they could be friends after all.

"Nice car," she said, once Adam had moved from opening her car door to getting in on the driver's side.

"Ah, it's no big deal."

"It suits you. You were always fast: on the field, on the courts, with the ladies. . . ."

Adam laughed as he purposely brushed his hand against Gwen's thigh while shifting into reverse. "That was a long time ago," he said as he put the car in first gear and brushed her thigh again. "I'm much more selective now."

Gwen shifted her legs away from the gear shaft and tried to relax. Even though he wasn't the fine hunk he once was, this was still *the* Adam Johnson, known for his smooth lines and sexual prowess.

More than one classmate had bragged about his powerfully thick . . . Gwen willed her thoughts away from their strayed course and struggled for safe conversation.

"This city sure has changed," she ventured.

"Yeah, the more things change, the more they stay the same."

"How's that?"

Adam shrugged. "There are new businesses and roads and whatnot. The population has doubled. But the narrow-mindedness, attitudes—there hasn't been much change there."

"You mean old Ms. Disney is still as prejudiced as she used to be?"

"Only with you girls. You know she always liked the brothahs."

Gwen shook her head. "Yeah, I still remember y'all got away with murder. And if I talked out of turn even once, it was on to the principal's office."

She became more relaxed as they reminisced about old times and shared memories, people they'd both gone to school with and events they'd experienced growing up in Sienna.

"You remember when O. J. Simpson came to our school? Talked to us about putting education first and taking pride in our community?"

Gwen laughed. "What female who was there could forget that? We didn't sleep for a week!"

"Man, he had it all—money, fame, everybody's respect—and now look where's he at. I bet he didn't imagine this chapter at the end of his life story."

Gwen shook her head sadly. "I doubt it."

"I don't feel sorry for him though."

"Why not?"

"Shoot, the man had nine lives, and used them all. A black man killed two white people and got away with it? Living large on a golf course in Florida? And *still* kept fucking up—excuse me, messing up? I'm glad they finally nabbed his ass in Vegas, and he's doing time. He deserves whatever he gets."

Gwen looked hard at Adam. It surprised her that a fellow footballer, one who'd been as goo-goo-eyed as anyone when Mr. Simpson made an appearance at their school and singled out Adam as the then star junior high player, would shift his allegiance.

"I don't think he killed Ron and Nicole," she said after a brief hesitation. "I think he knows who did it, but I don't think it was him. And as for that 'armed robbery conviction'"—Gwen made quotes in the air with her fingers—"we all know what that was about. O. J. went to prison for what happened in Brentwood, not for what supposedly went down in a Vegas hotel."

Adam grunted but remained silent. He understood the O. J. effect. It was the same one he used to have on women. It was hard for any estrogen-laden female to believe that someone who made their pussy throb could commit such a crime. That was why there were so many unreported acts of domestic violence. A big dick trumped a lot of wrongs. His bravado returned full force as he turned into the steak house parking lot.

"You really didn't have to do this," Gwen protested yet again at being taken out to lunch.

"Please, this isn't part of the interview. It's an invite from an old friend." Adam placed his large hand over her much smaller one and cast puffy bedroom eyes on her lips, yet again licking his own in anticipation of what was to come. "As far as I'm concerned, you've got the job."

An hour and a half later Gwen almost peeled out of the Sienna Elementary School parking lot as she tried to figure out how things had gotten out of hand so quickly. After almost sideswiping an older man in a blue Chevy pickup, she took a deep breath, gripped the steering wheel of her rental car, and forced herself to calm down.

The lunch had started out friendly and average: she'd ordered chopped steak with gravy and mashed potatoes, Adam a T-bone and fries. Their conversation veered from education to politics, and back to mutual people they'd known growing up. They'd enjoyed a civil ride back to the school parking lot . . . and then Adam had turned into a piranha.

"I'm very excited that you've come back home," he'd said as he opened the door for her to step out of the borrowed Porsche. He remained close as she stood, barely giving her room to breathe, let alone move.

"Uh, thanks, Adam," Gwen had replied, trying to ease her small frame through an even smaller exit.

Nothing doing. Adam pinned her against the warm metal and pressed a kiss against the plush, coral-colored lips he'd been eyeing all afternoon.

"Adam!"

"Don't worry, no one can see us from here." He stepped even closer, his pouch of a stomach pressing into Gwen's midsection and cutting off her air.

"That's not the point," she said as she angrily

pushed him away from her. When his eyes narrowed angrily, she thought of her impending job, and tried to soften her rejection of his affections.

"Look, Adam. You've always been a star with us, you know that. And I'm flattered that after all these years you find me attractive. God knows you never did before," she added under her breath. But Adam heard.

"Don't hold how stupid I was years ago against me," he whined, stepping close once again.

Gwen spun out of his embrace and put two additional feet between them. "The past is the past, Adam. And while I'm thankful that you're here and we can establish a friendship, the fact is, I'm still married. The divorce proceedings have been less than cordial, my mother is ill, and quite frankly, romance is the last thing on my mind."

She smiled and once again tried to smooth ruffled ego feathers. "Let's just be friends . . . okay? Let me get settled into this new life, have my divorce finalized, get my mother relocated, and then, maybe, I can . . . think of other things."

This time, Adam didn't try and hide his brash head-to-toe perusal of Gwen's body. "Yeah, I guess we've got all the time in the world, huh? But I'm coming after you, Gwen *Andrews*. And you know I always get what I come after."

In what was quickly becoming a nauseating habit for Gwen, Adam licked his lips for the umpteenth time before heading toward the school's side entrance. But LL Cool J he was not, and if it weren't for the fact that her job was on the line, Gwen would have made him aware of this fact and then offered him some Chapstick.

* * *

Still feeling nervous and annoyed, Gwen ran her hand through her straight, silky bob as she drove down Main Street. She reached a light and noticed a coffee shop on the opposite corner. A locally owned, Starbucks-feeling establishment without the high prices, it was one of the new businesses Adam had mentioned. Hot chocolate had always been a soother of Gwen's spirits. She was a connoisseur when it came to the cacao bean and decided to rate their services. The light turned green and minutes later, Gwen walked into the airy, aromatic establishment.

Meanwhile, Adam steamed, and hot chocolate had nothing to do with it. He knew he was no longer the handsome hunk Gwen may have expected, but he hadn't grown used to being turned down. Especially by former ugly ducklings like Gwen Andrews. How in the heck had she changed so much for the better while his looks had gone to the dogs? Twenty years ago, she would have given him her cherry for a five-minute conversation. And yet here she was telling him to hold on? This was not the turn of events he'd imagined. Heck, he'd never even given a thought to dating Gwen. The high school classmate he remembered was shy, a tad homely, and uneducated in the art of boy-girl relations. One look at her as she walked into his office and his thoughts immediately turned from classroom visits to extracurricular caresses. And she'd told him to wait? Because of a piece of paper and a sick mother? Didn't she know that nobody turned down Adam Johnson . . . for any reason?

Adam floored the gas pedal and the Porsche roared forward. He swerved between the four other cars around him and took the corner on two wheels. He knew where he could go and get both his ego and libido massaged, and reached for his cell phone to set up the visit. *Gwen probably can't crack a good nut anyway,* he thought, as he imagined her sexual ineptitude. Then he thought of being her teacher in the art of all things erotic, and his desire for her returned.

5

Ransom glanced at his watch as he turned his Jeep onto Main Street. He had a free half hour before his final meeting of the day, a potential contract with an LA developer who wanted to build a sports complex on the outskirts of the city. Ransom was excited about the meeting. If all went well he'd not only land the Vegas contract, but could network his way into LA construction projects as well.

He honked and waved as he drove, knowing almost everybody he passed. Growing up in a relatively small town could be both a blessing and a curse. The good thing was you knew everybody. The bad thing was everybody knew you. And everybody wanted to know everybody else's business. Even if they didn't know, they acted as if they did, or made something up.

He was just about to make a left at Main and Tenth Street when a tight body in a fitted navy blue suit caught his eye. The sexy stranger was going into Kristy's Coffee Shop and before Ransom knew what was happening, he'd swung from the left turn to center lane, crossed the street, and turned into the small coffee shop parking lot. He'd never been a coffee drinker, but he loved hot chocolate, and the cup of cute he'd seen switching into the small yet socially lively establishment was the kind of cup he craved. He jumped over the door of the Jeep, brushed his hands against his slim fitted jeans, and sauntered toward the door.

At the same time, Gwen was making a hasty exit. Her cell phone had rung just after she'd placed her order with the owner, Kristy McDowell. A worried Mary Walker, Gwen's mother's neighbor for the past twenty years, had first called Lorraine, and then knocked on her door, to no avail. She'd immediately called Gwen, who assured Miss Mary that she'd be there in five minutes. Then she'd dashed out of the coffee shop. . . .

And into the arms of Ransom Blake.

Gwen, who'd been looking down into her purse to fish out car keys, at first thought she'd run into a wall. But walls didn't have strong arms that enveloped her, a chest that pressed against her instantly alert nipples, or a smell like citrus and sandalwood. She looked up, blinked, and willed herself to speak. Her mouth formed an O, but nothing came out. She gulped, knowing the right thing to do would be to pull away from this black Fabio fantasy. But she could not. Was he real? Lord have mercy, was she? At a moment like this, who knew? She could have pinched herself to see if she were dreaming. That is, if she could move. Instead of retreating, she unwillingly and unconsciously leaned further into him.

Ransom took notice of a couple things before he tried to let her go. First, he noticed that the body beneath the conservative blue suit was firm yet supple.

He guessed her height at around five-seven or eight, and that the shiny hair that teased her shoulders was her own. She smelled clean, like the air after a rain shower. His manhood instantly leapt to attention, and he knew he should break the embrace before he embarrassed them both.

"I'm sorry," Gwen muttered, even as she willed her body to step back from the onyx Adonis.

"Are you all right?" Ransom countered.

"Yes," Gwen stuttered. With sheer determination, she tried to step back. And literally couldn't move. The butterfly brooch that her mother had sworn was the perfect complement to her professional ensemble was hopelessly entangled in the fabric of Ransom's tank top. "Oh, no. I'm sorry. I think I'm stuck."

"Well, now. Isn't this my lucky day?"

Gwen looked up into eyes as dark as coal, framed by lashes that seemed to reach the tips of his perfectly shaped brows. She dropped her gaze a couple inches and took in a tapered nose, flaring slightly with . . . desire? An inch or so more and a mouth that said "kiss me . . . now." Unlike earlier with Adam, Gwen wanted this man to lick his lips. Heck, *she* wanted to lick them! Gwen closed her eyes before she made a complete fool of herself and focused on the brooch with renewed determination.

"Wait a minute, baby, you're going to tear my top off me if you keep that up," Ransom said, his voice tinged with laughter. "Of course, I could think of worse fates for this old rag." His voice lowered and softened. "And believe me, someone who looks and smells as good as you don't have to tear nothing. I'll gladly come out of anything you want me to."

Gwen's breath caught in her throat. This man

whose name she did not know had her wet and trembling before God and everybody, on Main Street, in broad daylight, in the heart of their small town! But even as he aroused her, he relaxed her. He delivered an obvious line in a way that didn't seem pretentious. It felt, well, she thought it was cute.

"I'm sorry," she said, still trying to untangle a golden wing from his red nylon. "I wasn't looking where I was going. . . ." Despite her resolve to remain calm, she was ready to either snatch her brooch out of this man's material or throw his body into the backseat of her car and then herself on top of him!

"The way I see it," Ransom said calmly as he worked to undo the brooch from his shirt, "fate has dealt us a telling hand. Maybe since we're *stuck on each other,* we should go out on a date."

Gwen knew the man had just said something, but she was having trouble getting her mind to connect with her mouth. She had the almost irresistible urge to run her fingers through his long, silky hair. Just as her legs began to tremble and her hand reached for a strand, Ransom untangled the last piece of mesh from the butterfly.

"I always did like butterflies," he said as he straightened the lapel of Gwen's summer suit. "Now they hold even more meaning."

It was Gwen's turn to lick suddenly dry lips. She realized she could stare at this man for hours and listen to him all day. Then she remembered Mrs. Walker's phone call, and her mother.

"I've got to go," she snapped as she stepped around Ransom and ran to her car.

Intrigued, Ransom stared after her, eager to find out more about this obvious newcomer to the town of

Sienna. She had class and poise, something rare in the females he encountered around town. For some inexplicable reason, Ransom felt driven to make sure they keep the date he'd suggested in a lighthearted fashion. It wasn't until he entered the coffee shop that he recognized the problem in making that happen: he didn't know her name.

Adam sat at the corner of Tenth and Main—pissed. The same woman who had pushed him off her and hid under the cover of her marital status was practically mauling his half brother in broad daylight. She looked anything but unavailable as she held on to his red mesh top and gazed up into Ransom's eyes while his brother brazenly palmed her breasts. They'd stayed cuddled up the entire time it took the light to change, finally breaking apart as he made a left-hand turn toward the highway. But ten minutes later, as he pulled into the parking lot of the old yet stylish apartment turned condominium complex, his mind wasn't on the sex he felt sure awaited him just inside Joanna Roxbury's place. It was on Gwen Andrews Smith, the fake-ass bitch who'd tried to play hard to get. Well, he was hard all right. And he knew at that moment he wouldn't be satisfied until he'd shared that hardness with a certain former classmate.

6

Gwen emerged from the hot shower somewhat calmer than when she'd stepped under the water spray. She'd donned a shower cap, but tendrils of hair that had escaped now spiraled around the nape of her neck in their natural curled state. Eyeing herself critically in the mirror, she tried to tame her wayward locks with hard pulls of a brush, then swept her hair back in a ponytail, put on a worn cotton robe with fuzzy slippers, and exited the bathroom.

Although she'd just done so before going into the bathroom, she opened the door to her mother's bedroom and checked on her again. Lorraine was sleeping peacefully on her back, the hint of a smile on her face. Gwen watched the rise and fall of her mother's chest a moment, then backed out of the room.

She walked into the kitchen, put on water for tea, and washed the few dinner dishes that remained in the sink. Just as she was spooning honey into her cup of chamomile bliss, her cell phone rang.

"Okay," Chantay said without hello. "We're going to have to get one thing straight, because you've obviously got it twisted. I am the one you call with the play-by-play. You should have been on the phone to me as soon as you left Adam's office!"

"Hey, Chantay."

"Hey? Is that all? Did you get my message?"

"I did, but I've been a bit preoccupied. Mama walked off this afternoon while I was at the interview. She's okay. We found her a couple blocks over, talking to Ms. Disney's neighbor. He was just about to bring her home when Miss Mary and I turned the corner."

"Good Lord, Gwen," Chantay said, her voice changing quickly from pseudochagrin to true compassion. "You must have been worried sick."

"I was, still am. At times Mama is her old self, you know? Talking, laughing, cooking like she used to. But then in the next moment she snaps, and begins asking the same questions over and over, and leaving burners on under pots of already cooked food."

"You're still making sure the gas line to the stove is off when you leave, right?"

"Yes, and she's none too happy. Thinks I'm trying to run her life. I'm just trying to keep her from burning it up! If it wasn't for the fact that Robert was here last time . . ." Gwen stopped short of finishing the sentence. She didn't even want to think about what might have happened if her brother had not been visiting when Lorraine left a pot of greens boiling on high and had then gone to her room, closed the door, and fallen asleep.

"Good thing Robert forgot his cell phone and had to come back for it," Gwen continued. "Otherwise they would have been gone to the airport and . . . it's just a good thing he came back, that's all."

"I still don't understand why I'm not your sister-in-law. You know I should be raising Robert's kids right now, instead of Mike's and Tashon's."

"Uh, if I remember correctly it was you who dumped my brother for Mike, or are we having selective memory and rewriting history now?"

Chantay sighed audibly. "I cannot tell a lie. I don't know what I was thinking that night when I let Mike take me for a ride in his shiny new Mustang. And we all know the end to that run around the block. I came back with more than a hickey on my neck."

What Chantay had come back with was delivered nine months later, her daughter who shared the name of their town, Sienna. Two years younger than Chantay, who was a year older than Gwen, Robert was devastated when he found out the love of his teenage life was pregnant. She'd been his first.

"Too bad I didn't know then what I know now," Chantay murmured, in a conversation they'd had more than once. "Mike took half the girls in school for a ride *in* his Mustang and *on* his joystick. He even cheated on me while I was pregnant with Sienna. You know that's why we eventually split up: three people in the bed all the time is a crowd, even if the dick is good. Dang, and what is Robert now?"

"CFO of Automated Technologies," Gwen responded. "He deserved the promotion after hanging with the ups and downs of that company for the past eight years."

"And he's been married to his wife a long time, huh? I bet he's tired of tapping that familiar territory. Wonder if there's any chance—"

"Don't even start with that nonsense," Gwen said,

cutting Chantay off. "Denise is a good woman to Robert, mother to their son, and she's family."

"Hell, I'm family. I've been in your family longer than her!"

"Yeah but she's *family* family, as in with a ring, a license, and a vow. Besides, you know how faithful Robert was with you, how deep he falls when he loves someone. He is still in love with his wife."

"Oh, who asked you," Chantay huffed. Both women were silent for a moment, thinking about *woulda, coulda,* and *shoulda.*

"So . . . since I'm not going to get Robert, are you going to get Adam? How was the closed door meeting?" Chantay let her voice provide the correct inference to her question.

"Not as you or I had imagined," Gwen answered, glad to change the subject. Chantay could be stubborn when she wanted to and Gwen didn't want any shake-ups to her brother's happy home. "First of all, Adam oh, *oh,* has turned into Adam, oh *no!*"

"What do you mean by that?"

"How can I put this nicely? Our firm piece of Hershey's chocolate has morphed into a Klondike bar."

7

The jazz music streaming from the radio sitting on Mama Lorraine's kitchen counter provided the soothing atmosphere Gwen needed. She smiled as she moved her body to the rhythm and put up groceries. Since arriving in Sienna, her schedule had been hectic. But she'd gotten a lot done. In just over a week, she'd bought a car to replace the gas guzzler she'd sold before leaving Chicago, checked out several assisted living facilities, and with the help of her mother, had narrowed the choices down to two. And the biggest and best news? She'd received and accepted the official offer to teach at Sienna Elementary.

Orientation was a week away, so the faster she got her mother settled in and adapting to her new living arrangements, the better. She didn't want to leave Lorraine alone all day. Even with Miss Mary nearby, she couldn't depend on her mother's neighbor to be responsible for watching Lorraine's every move. It pained her to think of her mother anywhere but in the home she'd shared with Harold for the past thirty years, but at the end of the day, the only thing that remained constant . . . was change.

As if thinking about Mary Walker conjured her up, the doorbell rang, followed by Mary's familiar "'lo, Lo": *'lo* short for hello, and *Lo,* the nickname she gave Gwen's mother when they'd met decades earlier.

Gwen walked over and opened the door. "Come on in, Miss Mary. Mama's in the bathroom." She continued talking as Mary followed her into the kitchen with a covered casserole dish. "I see you've been cooking again. What do you have that smells so good?"

"Oh, just a spaghetti casserole I whipped up. You know I can never cook just for myself. Thought I'd come and share it with you and Lo."

"Well, that's sure nice of you, Mary," Lorraine said as she rounded the corner. "It seems like I can never get this stove to work since Gwen's been home. I need to have the man come out and fix it."

Gwen and Mary exchanged a knowing look. "I'm sure everything's working just fine," Mary said. "You just need somebody here when you're cooking."

Lorraine's face contorted into an uncharacteristic scowl. "I'm plenty grown, Mary Walker, and been cooking since I was ten years old. I know my way around a kitchen and don't need nobody to help me cook!"

"Mama, why don't you and Miss Mary visit while I make a salad?" Gwen underscored her suggestion by gently placing her arm around her mother's shoulders as she walked her toward the living room sofa. "And if you want, I'll make a nice pitcher of your favorite lemonade."

Fortunately, the rest of Mary's visit went smoothly. It was one of Lorraine's good days, and she lucidly chatted about Gwen's childhood in Sienna, Mary's daughter who lived in Phoenix, and the new boyfriend Mary was considering for a live-in love interest.

"He's a nice enough man, and these days it's dangerous for a woman to live alone," Mary responded when asked why she'd consider "shacking up," the term Lorraine had used to describe her friend's plan.

"But hasn't it always been pretty quiet in Sienna? Other than a few teenaged pranks, vandalism, broken windows, a stolen car here or there?"

"Gwen, things have changed, even in this small town. Ever since the drugs and gangs sprung up in Los Angeles, our little piece of heaven on earth hasn't been the same. You know Viola's boy, Thomas?"

"No."

"Oh, that's right, you were gone by the time he came along. He's probably fifteen, twenty years younger than you. Well, anyway, he was arrested for robbing Ms. Disney's house, got caught as he tried to climb back out her dining room window. And she was right there the whole time, sleeping on the couch!"

"Ms. Disney?" Gwen was incredulous. This dedicated educator had taught at least three generations in Sienna. Her retirement after fifty years was the opening at Sienna Elementary that created the vacancy Gwen now filled. How anyone could lift a finger to hurt one of the town's treasures was beyond her. In fact, how anyone could think of taking advantage of an old person filled her with disgust. At times like these, she felt older than her forty years, lightyears removed from the twenty-something crowd this Thomas fit into. She wasn't much into hip-hop, still preferred a telephone call to a text message, and couldn't understand why men wanted to walk around showing their drawers.

"Is he in jail?"

"Yeah, they arrested him," her mother answered. "But there's plenty more where he came from. Driving down the street with music so loud it'll wake the dead, walking around in the middle of the day when they should be punching somebody's time clock. A man don't work, he'll steal. That's what the scriptures say."

"Let me get on across the way before it gets dark," Mary said once they finished eating. All the conversation about thugs and drugs and crimes being committed had her understandably squeamish.

"I'll walk with you if you'd like," Gwen offered.

"Oh, no, I wouldn't think of it," Mary responded strongly. But once she got to the door, she added, "You can watch me though . . . until I get inside my door."

Mary smiled and waved as she bolted her screen door and then closed her wooden one. Gwen joined her mother on the couch where they watched a rerun of Lorraine's favorite sitcom, *Sanford and Son*. Once her mother retired for the night, Gwen washed the dinner dishes, made a cup of hot chocolate, and decided to unwind in her mother's backyard garden. Since she could remember, there were always flowers everywhere. In spite of the heat, the blooms were flourishing: lavender, gladiola, sunflowers, and sweet pea. They offered a profusion of beauty to the backyard her father had helped landscape. She thought of him as she walked across the cobblestone pathway and over to the wooden bench resting near a bird bath she remembered picking out with her dad. In those days, it was always filled with water. Now it sat silent and neglected, with leaves, weeds, and an errant piece of paper filling the bowl. The nostalgic moment made her think of her mother, and just how hard it would be for her to leave the home she'd created with Harold Andrews.

Gwen closed her eyes for a moment, basking in the warmth of the night. As had often been the case since meeting him a week ago, her mind went to the handsome stranger at the coffee shop. She'd gone back almost every day since their chance encounter a week before, and had almost convinced herself it was really because she liked Kristy's hot chocolate. Truth be told, it was to hopefully run into him again, but that hadn't happened. So she was left with her memories and imagination. She remembered the feel of his hard chest, and imagined it crushing her breasts as he lay on top of her. She remembered his strong arms, and imagined them enfolding her as they lay naked and satisfied. She remembered his mouth, and imagined it covering hers, tongue swirls and love bites. She remembered his eyes, and imagined drowning in their depths as he professed his undying love. He was tall and hard and beautiful. She imagined that his . . . well . . . all of him was as perfect as what she'd already seen.

When she'd asked Chantay about him, her usually know-everything-about-everybody friend drew a blank. At one point, she'd almost called Joanna, the fellow first-grade Sienna teacher. But she didn't feel she knew her well enough to enlist her help on a personal matter.

And just what matter is that? she asked herself. *Joe violated his wedding vows but you're still a married woman, Gwen Smith. And you've got priorities—your mother and your job. Whoever that man was, okay whoever that fine, strapping, gorgeous chunk of oh-my-goodness is, makes no difference to you . . . no difference at all!*

Draining the last of her chocolate, Gwen tried to chase away the erotic thoughts by turning to the bird bath and methodically cleaning out the debris. Soon memories of her and her dad visiting on this very bench replaced thoughts of *him*. Just when she felt the tension leaving her shoulders, a sound interrupted her peace. She started and looked around her. It had gotten dark, and while there were back porch lights on at various houses, it was hard to see past ten or so feet. After looking around for a moment, she went back to cleaning the bird bath. And then another sound, something scraping or being dragged, a creaking of wood.

Gwen strained to see into the darkness. This was Sienna, the small podunk town that was almost as clean cut and drama free as Mayberry. At least it used to be, when she was growing up. But hadn't Miss Mary said things had changed since then? Gwen's heart began to beat a little faster as she heard the distinct sound of footsteps. How could that be? The yards were all covered with grass and inlaid with either cobblestone or large rocks to make paths. This was the creaking of footsteps across wood. It didn't make sense. Gwen tried to calm herself down. "You're being silly," she said aloud.

And then she saw him. An unmistakable figure crawling on the roof of her neighbor's house. *Miss Mary!* Just as she was about to yell out, the figure disappeared into a window sitting on the roof's backside. *Her attic! He's gone inside her attic!*

Gwen sprinted inside her house and dialed 9-1-1.

8

Officers Young and Lopez approached the front of the Walker residence, while two others ran around the house to the back. Carlos Lopez placed a hand on the handle of his weapon as he cautiously approached the front porch. His partner, Young, drew his weapon and planted himself at the side of the house, with a clear shot to whoever answered his partner's knock.

Carlos silently stepped up on the porch, peering into the medium-sized picture window as he did so. The curtains were drawn, but part of the material had caught on a knickknack positioned on the television console. Carlos motioned to his partner, then cautiously stepped closer and peered inside.

There were two people sitting on the couch: an older woman and a younger man. The man leaned over and spoke to the woman, eliciting a hearty laugh. She reached for a plate of cookies and offered one to him. He objected briefly, running a hand across his midsection, before taking one.

Carlos frowned as he walked over to the door and knocked. "Mrs. Walker, this is the police. Open up."

There was a flurry of footsteps before a cautious pair of eyes appeared above the rim of a small window in the middle of the door. "It's the police," she said to her visitor. He joined her in the small foyer and soon his eyes peered down squarely at the officer at the door.

"Open up, Ransom." Carlos sighed.

Ransom assured Mrs. Walker all was well, and then opened the door.

"What's going on, man?" Ransom asked his former classmate and good friend. "Y'all fools have so little to do that you're harassing old ladies now? What, is Kristy's closed or out of donuts?"

Carlos gave an all's clear to the other officers. His partner walked to the patrol car to make a report, shaking his head as he did so.

"We got a call, ma'am," Carlos directed his comment to Mary. "One of your neighbors thought they saw a burglar on your roof."

"That was me, fool," Ransom said. "Miss Mary has squirrels getting in through a hole in the attic window. I found the culprit of the break-in, an old tennis ball. One of the kids probably threw it when Miss Mary wasn't home and the hole's been there ever since. I guess it's good the neighbors are being vigilant, though. Who called you?"

"That's confidential."

Ransom snorted.

Carlos once again directed his words to the home owner. "You have good neighbors," he said with a smile. "It's nice to know that you're all looking out for each other. You can't be too careful. And even though this was a false alarm, you might want to consider taking additional measures since you live alone. There are affordable alarm systems available, and dogs not only make good pets and companions, they're great protectors too."

"Well, I sure do appreciate it," Mary murmured shyly. Getting attention from the handsome man had her blushing like a teenager. Still fit and feisty at sixty-two, she often wondered who the old woman was staring back from her mirror, and what happened to the thirty-something she thought she'd see forever.

"Some company will be moving in soon."

"A relative or somebody?" Ransom asked.

Mary gave him the once-over. "Or somebody . . ." she answered in a that-is-none-of-your-business voice. Her sparkling eyes and pursed lips showed there'd be no further explanation.

To underscore that fact, Mary walked over to the table and picked up the aluminum tray of cookies and a stack of napkins. "For you and the other officers," she offered Carlos.

"Oh, thank you, ma'am. But we couldn't take all your sweets."

"I insist, you handsome devil. Give them to your boys out there." Mary gestured to the street where the other officers lounged between the two parked patrol cars.

"Well, thank you, ma'am. Since it appears everything is under control here, we'll be on our way."

"I appreciate your looking after me," Mary called out to the officer's retreating back.

He threw back a wave and within minutes, the cars were gone.

9

Gwen stood in the shadows of her front porch, waiting to see the perpetrator marched off in handcuffs. She'd ventured just outside her door as soon as the officers drove up, had watched two of them walk up the front sidewalk while a third had disappeared around the side of Mary's house. Muffled voices followed. Gwen couldn't make out the conversation but since there was no shouting or gunshots, she breathed a sigh of relief that the criminal would be taken away peacefully.

Gwen came to full alert as two officers walked back to their patrol car. The officers could be seen clearly under the streetlights, and while they seemed intent on doing their business, there was no sign of stress that she could pick up from their body language. Gwen couldn't believe they were being so casual at the scene of a crime.

When the third officer came away from the shrubbery laughing and holding what looked like a cookie tray, Gwen's curiosity could take no more. *Where is that low-down gangster thug? How could he have escaped?*

The police cars had barely pulled away from the curb when she came out of her hiding place and marched across the lawn.

"Miss Mary! Miss Mary?" she said as she rapped the door's knocker. "Miss Mary, it's me, Gwen."

Gwen turned to see if the police had indeed left their block. *Maybe they're circling, making sure the area is safe and the assailant isn't still lurking behind some bush.* When she heard the door open, she spun around.

"Oh, thank good . . ."

The rest of the words died on her lips as she looked up into the eyes of *goodness,* looking commanding and a bit intimidating dressed in black: fitted black T-shirt and black jeans that showcased his thick thighs and long legs. When she kept staring silently, Ransom widened his stance and crossed his arms, a slight frown crossing his brow.

"It was you, wasn't it?"

"Me . . . who . . . what?"

"Don't 'what' me. You called the police."

His look was piercing now, coal black eyes boring, it seemed, to her very core. Gwen shuddered, as if just now aware of the tremendous power he exuded. He was not only extremely handsome, even more than she remembered, but he also exuded virility, sexuality, authority. Ransom reached out, grabbed her arm and pulled her inside Mary's home. It would have been silly of her to try and resist.

"I think we have our whistle-blower, Miss Mary," Ransom said as he walked them farther into the living room. He placed his arm firmly around Gwen's shoulders while a thumb drew a lazy line up and down her bare arm.

Gwen thought she'd faint from the contact; no man before in her entire life, on television or in person, had left her as breathless as did the man beside her. She focused on Miss Mary like a lifeline, and as much as Chantay aggravated her at times, Gwen wished at this moment she could "phone a friend" to divert her attention and stop her nana from tingling. *You are not interested,* Gwen thought, then continued her silent chastisement. *You're focused on work and your mother, period, not the opposite sex!*

Ransom leaned down and whispered in her ear, "Miss Mary is talking to you."

His breath felt hot and damp against her earlobe. She tried to ease away from Ransom so she could think and talk at the same time, but he held firm.

"Uh, yes, what was that, Miss Mary?"

"I was thanking you for watching out for me, calling the police and all. Of course, it was Ransom here who climbed into my attic."

Gwen's eyes widened as she looked up. "You?"

Ransom shrugged. "Squirrels."

"In the attic," Mary patiently explained, as the bewildered look on Gwen's face continued to grow.

"There's a hole in her window. It looks like an entire family has been making their home there for quite some time."

"Ransom here . . . he's so nice. He's a businessman with his own company, you know, but still gets around to helping us older people in the community.

"Where are my manners? Do you two know each other? Gwen, as I said, this is Ransom. Ransom, this is Lo's daughter, Gwen."

"You're Miss Lorraine's daughter?" Ransom asked as he took her hand in his.

Gwen nodded and walked toward Miss Mary. This time, Ransom let her go. She had to sit before her legs betrayed her. She'd just called the cops on her Bro Fabio!

"You look a little peaked," Mary said. "Are you all right?"

"I'm fine." Gwen cleared her throat, grateful for the chair. She felt strength coming back now that there was a bit of distance between her and Ransom. "I'm fine," she repeated, before turning her attention to Ransom. "And very sorry for whatever trouble I caused. I thought you were a burglar."

"It was an honest mistake. I'm glad you thought to act first and ask questions later. That doesn't always happen these days. People are not as willing to get involved. But then"—Ransom focused those hypnotizing eyes on her again—"something tells me you're not like the other people around here."

"Miss Mary, since I know you're all right," Gwen said as she stood, "I'll be leaving." She tried to brush past Ransom. "Nice meeting you."

"Wait a minute, neighbor, not so fast. We can't let an angel such as yourself walk home alone. I was just leaving anyway, and will be glad to escort you."

Gwen laughed in a way she hoped sounded light and unaffected. "Don't be silly. I live right next door."

"Oh, let the young man walk you home," Mary encouraged. "Honey, never pass up the opportunity to have a fine man on your arm!"

Ransom had her arm again, in that firm yet gentle way that spoke volumes about who he felt was in charge.

There was a strained silence as Ransom and Gwen covered the short distance from Mary's to her mother's. As soon as she stepped on their lawn she stopped.

"Okay, I'm in my yard. Thank you."

"What? I'm going to be a jerk and leave a lady like you on the grass? Oh no, we must make sure you're safely inside."

Gwen held a rein on her temper as she hurried up the steps. Obviously this man had no idea how close to being out of control she was around him. She'd never reacted this way to a man and quite frankly, it scared her.

"We're here. My front door. Good-bye."

"Good-bye? Just like that? You call the police on a law-abiding citizen, forcing him away from his scheduled task of squirrel-hunting . . . and now it's just . . . good-bye?"

Gwen put her hands on her hips and raised up to her full five-foot-seven. "Look, I said I'm sorry about the phone call. What else do you want from me?"

"Just this."

The assault was not what she expected. Instead of a hard, bruising kiss, Ransom's attack was soft, yet deliberate. He rubbed his lips against hers, ever so slightly, as he made circular motions at the nape of her neck, massaging her into submission. Before Gwen realized it, she'd opened her mouth to welcome him and Ransom instantly took full advantage. His thrusting tongue was hot and purposeful against the insides of her mouth, devouring her with a gentleness that belied his strength. He dug his hands into her hair and deepened the kiss. His other hand caressed her back, even as he outlined her lips with the tip of his tongue before plunging in again.

He kissed with a rhythm that reminded Gwen of

lovemaking. She wanted to push him away but couldn't. She'd never, ever experienced a kiss like this before. It made her want to laugh, to cry, to pledge her undying love, to take the first thing smoking out of Sienna. In short, it made her crazy. And she knew that if she didn't stop the madness now, then later on, it would be too late.

"Please," she said, placing a hand on his chest and putting as much distance between them as she could, still wrapped in his arms. She didn't know that his desire-filled eyes mirrored her own. "I can't," she stuttered.

"Baby, you taste so good. I can only imagine . . ."

"Well, don't be imagining anything. You said a kiss was the other . . . payment . . . you wanted for my calling law enforcement and you . . . well . . . we've done that. Now if you'll excuse me, I have a busy day tomorrow."

"The kiss was just the beginning," Ransom said, undeterred by her stern manner. He liked his women feisty, and loved a challenge. "Give me your number. I'd like to take you out. I've been thinking of you since we . . . ran into each other the other day."

"No."

"No?"

"You heard me."

"Why won't you go out with me? Scared you'll seduce me on our first date?"

"You're pretty sure of yourself, aren't you?"

"No, but I'm pretty sure of us. Something is going to go down between us. I felt it from the first moment I held you in my arms . . . because of the butterfly."

Gwen was thinking of butterflies all right, the ones that kept fluttering in her stomach every time this man opened his mouth. The mouth that had kissed her so thoroughly, so . . .

"Look, I'm here to take care of my mother. And dating is out of the question."

"Why?" Ransom stepped forward.

Gwen stepped back, and fumbled for the door-knob behind her. "Because I'm . . . not interested!"

With that, she ran inside and closed the door firmly behind her.

10

It had been three days and Ransom couldn't stop thinking about her. Gwendolyn Marie Andrews, according to Kristy's Aunt Betsy, had been Adam's classmate. She'd pored over old yearbooks and found Gwen's picture. Ransom couldn't believe she was the same age as his older brother.

A little digging and he'd found out more: that she was the new first-grade teacher at his daughter's school. She'd be Isis's teacher. Since Ransom didn't plan on quitting until he'd scored at least one date with Miss Gwendolyn Andrews, he loved this little tidbit of information. It would give him legitimate, almost unlimited access to the woman who had captured his interest from the get-go. After all, he was a concerned single father, and when it came to his daughter's education, a very involved parent . . . especially now.

"I'm going to Kristy's. Anybody want anything?" Ransom's crew murmured various orders. He waved away the offers to chip in on the purchase and jumped into his Jeep. On the way, he continued to think about Gwen, his mind swirling with questions. Why is she not interested in going out? Does she think she's too old for me? Is she married? Ransom didn't know the answer to any of these questions, but he fully intended to find out.

Gwen ran a hand through the straight hair she was still getting used to. Whenever she touched her hair, she thought of that guy, Ransom, who'd shaken her to her very foundation with a simple kiss, even as he massaged the tresses at the nape of her neck.

Ransom, she thought, as she walked to her pre-owned Toyota and slid into the driver's seat. *What kind of name is that, anyway?* Gwen realized she had more questions than she did answers. Like where was he from? Gwen prided herself on staying somewhat current with the Sienna population, at least until ten years ago, the last reunion she'd attended and the time she'd married Joe and begun to gain distance from her hometown. Aside from Chantay, she didn't really have any inside connections to the goings on in her city. She definitely couldn't depend on her mother for information. Miss Mary would probably tell her everything about Ransom she wanted to know, and then promptly turn around and tell him she'd asked. One question to her about Ransom, and not only he but half the town would know about it. She needed someone closer to her own age, or at the very least, closer to what was happening in twenty-first-century Sienna.

Which is why she'd finally decided to take Joanna up on her lunch date offer. Chantay was her closest connection to Sienna, but she lived in Los Angeles,

and aside from her mother, hadn't been a real part
of the community either. She doubted the constantly
flirting Adam would appreciate an inquiry regarding
another man, and although a conversation with Mrs.
Summers had uncovered a variety of people and in-
terests they had in common, Gwen wasn't quite ready
to call a senior citizen her sistah-girl confidante.

Not that she was interested in Ransom. *I'm a married woman,* she reminded herself . . . again. Plus, he
looked like trouble waiting to happen, with those en-
chanting eyes and hair so straight it looked like a
weave. *Could it be?* No, she concluded, there's no way
a man that manly would don fake hair. No, she wasn't
interested in Ransom from a personal perspective but
from one of a concerned resident wanting to know
more about the man kind enough to track down
troublesome squirrels for Miss Mary.

Gwen eased into the coffee shop parking lot and
parked next to a Jeep that seemed more suited for
the desert than a sedate town of ten thousand. Still,
there was something about the ruggedness and
strength that struck her as thoughtful. In a world
where everything was about the bling-bling, like
Adam's sporty Porsche or Chantay's champagne
wardrobe on a beer budget, this display of restraint
was welcomed.

The twinkling of the door chimes to Kristy's Coffee
Shop welcomed Gwen into the establishment and
provided a strange comfort. Since leaving Joe, or vice
versa, and the news about her mother's deteriorating
mental state, her life had been anything but routine.
Coming here almost every day gave the place a familiar feel. In the few weeks left until the first day of

school, Gwen was determined to find the peace and predictability she once took for granted.

Gwen stepped into the cool confines and tantalizing smells of the eclectically decorated establishment. Again she noticed the homey, personal touches Kristy had used to make her business feel as if one were sitting in someone's home. Cozy, overstuffed chairs in deep mustards and burgundies vied for space with two colorfully striped love seats that anchored each wall. Two tall, worn bookcases held the latest newspapers, gossip rags, and a variety of used books. The ledge under a game table housed chess, checkers, Scrabble, and a couple decks of cards. Four round wooden table and chair sets lined the back wall. Local artists added their creative flair to the salmon-colored walls with prices for the artwork discreetly displayed on wooden blocks beneath each piece. The overhead lighting was subdued, with lamps strategically placed throughout to give the readers additional illumination if needed. The low-playing music had a world beat sound that lent an organic quality to the overall vibe.

"Hey, Gwen."

"Hey, Kristy. You know, I've been meaning to tell you that I love the decor here. Is it your design?"

"Design may be a bit lofty a description. Basically I scoured estate sales and flea markets for whatever I couldn't steal out of my parents' basement."

"You gotta appreciate a woman who can improvise."

"That's what I say. Your favorite double-Dutch chocolate today?"

"Actually, I think I'll wait to decide. I'm meeting someone."

"No problem. I'll just finish up this order. Let me know when you're ready."

As Gwen studied the menu on the wall, a man came up behind her.

"There's my butterfly. How long have you been waiting for me?"

Gwen jumped at the husky sounding voice perilously close behind her. Knowing the man behind the voice, she closed her eyes and swallowed before stepping out of his reach and turning around.

"Hi, Ransom," she said in her best professional, nonchalant, you-don't-affect-me-at-all Mrs. Smith voice.

Ransom took a step toward Gwen. Gwen took another step away from him.

"Why do you keep running from me?"

"I'm not running from you. I just like my personal space, that's all."

Ransom narrowed his eyes and nodded slowly. "Is that so?"

"Yes, that's so."

"Well, I like it too. Although I am respectful. I wouldn't want to step on your wedding vows and whatnot, try and take something that doesn't belong to me. Is that why you're unavailable, because you're married?"

Tell him, Gwen. Just say yes! But she could not. While technically true, she felt that to say this would be lying. But to say she was separated would invite questions about Joe, the last person she wanted to discuss. And while she wouldn't dare admit it, a part of her wanted very much to be available to the man in front of her. So she danced around his question.

"I didn't say I was unavailable. I said I was uninterested. There's a difference."

"So then you're gay."

"Ha! Hardly, though I'm sure you believe a woman who isn't interested in you must be gay."

"No, but I think a woman who is hiding her true feelings must have a reason."

Before Gwen could think of a sassy retort, Kristy spoke.

"Your order's ready, Ransom."

Ransom placed a credit card on the counter without taking his eyes off Gwen. "Add whatever the lady is having," he said to Kristy.

"She hasn't ordered yet."

"Add an extra twenty and tab whatever's left."

Kristy's eyes sparkled as she looked from Ransom's predatory gaze to Gwen's deer-in-headlights one. "Wow, Gwen. You've got Ransom peeling off the big bucks. You go, girl."

"That's quite all right, Kristy," Gwen replied. "I'll be glad to take care of my purchase."

Kristy looked from Gwen to Ransom.

Ransom gave Kristy an authoritative look. She simply nodded and rang up his purchase, plus twenty dollars.

He turned impatient eyes on Gwen and took another step toward her, gently grabbing her arm before she could retreat again.

"I see we're going to have to establish early on who's the boss around here," he whispered, his breath dangerously warm on her temple.

Gwen resisted the urge to shiver and instead steeled herself with resolve. "Kindly take your hand off me."

"Don't make a scene," Ransom continued in a near whisper. "Just give me your number."

"Give you my . . . what?" Gwen struggled again

to break free from Ransom's grasp. His grip was deceptively light but firm. There was no way she could move without the two customers who'd just come in knowing there was a disagreement happening. Gwen hated acting out in public but realized now might have to be one of those times. Maybe it was because she and Joe rarely had sex in their last three months together, but strange things happened when this man touched her. She lowered her voice to match his. "Please, let me go."

"Hey, Gwen!" Joanna walked to the end of the counter where Gwen and Ransom stood. She leaned in provocatively and added, "Hey, Ransom."

"What's up, Joanna?"

"You, gorgeous . . . always."

Gwen tried to ignore the stab of jealousy that whipped around her heart as soon as Joanna started flirting. Ransom was not her business; maybe if he focused on Joanna he would leave her alone.

"You sure do get around, Ransom," Joanna continued. "What do you do? Get a heads-up from city hall whenever somebody new moves in?"

"What I do is mind my own business," Ransom replied. "You would do well to do the same."

Kristy chuckled behind the counter, which drew a heated glare from Joanna.

Ransom turned and gave Gwen a hug. "I'll see you later," he vowed. And was gone.

Joanna eyed Ransom until he was out of view and then whipped around to Gwen. "How'd you meet Ransom?"

Gwen's female antennae instantly went on high alert and her plans to ask Joanna about Ransom changed in that moment.

"Here, at Kristy's."

"You guys didn't seem too casual. In fact it sounds like you're hooking up later on. If that's true, I need to warn you. There's a line a mile long ahead of you trying to tie him down."

"Don't listen to her," Kristy chimed in. For the moment, they were the only three in the shop. "Everybody tries to act like they know Ransom's business, but nobody does."

"Including you," Joanna snapped.

Gwen groaned inwardly. More and more, this lunch idea with Joanna was proving to be a bad one. She had no desire to sit down and be interrogated for an hour by an obvious busybody. When her phone rang and she saw Chantay on the caller ID, she could have kissed her friend.

"Hello?"

"Hey, girl, what's happening?"

"Yes, this is Gwen Smith."

"I know who the hell you are. What are you doing, drinking Sienna tap water and losing your mind?"

"Oh, I see. Well, I'm at lunch actually, but I could come right now."

"Who are you trying to give the heave-ho to? It better not be that fine man you keep acting like you don't like."

"Okay, I'll leave right now and get there as soon as I can."

"Okay, Oleta Adams. Railway, trailway, cross a damn desert and come see my ass!"

Gwen ended the call and crushed down a guffaw. When she saw Chantay, she would strangle her!

"Is everything okay?"

"Actually, no, Joanna. That call was regarding

something urgent. I'm sorry, but I'm going to have to take a raincheck. Kristy, can you make me a large double-Dutch to go?"

As soon as she got in the car, Gwen couldn't get her Bluetooth on fast enough. She hit Chantay on the speed dial and eased out of Kristy's parking lot. Chantay was laughing hysterically when she answered her phone.

"That wasn't funny," Gwen said, unable to contain the laughter spilling out of her own mouth. "You don't know what was going on. It could have been important. I could barely keep a straight face. Chantay, stop laughing!"

Chantay tried to stop, and spit words out between giggles. "Okay, girl. Ooh, man, I haven't laughed like that in a long time. Whew, that was good." She took a couple deep breaths to regain her composure and wiped tears away from her eyes.

"Yeah, well, I'm glad I helped you get your laugh on."

"Who was it . . . Adam?"

"No, Joanna, the first-grade teacher. And I can see right now that she's messy, and will be the last one in town who I tell my business."

Gwen relayed what had happened at Kristy's and made plans to visit her true-blue friend the following weekend.

11

Gwen faced a barrage of mixed emotions as she drove to Chantay's apartment. Where had her calm life gone? And why was the usual placid, handle-any-circumstance Gwen on a perpetual emotional roller coaster? She wanted to blame her period, but it wasn't due for another two weeks. Of course, part of it was her mother's move and another part was her divorce from Joe Smith. And as significant as these events were, it chagrined her that they weren't the main reasons for her turmoil. She hadn't seen Ransom for several days, but he was never far from her mind.

Determined not to think about him, Gwen reached for the radio knob and turned up the sound. She'd brought along her favorite CD for this very reason—so she could tune out any unwanted thoughts and keep her mood happy. The *Greatest R&B Hits of 1984* CD switched from one song to another, and Gwen tapped out a beat on the steering wheel as she sang along to a Rockwell classic. As she thought about who might be watching her, a pair of coal black eyes swam into her consciousness. *Dangit. What's the matter with me?* she thought. Gwen considered herself a self-contained, practical adult, not prone to flights of fancy or childish crushes. That she couldn't seem to shake a man who obviously thought he was God's gift was getting on her nerves. Peeved, she punched the CD track button again.

". . . and now it's solid . . . solid as a rock!"

Ashford and Simpson could normally take Gwen straight back into junior year and the Showtime skating rink with Chantay and company. But now all that thinking about something solid did was take her back into the memory of that hard chest she ran into on her first visit to Kristy's. She tried not to react, but her body wouldn't listen. A squiggly feeling fluttered inside her va-jay-jay. She squeezed her thighs together, getting angrier by the minute at the man who'd cast his spell over her and awakened a sexual hunger she hadn't known existed.

"Jesus Christ! Is there nothing that can stop me from thinking about that man?" She punched the CD button once more and New Edition had a message for her. She smoldered at first but by the time the cutesy chorus came around, she couldn't help but laugh at the answer that seemingly came from above. Yes, she definitely needed to cool it immediately. Gwen laughed out loud, pushed the repeat button, and jammed with her teenage heartthrobs until she pulled into Chantay's driveway.

Gwen stood amazed as she eyed the young woman who stood almost as tall as she. "This can't be Sharonna," she exclaimed, as a totally disinterested teenager shifted from one foot to another.

"Mama, dang. Can I go with Niecy 'nem? I've asked you twice."

"And if you ask me again the answer will definitely be no, how 'bout that? And did you say hello to Gwen? You probably don't remember her from Mama's funeral last year, but this is my best friend from high school, best friend in the world. You'd better recognize and show some respect!"

"Hi," Sharonna said, with all the enthusiasm of a meat-lover in a vegetarian restaurant.

"You're becoming an attractive young woman, Sharonna."

"Yeah, and she's grown into a hot-to-trot boy chaser too. She can't like the good ones, always has to go after the hardheads."

Gwen didn't comment, remembering how nice guys like her brother had finished last with Chantay as well.

Sharonna said nothing either, just squirmed as the question of whether she could go with her friends threatened to erupt from her mouth yet again. Knowing if she stomped off, that would surely get her an ix-nay on the all-may, she walked over to the living room and slouched down on the couch.

"Get your butt on out of here and don't make me have to come looking for you!"

The last part of Chantay's sentence was to Sharonna's back, as her daughter covered the distance between the couch and the front door in two seconds flat. Her "bye" came after the door was already closed.

"She's just like you," Gwen said, laughing.

"I know. That's what I'm afraid of," Chantay replied. "I made sure she's on the pill but still. . . ."

"She's sexually active?" Gwen tried not to be judgmental, but thought sixteen too young for intimacy.

"Girl, please, for at least a year. Be glad you don't have kids. Especially living here in LA."

"Things sure are different than when we were growing up."

"Hmph. Not too . . ."

Gwen fixed Chantay with a questioning look. "How old were you?"

Chantay sighed and walked behind the bar counter into the kitchen.

"Can I get you something? You want a glass of wine?"

"No, I never drink and drive. What else do you have?"

Chantay poured a glass of orange juice for Gwen and for herself a glass of wine. While talking, she motioned them over from the combination dining room–kitchen area to the living room, where bright sunlight streamed in through the patio doors.

"Girl, I thought you knew Mike took my cherry when I was fifteen."

Gwen was shocked. "No!"

"What, you thought Robert was the first?"

"Ooh, girl, stop. The last thing I need is a reminder that you and my brother did it."

"You always were kinda prudish, weren't you?"

"With two brothers acting like bodyguards, threatening their friends if they hurt me, what do you expect?"

"What about after we graduated, when your brothers weren't around? Joe was what, only your second or third lover? And you never talked about y'all's sex life. Must not have been that good."

"Contrary to what you believe, Chantay, sex isn't everything."

"Trust, you're just talking nonsense 'cause you haven't had that kitty petted right yet."

"Uh, I think that's a good note on which to change the subject. Are you coming with me to the shop?"

"No, my neighbor's going to redo my braids."

"I thought that was part of our hang-out time, getting our hair done," Gwen protested.

"I'll still get a mani/pedi and a facial. That's about how long it'll take for you anyways." Chantay paused and took a long swallow of merlot. "So give me the update."

"On what?"

"What else? Ransom!"

Gwen got up from the couch and peered through the patio door into the August sunshine. "Why did I ever even ask you about him?"

"Because I'm your friend and you want my advice on catching his fine ass. If he's anywhere close to the man you described . . . baby! You'd better strike while the iron is hot."

"I'm not going to strike anything. I only asked about him because he didn't look like any of the families we grew up with."

"Uh-huh."

"And I find him exasperating; he acts as if he knows I'm going to give in to his flirtations and that just makes me more determined to stay away."

"I see."

Gwen came back and flopped on the couch. "Obviously you don't. He's probably screwed half the women in town, and I never was the type who wanted to be at the end of a long list. You remember how many of our classmates used to lie and say they'd had me just because nobody had. And you know the mantra Mama drilled into me every week. Keep your panties up and your dress down, hon, else you'll end up on the—"

"Front page of the *Sienna Sun*!" Gwen and Chantay finished together.

"How old is he?"

Gwen shrugged her shoulders. "Younger than me. Now that you mention it, he's probably quite a bit younger than me. Strike two."

Chantay rolled her eyes. "For a woman married ten years, you sure sound naive. The younger they are, the better, girl. All that stamina, plus you can train 'em."

"No, Chantay, *you* can. Any child I teach will be in my first-grade class room. This is a moot conversation because of strike three—I'm still married. Have you forgotten that?"

"No, but I wish you would. Because you're not really married, just waiting to go before the judge to make your divorce final. Does it look like Joe is waiting until the divorce is official? He barely waited until the ink was dry on your petition. Oh, my bad. He didn't wait. He started screwing his little Mitzi mistress before there even was a petition."

"Are you trying to piss me off?"

"Wouldn't be the first time, won't be the last. Sure you don't want one glass of wine before we leave?"

12

Gwen turned the corner onto her block and was surprised at what she saw: Adam's Porsche parked by the curb in front of her mother's house. A slight frown formed on her face as she parked behind it. What was he doing here? Had she rebuffed him to the point where he'd gotten school administrators to rescind their job offer? Gwen needed this job, not just for the money, but for her sanity. She tried to remain calm as she opened her car door and walked up the steps, but by the time she put her key in the front door lock, she was a bundle of nerves.

"Where the hell have you been?" was the unexpected greeting that met her own incredulity in the audacity of the man before her.

"What do you mean, 'where have I been'? What are you doing in my house?" In a rare move, Gwen walked toward Ransom instead of away from him, pointing her finger at his chest.

Crossing his arms over his chest in a gesture as defiant as his wide-legged stance, Ransom glared. He looked like a gloriously adorned stallion warrior, even wearing jeans and a simple T-shirt, but Gwen fought hard against this unwanted observation. Thankfully, her anger pushed past the usual paralysis that gripped her whenever she came within feet of this man.

"You are the most conceited, bullheaded man I've ever met, and that you'd have the nerve, the balls, the unmitigated gall to come *to* my house, let alone *in* my house, uninvited, bothering my mother . . . wait. Where is my mother?"

"So, you've finally gotten around to thinking about someone besides yourself. She's at the hospital. Let's go.

"She passed out," Ransom continued as he led a bewildered Gwen to the car, opened the door, and helped her in. "I was repairing Miss Mary's back porch steps when she came running. She'd dialed nine-one-one, but was beside herself and couldn't remember what she'd done with your cell number."

Gwen said nothing, reached for her cell phone. She couldn't think, even to dial information for the hospital number. Then she realized she didn't even know which hospital her mom was in.

"Where'd they take her?"

"Bradley Memorial. We'll be there in five minutes." Her wide-eyed question asked so desperately squeezed Ransom's heart. He reached over and took her trembling hand in his. "It's going to be okay."

His voice was the soothing one he used to tell Isis her ouchies would heal. If this were Isis, he'd take his daughter in his arms, squeeze her tight, and rock her until she fell asleep. He wanted to do the same thing to the woman beside him.

"Where's Miss Mary?" Gwen's voice was timid,

strained. "I should have been here," she whispered, as tears threatened.

Guilt racked her as she thought of the fun, carefree afternoon she'd spent with Chantay. After their beauty shop appointment, they'd gone to a spa for massages and then out to eat. She'd called her mother from the restaurant and everything was fine: Miss Mary was over and they were playing gin rummy. That's why taking in a movie once they'd left the restaurant hadn't seemed like a big deal. Until now.

"She rode in the ambulance with your mother."

Gwen's brows furrowed in confusion and worry. "Where's Adam?"

"What?"

"Adam. Where is he? And why are you driving his car?"

"This is my car. I've let Adam use it the past couple weeks."

"Why in the world would you do that?"

Ransom looked over quickly. She didn't know he and Adam were brothers? He scowled, thinking of something else. It was just three or so weeks ago that Adam had asked to borrow the Porsche. Was Gwen the woman he was trying to . . . ? "Is there something going on between you and him?"

"I don't know that that is any of your business."

"Actually it is."

"And how is that?"

"Because I know Adam and I like you, and if he thinks he's going to . . . treat you the way he does most women, there's getting ready to be a problem because I won't let that happen."

The hospital was just ahead. Gwen's focus went

immediately back to her mother. But as they turned into the parking lot, she found herself asking, "How do you know about Adam?"

"He's my brother."

Gwen didn't have time to absorb this shocking news. The Porsche had barely stopped rolling before she was out of the car and running through the short hallway to the hospital's front desk.

"I'm here to see about my mother, Lorraine Andrews?"

The nurse clicked a few keys on the computer keyboard before replying. "She's still in with the doctors. If you'd like to have a seat, I'll let you know as soon as she's been moved to a room where you can visit her."

"I need to see her now!"

"Please, Miss . . . what's your name?"

"Gwen, Gwen Smith. I'm her daughter. I need to see for myself that she's okay."

Just then, Miss Mary, who'd been sitting in the waiting room opposite the nurses' station, walked up to Gwen. "Calm down, baby," she said, even before reaching her. "The doctors are with her now and we can't go in there."

Gwen hugged Miss Mary and tried to keep her composure. "What happened?"

"We were in her house talking and watching TV. Then all of a sudden, Lo said she felt light-headed. I got up to get her a glass of water. When I came back, she was slumped over on the couch. I couldn't wake her. I couldn't get her to . . ." Miss Mary felt tears threatening and couldn't go on. "She's going to be all right," she finished lamely, although at that moment neither woman believed that was true.

Gwen looked helplessly at the nurse, whose

tawny-colored eyes were full of compassion. "I do understand, Miss Smith. But your mother is being examined by two very capable doctors. Just try and stay calm . . . and maybe say a prayer or two?"

When Gwen's stormy yet worried facial expression remained unchanged, the nurse stood. "Tell you what. I'll go in and take a quick peek myself so I can give you a personal update. How's that?"

Gwen nodded, not trusting herself to speak. Nothing could happen to her mother, not now. She could barely deal with the changes that had already taken place. Gwen turned toward the hall the nurse had gone down and ran a worried hand through her hair.

"It's okay," Ransom said, coming up behind her and taking her gently in his arms. For once, she didn't pull away, but rather turned into his comforting embrace. No words were spoken; none were necessary. At this moment she needed a shoulder to lean on and didn't care whose. And she wouldn't dare admit how glad she was that it belonged to the stranger named Ransom.

"Mr. and Mrs. Smith?" The warm voice that interrupted the peaceful interlude with its mistaken salutation jerked Gwen back into both the reality of the moment and the inappropriateness of what had just happened. She didn't want to lead this man on. But that was a matter for later.

"Oh no, we're not . . . I mean . . . yes, I'm Gwen Smith."

"Dr. Rolette here."

They shook hands. "How's my mother?"

"We're going to have to conduct more tests before we have an answer. For now, her vitals are stabilized and she's breathing on her own."

"On her own? You mean—"

The doctor placed a comforting hand on Gwen's arm. "Your mother wasn't responsive when the paramedics arrived at her house. They had to use methods to help her breathe until she could do so on her own."

Gwen's shoulders slumped and she fought to control the tears. As much as she wanted to fold herself into the hard body standing next to her, that was not an option. She needed to be strong.

Miss Mary sensed Gwen's vulnerability and took her hand. "What do we need to do?" Mary asked.

"Nothing right now. You can go in to see her. She's resting comfortably. What we want to do is transfer her to a larger hospital in the Los Angeles area, one with more sophisticated equipment than what's available here. Have them do a more extensive physical, a CAT scan, and MRI."

Gwen looked down the hall. "What room is she in?"

The doctor answered Gwen's question. "But don't stay too long," he added. "Rest is what Mrs. Andrews needs right now. In fact, she may be sleeping. If so, don't wake her. Just know she's okay."

Gwen nodded, whispered a thank you, and began walking quickly down the hall. Ransom followed after her, and Miss Mary worked to catch up.

"Ransom," Gwen said, as she stopped and turned, "could you do me a favor and give Miss Mary a ride home? I'm sure she's exhausted. I'm going to stay here with Mama until she wakes up, and then catch a cab when I'm ready to go home."

"I don't like leaving you here alone," he responded.

"I can catch my own cab," Mary added.

"Please, I know you guys mean well, but I'm really okay to handle things from here. I'm going to call my brothers and I'm sure Robert will come right away. I'm okay, really."

Ransom pulled out his cell phone. "Give me your number." He looked at her with determined eyes, and without the usual flirtatious smile that accompanied this request.

Gwen complied. "Can you also write it on the board in Miss Mary's kitchen when you get there? That way, she'll have it right in front of her should she ever need to contact me again."

Ransom nodded, and after looking at Gwen intently, took her in his arms. This time Gwen was stiff, back on guard. After only seconds, she pushed away. "Thank you," she said without emotion.

She turned to Miss Mary and gave her a longer, more enveloping hug. "I'm in your debt," she whispered to the slight, older lady. "Thank you so much."

As she hurried down the hall, Ransom called after her. "Hey, Gwen!"

She stopped and turned around.

"You're in mine too." The flirtatious, confident smile had returned.

13

The house was eerily quiet and everywhere Gwen looked, she saw reminders of Lorraine. The oversized floral couch that had caused quite the ruckus when it replaced her father's perfectly worn plaid one. It was her mother's favorite place to sit and work on the *New York Times* crossword puzzle, which lay partially finished on the middle couch cushion. Her mother's eyeglasses rested on an end table cluttered with sale papers and an unfinished job of coupon clipping. Lorraine loved a bargain and in that respect, the apple hadn't fallen far from the tree. Gwen smiled wistfully as she ran her fingers along the back of the couch, taking in the fringed Tiffany lamps, the Queen Anne–styled tables, the vase of fresh flowers cut from Lorraine's own garden. She stopped and fingered the lavender-colored petals, thinking that the bouquet was so like her mother, beautiful, sweet, and fragile. A tear ran down her cheek, hovered underneath her chin, and finally plopped down on a perfectly formed sunflower. Gwen idly outlined the floral pattern on the doily beneath the vase, and glanced around the room to take in the other doilies, one on each of the identical, mint green-colored armchairs, and another on the back of the couch. Her mother had often encouraged Gwen to take up crocheting, but in the area of decorating and dress, she and her mother couldn't have been more different. Lorraine preferred cutesy, very feminine looking apparel and decor while Gwen had always liked simple elegance, bordering on minimalist designs.

More tears gathered at the corners of Gwen's eyes and began to fall. Until now, she'd been strong—on the drive to the hospital, while talking to the doctor, and when sitting next to her sleeping mom. But at this moment the sadness and fear threatened to overtake her. She placed a hand over her mouth as a sob erupted. More tears flowed as Gwen cried quietly, wanting to stop, but the spigot of heartache causing the flow refused to turn off. She realized that her crying was not simply that she was dealing with such a tenuous time with her mother . . . but that she was doing so alone.

She sank down into the soft cushions of the couch and hugged one of the pillows to her chest. Absently, she picked up the pen and the crossword puzzle lying beneath it and began finishing the work her mother had started. The act of thinking of each answer took her mind off her pain, momentarily. The puzzle was just about completed when the phone rang.

"Hey, baby brother," Gwen said softly.

"Is Mama all right?" Robert asked without preamble. "We were at the movies, and I had my cell phone turned off. I just got your message."

"We don't know," Gwen answered. She told him what she did know, including that their mother would be in the hospital for the next several days for observation.

"I'm coming home," Robert said simply.

"I'm glad," Gwen responded. Any other time she would have encouraged him to stay with his family and on his job, that she could handle it, like she did most everything else. But her strong, take-charge persona had given way to a much more vulnerable one, and she wasn't ashamed to let her favorite brother know it. "I could really use your eternal optimism right now. The dementia's getting worse, Robert, and . . ." Gwen stopped, unwilling to voice her fears.

"Shh, it's okay. Everything is going to be fine. I'll go online as soon as we hang up and get the first flight I can into LA. Can you pick me up?"

"Yes."

"What about Joe? Have you talked to him?"

"What in the world would I have to say to him?"

Robert paused, taken aback by Gwen's abrupt change of tone. "Well, I guess nothing since you asked it like that. I just thought he'd be concerned. Even though you two are separated, he was in this family for ten years, and always treated Mama well."

Robert had a point, but the last person she needed to have a conversation with right now was her ex-husband.

"Forward your confirmation when you get it," Gwen said, effectively changing the subject. "So I'll know what airline you're on and what time your flight gets in."

"I'll do that. But I'm worried about you, sister, there all by yourself." A slight pause and then, "Have you called Chantay?"

"I'll call her now."

"Good. Maybe she can come down and keep you company tonight."

"Yeah, maybe. See you tomorrow, okay?"

"I love you, big sis."

"Love you back."

Gwen's smile was bittersweet as she hung up the phone. She was a lucky girl to have a brother as special as Robert. She loved her older brother Gerald too, but theirs was not the close relationship that she and Robert shared. Gerald's personality was more like their late father Harold's, while her and Robert's understated demeanor resembled Lorraine's. Gerald's brash gregariousness was almost too much for Gwen sometimes. In many ways, Adam's verboseness was a lot like that, and what turned her off about him.

He's my brother. Amid all the thoughts of worry, Gwen had forgotten the bomb Ransom had dropped just as they reached the hospital. Calling Chantay was a good idea.

Gwen got up from the couch and walked over to where she'd thrown her purse on the Queen Anne chair by the six-paned picture window when she'd come home from the hospital. As soon as she pulled the phone out, it rang. The number was unfamiliar. *The hospital,* Gwen thought.

"Hey, Butterfly." Ransom's voice was soothing, thoughtful. "I'm calling to check on you."

Gwen closed her eyes and tried to block out the rush of longing that seized her heartstrings. While the thought of talking to Joe had made her nauseous, the thought of being wrapped in this man's arms made her weak with wanting. And she loved the nickname he'd given her—the one that her mother's impromptu suggestion on the day of the interview had evoked. Once again, tears threatened.

"Gwen? Baby, are you all right?"

I've got to keep it together! "Look, don't baby me," Gwen said, in a gruff voice meant to generate anger and with it, control. "Have you forgotten I'm not interested in you?"

"Have you forgotten you're separated?" Ransom waited a moment, to let what he said sink in. "Miss Mary told me," he continued softly. "When I took her home."

Gwen remained silent. The only sounds in the house were the ticking of the grandfather clock in the dining room and Gwen's rapid heartbeat. She couldn't fault Miss Mary for divulging this information any more than she could fault her mother for sharing what had happened between Gwen and Joe with her close friend. After all, it wasn't a secret. She'd told Adam during their first conversation after twenty-plus years of not speaking. But for some reason, the fact that Ransom now knew unnerved her—took away a shield that she'd hoisted against him. "I'm still legally married," she finally offered, but the statement sounded lame, even to her ears.

Ransom chose not to comment on what Gwen just said. He knew he'd scored a victory and put a chink in her armor. "Your mother is doing better."

"How do you know?"

"I called Miss Mary after I got home, to make sure she's still doing okay. I don't have to tell you how close those two ladies are, and I know she's upset. She'd just hung up with the hospital."

Ransom's obvious kindness, both toward her and Miss Mary, made Gwen feel small. He and Adam couldn't be more different. "It was very kind of you to call," she said softly. "I'm sorry for snapping at you."

"You're tired and scared and probably feeling as if things are way beyond your control. It's understandable that you're on edge."

More silence filled the room. Gwen was afraid to speak, afraid that if she opened her mouth it would be to beg him to come over and make love to her until all of the pain and the hurt and the fear disappeared. Why did Joe have to abandon her? Why did she have to go through this alone? Anger at Joe began to replace the vulnerable way she felt regarding all things Ransom.

"I have to—"

"If you need—"

They both began talking at once, and then again fell silent.

"If you need anything, anything at all, you have my cell number. Save it in your phone, and don't let your independent streak make you hesitate to use it. Matter of fact, I want to give you my home number too. Put it in your phone."

"I don't know how to do that while talking on it."

"Then get a pen."

"Really, Ransom . . ."

"A pen, Gwen. Do you have one?"

Gwen frowned at the authoritative way in which Ransom spoke to her, and yet felt strangely protected and cared for at the same time. His concern was touching. In that moment she realized she didn't know much about this man who affected her so. Her next thought was that she wanted to.

After writing down his home number, Gwen thanked

him again for calling. There were questions she wanted to ask, personal questions regarding him and Adam, but she didn't have the nerve.

"Butterfly," Ransom said, his voice low and soft against her ear.

"Yes?"

"You're not in this alone. I'm hugging you, can you feel it?"

It was strange but Gwen did feel something, a warmth that seemed to come out of her heart and settle around her shoulders. "Yes."

"Good. And just so you know, I'll be hugging you all night long."

14

A good night's sleep and a few sips of the large double-Dutch chocolate she'd just purchased from Kristy's had Gwen feeling much better than she had the previous night. She attached her Bluetooth, started her car, and was soon heading toward the freeway. She punched a number on her speed dial and waited. Chantay's groggy voice confirmed what Gwen suspected. She'd woken her up.

"Hey, girl."

"What's the nine-one-one?" Chantay whispered in a hoarse voice.

"I woke you up."

Gwen's asking the obvious didn't sit well with her hungover friend. "You know good and damn well you woke me up. And it better be important."

"Mama's in the hospital."

That was all Chantay needed to hear. She sat up immediately, and her voice mirrored her concern. "But she's okay, right?"

"She's doing better," Gwen answered. She shared what the hospital had told her. "They're transferring her to Good Samaritan later today. We'll get more definitive answers after they've conducted all the tests."

Chantay reached for her robe as she got out of bed, then headed for the bathroom. "Why didn't you call me last night?"

"I fell asleep."

"When did this happen to her?"

"Last night. This is the news that greeted me when I returned home from our good time in LA yesterday. I shouldn't have left her alone for so long, Tay. But Ransom was at my house and—"

"Ransom?"

"Yeah. He was fixing Miss Mary's steps when Mama passed out. Miss Mary got all excited, couldn't remember my cell phone number. She went to the hospital with Mama while he waited for me."

"Hmm."

"Don't start, Chantay. It means nothing."

"Did I say anything?"

"You don't have to. I hear you thinking."

"What is up with you and this dude?"

Gwen immediately became rigid, her usual response to all things Ransom. "Nothing's up!"

"Are you sure? I know our town is small but it seems as if every time you turn around, there he is—like you can't get away from him. Maybe you aren't supposed to."

Gwen took her frustration out on the wheel she gripped as if it were her third and final lifeline. She spat the next sentence out between gripped teeth. "I have nothing to do with our coincidental meetings. He was at Miss Mary's house. She couldn't find my number. He offered to stay and let me know about Mama. End of story, Chantay."

The last sentence was issued as a threat, not a statement. To further switch the topic, she played her trump card. "Anyway, I'm on my way to pick up Robert at the airport."

"And you didn't swing through and get me? Girl, you're slipping on our friendship."

"No, you're *tripping* on our friendship. You're my best friend and I love you like a sister. But if you think I'm going to do anything to create dissention in Robert's *happy* marriage, you've got another think coming!"

"Why, Gwendolyn Marie Andrews Smith," Chantay said in mock indignation. "What exactly are you thinking? I'm appalled at your assumptions."

"And I'm appalled at your ass. . . . Trying to tip in on marked territory. And just so you know . . . Denise is pregnant. Robert just told me. So give it up, Chantay. You had your chance a long time ago, and you blew it." Gwen heard how hard she sounded and tried to clean it up. "There's someone out there for you, girl. And me, too."

Gwen's phone beeped and she looked at her phone screen. "Great, just what I need right now."

"What?"

"This is Joe. Let me call you back." She didn't wait for an answer, but hit her Bluetooth flash button and clicked over—before a myriad of negative thoughts could form.

"Joe," she said in a voice she hoped sounded civil, "I was going to call you."

"Why?"

Gwen almost copped an attitude at the way he framed the word, but being determined to stay on the high road, she took a deep breath and plunged ahead. "It's Mama. She's in the hospital."

A slight pause and then, "Is she going to live?"

Gwen looked down at the phone that was nestled in her cup holder. *No, he didn't ask what I just heard in the way that I heard it!* And then she thought that maybe she was a bit sensitive; she was less than twenty-four hours from the trauma herself.

"Yes," she said simply.

"So why were you going to call me?"

Gwen got pissed off all over again. "Oh, my bad, Joe. I just thought you cared about the woman who called you *son* for ten years."

"I, well, uh, I do care, Gwen," Joe sputtered. "It's just that I didn't know what you . . . I mean . . . I've got things going on right now and can't fly out there."

If Gwen could have, she would have driven her car nonstop to Chicago and slapped the sorry out of her soon-to-be ex's ass. "Did I ask you to come out here?" she yelled. "Have I ever asked your sorry, selfish ass for anything? I can't talk to you now, Joe. Whatever you wanted to tell me? Put it in an e-mail. And don't call me again!"

Gwen ended the call and pulled over to the side of the highway. She was shaking uncontrollably; Joe had pushed every wrong button that she possessed. Granted, after her conversation with Ransom, about how he'd hug her all night, she'd slept soundly. She hadn't even dared think what that meant. She'd awakened feeling refreshed, calm. Yet it had only taken Joe five minutes to unglue her. Obviously, she was still as tightly wound as a nap on *Good Times* J.J.'s head.

Call Ransom. The thought rose unbidden in her mind. "No!" she said aloud to herself. She took several deep breaths, and after signaling and looking in her rearview and side mirrors, pulled back onto the highway and made it to LAX Airport in time to see her brother walk through the airport's exit doors.

15

Robert saw her at the exact same time. A broad smile appeared on his face as he walked toward her car parked curbside. Gwen turned into his embrace as a child would a parent's. "Robert," she said, her voice cracking, "I'm so glad you're here."

"Of course, big sis. You know I'd come."

Gwen nodded, not trusting herself to speak lest she melt into an all-out boohoo. When Robert suggested he'd drive, she gratefully threw him the keys. She was working to keep it together, but knew that the time would come when she'd have to give in to the fear and pain that was hurting her heart. A good old-fashioned cry would make her feel better. *Later, maybe,* she thought as Robert eased into the heavy airport traffic. *But not now.*

As Robert changed lanes to hit the highway, he and Gwen chatted briefly about their mother and then switched the topic to life in Seattle. It was good for her to escape the pressing issues of the moment and hear about her nephew, Robert Jr., and the daughter Robert and Denise were expecting in six months.

"Any names yet?" Gwen asked.

Robert's voice was soft and thoughtful as he answered. "Yes . . . Lorraina."

Gwen immediately teared up at the unexpected answer. "That's beautiful, bro," she whispered.

"So, what exactly is happening with Mama?"

"They have to conduct more extensive tests before they know for sure. The doctor said there could be several reasons why she fainted, from low blood sugar to a severe sinus infection. He doesn't think it's related to her dementia, though. Which in a way is good news, because that correlation would mean her condition was worsening more rapidly. On the other hand, she doesn't need to be battling something physical along with the mental right now."

"But she's cool now, right?"

"Yes, thank goodness. I called her just before leaving the house. She's glad you're coming. She still sounds pretty weak and groggy, but the doctor believes something as simple as antibiotics may cure whatever ailed her."

"Then why are they transferring her to LA?"

"To be absolutely sure, Robert." Gwen knew her brother kept asking because he was scared. Out of all the children, his and Lorraine's had always been the closest relationship, even closer than hers. She put a hand on his shoulder. "They're just wanting to be on the safe side, eliminate all other possibilities. But our mama is going to be fine. I mean, they're still working to slow the progression of the dementia, but these tests will even help in how to deal with that."

Robert nodded, seemingly satisfied with her answer. "I can't wait to see her, that's all. Then I'll feel better." After another moment, she saw his shoulders visibly relax. "So how's my old girl Chantay doing? You called her last night, right?"

"This morning. And what can I say, Chantay is still Chantay."

"I told you to call her last night, Gwen. You know she would have driven down so you could have some support. You can be so bullheaded sometimes."

"It's all good, little brother. I ended up talking to Ransom and then afterward I fell asleep." Gwen probably wouldn't have shared this information with anyone else, but with Robert she felt safe, free to let her guard down.

Robert took his eyes off the road to glance at Gwen. "How'd you and he hook up anyway?"

"We're not *hooked up*, as you say," Gwen retorted, surprised to find that her guard was down but not all the way gone. "He helps out Miss Mary with odd jobs around her house, and was there when Mama passed out. I told you this when we talked last night."

They were silent for several miles before Robert spoke again. "We are talking about Adam Johnson's half-brother, right?"

Now it was Gwen's turn to stare at Robert. "Why didn't you tell me you knew him when I mentioned him last night?"

Robert cast a questioning glance at his sister. "Because I don't, not really."

Gwen never considered Robert a source of information. Now she was all ears. "Tell me what you know about him."

"Just that he's a product of their mother's second marriage. His father is Native American, and I'm pretty sure the parents are still together. Phillip told me."

"Phillip Burns? Not the Phillip Burns who got caught screwing y'all's art teacher his senior year!"

Robert laughed. "The one and only."

Gwen shook her head. "I didn't know you and Phillip stayed in touch."

"We lost touch for a while, but reconnected at the fifteen-year reunion." .

"So how does he know Ransom?"

"His niece and Ransom went to school together."

"Niece? How old is she?"

"Twenty-five, six, something like that."

Gwen's mind whirled. Yet one more reason any romantic thoughts about Ransom were inappropriate: she was almost old enough to be his mother!

"So Ransom and Phillip's niece dated?" Gwen asked.

"That's why his niece was all upset during that weekend I was back here. She secretly liked Ransom and hoped he would break up with his girlfriend. That's how his name came up. Instead, she found out the girl was pregnant."

Will the surprises about this man ever end? "Ransom has a child?"

Robert shrugged. "Far as I know. But that's about all I know, sis, that and the fact that there's not too much love lost between Ransom and his brother. Phillip says the dude's all suave and what not, getting the type of attention from the Sienna ladies that at one time only Adam enjoyed." Robert eyed his sister again. "You're asking a lot of questions. Is he getting that type of attention from you?"

"Of course not. He's just a kid. But like I said, he spends a lot of time next door, at Miss Mary's. It's good to know about the people hanging out in the neighborhood."

"Where's Joe?" Robert asked, once again changing the subject.

"Who cares?" Gwen retorted before she had time to mask her disgust.

"I'm sure he does, about Mama that is. I figured you'd called him, and that he would be flying out."

"Yeah, well, you figured wrong. He 'has things going on,' as he put it. My guess, she's blond, about five-two, and answers to the name Mitzi. And probably a few others, like tramp, whore . . ."

"I still can't believe Joe cheated on you. He never seemed the type."

"What man ever does?"

"Adam!" they both said together, and laughed. This answer relieved some of the tension in the car.

"So there's no chance for y'all to get back together? The divorce is definitely going through?"

"You even have to ask? Absolutely."

"C'mon now, sis. Cheating doesn't always mean the end of a marriage."

"It means the end of this one. But truth be told, it was probably over long before he violated our marriage vows."

Robert didn't ask his sister to elaborate. They'd always been close; if she wanted to explain the comment he was sure she would when she was ready.

"When will it be final?"

"In about three months. The docket was backed up and that was the first date we could get for our hearing. If you ask me, the end can't come soon enough."

Robert snuck another peek at the sister he loved. "Because of Ransom?" he asked, only half joking.

"No!" Gwen answered. "Why would you think Ransom has anything to do with it? I barely know him." She then crossed her arms, turned her back toward Robert, and gazed out the window.

I'm not buying it, Robert thought. He wisely turned on the radio and allowed the sounds of smooth jazz to fill the rest of the miles to the hospital in Sienna.

Unfortunately, the turmoil in Gwen's mind didn't match the soothing, slow jam coming from the radio. Her mind was abuzz with the news about Ransom: that he was Adam's half brother, that he was too young for her to even think about thinking about, and that he had a baby, which meant somewhere . . . a baby's mama.

Gwen ignored the twinge of her heart and determined she was glad for the information. Now she had the ammunition she needed to put any romantic notions of anything ever happening between her and Ransom behind her. Not that she'd ever really considered it, she reminded herself. But now, even if she had, there was absolutely, positively, no way she would ever think about so much as a date with Adam's kid brother. And the next time he came on to her with his searing eyes and wicked smile, she planned to make sure he got the message that she was not interested.

16

"Miss Gwen, I have to use the restroom."

"Okay, Isis. But remember the buddy system. Ask Kari if she'll go with you."

"Really, Miss Gwen," Isis answered in a tone of measured patience, "I think I'm old enough to pee on my own."

Before Gwen could formulate an answer besides "oh no she didn't," Isis held up five tiny fingers. *Did she just tell me to talk to the hand?*

"Kari, can you go to the restroom with me so Miss Gwen will feel better?"

Kari nodded, closed her coloring book, and soon bouncing blond and black curls skipped out of the classroom.

Gwen shook her head and hid a smile from her face. She knew she should rein in the little Miss Bossy child that was Isis Blake, but the truth of the matter was Gwen simply adored her. It had been love at first sight when on the first day of school, Isis had shushed the class and commanded they give the new teacher their attention. Even more intriguing than seeing a six-year-old with all the confidence and poise of someone much older was the fact that everyone not only listened but also obeyed.

Isis was a very intelligent child. This fact was also readily apparent within the first hour Gwen had arrived in the classroom at Sienna. She finished her lessons quickly and possessed a highly developed vocabulary for someone her age. Gwen thought she should probably be in an advanced class or at least be tutored at a level where she didn't become bored with school. She intended to discuss this with Isis's parents next week, at the Back to School Blast.

Gwen continued to organize papers for the next day's assignment while waiting for Kari's mother, Carol, to pick up the girls. Carol was one of several mothers who showed real interest in their children's education. She'd wanted to ask her about Isis's mother, but Adam, who seemed to know every female in town, had come up and interrupted them. That was at the ice cream social held the day before school started, when neither Isis nor her mother had shown up.

Gwen felt calm for the first time in weeks. Her brother's visit had helped a lot. Robert stayed a week, and during that time helped with the Herculean undertaking of making their mother's new home a place where she'd feel comfortable. They transferred as much of her old home as they could to the new, roomy, two-bedroom apartment at Sunrise Place, the assisted-living complex in Lancaster, less than thirty minutes away from Sienna.

Once her mother was settled, Gwen had immersed herself in teaching preparation: lesson prep, orientations, and supply and clothes shopping. She was blissfully busy. On the first day of class, she'd instructed her students to take the desks from their orderly rows and place them wherever they wanted to sit. Not used to such freedom, the children had hesitated. But when she explained that their desks could go anywhere and be positioned in any direction, really, they'd virtually screeched with happiness. Now kids scampered to desks turned forward and backward, in rows and circles, and one in the lone formerly empty corner. To others it may have appeared as chaos. For her, it was sheer ecstasy and her first of many steps toward teaching her students to think outside the box and color outside the lines.

Gwen stood, stretched, and walked over to erase the day's lesson from the whiteboard. This simple act, one she'd done a thousand times, made her smile. Because of their district's stair-step calendar, Sienna Elementary classes had started mid-August, and not a moment too soon. Finally, she was in a place where she felt she truly belonged. She was beginning to experience and like this "new normal."

"Is that smile for me?"

The tranquility Gwen basked in flew out the open window welcoming in a slight September breeze. She knew that voice, had heard it in her head almost nonstop since the last words it had uttered: *I'll be hugging you all night long*. But she'd heard other voices since that fateful day, namely that of her brother with the sobering news that Ransom was a father and perhaps, in her opinion, a player too.

She'd succeeded in avoiding him for the past two weeks, and after leaving two voice mails on her cell phone, he'd stopped calling. Now she was thinking that maybe it would have been better to take the call and deliver her sayonara speech over the phone.

"She ignores my calls and now thinks she will ignore me in person." Ransom swaggered up to the desk and leaned a hip on it. "I know you've been busy, Butterfly, getting ready for school and all. Apology accepted."

The smell of his citrus and sandalwood cologne tickled her abdomen. As always, her body was reacting to his mere presence. She was not amused.

"Would you kindly leave my class and this building before I call security?" Finally, she looked up. "And stop calling me Butterfly. Ransom, I'm flattered that you're interested, but there is absolutely no chance that I'm going on a date with you, and while I'm sure that bruises your ego, it is the truth. Now granted, this is a small town and we're sure to bump into each other from time to time. I agree to be cordial, if you agree to leave me alone."

There, it was out. She'd said it. And she hadn't even stuttered. Proud of herself, she waited for him to get up and leave.

Instead, he irritated her with a smile that oozed confidence . . . and charm. "What makes you think I was coming here to see you?"

Gwen rolled her eyes. "Oh, please, Ransom. I don't have the time or energy to play childish games. You have absolutely no business coming here and really, stalking doesn't become you. So I'm going to ask you nicely. Would you please leave?"

Ransom laughed in a way that made Gwen smolder, from both anger and desire. "It's a good thing my ego isn't fragile," he said as he lazily slid off the desk and began walking around the classroom.

"Because otherwise . . . you would have definitely hurt my feelings."

"I'm not playing, Ransom. Get out of here."

Ransom turned around slowly, burning her with his coal black eyes. "I'm not leaving until I get what I came for."

"What you came for? You know what? I've tried to be nice to you because of a couple gestures on your part that suggested a heart inside that hard"—*oh, shoot, I didn't mean to say that*—"chest of yours. But just so you know, I've heard some things that make me know otherwise. Here you are trying to hit on me when you've got another woman somewhere who not only probably needs but definitely deserves your attention."

"Wait a minute, Gwen. I don't know what you've heard but—"

"And on top of that, you have a baby that you're probably not taking care of and God only knows if there aren't a whole slew of baby mamas out there. You've got every female in town breathing heavy at the mention of your name and you probably think I'm on that list. Well, think again, Ransom. Because while you may be fine and everything, your obvious disregard for women in general and your child in particular are not attractive. So I want you to take your suave one-liners and try and hit on the next skirt you see swishing. Because I am not the one!"

Ransom's retort was interrupted.

"Daddy!"

Daddy? Gwen's mouth dropped open.

Isis came running over to her dad and grabbed him around the knee. "What are you doing here?"

"Hey, Ransom!" Kari ran over and grabbed Ransom's other leg. "Where's mom?"

Ransom picked up his daughter and mussed Kari's curls. He spoke to the children, but his answer was obviously meant for Gwen. "She had to stay late at work and asked me to come get you. Is that all right? For me to come into the classroom and pick up my daughter and her friend?"

"Of course it's all right, Daddy. Will you take us to Tastee Treat?"

"Yes, Ransom. Can you get us a snack like always?"

Ransom kissed his daughter on the cheek before he put her down. Grabbing Isis's hand on one side and Kari's on the other, he began walking from the room. "Well now, that's going to depend on how much you can tell me about what you've learned today."

Isis and Kari started talking at once, each trying to best the other with their been-in-first-grade-a-week wealth of knowledge.

They were almost to the door and still Gwen hadn't moved. She had barely remembered to close her mouth. She was not only shocked speechless, but she was paralyzed. Ransom was the father of Isis—the adorable, intelligent student that she'd secretly coveted, believing that if she had a daughter, she'd want her to be like? Where was the mother? Why hadn't she come to pick up her daughter and Carol's child? A zillion thoughts fought for dominance as Gwen sought to connect her mind to her mouth and deliver a sound.

"Ransom!"

Ransom and the girls were halfway down the hall.

"Ransom! Wait!" He didn't turn around. Gwen

hurried to catch him, all the time wishing the floor could swallow her up and she could take back the last five minutes. *If only Isis and Kari had come back sooner.* "Ransom, please, I was way out of line."

"Yes," Ransom said, without turning around. "You were. But it doesn't matter, not now."

"I'm sorry, Ransom."

He turned then, pulling Isis closer to his side. "I got what I came for, and then some. Good-bye, Gwen."

Gwen swallowed hard, watching the strong, proud retreating back as it exited the building, as she'd asked. And he'd called her Gwen, not Butterfly, as she'd asked. So why didn't it feel good to get what she said she wanted?

17

Gwen's heart sank as she walked back to her classroom. She'd put more than a foot in her mouth. She'd put her foot, shin, thigh, and half her ass in there! And what could she do about it? There was no use calling him. To say what? she thought. *Whoops, my bad? Gwen's got jokes? I didn't mean it, really?* No, Gwen knew she'd made a horrible mistake, said things that were inappropriate to a man who obviously didn't deserve it. She didn't know the story behind the glee in Isis's voice when she saw her dad, or the light that shone in his eyes when he looked at her, but she was sure it stood in marked contrast to the picture of him she'd painted. As she'd watched him exit the building, her mother's voice echoed in her mind. *Be careful what you ask for.* "You just might get it," Gwen said aloud. For she was certain that Ransom would now most definitely leave her alone.

"If I didn't know better, I'd think I just overheard a lovers' quarrel." Adam spoke softly as he walked into Gwen's classroom. "But since I know you're still *married,* and only interested in helping your mother and your students . . ." He placed a hand on her shoulder.

Gwen quickly put her desk between them and began shuffling papers.

Undeterred, Adam leaned on the desk, at the same spot Ransom had recently occupied. "You want to talk about it?"

"No, I don't." Gwen hurriedly placed the papers, folders, notebooks, and teacher aids into her tote bag.

"Fraternizing with the parents is frowned upon," Adam continued. "It's a small town, you know. . . . People talk."

"Yes I do know, Adam. And I know something else. You and I go way back, it's true. And I appreciate this special time you're taking to check on a friend. Things have been cool this week, and I think I'm going to enjoy working here. But as I said at our first meeting, I'd like to keep our discussions professional and let my private life stay that way."

"Oh, so you *are* fucking my brother?"

"I beg your pardon?"

"Uh-huh, must be true. Not here a month and already spreading your legs for the locals. You were trying to act all goody-goody in the interview, so morally righteous. His game ain't half good as mine and it only took my brother"—Adam snapped his fingers—"this long to get that pussy. My *baby* brother, at that."

"Adam, this conversation is highly inappropriate and if you don't leave right now, I'm going to have to report you."

Adam laughed. "To who?" He laughed again. "Do you think things have changed that much since we left here? Girl, I still own this town. The sooner you realize that, the sooner you'll realize the advantages of playing on my team, and running all the way into the end zone to score that goal. You understand what I'm saying?"

Gwen was almost shaking with anger, but her mind was too confused to argue. She needed time to think, to regroup, to get her head together. That definitely wasn't going to happen with Adam around.

She took a breath and calmly spoke to Adam. "Did you come here as the principal, in a professional capacity, or as my friend?"

Adam smiled and licked his lips. "I'm here as your friend, baby," he said huskily.

"Well, in that case," Gwen answered, "please let the door hit 'cha where the good Lord split 'cha. I've got work to do. Bye-bye."

When he refused to budge, Gwen reached in the bottom desk drawer for her purse and took her keys out of the side pocket. She walked around her desk and toward the door.

"Adam, I respect you as the principal of this school, and when you approach me in that capacity, you will get my full cooperation."

There, she thought. *I guess I told him.* Her sandal heels clicked along the floor as she walked a little taller out of the room, proud of the parting jab she'd delivered. Adam didn't scare her, and she was looking for a job when she got this one. He'd better recognize!

But he had a parting gift for her too, one he delivered when he caught up to her in the hallway.

"As of this moment, you're on a ninety-day probation," he said, strolling casually next to her.

"What?" Gwen stopped. "Why? Because I'm your *friend*?" she hissed in a low voice.

"Because as of this moment you're simply an *employee*," Adam answered in an equally low tone. "That's how you want to play this, correct?

"Look, it was a decision left up to me because of the strong recommendation I gave you, a report which heavily swayed the board. I wasn't going to implement the probation because, well, you know, because I thought we were friends. But you've made it clear that is not what we are. So over the next three months, you need to show me how much you really want this job."

Gwen's blood was reaching the boiling point—again. "Don't you mean I need to make sure to perform my duties in an exemplary manner, based on the parameters set for each teacher?"

"I think you understand exactly what I mean, Gwen Andrews *Smith*. I can make or break your employment here. The choice is yours."

With that, Adam turned on his heel and walked toward his office.

Well, now you've gone and done it, Gwen thought, as a shaky hand placed the key in her car's ignition. She'd killed two proverbial birds with one "leave me alone" stone. She could justify Ransom's assured absence. She didn't need a lover. But Adam? Not so easy. Because she definitely needed a job.

18

Even though it was a weeknight, Gwen drove the two hours necessary to find common sense. For it seemed that no one in Sienna was in possession of any right now, especially her. She pulled into the complex parking lot and before she could knock on Chantay's front door, it opened.

"Girl, get in here and tell me what the bump is going on in Sienna!"

"I don't know. That's why I'm here."

"Well, it must be something since you didn't even want to talk about it over the phone."

It was true. Gwen had called Chantay as soon as she left the school and asked about her plans for the night. When Chantay said her only plans were to take Sharonna to Target for additional school supplies, Gwen told her she'd be right over, as if LA wasn't two hours away from where she was.

Gwen walked past Chantay and plopped down on the couch in the living room. Then she jumped back up and started pacing the room.

"Girl, you need a drink."

"What I need is for both Adam and Ransom to move out of Sienna!"

"Uh-oh, dick drama."

Gwen stopped pacing, looked at Chantay, and rolled her eyes.

"Girl, please, don't give me attitude. I'm going to keep it as real as the hair under Tyra's weave."

This elicited the smile from Gwen that Chantay had hoped for, but didn't stop the pacing.

Chantay watched in silence for a moment, before walking over and grabbing Gwen by the arm. "If you don't come over here, sit your butt down and tell me what's the matter, then you're going to have to leave my house."

Gwen allowed herself to be led over to the couch. Chantay put a finger in her face as if Gwen were her third child. "Don't move."

She went into the kitchen, and after Gwen listened to the opening of the refrigerator door, the clink of plates and glasses, a cork being pulled from its tight enclosure, and the sound of pouring liquid, Chantay came back into the room with two glasses of wine.

"You know I don't drink and drive," Gwen said.

"You're not drinking and driving, you're drinking and sitting. Just one glass. It will calm your nerves. I'll make sure you're sober before you leave. Now, here."

Gwen took a tentative sip of the wine, and then another larger one before placing the glass on the black lacquer coffee table. After taking a deep breath, she began. "I did something really horrible today."

Chantay nodded, encouraging her to go on.

"I made some assumptions about Ransom that were way off base, said some horrible things to and about him, and made a fool of myself in the process."

Gwen stopped, took another sip of wine and then proceeded to tell Chantay about the afternoon's encounter. She ended with her newfound knowledge that Isis was Ransom's child.

"No! Not the one who you said if given the choice for a daughter, it would be her?"

"Can you believe it?"

Chantay took a sip of wine as she pondered what Gwen had told her. "It might not be as bad as you think," she said finally. "I mean, everybody makes mistakes. Plus, you showed him you are not to be messed with. Now, just apologize profusely, give him some, and let bygones be bygones."

Gwen's brow furrowed as she looked at Chantay. "Give him some what?"

Chantay sat back on the couch. She looked at her friend and shook her head slowly. "Child, I can't believe you're forty. Pussy," she added, after Gwen continued to look confused. "P-u-s-s-y, give him some. That's a sorry that works for most of the male species any day of the week."

"You know what? If you weren't my best friend, I'd be offended. Contrary to popular belief and obviously yours too, sex is not the end-all, be-all, cure-all for life's ailments."

"Well, baby, it can handle about ninety-nine point nine, nine—"

"Furthermore," Gwen said firmly, rising from the couch to pace again but this time taking the wineglass with her, "I have no plans to start anything romantic with anybody in that town, or anybody anywhere in the near future."

"Yeah, I know . . . you're *married*. Even though

you're the only one acting like it," Chantay added after a beat.

"That's not the point and that was not where I was headed. You know how it is in Sienna, with everybody knowing everybody's business. How many times did we hear some rumor about who I supposedly slept with? It's one of the reasons I was a virgin when I left high school, because I was determined not to be the notch on somebody's belt or the prize of some fool's wager. And because I didn't want to end up on the front page of the—"

"*Sienna Sun*," Chantay said with Gwen.

"Coming back as a teacher makes my position on this all the more important," Gwen continued. "I'm responsible for my neighbors' children, and a role model for others." Gwen paused, remembering the conversations she and Chantay had had after telling her that Phillip Burns was how Robert knew Ransom.

"You mean the red-haired cutie who was sexing up the teacher?" Chantay had laughingly asked.

Gwen didn't intend to be the butt of a joke about the teacher who *sexed up* her student's dad. "As teachers," she continued, "we're held to a different standard, and the last thing I want is to have folks whispering behind my back about whose house I tipped out of in the middle of the night."

"Well, if you'd leave in the daytime like respectable folk, you wouldn't have that problem."

Gwen returned to the couch. "The truth is, being broadsided by Joe wanting out of the marriage didn't do wonders for my self-esteem or my trust in men. I think it's best right now to concentrate on my work and Mama. Wait a minute. How did the conversation go from my horrible run-in with Sienna's heartthrob to me and relationships?"

"Girl, I don't even know. You hungry?" Chantay got up and walked toward the kitchen. "And where does Adam fit in to the scenario? Why does he have to leave town?"

"Because he's trying to get into my panties, but what else is new with Adam Johnson?"

"Figures. What I can't figure out though, is why you're saying no. After all these years? You should do it for old times' sake, if nothing else."

"Chantay . . ."

"Girl, I'm just kidding." Chantay laughed, as the smell of frying hamburgers wafted into the living room.

"He all but threatened me," Gwen continued. She walked into the kitchen, took a glass from the cabinet and filled it with water. "Saying that it was his recommendation that got me the job." She drank almost half the glass and refilled it. "And that's not all. He put me on a ninety-day probation."

"Uh-uh, stop it, girl. He can do that?"

"I need to re-examine my contract, but I wouldn't doubt it. Not that I'm worried. If there's one thing I'm sure of, it's that I am an excellent teacher, if I must say so myself. I'll be the epitome of excellence until Christmas and beyond. I'll even switch schools if I have to. I thought this was the dream job, but now that Mama is in Lancaster . . ."

"Hmph. Trust, you don't want to deal with those bad-ass kids."

"And he thinks I'm screwing Ransom."

"Of course he does. Adam always thinks the only

reason a woman isn't with him is because she's with someone else. It's better for his fragile male ego."

Chantay placed slices of pepper jack cheese on the well-done patties and placed a lid over the skillet. "You want grilled onions?"

"However you're having yours," Gwen replied.

A few minutes later, the women sat at Chantay's well-worn dining room table with plates of burgers and potato salad. After eating silently for a few minutes, Chantay put down her fork.

"Here's the deal, Gwen. And I'm going to give it to you straight. You're wound as tight as a cork, and you need to lighten up." She put her hand up when Gwen got ready to protest. "I'm not saying you're wrong, and I'm definitely not taking sides with Adam. All I am saying is that your experience with Joe, asshole that he is, has you lashing out at the entire male species and it's making life miserable for you. You're a beautiful, talented woman. You've got the tools . . . use them! There's nothing wrong with a little harmless flirting. You don't have to be slutty, just be nice! Apologize to Ransom, throw a smile or two at Adam. Make a man think he might get some, even in the distant future, and you'll tame him quick.

"You don't need to add any more stress to your life than is already there. And you've repeatedly said how bad you need this job—not that you can't get one elsewhere, but do you really want to do that right now? There are not many areas in life where I can be an example. But if I know anything, I know men. And I know how you can make your life a lot easier. . . . Let somebody hit that pom-pom so you can chill the bump out!"

19

A kaleidoscope of five- and six-year-old sights and sounds swirled around Gwen's rambunctious first-grade classroom.

"Okay, class, I need your attention for a moment."

The cacophony continued. Gwen walked from behind her desk and rested her hip against the front of it. "I have another really big surprise for you, but until everybody is quiet, no one will hear what it is."

That's all she needed to say. The leaders of the class were promptly shushing those who dared speak, and one particularly saucy six-year-old seemed to have all of them, boy and girl, eating out of her hand.

"Brandon, put that game down and listen. Tianna, stop it. Don't you guys want to know the surprise?"

As one, the classroom nodded at their pint-sized teacher, who, once it was quiet, turned her doe-eyed gaze to Gwen. "Okay, Miss Gwen, we're ready for you."

"Thank you, Isis."

Gwen smiled as Isis preened in the light of leadership. Now, whenever Gwen looked at her, she thought of Ransom. She couldn't help it. In retrospect, Isis looked just like him. And while Gwen prided herself on not having classroom favorites, little Isis was making impartiality difficult.

A brown-haired troublemaker across the room threw a balled up piece of paper at the girl sitting next to him.

"Joshua!" Isis yelled, rising from her desk and marching over to the boy. "Pick that up, now!"

"Okay, Isis," Gwen said as she walked over to get between the students before a fight broke out. "I appreciate your help but remember, I'm the teacher."

"But, Miss Gwen"—Isis pouted and crossed her arms—"the kids listen to me."

"Yes, and you as well as the other students in the room need to listen to *me*. Now, please take your seat."

Isis stood before her with a frown that mirrored the one that had crossed her father's face when Gwen had spewed her venomous accusations the previous week. The same stubbornness was there too, as it took a few seconds for the teacher's order to be obeyed.

Gwen sighed silently as she walked to the front of the classroom. She wondered how long it would take Ransom to get over what she'd said to him. He hadn't returned her phone calls and after leaving several messages, she hadn't tried again. It was probably for the best, she realized. Apologizing again in person for her presumptive behavior would be better than voice mail. Today, she'd get that chance.

As for Adam, Chantay had been absolutely right. Gwen had arrived at school the day after their conversation and approached Adam in the cafeteria.

"Adam, could I have a word?" The request came with a brief touch on his arm and a bright smile.

"Sure," he said cordially, as if the threat of the day before had never happened. They walked a couple steps away from the first graders sitting at the long, white table. A pair of narrowed eyes followed their movement.

"I had no right to speak the way I did yesterday. After all, you are my superior. So I apologize."

Adam's cocky smile was almost enough to make Gwen regurgitate her macaroni and cheese, but she kept a cheerful smile firmly in place. "Sure, Gwen. Insuring a friendly and productive work environment is my number-one goal, especially with the teachers on staff. I probably said a few out of line things myself—"

"Probably?"

"Okay, absolutely. Sometimes it's hard drawing the line between friend and colleague, especially a friendship that goes back as far as ours."

"We weren't exactly friends growing up, Adam."

"True, but when there's only five thousand people in town . . ."

"Okay, point taken. So can we turn the page on our differences and get along?"

Adam turned so that his back was to the crowded lunchroom. "I absolutely want to get along," he said as he performed his habitual lip lick.

"As friends and colleagues, Adam. That's all I can offer," Gwen tempered her stern answer with another smile. "At least right now. You know how it is going through a divorce, the damage it does to feelings, esteem, and all the rest. So let's just start with being cordial . . . okay?"

"Sure, baby," Adam's voice was low, silky. "Friends." *With benefits,* he thought as she walked away. *Yeah, man. You still got it. You're still "the Johnson."*

Gwen snapped out of her daydreaming and returned her thoughts to the once again restless classroom.

"All right, all right, settle down. Now, who can tell me what's happening this afternoon?"

"The Back to School Blast!" various voices shouted.

"And who wants to tell me exactly what that is?"

Several students raised their hands.

"Kari?"

"It's a party with our parents."

"You're right, Kari. We've invited all of your moms and dads so they can see where you study, look at the work you've done so far, and celebrate the new school year. Because you've been obedient, and very good so far this year, I have a special project for you—individual gift bags you'll make for your parents, and a large sign to welcome them."

"How large?" one of the students asked.

"Very large," Gwen answered, underscoring her answer with outstretched arms. "It's going to be a lot of fun. You get to play with paint and get your hands dirty. Are we ready to study hard so we can have fun later?"

Various affirmative answers were hurled in her direction. With that, the second Friday since school started began in earnest.

The next three hours were filled with reading, writing, math, and music. After lunch and recess, the children returned to the classroom to prepare for the party set for four o'clock.

"Okay class, today we have a room mother who's

here to help us with the party and the special project. Everyone say hello to Kari's mother, Carol Connors."

The children greeted Kari's mother and after instructions, they became happily immersed in the painting assignment. The welcome sign Gwen planned would hang across the back wall in the gym, where the party was set to be held. The word *welcome* was painted in several languages and, the best part, the entire sign was adorned with student hands that had been dipped in water-based paint and pressed onto the paper.

Once finished, it was fan dried and taken to the gym to be hung by the janitor. By the time she and Carol helped the children wash up, the student assistant informed them that the parents were arriving.

Gwen excused herself and went to the bathroom. The day's activities had kept her busy but now that the moment of truth had arrived, her stomach was in knots. Today she'd see Ransom and apologize. It would be a serious, somber moment. So why was her heart fluttering? Like . . . *butterflies*. The memory of his voice warmed her, even as the memories of her last words to him, the last time she saw him in person, sent a chill up her spine. She washed her hands, reached for a towel, and held the cold damp paper against her forehead. Then she stood up straight, squared her shoulders, and prepared to face "the accused."

The sound of children's laughter spilled out of the gymnasium, the location for the back to school bash. This day in mid-September had burst forth with radiant sunshine, and Gwen had dressed both for the weather and hopefully success in a sleeveless tunic in bold primary colors and a pair of slim-cut pants. She skimmed a nervous and suddenly clammy hand over the cool cotton cloth, turned the corner, and stepped inside the gym.

She was determined to not look for him. Alas, she didn't have to. His presence was the strongest one in the room: commanding, magnetic. He stood in his usual stance of power: legs spread, arms crossed, talking to his brother. *Best to get it over with,* she thought, and proceeded directly to where they were standing. But several of the students and their parents had other plans. She was stopped a number of times before finally making her way across the room. Two sets of eyes followed her, but she was acutely aware of only one of them.

"Hello, Ransom," she said with hand outstretched, when she reached his side. "Thanks for coming to our bash. Isis is so excited about school, and about the special gift she made for you."

"Gwen," Ransom replied, casually reaching out to envelop her small hand in his much larger one. His touch was placid, as were his unreadable eyes. His face masked his emotions. If he were playing poker, one wouldn't know if he had a no pair or five of a kind. He shook her hand in a perfunctory fashion and then quickly released it.

Adam promptly put his arm around Gwen's shoulders. She felt the action improper, and wanted to squirm her way out of his grasp. But the last thing she wanted to do was cause a scene . . . again. So she turned her head toward Adam and tried to sound casual.

"Hey, Adam."

"You know Gwen and I go way back," Adam said to Ransom.

"Is that so?"

"Yeah, baby girl had the hots for me back in the day!"

"I did not," Gwen protested, even as a chorus of *oh, oh, oh* tuned up in her mind.

Adam winked and gripped her tighter. "She was *hot* for your boy."

"Stop lying," Gwen said, playfully wiggling away from Adam, or so she hoped it appeared. She wanted nothing more than to get Ransom to herself for a moment, so she could do what she needed to do, and then focus on her other students' parents.

"Ransom, could I—"

"So you *are* here! I called your house before I came, but I see Isis was right. You needed no reminder of today's event." Carol came up, hugged Ransom, and remained as close to him as wet on water. Gwen immediately copped a 'tude.

"Hey, Adam," Carol said, while placing her arm through Ransom's. She looked up at Ransom with adoring eyes. "C'mon, let me show you Kari and Isis's classroom. We made a special gift for you."

We made? Let "me" show you? Gwen saw the necessity to immediately set a few things straight. One, that she was the teacher, not Carol. Two, that *we* hadn't made anything, but that Gwen, along with her students' work and Carol's mere presence, had put together the gift bag that Ransom would enjoy. Three, that this was her moment to right a wrong. And four . . . Gwen realized she didn't have time to mentally list the myriad of reasons she suddenly disliked the room mother she'd formerly praised. Let alone dissect the reason for said sudden dislike.

"Actually," she began before Carol could drag him

away, as if he, still and strong as an oak tree, was going anywhere. "I was just getting ready to lead that tour myself. I'd like to discuss Isis's work with her father. Ransom, do you mind?"

When he didn't say no, she took a step toward the gym doors.

"I'd like to discuss Kari too," Carol said, preparing to go along.

"Yes," Gwen answered, stopping as she did so. "I look forward to discussing your daughter. She's very bright. But my job is to speak with each parent one-on-one. That's why I gave out a schedule, with the meeting times outlined. Did you not bring yours?"

"I did but, really, there's nothing you'll tell Ransom that I don't—"

The look Ransom gave Carol extinguished further argument. "Fine, I'll just . . . uh . . . wait here." She barely concealed the pouted mouth and narrowed eyes that watched the man of her desire leave the room. She rummaged through her purse and pulled out the crumpled piece of paper that was the parent/teacher "quick conference" schedule, designed so that Gwen could spend a brief solitary moment with each student's parents. Carol's pout turned to an all out frown when she saw that Ransom's scheduled appointment was still thirty minutes away.

She interrupted me on purpose. She wants him! Carol immediately began plotting. She'd worked on Ransom for years, longer than he'd had full custody of Isis. Nobody was going to waltz into town and disrupt all the groundwork she'd laid on the path to his bedroom. She looked across the room and immediately spotted an ally. Her frown turned to a smile as she hurried toward her goal.

Gwen and Ransom crossed the shiny wooden court and exited the gym. A mixture of parents, students, and teachers were in the hallway, walking from various classrooms and then outdoors to the ultracontemporary playground. *The playground Ransom's company built,* Gwen thought with further embarrassment. Adam had told her this during a recent recess, when they'd had a cordial, barely flirty conversation the week before. When he had tried to pry out her true feelings for his sibling. And failed.

They entered the classroom. A couple parents were inside, walking around the room as their children pointed out various posters, charts, and drawings. Gwen headed in the opposite direction of where they stood, toward her desk.

When she was as far away from them as she could get in the medium-sized room, she stopped and began talking softly. "Ransom, I'm terribly sorry for what I said the other week."

"What?" Ransom sat on the desk, which put him at about eye level with Gwen and made it easier to hear her whispering.

"I said I'm—"

"Daddy!" Isis and Kari burst into the room. "I don't feel good."

Carol came in behind the girls. "She's a bit hot, Ransom. I think she might have a fever." She didn't look at Gwen but the satisfied smirk on her face said it all. "I know you're in a meeting. Do you want me to take her home with me? You can stop by and get her later."

Ransom eyed Gwen a moment before getting up

off the desk and stooping to eye level with his daughter.

"You don't feel good, Princess?"

Isis shook her head no.

Ransom placed his hand on her forehead and then her neck. She felt a little warm, but then again it was the time of the Santa Ana winds. It was one hundred degrees outside.

"Maybe we'd better go," he said to Gwen.

"Of course," she replied. "Here." She walked over to a table filled with gift bags and picked one up bearing his name. "This is for you."

"I made it, Daddy," Isis said softly.

Gwen noticed Isis's usual exuberance was gone. Maybe the child really wasn't feeling well.

"It's beautiful, baby." He turned to Gwen. "Isis is very happy to be in your class. She talks about you all the time. Thanks for everything you're doing."

"Oh, no worries, it's my job. Isis is doing great. We'll chat about it another time." She patted Isis on top of her head. "Feel better, Isis."

Both Carol and Gwen watched father and daughter walk through the doorway. "I'll have to chat with you later as well," Carol said pointedly. "Ransom needs help with Isis, and that's *my* job."

20

Gwen almost had to sit on her hands to keep from calling Ransom. But she wouldn't. She wouldn't! She eyed the clock, and then her purse, tempted for the umpteenth time to drive to Kristy's. But she wouldn't do that either, because she wanted *him* to be there. Reaching for the floral pillow beside her, she grabbed it and flung it across the room. Two more pillows quickly followed. She knew she was being childish but she didn't care. She felt about to explode, and there was no one around to help calm her down.

Chantay was the first one she'd tried. She was surprised when Sharonna answered, especially since it was a Friday night. But she had, and promptly informed Gwen that Chantay was out . . . on a date. *Of all the nights,* Gwen had inwardly wailed. Her fingers had itched to call Chantay's cell phone, but Gwen figured her friend had finally finagled a yes out of the coworker she'd been chasing. And Gwen knew Chantay. Friends came first until a man bumped them to second. Especially on a first date.

After the back to school bash ended, she'd tried to

stay busy, keep her mind off Carol and images of her and Ransom spending the evening together. She'd left the school, gone through a drive-through for a chicken sandwich, and hit the highway. Not for one minute did she mind rush hour traffic. The longer it took her to do whatever she was doing to busy herself, the better. She'd spent a couple hours with her mother, literally tucking her into bed. Resisting the impulse to curl up on the couch and spend the night because it felt too much like hiding from her heartache, she'd stopped by another drive-through, ordered a large chocolate shake, and let the syrupy sweet ice cream and *The Very Best of TLC* accompany her home. On the way, she'd stopped at a Walmart, roamed the aisles, bought stuff she didn't need and would probably return, and seriously eyed a theater before deciding that going in and watching a movie alone would not make her feel better.

And the worst part of the evening was the fact that her phone hadn't rung one time. She'd wanted it to, willed it to, with Ransom on the other line. She'd even checked it to see if maybe the battery had died. Unfortunately, all three bars were clearly visible—fully charged.

"This is crazy!" Gwen declared to the empty room. She got up, walked into the dining room, and snatched said phone off the dining room table. She punched speed dial. While waiting for an answer, she walked into the kitchen and placed a large bag of chips and a large container of French onion dip on the table. She was about to hang up when the familiar voice sounded on the other end.

"Hello?"

"Hey, brother."

"Gwen?"

"How many sisters do you have?"

"One too many, it sounds like." When the smart retort Robert expected wasn't flung back at him, he got serious. "Are you all right? Is it Mama?"

"No, Mama's all right. I mean, everything's fine."

"Are you sure? You sound upset."

Why did I think calling my brother was a good idea? "It's nothing, just work stuff."

"Adam messing with you? You know I'll come home and kick his butt if he's getting out of line."

Gwen smiled. "I know, brother . . . forever my protector."

"You got that right. I'll always be your big little brother." Robert muffled the phone and conversed with someone else.

"Is that Denise? I didn't even think . . . am I interrupting?"

"Oh, we had an informal dinner party, and some folks just don't know when to leave!"

Gwen knew from the laughter she heard in the background that Robert's loud comment was a jest meant for the friends he was entertaining. It was time for her to get off the phone.

"I'll holler later, brother."

"All right, sis. But you're cool, right? Everything's okay?"

"Yes, everything's fine."

Gwen hung up the phone wishing what she said was true. Everything wasn't fine. Everything was far from fine. But in that moment, Gwen decided things could be better, and that she would do what she could to help turn the misery-making events in her life around. Once again, she reached for the phone.

* * *

Ransom smoothed Isis's hair away from her face. His little cherub was finally asleep. It was touch and go for a while. Isis's temperature had spiked earlier in the evening and they'd almost ended up in the emergency room. But after he'd talked to his father and made tea the older man had suggested, Isis's stomach seemed to calm down. He'd fed her vegetable soup, loaded with herbs his father had also suggested, and was glad she was sleeping comfortably. His world now revolved around this angel at whose bedside he sat. Watching her sleep, he was hard pressed to remember a time in his life when that was not the case.

Ransom's phone rang, shaking him from his musings. He thought of Gwen at once and smiled, reaching for the phone. *She's calling to apologize.*

"Hello?"

"Hey, you."

Carol. Dangit! I should have looked at the ID. "Oh, hey, Carol."

"Who were you expecting . . . Gwen?"

Ransom's call-waiting tone beeped in his ear. This time he looked at the number. "I need to take this call, Carol." He switched over without waiting for a reply.

"Hello?"

Gwen only hesitated for a moment before responding. "Ransom, it's Gwen. I hope it isn't too late to call but I was . . . concerned about Isis. Is she okay?"

Ransom tried not to let his ego deflate too badly over the fact that Gwen was calling to check on his daughter's welfare and not his own. "She's got a slight fever, but a good night's sleep and a dose of my special healing potion and . . . she'll be all right."

"Your healing potion?"

Ransom frowned at the smile in Gwen's voice. Did she think she could get back in his good graces so quickly? Of course he'd let her back in. He knew that, but he couldn't let her know it, not without a little squirming on her part. His voice, while not harsh, was matter-of-fact as he answered.

"My father's Iroquois Indian, and he passes on some of their medicine knowledge to me. I made a healing tonic for her, that's all."

"Oh." His somber tone wasn't lost on Gwen. She squirmed. "Well, uh, I won't keep you then. I was concerned, and just wanted to check on your daughter. She's one of my best students."

"Is that the only reason you called?"

Gwen stifled a sigh. "No, I also called to apologize for my awful behavior the other day, my stereotypical presumptions and accusations. Actually, I wanted to do this in person but—"

"Then why don't you?"

"That's what I was trying to do today, when we were interrupted. When your daughter came into the classroom saying she wasn't feeling well."

"What's wrong with now?"

"Now?" Gwen looked at her watch. "Oh, Ransom, I couldn't possibly impose on you at this hour. It's almost nine o'clock."

"What, your car doesn't start after the sun goes down? You're on a teacher's curfew?"

"No, it's just that . . . I don't know how appropriate it would be for me to be visiting a parent this late at night."

Chagrin tinged Ransom's voice. "Well, never mind then, Gwen. I accept your apology. Have a good night."

"Wait, Ransom, don't hang up. What's your address?"

"Why?"

"I'm coming over."

21

Gwen pulled up in front of the home Ransom had described. She hesitated only a moment before opening her door and exiting the car. A motion light came on as she walked up the circular pathway to the front door. Its brightness revealed tan-colored bricks beneath a deep-red, Spanish styled roof. Two lion statues guarded each side of the door. A bright pink tricycle sat partially hidden behind a large bird-of-paradise bush, and a garden hose lay coiled just beside the tricycle. Gwen reached a tentative finger up to the doorbell and rang it.

Her heart skipped a beat when Ransom opened the door. He stood tall and proud, backlit by the hall light behind him, wearing jeans and a tank top. His coal black hair was unbound, falling over his shoulders, while wisps of it framed his face. A few seconds elapsed as they looked at each other. Ransom broke the tension with a smile.

"Well, are you going to deliver the apology from my doorstep?"

Gwen smiled too. "No, I guess not."

Ransom stepped back, opening the door farther. "Come on in."

Gwen walked through the doorway and followed Ransom down the hall and into the large rectangular living room. She was immediately taken in with the simple yet sophisticated style of the place, a haphazard elegance unsuspected in a man Ransom's age. The chocolate brown leather sofa and love seat were softened by silk throw pillows and a multicolored woven rug that took up half the room. On it sat a square wooden coffee table with architectural magazines vying for space with coloring books and black Barbie dolls. The other side of the room housed an entertainment center crammed with modern techie toys surrounding a large flat-screen TV. A pair of red bongos sat in a corner; a chair that appeared to be carved from a tree trunk rested on the other wall. The bare walls and lack of trivial whatnots revealed the lack of a woman's touch, but for a twenty-six-year-old man with a six-year-old . . . the house felt comfortable, settled, mature. The sound of straight ahead jazz, Freddie Hubbard or Maynard Ferguson she guessed, oozed from the hidden surround-sound speakers—the music choice yet another surprise.

"Your place is nice," Gwen said, after she'd finished her quick perusal of the room.

"Not the blunts and blasting hip-hop you expected?"

Gwen chose the caustically delivered comment as her moment to dive right in. "I'm sorry for the things I said to you, Ransom. I was totally out of line and obviously way off base. I've been going through a lot these past few months. . . . That day you came to my classroom, well, the stress got the better of me. I'm not making excuses for what I did or the things I said. I'm just saying it's out of character for me to behave that way and I hope you will accept my apology."

Once again Ransom's face was a mask. He crossed his arms and continued to eye Gwen with a ferocity that made her uncomfortable.

"I hope we can salvage a civil relationship out of this," she continued into the silence. "For Isis's sake if no other reason. I'm sure I don't have to tell you that your daughter is a very bright child, a leader. Her future is filled with promise. I'm not supposed to have favorites but it's hard not to be drawn to her special personality. It tells me you . . . and her mother . . . have been doing something right."

A frown flittered across Ransom's face and then quickly disappeared. "Her mother has little to do with it. Can I get you a drink?"

"Uh, no, thanks. I can't stay long."

"Why not? It's Friday night. What's got you so anxious to leave, besides your attraction to me?"

His closeness to the truth made Gwen angry. "Look, I've done what I came here to do."

"Yeah, you've apologized. But I haven't accepted it yet. I can understand your need to run away from me. You're scared of your feelings, and of me, and what might happen if you stay."

"Oh, please. You flatter yourself. I'm not afraid of you."

"Good. In that case, have a seat. I'll be right back."

Before Gwen could respond, she was watching a pair of strong, graceful legs beneath a broad muscled back walk away from her, through the dining room and into the kitchen. Her mind worked to discount his accurate assessment of her fear even as her hand itched to run its fingers through the satiny hair that swayed back and forth as he turned the corner.

I'm the older adult here! Gwen reminded herself. *I can handle this. After all, he's the parent of one of my students, nothing more.* Gwen's argument felt convincing until he walked back into the room, with two cups. Then, her tingling nana suggested otherwise.

Ransom stopped in front of her and offered a cup with steam rising from its brim.

"What's this?"

"Something to relax you," Ransom said, taking a seat near the opposite end of the couch.

Gwen lifted the cup off the saucer and to her nose. "It smells good." She prepared to take a sip. "There aren't any drugs or anything in here, are there?" Immediately, she regretted the comment. "I'm sorry. What I meant was . . ." Gwen took a tentative sip. The concoction was at once spicy and sweet.

"Always thinking the worst," Ransom countered smoothly. He took a sip of the cinnamon-flavored brew he'd made. "No drugs, no alcohol. Just a tea designed to calm and soothe." Ransom continued to sip the drink, his deep black eyes piercing and unyielding. "Where is your soon-to-be ex-husband, and what did he do to hurt you so?"

The question caught Gwen off guard. She'd almost forgotten that Miss Mary had seen fit to share her business with him the night her mother fainted.

"He's in Chicago." Gwen didn't know how much of her personal life she wanted to reveal. She deflected his investigative probing with a question of her own. "Where's Isis's mother?"

"New York."

A lone trumpet filled the ensuing silence as the

players of conversational chess plotted the next move. Gwen knew she should say something and wasn't quite sure why this man so unnerved her. True, she didn't have a wealth of experience with the opposite sex, especially ones who looked and acted as Ransom did, but she was no longer a cringing wallflower.

"She's a model," Ransom finally continued into the silence. "Left three years ago to pursue a career after deciding that motherhood was not for her."

"So you take care of Isis alone . . . a single father?"

Ransom laughed, the first sign of camaraderie he'd shown all night. "Dang, woman, don't sound so shocked. I have help. A housekeeper comes in a couple days a week. Sometimes she helps me with Isis. Carol does too. Her daughter, Kari, and Isis are best friends."

Gwen curbed the urge to ask about his and Carol's friendship. Sticking to the absent mother subject felt safer. "Does Isis's mother see her often?"

"Not lately. Brea got an agent and has been doing a lot of work in Europe. Her mother, a sister, and two brothers live in LA, but we haven't seen any of them in the past two years."

"It must be hard juggling work and family. You own a construction company, right?"

Ransom nodded. "Blake Construction. It's small, but we've gotten lucky on a couple choice bids—the Sienna Elementary School job, for instance. Did Adam tell you how he tried to block our bid?"

"Why would he do that?"

"Because he's a jerk. But then again, as long as you've known my brother you would know that."

Ransom studied Gwen casually, sipped his tea. "When's your divorce going to be final?"

Whatever kind of tea Ransom had given her, it must have been working, because Gwen, feeling more relaxed, sat back in her seat and decided to answer his question.

"In a few months."

"I don't understand how a man could cheat on a woman like you."

"Oh my God. Is there anything Miss Mary *didn't* tell you?"

Ransom smiled. "That's all she said, that you left your husband after he'd been unfaithful. I'll never understand how some people can treat commitment so lightly," Ransom said. "People don't take responsibility seriously these days."

There it was again, that maturity that belied his years. Gwen placed the cup in its saucer and rose from the couch. She walked over to the entertainment center, where what looked like hundreds of CDs lined a number of shelves.

"I really misjudged you, didn't I?" she said without turning around. "You're nothing like I would have guessed. In fact, you're the opposite. Take this music, for instance. It's the last kind I thought you'd be listening to. My dad loved this old-style jazz with its straight ahead sound. Who would have thought . . ."

The rest of the sentence died on her lips as she turned around and encountered the same strong chest that she'd fantasized about ever since feeling it a month ago. She slowly raised her eyes to meet Ransom's.

"I didn't hear you walk up behind me," she said softly.

"The mark of a true Native," Ransom responded.

Gwen took a step back and bumped into the entertainment center. She took a step sideways and walked around him, toward the safety of the other side of the room. "Do you accept my apology?" she asked, finishing the last drops of the now cold tea.

"Have you learned your lesson?" Ransom countered.

"What lesson?" Gwen remained standing, wanting to reach for her purse, but not wanting to appear to be running away . . . again.

Ransom crossed his arms as he spoke. "The one about not judging someone prematurely, and not putting all young black men into one big stereotypical box."

"Yes," Gwen answered, forcing herself to meet Ransom's unblinking gaze. "I've learned my lesson."

"Good," he said. "Then come back over here."

"Why?"

"Because I've got another lesson to teach you."

22

Gwen mirrored Ransom's cross-armed stance. "Why?"

"Is that the kind of response you expect from your students? I'm the teacher right now. Come here."

Gwen's heart pounded as she forced herself to obey his command. *I'm not scared of this boy,* she lied. *I'm almost old enough to be his mother.*

"Now, turn around," he said once she stood before him.

She did as instructed. It seemed an eternity passed where once again silence, and the bayou sounds of Wynton Marsalis, pulsated through the room. Then she felt his fingers, at once both strong and pliable, grasp the sides of her neck. He applied pressure with one hand. With the other, he clasped her upper arm, gently yet firmly. With her locked in place he massaged the nape of her neck, and her scalp just above it. Gwen dropped her head, a strange calmness enveloping her, even as she felt her muscles further relax.

"The gentle sex," Ransom said softly, "holds much

of their tension in this area of their body. You're carrying the weight of the world on your shoulders, Gwen."

He stepped closer, placed both his hands on her shoulders, and massaged between the blades and the tops of her arms. "You've been keeping worry and frustration inside you. It's not healthy."

He ran a strong finger down the middle of her spine. Gwen shivered. "Just as I figured," Ransom mumbled to himself.

"What?" Gwen whispered, suppressing a moan. Ransom's fingers were like magic, melting the day's stress away.

"You're full of sexual tension as well," Ransom concluded matter-of-factly. He ran a finger down her spine again, harder this time, even as he stepped closer and braced her with a hand on her stomach.

This time Gwen did moan. And move, fast. "Thanks for helping me relax, but I've got to go," she said, rushing the words together as she reached for her purse. Gwen's va-jay-jay was throbbing, even as wetness covered her thong underwear. She hoped the desire didn't show on her face.

"I'm not running away," she continued, running for the door. "It's just that I promised my mother I'd visit her early in the morning."

"That's cool," Ransom said, knowing what his touch had done to her. His Iroquois mentors, friends of his father, had educated him well in the ways of a woman's body. And how to take the tension away . . . from everywhere. "But give me a hug before you go." He stepped in front of her as they reached the door, barring her escape.

"Ransom, I can't get involved with the parent of a student."

"Who said anything about getting involved? I just asked for a hug, that's all."

"Fine," Gwen said, stepping into his open arms. *Just a quick one. I won't even let our bodies touch.*

Of course, Ransom had other plans. He enveloped her fully, bending down to place his head in the crook of her neck. His hair smelled as fresh as sunshine and was soft and warm against her face. His lips nuzzled her neck, and then came around to claim her mouth in a kiss that seared her senses. He pulled her closer, thrust his tongue inside her mouth, and lavished her with a tenderness that sparked intense desire. Even as she thought not to, she pressed herself against his hard, lean frame. Her lower body developed a mind of its own and began a sensual grinding against his bulging manhood. Ransom cupped Gwen's butt and pressed her against his hardness. His tongue plunged deeper; Gwen swirled her tongue around his, mimicking her lower body. Ransom lifted her off the floor, pinned her against the wall, and increased his assault. She wrapped her legs around his waist. He placed a hand underneath her top. The flimsy camisole offered little resistance as he grabbed a nipple and expertly brought it to a hardened peak. He lifted her higher, so that his mouth could replace his fingers. He suckled, licked, nipped at her now exposed flesh. The hard thick shaft that was now centered between her folds, separated only by cloth and waning constraint, confirmed what Gwen had wondered about. . . . Ransom was all that and a bag of whatever . . . supersized.

Suddenly, she didn't care anymore. Not about her

reputation as a schoolteacher, her marital status, her self-made promise not to get romantically involved with any Sienna citizen. After months of abstinence she was on fire, and it felt like the man in front of her had more than enough hose to douse her flame. Ransom was over twenty-one after all; she might be rocking the cradle but she wasn't robbing it.

Her pants and his jeans was too much material between them. She wanted to feel him, hard and heavy, between her legs, inside her. She buried her hands in the hair she'd longed to touch and placed a flurry of kisses on his brow, nose, and lips. She looked into already black eyes further darkened with desire, and knew that soon she would see him naked. She was going to do it—throw caution to the wind and make love to this amazing, gorgeous man.

"Daddy, where are you?" A groggy young voice pierced their haze of desire. "Daddy?"

Ransom stepped back quickly, easing Gwen to the floor as he did so. "I'm right here, Princess," he called out. "Don't move," he whispered to Gwen, and then walked down the hall in the opposite direction of the living room, obviously to where the bedrooms were located. "Are you feeling better?" Gwen heard him ask his daughter.

She didn't wait to hear the answer. She gingerly opened the front door and stepped outside, forcing wobbly legs toward her car parked at the curb. Once inside, she struggled to catch her breath and still her shaking insides. A myriad of emotions warred inside her. Anger that she'd lost control and that that loss of control had been interrupted. Relief that what had almost happened hadn't occurred. Sadness that what had almost happened hadn't occurred. Gwen placed her key in the ignition, started the car, and drove slowly down the street. Her mind was in a daze even as her body still protested the sudden turn of events. She turned first one corner and then another, and steered onto the on-ramp, the highway, and the other side of town.

Carol watched Gwen's taillights until she'd turned the corner. She tapped her fingers on the steering wheel and palmed her cell phone in the other hand. Her instincts had been spot on: Gwen was the caller who'd interrupted her potential rendezvous with her daughter's best friend's father. A piece of her well-conceived plan sat in the seat beside her: a double order of chicken-vegetable soup from the local restaurant, a loaf of French bread, and a nice bottle of Bordeaux. This was a far cry from the fast-food takeout she normally purchased. A burger and fries kind of girl, she had reached beyond her comfort zone and her budget to purchase what she felt would make Isis feel better and impress the child's father as well. Ransom was always working out and talking about eating healthy. And wasn't chicken soup the end-all-be-all cure?

This afternoon she'd thought it, but now she knew it. Gwen Smith was after what Carol had already claimed as hers. It was time for a good old reputation-ruining Sienna scandal—one that would hopefully run this unexpected competition right out of town. Carol had two people in mind as she reached for the phone. She stared at the house she longed to call home, as she waited for her call to be answered. When it was, she wasted no time with pleasantries.

"That bitch just left."

Joanna rolled away from Adam to the other side of his bed. "Who? What are you talking about?" she whispered.

"Gwen, that's who! That whore was at his house. She just left."

"How do you know?"

"Because I'm at his house right now, saw her with my own eyes walk out of his house like she owned it and then drive away in her raggedy-ass car."

"What are you going to do?"

"The question is what are *we* going to do?"

"We?"

"Yeah . . . you and me."

Joanna glanced at Adam as he turned over. She crept out of bed, went into the bathroom, and closed the door.

Carol's temper increased along with her volume. "Joanna, you there? Hello?"

"Calm down, Carol. I'm over at Adam's. He's asleep so I came into the bathroom. Now, what's this 'we' business?"

"Oh, please, you don't know? She's screwing Adam, too." Carol knew how to push Joanna's buttons. It didn't hurt that Joanna looked up to Carol, five years older than Joanna, as the big sister she never had.

"No, she isn't." Joanna spoke what she hoped more than what she knew for sure.

"Not yet. But as soon as I get her out of Ransom's bed, where do you think she'll run?"

Silence.

"Exactly, to her boss. Slim pickings in this town, for both jobs and men. Don't think she'll hesitate because they're brothers. Remember, she and Adam grew up together. He probably already had her years ago. It's supposed to be me and Ransom, you and Adam. She's the fifth wheel who needs to roll out of town. Don't forget how you saw her flirting with Adam in the gym. She's stacking her safe cards up, Joanna, and one of them is your man!"

"But how do we get her to leave?"

"I don't know . . . yet."

Joanna ended the call, returned to the bedroom, placed her cell back on the charger, and snuggled up against Adam's back.

"Who was that?" Adam asked.

"Sorry, didn't mean to wake you. But since I did . . ." Joanna reached over to palm Adam's flaccid manhood.

"Who was it?" Adam repeated brusquely. "Better not be some other nucka calling here." He squirmed under Joanna's ministrations, flipped onto his back to give her easier access.

"No, it was Carol."

"What did she want?"

"Just to talk. She's upset."

"About what?"

Thinking the news might work to her advantage where keeping Adam exclusive was concerned, she decided to share. "About Ransom—she saw Gwen leaving his house."

"When, today?"

"No, just now."

Adam swatted Joanna's hand away from his burgeoning erection and sat up. "What? At this time of night?"

"You didn't know they were screwing?"

"Hell, no!"

"Well, what do you care, Adam? As long as she does her job. Unless you're wanting little Miss Chicago for yourself. Is that it?"

That was it exactly, but Adam's pride wouldn't allow him to acknowledge it. "Been there, done that," he lied. "Little brother can have my leftovers. I prefer this plump, rare steak I've got right here." He grabbed Joanna's butt cheek and jiggled it playfully. "Now get on down there and take care of business."

Joanna scooted down toward Adam's rod and began to lick it. "You're not mad at me, are you? For talking to Carol, waking you up?"

"Why would I be mad at you?" He asked the question, even as placing his penis in her mouth cut off her ability to answer.

I could care less what you bitches talk about, he thought, as he began gyrating his hips in time with Joanna's swirling tongue. Even so, the pulsations in his lower head couldn't stop the thoughts running through his upper head: Gwen had denied him a taste, but was letting Ransom hit it on the regular. Knowing this didn't make Adam mad, it made him livid. He rolled over on Joanna and thrust into her swiftly, repeatedly, imagining what would happen soon . . . imagining the person he pounded was Gwen.

23

"I won't take no for an answer." Ransom was firm, but a smile could also be detected in his voice. "You know you liked it, and you know you're sorry we were interrupted."

Gwen laughed, feeling younger and freer than she had in months. "Yeah, I liked it. And so what if I did? I'm just glad Isis is better. You did say that's why you called, to give me an update."

"Okay, I lied. I called because I can still taste the chocolate from your nipples and I'd like to taste more . . . from other areas of your anatomy."

Gwen flushed in spite of herself. She and Joe had never been adventurous sexually. The few times they'd tried oral sex, it hadn't worked out. Joe didn't like to put his tongue "way down there," and Gwen wasn't exactly turned on by his perpetually semisoft erection. The experience wasn't the way it looked in the porno movie they'd rented as a turn-on. Not at all.

"What time should I pick you up?"

"Huh?"

"Girl, quit daydreaming about what's to come. I said I'm kidnapping you and taking you to LA, no exceptions, no excuses. Now what time can I pick you up?"

"I wouldn't mind spending time with you, Ransom, but there's something you should know."

"Please, not that fake marriage nonsense again."

"Until the eighteenth of October, my marriage is very real, even though my husband and I are no longer together. Now, I know it may seem odd, or even old-fashioned to you, but until I am legally divorced, I intend to honor my marriage vows. I cannot be intimate with another man."

"Enough, already. I respect your blah, blah, blah. Now pack something sexy to sleep in because we won't be coming back to Sienna tonight. Notice I said sleep, not have sex in. As much as you want me, and as much as it will pain you when I actually refuse to do what you'll beg for later, I am going to honor your honor, and respect the marriage vow your man threw in your face."

Three hours later, Gwen was in Ransom's Porsche, zooming down the highway toward Los Angeles and their nonsexual rendezvous. Yet even now, with the outline of Sienna's skyline still visible in the rearview mirror, Gwen began to second-guess her earlier stance. Why had she put up Joe as a wall of defense? Their marriage was over, had been for months. Did she really think it cheating to be with another man when Joe was living with Mitzi right now? Gwen snuck a glance at Ransom, bobbing his head to the beat of Angélique Kidjo, one of many artists on his iPod whose sound he described as world beat. His hair was like that of a stallion, swaying in the breeze of the open window. His eyes were hidden behind dark shades, but his prominent cheekbones and wonder-working lips were fully visible. A squiggly feeling in her heat caused Gwen to look away. Now, with him here beside her, she could think of no logical reason why absolutely ravishing this man was not in order . . . no reason at all. Her mind tussled with what her body desired for several moments, until the sports car's digital speedometer numbers continued to climb.

"Do you always drive like you're in the Indy Five Hundred?" Gwen yelled over the sound of stereo drums and whistling wind.

"What?"

"Slow down!"

Ransom laughed, turned down the sound, and eased off the gas. The boisterous sounds of Angélique segued into Earth Wind and Fire and the Emotions, who encouraged the listener to dance in boogie won-derland. Ransom sang along.

"You actually know the words," Gwen stated incred-ulously.

"I own the music. Why are you so surprised?"

"You're too young to know old school."

"Age is just a number, Butterfly, and good music is timeless. EWF is one of my favorite groups."

"But how do you know about them?"

"My mom mostly. I grew up hearing her play music from the sixties, seventies, and eighties. My dad loves jazz, world beat, and of course the sound of the Na-tives. I like all of that, plus hip-hop, techno, and I'm not beyond knowing a Disney lyric or two. . . . I have a six-year-old, after all. And then there are my coun-try favorites."

"You do *not* like country music!"

Ransom pushed a few buttons on his iPod. Soon the sounds of Tim McGraw spilled from the speakers. Gwen laughed as she joined him on the refrain. Something about this man beside her made her want to live life to the fullest. She turned to stare at him, seeing him anew. "Who are you?"

Ransom answered without missing a beat. "Your dream come true."

Ransom and Gwen continued to learn about each other during the two-hour trip into the city. Gwen shared her experience of growing up in what was then a much smaller Sienna, her not-so-close relationship with Adam, her ten-year marriage interrupted by Mitzi and a midlife crisis, and why teaching remained her first love. Ransom talked about his Native heritage, wild teenaged years, brief modeling stint, construction company, his hot and cold relationship with Adam, and how his life changed once Isis arrived.

"Even with the sacrifices, she's the best thing that ever happened to me," he concluded as he exited off the highway toward Universal Studios. "Probably kept me from doing a bunch of stuff I shouldn't have been doing anyway. But I never was one for much foolishness. Got that from my dad. Growing up, I'd rather hang out with him and my mentors than with boys my own age. The Iroquois brethren call me an old soul."

Gwen looked down at the vibrating cell phone that had interrupted her response to Ransom's statement. Joe. What did he want now?

"You're not going to get that? Must be your ex."

Gwen frowned at the accuracy of Ransom's offhand

comment. "What are you, a psychic or something? As a matter of fact, it is my ex."

"I was taught to trust my intuition from an early age, and yes, some of the elders say I have the gift." Ransom shrugged. "I don't make a big deal of it though, just pay attention when I feel Spirit talking."

Gwen was silent. It was amazing how a man almost half her age seemed to have wisdom beyond her years. While her mother had been a staunch Methodist most of her life, Gwen had left organized religion shortly after high school graduation. She still believed in God, just hadn't been a regular churchgoer, or a communicator with "Spirit," as far as she knew. Somehow the "Now I lay me down to sleep" prayer she'd recited by rote as a child didn't seem to count.

Her phone buzzed again. This time she answered. "Hey, Tay, what's up?"

"That's what I want to know. I called your mom's house last night. You didn't get my message?"

"I did, but it was late."

"Uh-huh. So was it Adam or Ransom?"

Gwen pressed the phone closer to her ear, hoping to muffle the probes of her loudmouthed friend. She only hoped Ransom's "Spirit" would also keep the convo on the down low.

"I'm in LA right now," she answered. "We're on our way to Universal Studios."

Chantay immediately got the unspoken message and lowered her voice. "Oh, so you can't talk right now."

"Right."

"Are you with Adam?"

"No, I don't think I'll be here long enough to stop by your house."

"Oh, so it must be Ransom. Girl, you know you

should have called a sistah. Derek is coming over later. We could have double-dated and checked each other's man out."

"I don't know about all that, Chantay. But I will give you a call when I get back home."

"You'd better."

"Your girlfriend checking up on you?" Ransom asked, when Gwen ended the call.

"Right again," Gwen admitted. "I see I need to be careful with you—reading people's minds and all."

"I'm harmless, I assure you," Ransom said. He pulled into one of the long lines at the theme park and casually placed a hand on Gwen's thigh as the cars slowly moved forward toward a parking area.

Several hours later, Ransom and Gwen sat at a beachside restaurant, munching on popcorn shrimp appetizers as they waited for their main courses to arrive. Their time at the amusement park had been wonderful. It had been years, more than a decade, since Gwen had ridden a roller coaster. But Ransom had insisted, and before long he and Gwen were flinging their hands high in the air, with Gwen screaming as the Jurassic Park ride dipped, turned, and plunged through a spray of water before stopping. After disembarking, they fed each other funnel cake and held hands like teenagers. It felt right to have Ransom beside her, Gwen thought. Even the envious stares from women half her age couldn't dim her joy or shake her confidence. Their conversation on the way to LA had erased the years between them: their common love of seafood, good music, Dave Chappelle reruns, and Isis bonded them, not to mention that he seemed genuinely concerned about her mother, who was continually improving. By the time Gwen finished her appetizer, she was not only looking forward to her crab leg entrée, but to dessert as well . . . and not necessarily something on the restaurant menu.

Gwen's phone rang again. She frowned as she recognized Tay's number. "Hey, girl, what's up?"

"You and Ransom are coming over."

"I told you we're—"

"Look, heifa, I don't care what you told me. I'm telling you that you and Ransom are going to come over to have a drink with me and Derek. I need to check this brothah out. I'm not taking no for an answer and you know you don't want me to get ugly."

"I think it's too late for that."

"Oh, no you didn't."

"Uh, yes I did. Hold on a minute." Gwen looked at Ransom. "It's my best friend, Chantay. She lives not far from here and insists we come over for a drink."

Ransom shrugged his shoulders. "Sure."

"We'll be there within the hour."

"Why hello, Gwen." Chantay's voice was the epitome of innocence. "Glad you two could make it."

"Yeah, right," Gwen answered as she hugged her friend. "Ransom knows turning down your invite was not an option."

"Damn skippie, now let me hug this hunk of fine standing behind you." She playfully pushed Gwen out of the way and stood before Ransom. "You are gorgeous," she said, before hugging him briefly. "I'm Chantay, Gwen's *best* friend."

"Ransom, nice to meet you."

"And this is Derek, my Mr. Fine."

The men shook hands and went into the living room, as Chantay had directed. She and Gwen went into the kitchen.

"Girl," Chantay whispered as soon as they turned the corner, "you didn't tell me the brothah was *that* fine. I mean you said he was fine but that boy is fa-eye-ine. Ooh, I'm so mad at you!"

"Why?"

"Something that fine and you haven't fucked him already. What is *wrong* with you, girl?"

"Derek is cute," Gwen said, changing the subject.

"Yeah, cute. Not fine. And I've already let him hit it. And it was good too."

"The glasses are in here, right?"

"Whatever, Gwen. You better call me the moment you're alone. We need to talk!"

Gwen and Ransom stayed at Chantay's for just over an hour, sharing wine, conversation, and lots of laughter. When Derek suggested they take the party to a club not far from them, Ransom declined.

"Thanks, man, but Gwen and I have had a long day. I think we'll head to the hotel now."

Chantay's eyebrows raised in question. Gwen shot her a look that dared her to comment.

"Well, don't let us stop you from getting your girl to bed. I mean, you know, with your full day and all, I know she's probably *exhausted.*" Chantay's comment was followed with an exaggerated wink.

"Don't pay attention to her, Ransom," Gwen said calmly. "She can't help but babble. Her mama dropped her on her head when she was a baby."

24

Gwen stepped back as Ransom opened the door to their hotel room.

"Two queen beds, as you requested," he said, allowing her to enter the room before him.

"Right, as I requested," Gwen muttered.

She placed her small overnight bag on the bed nearest the window, then walked over and watched the cars whizzing by on the highway. Suddenly she felt awkward and shy, like the flower who used to hold up the wall at school dances. *What am I doing in a hotel alone with this man? Am I a glutton for punishment or what?*

Gwen's shoulders tensed as she felt Ransom's hands on them. Remembering his strong fingers and deft touch from the night before, she tried to move around him.

"Hey, be still. You need to learn to relax more and worry less."

"Who says I'm worried?"

"Your body does. You're worried about losing control every time I come near you."

"You sure are cocky."

"Hardly. I just know how I feel around you, and I know it's how you feel around me. I can sense it, smell it."

He deepened the pressure of his thumbs between Gwen's shoulder blades. An involuntary moan escaped her.

"Don't worry," Ransom whispered. "I'm only going to kiss you tonight. Nothing more. And when we go to sleep, it will be in separate beds . . . as you've requested."

Gwen could only nod. She was melting under his expert ministrations.

"Turn around," Ransom whispered.

Gwen slowly did as she was told. They stood about a foot apart, not touching. Ransom appeared to look into the depth of her very soul, his eyes shielded by those ridiculously long lashes.

"What?" Gwen asked tentatively. His staring made her nervous.

"I'm just looking at you," Ransom responded. "Loving you."

Gwen tried to go around him. Ransom blocked her path. "No, don't move. Just look at me. Love me back."

"I don't know what you mean. I—"

"Shh, don't talk. Send your love into the silence, and the space that's between us. Love me with your eyes."

Gwen closed her eyes, swallowed, and took a deep breath. When she opened them, she looked at Ransom with what she hoped was a neutral expression. A part of her wanted to laugh, the part that was nervous, and another part wanted to run away . . . the part that was nervous. She forced herself to stand there and look at him, as he'd instructed. And then she felt it, a subtle warmth spreading throughout her insides.

"This feels weird," she admitted. "And I feel warm."

Ransom smiled. "People tend not to look at each other. We do briefly, in passing, and if necessary. But most people, especially lovers, spend very little time really getting to know what their partner looks like, not only on the outside . . . but on the inside."

"What do I look like inside?"

"Shh."

They stood this way for another moment, until Gwen felt she could not take his scrutiny or the warmth enveloping her a moment longer.

"Kiss me," Ransom softly commanded.

Gwen's heart quickened.

"With only our mouths touching. Don't use your hands, or any other part of your body. And I won't touch you. I want to explore the depth of you, one part at a time, starting with your mouth."

Gwen tilted her head as Ransom lowered his. She licked her lips just before their mouths joined. The kiss started soft, slow, lips barely touching. Her fingers itched; she longed to put her hands on Ransom's shoulders. She pushed her head forward and tried to deepen the kiss. Ransom resisted, pulled his head back a bit, while continuing to brush his lips over Gwen's. He flicked his tongue at the corner of her mouth, then outlined her lips with its wetness. Gwen mirrored his movements, noting the beginning growth of a mustache, and how Ransom's lower lip was thicker than his upper one. Soon, their tongues met, swirled, and teased. Again, Ransom pulled back, and placed light kisses on each side of Gwen's mouth.

Gwen's body began to hum in both anticipation and aggravation. She stepped closer and placed her arms around Ransom's neck to deepen the kiss.

"Uh-uh, only lips touching," he admonished, before gently removing her arms. But this time when he reclaimed her mouth, his assault was fierce, his tongue hard and probing. The sudden intensity took Gwen's breath away, even as a bolt of desire shot through her pulsating heat. Ransom lapped her mouth as a thirsty dog would water, using his tongue to probe every crevice and corner of her oral cavity. Their kiss went on forever, two, three, five minutes. Gwen shook with the need to hug him, to feel his body close to hers, on top of hers.

"Ransom," she whispered.

Finally, she felt his arms around her, pressing his hardness against her stomach. She wrapped one arm around his hard body, and placed a hand through thick hair as she pushed his head forward to deepen the kiss. Her kitty was throbbing so badly that it would have meowed if it had a voice. Gwen wanted to tear off Ransom's clothes and make wild, passionate love, the kind she'd only dreamed of before. *If I can just stop kissing him long enough,* she thought. *Long enough to ask him to make love to me.*

Ransom's arms went from around her body to her shoulders, the kiss becoming light and playful once again. Gwen's heartbeat quickened even more in anticipation of what was to come. Ransom ended the kiss and looked deep into her eyes.

"Thank you," he said simply. "Now, let's go to bed."

Yes! Gwen thought. She watched Ransom turn and

go into the bathroom. Soon, she heard the shower going. She stood awkwardly for a moment, trying to decide whether to join him in the shower or to wait and take one separately. Before she could decide, the water stopped. After another moment, Ransom opened the bathroom door and came back into the room. A towel wrapped around him was his only covering.

"I forgot to tell you that I sleep in the nude," he said as he folded back the covers on the bed next to the door. "Of course, that won't bother you, since you have your own bed. I just didn't want you to think I was trying to send a mixed signal or anything. I intend to honor you, and your marital status. In case I'm asleep when you get out of the shower, I had a wonderful time today. We can sleep in tomorrow if you'd like. Good night."

Good night? Did this man just light me up like a fire-cracker and then tell me good night? "You know, Ransom, I've been thinking about what I said today, about my marital status and all. It really is just a technicality, you know. It will be officially over in six weeks."

"Then that's when we'll make love."

"Excuse me?"

"You heard me. But don't look so disappointed. You did very well with your lesson on the art of the kiss."

"My lesson on . . . excuse me?"

"Have you forgotten already, Ms. Smith? Outside your classroom, you're the student. I'm the teacher. Now, if you shower and go to bed like a good little girl, you might wake up tomorrow to another lesson."

Gwen, speechless, all but stomped into the bath-room. She closed the door, crossed her arms, and didn't try and stop the pout that formed on her face. She was precariously close to wriggling her hands in her ears and sticking her tongue out. She eyed her reflection in the mirror and almost laughed at the petulant expression she saw there.

"It's my own fault," she hissed to herself as she undressed and turned on the water. "Trying to be so goody-goody. And now I've got to go out there and sleep in the big and empty bed I made."

25

Ransom had relieved his sexual tension in the shower, but sleep still remained elusive for hours. The perfume Gwen wore tantalized his nostrils and made him hard for her all over again. Gwen fared no better. She got goose bumps at the memory of his kisses, and knowing he was naked underneath the comforter drove her crazy for most of the night. Only pride stopped her from getting out of her bed, jumping into his, and demanding they finish what he started. Both woke up cranky, and both tried to hide it.

"Good morning, Butterfly."

"Good morning."

"Did you sleep well?"

"Like a baby," Gwen lied. "And you?"

"Like a log."

"You liar."

"Takes one to know one."

They both laughed. "So is it time?" Gwen asked.

"For what?"

"You know what."

"No, I don't."

"What you talked about last night, before we went to sleep . . . to bed at least."

"Ah, the lesson." Ransom's eyes twinkled. "Eager student, are we?"

"You don't have to be so smug about it."

"First I was cocky, and now I'm smug. Tell me, what is it exactly that you like about me?" Ransom's iPhone beeped. "Hold that thought; this is work." He tapped the screen to accept the call. "Blake."

Gwen walked into the bathroom, to give Ransom privacy and to take a quick shower. Just the thought of another "lesson" from her "teacher" made her heart beat faster. She didn't know exactly what today's class would entail but she was pretty sure that for whatever it was she would want to be clean. She hummed a verse of "Boogie Wonderland" as she stepped into the shower.

A couple minutes later, there was a knock on the bathroom door. "Gwen."

"Yes?"

Ransom opened the door but spoke from the hallway. "Sorry, Butterfly, but I need to run out to a job site."

"What? Wait a minute." Gwen stopped the water and stuck her head out from behind the shower curtain.

"That was the foreman from a job we're doing here, in LA," Ransom continued. "We're behind schedule and he has a problem. I need to run over there real quick."

"Now?"

Ransom grinned in spite of himself. He stuck his head inside the door, looked at Gwen and the water droplets running down her bare shoulders, and imaged the taut naked behind just beyond his view. "Sucks, doesn't it?"

"What I mean is . . ."

Ransom began walking toward her. "I know what you mean, Butterfly." He stopped at the curtain and blessed her with a deep, sensual kiss. "The teacher is as frustrated as the student. I'll be back as soon as I can."

Gwen finished her shower quickly and tried not to be angry. It wasn't Ransom's fault that his foreman's timing could not have been worse. Although it was only a few minutes past eight, she dialed Chantay. As expected, a groggy voice answered.

"It's eight o'clock in the morning, what the hell you want?"

"Good morning to you too," Gwen said, laughing.

"Girl, what are you doing up? Y'all must not have fucked long enough."

"Chantay, you'd better not be saying that if Derek's right there."

"He's not." Chantay yawned, loud and long. "He had to go to early morning service. He plays drums at his church."

"Maybe you should have gone with him."

"And chance getting struck by lightning? God knows I don't belong up in His house. Plus, that brothah wore me out last night."

"Please, spare me the details."

"You're just saying that because you don't want to give me the four-one-one. But you know I'm not having that."

"I tell you what. Come over here to the Sheraton and I'll tell you all about it. Breakfast is on me."

"I'm on my way."

* * *

Chantay was patient, waiting until after she had ordered two eggs, scrambled, French toast, sausage, and hash browns, and Gwen had ordered the same, except with bacon, crispy. She sipped her orange juice and watched Gwen pour two packets of sugar and three creamers into her steaming black coffee. She even let her take a sip before she exploded.

"Girl, tell me what happened."

"What happened?" Gwen teased, taking another sip of coffee. "When?"

"Gwen Andrews, you are about to get a Sunday morning beat down."

"Okay, okay," Gwen said, laughing. "But I'm telling you now, you're going to be disappointed." Gwen proceeded to tell Chantay about the lesson: the staring, the touching, and finally, the kiss.

"And then what happened?" Chantay prompted when Gwen finished with a dreamy, faraway look in her eyes.

"We went to bed."

"And?" Chantay huffed.

"Oh, right, you're assuming we went to sleep in the same bed. We didn't. He slept in one bed and I slept in the other."

"You're a lie and the truth ain't in you."

"Cross my heart."

"You're lying, Gwendolyn Marie!" Chantay whooped. "Ain't no way you're going to convince me that after all that foreplay nothing didn't go down in that hotel room."

Gwen shrugged. "Believe what you want but trust me . . . that's the *whole* story, unfortunately. Not that

I didn't want more to happen. I even told him I changed my mind about waiting until the divorce was final."

"And what did he say?"

"That he was going to honor my initial wish and wait until the divorce is official. Doesn't want me to have any regrets, I guess."

"Something is wrong with that man."

"Why do you say that?"

Chantay's answer was interrupted by the waiter bringing their food. Chantay poured a liberal amount of syrup on the French toast and then took a large bite. "Look," she began around a mouthful of food, "you tell me a man is going to stare at you until your coochie catches fire, which sounds like some juju shit to me, and then . . ." She finished her bite, licked her fingers, and continued. "And next, kiss you to within an inch of your life, and then say good night? That's it? Just like that? He's either crazy, or gay, or has a dick the size of my pinkie."

"I've felt the proof that it's definitely not the latter. I don't think he's crazy or gay either. I just think he's . . . special."

"Yeah, so was Urkel. Did you want to screw him, too?"

Gwen and Chantay finished breakfast, and Ransom still hadn't called. Gwen returned to the hotel room, packed her overnight bag, and switched between church services, football, and an old movie on television. As it neared checkout time, she called Ransom.

"Blake."

"Ransom, it's Gwen."

"Oh, sorry for not calling you, baby. I'm swamped here."

"Is everything okay?"

"Not really, but it's under control. We've got a very particular client who chose today of all days to come over and request last minute changes on a job that has to be done next week."

"Sounds like you could be a while."

"I'm sorry, Gwen, but it looks that way."

"What do you want me to do?"

Ransom sighed audibly. "I'm not sure, Butterfly. It's hard to say how long I'm going to be here. Have you checked out already?"

"No."

"It's a lot to ask for you to stay until I'm finished. . . ."

"I don't mind."

"Maybe your friend, Chantay, can come over. Lunch is on me."

"She came by for breakfast. But no worries, I'm a big girl. I'll be okay."

"Good. You might want to get some rest. If I finish soon enough, there may be time for a lesson before we head back to Sienna."

Gwen got her rest, but not her lesson. Ransom was at his job site all day, and after Derek got out of church, Chantay spent the day with him. Gwen had a nice long phone conversation with her mother, who seemed to be responding positively both to her new environment, where there were constant activities and new friends, and to the new medication prescribed to slow her illness. Feeling upbeat after reminiscing with her mother about her father, with Lorraine bringing up childhood incidents that Gwen had forgotten, she took the shuttle over to Universal City Walk. *Mama remembered well today, sounded like her old self.* Gwen called Ransom again, got voice mail, left a message, and then took in a movie. Once the movie was over she checked her messages. Ransom had called and was waiting for her at the hotel.

"Butterfly, I'm so sorry," he said as he met her in the lobby. "Did you enjoy your day at least?"

"More than you, I expect." She recapped her day for Ransom as they walked to his car.

The drive back to Sienna was quick, quiet. Ransom was obviously tired and drained from his unexpected workday, and Gwen was battling a slew of mixed emotions for which there were no words. Both were happy to let an array of artists, from Tupac to Terence Trent D'Arby, and Bob Marley to Joss Stone, fill the quiet space. As they entered the town limits, a part of Gwen became wistful, almost melancholy. She didn't want their time together to end.

They pulled up in front of Gwen's house. Ransom turned off the motor.

"Thank you for a wonderful weekend," Gwen said sincerely.

"A wonderful day, anyway," Ransom responded.

"We'll have more days . . . maybe," Gwen quickly added lest she sound too eager.

"Definitely. Now let's get you inside."

"It's okay, Ransom. I know you're tired. You don't have to walk me to the door. I didn't even know guys still did that anyway."

"Guys may not. But I do. And don't touch that handle either. I've been meaning to tell you about that."

Gwen smiled as Ransom walked around to her side of the car, opened the door, and helped her out. He took her key and unlocked the front door to her home, and then stood back so she could enter.

"Thanks again, Ransom. Get good rest."

Ransom enveloped her in a hug and kissed her on her forehead. "Don't think I forgot."

"About what?"

"About the lesson. I'll call you tomorrow."

Gwen said good-bye and closed the door. Two thoughts came to mind as she walked to her bedroom. One, she was falling in love with Ransom Blake. Two, tomorrow couldn't come soon enough.

26

Gwen's car tires had barely stopped rolling before Adam was at her door. He yanked it open. "Where were you all weekend?"

"Well, good morning to you too, Mr. Johnson," Gwen replied. She got out of the car, reached back inside for her oversized tote bag, and headed toward the school entrance with Adam on her heels.

"I tried reaching you."

"I'm sorry. I didn't get your message until late last night."

"I left messages on Saturday *and* yesterday."

"You've got my undivided attention now. What's the emergency?"

They walked into the teachers' lounge. Although she'd already had two, Gwen poured herself another cup of coffee just for something to do while she waited to hear what had Adam's drawers in a bunch.

Adam placed his cup beside hers for Gwen to fill. "So . . . where were you?"

"Really, Adam, I don't see where what I do on my off days is any of your business."

"I'm making it my business."

"Well, you do that. I've got a class to teach."

"Have you forgotten that you're still on proba-tion?"

"Is there something regarding my classroom, the curriculum, or some other school-related matter that we need to discuss?"

Adam eyed Gwen for a long moment. "Yes. Be in my office at four o'clock."

Carol squelched the urge to go knock on Ransom's door. Instead, she honked as always. A moment later, Isis ran out, her long, thick braids bouncing behind her. Ransom stepped just outside his door and waved at Carol and Kari. They waved back.

Carol rolled down her window. "I called you yes-terday."

"I was in LA," Ransom said, walking down the side-walk toward the curb. "On a job site."

"You know what they say about all work and no play."

"I played a little."

Yeah, and I know just who you were playing with. Carol knew she needed to step up her game in the goal of getting Ransom. But she also knew he was a man who didn't like to be pushed. So she tried to keep both her voice and the conversation light. "I hope the woman knows how lucky she is."

Ransom knew Carol was fishing for information; he didn't intend to give her any. "Listen, I have some busi-ness to take care of tonight. Is there any way Isis can stay over at your house until around eight o'clock?"

"Sure. She can even spend the night if you run late."

"I appreciate that, Carol. I'll give you a call if the meeting runs later than planned."

Ransom waved a final time and then bounced back into the house to text Gwen.

"Is your seat belt fastened?" Carol asked Isis as she pulled away from the curb.

"Yes."

"Are you feeling better?"

"Uh-huh."

"That's good. How was your weekend?"

"Fine."

"What did you and your daddy do?"

"Nothing. I went over to Grandma's house."

"Oh, really? The whole weekend?"

"Yes. Well, not Friday night. Just Saturday and yesterday."

"Oh, what did you do Friday night?"

"Nothing."

"Nothing? Didn't you have fun when Gwen came over?"

"Miss Gwen didn't come to our house."

"She didn't?"

"No."

Carol frowned at the thought of Isis lying to her. Had Ransom told her to do it? That had to be it. Isis wouldn't know to hide the relationship on her own. *Which only means one thing,* Carol thought as she turned into the school's drop-off circle. *Ransom is definitely screwing her. I've got to work fast.*

Gwen smiled as her phone beeped, indicating a text message. *Ransom,* she thought. He'd been texting her all day.

Only two hours until your lesson. It starts at six o'clock sharp. If you're late, I'll have to spank you.

Gwen looked at the clock. Where had the hour gone? She hurriedly straightened her desk and placed a stack of papers into her tote bag. Picking up her purse, she checked her desk a final time to make sure she had everything. She intended to go directly home after the meeting.

"Sorry I'm late," Gwen began as she rushed into Adam's office. She stopped when she saw Joanna sitting there as well. "Oh, I didn't mean to interrupt. I'll just wait outside." She turned to leave but Adam's voice stopped her.

"Come back, Gwen. Joanna is meeting with us as well."

"Oh, okay." Gwen sat in the chair next to Joanna and placed her tote bag and purse on the floor. She noticed Joanna had a couple of folders on her lap, and what looked to be an outline of some sort. "Should I have brought my lesson plans?"

Adam began speaking as he walked to his office door and closed it. "I asked Joanna to bring in a proposal she shared with me last week. I want to make it the standard for first-grade instruction here."

Gwen was immediately rigid. She had worked hard on her lesson plans, had charted out the next two months. Each week's emphasis was well thought out, coinciding with what the students had learned previously and what she planned to teach next. Field trips and other activities had been coordinated with this format in mind. Adam was well aware of this, Gwen knew. He was the one who had approved her outings.

Still, she tried not to overreact. "I'm sure Joanna's

plan is great," Gwen said calmly. "But I am very happy with the progress my students are making using the plans I've developed. I've worked very hard to make sure these student lessons are diverse, creative, and stimulating. I know we're still in the first trimester, but I believe their grades, and the parent feedback, will bear out the fact that my formula is working."

"That may be," Adam countered. "But I've made my decision. Joanna, give Gwen the folder with her new lesson outlines."

Joanna passed the folder to Gwen. When Gwen made no move to take it, Joanna simply let the folder drop in Gwen's lap. Gwen imagined slapping Joanna into the next semester, but decided not to give them the pleasure of knowing they'd pissed her off.

"Because this new format is Joanna's design, I want you to work with her closely, Gwen, for you two to meet at least once a week throughout the remainder of your probation. Joanna will make sure the lessons you've prepared are within the guidelines of this new formula she's developed."

"You're joking, right?" Gwen asked Adam.

"Am I laughing?" he shot back.

Despite her best effort, Gwen was unable to control her temper. "You're asking me to have Joanna *approve* my lessons?" she asked with barely veiled incredulity. "Do I have to remind either of you that I have a decade's worth of teaching experience under my belt, not to mention a master's in education and several accreditations from some of the finest institutions in the country?" She looked from Adam to Joanna, who sat with a smug look on her face.

This child doesn't know how close she is to seeing stars, and I don't mean Brad and Angelina. Gwen had to almost bite her tongue to keep from cursing both Adam and Joanna out. She was so angry she could barely think. She knew if she didn't get away soon, she couldn't be responsible for her actions. "I'm not sure what this is all about, but I don't think it's a good idea to make a change this major with the school year already started and the current lesson plan already under way. Children need structure, and I question the wisdom of switching everything around so abruptly."

"Your concern is duly noted," Adam said sarcastically. "Now, if there's nothing further, I'd like Joanna to go over the plans with you this evening. Perhaps you'll want to do it over dinner. You can charge it to the school."

Gwen stood. "I'm afraid that won't be possible. I have plans tonight that cannot be changed." She reached down for her tote bag and put the folder Joanna had given her inside it. "I'll go over the plans tonight, Joanna," she said, looking her in the eye with a calm demeanor that took a Herculean effort to pull off. "Perhaps we can meet before school tomorrow, a coffee at Kristy's."

"I'm afraid that won't be possible," Joanna said, mimicking Gwen's answer. "Do you think she can call me tonight, Adam, just so I know that she's read the new lesson plan and doesn't have any questions regarding it?"

"I'll call you," Gwen said before Adam could answer. "If that's it for this meeting, I really need to go."

27

Gwen was still seething when Ransom arrived promptly at five minutes to six. He knocked on her door and was surprised when she opened it, let him in, and then without a kiss or a hug marched toward the kitchen. "Your brother is an asshole," she threw over her shoulder.

It was not the greeting he expected. "That may be so," Ransom said smoothly, following Gwen into the kitchen, "but we're not going to let whatever happened during the day affect our evening. Especially if it involves my brother."

"But—"

"No buts. Well, maybe this one." He placed his hands on Gwen's butt and lifted her onto the counter where he proceeded to kiss her senseless. Gwen's stiff back loosened as Ransom worked his magic, and before long her pocketbook, as Miss Mary called it, was vibrating like it had batteries.

"Come on, let's take a shower."

"Together?"

Ransom nodded.

"But I thought you said—"

"And I meant it. No sex until October."

"What does that mean exactly?"

"Exactly what I said. Now, quit stalling."

Gwen's heart thumped so loudly she thought Ransom could hear it. She felt if she left the kitchen she might never find the way back to herself. "But what about the food?" she asked lamely.

"We'll eat later."

Gwen shivered, but not from cold. It was from the way Ransom drank her in with his eyes as she undressed. When she suggested he take off his clothes at the same time, he shook his head and said, "I want to watch you."

After she'd undressed, Ransom took off the signature black tank top and black jeans he wore. He stripped, quickly, methodically, but his eyes never left Gwen's.

To her credit, Gwen stifled a gasp when Ransom pulled down his boxers and his manhood sprang up, poised and ready. It was long and thick and the most beautiful penis Gwen had ever seen. She swallowed once, and again. There had only been one guy before Joe, and those two men's appendages together could not equal one Ransom. Her lack of diverse sexual experience made her wary, wondering if she could even accommodate him, let alone satisfy his needs.

"We're not going to do that yet, remember?" Ransom said, correctly reading her mind.

"I wasn't thinking about that," she said.

Ransom laughed and picked her up. "Yes . . . you were."

Ransom carried Gwen to the bathroom and gingerly put her down. He turned on the water and stepped back for Gwen to get in first. "I'll be right back," he said, and returned a moment later and joined her in the shower.

"What's that?" Gwen asked.

Ransom unscrewed the lid from a bottle of liquid soap. "An aphrodisiac."

He placed a dab of the amber-colored liquid in his hands and rubbed them together. Then he placed his hands on Gwen's wet body, creating a bubbly lather with his strokes. He ran his hands over the length of her body, caressing her thighs, running a finger along her feminine folds.

All of Gwen's senses were enraptured. The feel of Ransom's hands on her body, the sight of his long hair, black and wet against his tanned skin, the sound of his voice as he told her all the things he planned to do to her, the taste of his tongue when he wasn't talking, and the smell of the soap: cinnamon and vanilla and something else she couldn't quite define.

When they finished showering, Gwen stepped out of the tub and reached for a towel.

"Not yet," Ransom said, picking her up once again and walking into her bedroom. He dried himself quickly, laid a second towel on the bed, and told Gwen to lie on it. He put on a pair of sexy black boxers and then reached into his bag for another bottle.

"What's that?" she whispered.

"Edible lotion," he replied.

Gwen shivered, and again, not from cold.

Ransom started with her toes. He lotioned and licked each one. The lotion mixed with the moisture still on Gwen's body, making her skin feel soft and silky smooth. Ransom continued up her legs, thighs, hips and stomach, lotioning, licking, over and again. He played with her navel and discovered she was ticklish there.

"Ooh, stop it, Ransom," Gwen said, laughing.

Ransom stopped.

"No, don't stop," Gwen corrected. "I mean, ah!"

Ransom's hot mouth on Gwen's wet nipple took her breath away. She squirmed under his assault, her passion paradise longing to be touched and licked, as had the rest of her body. She resisted the urge to take his hand and put it where she wanted, to put his fingers inside her. Yet she could barely stand it. Her body yearned for release.

"Spread your legs," Ransom quietly commanded.

Gwen did as she was told. Ransom stared at her for an agonizingly long moment. Gwen felt herself grow warm and wet under his intense gaze. Suddenly she remembered the taunts of her youth: that her breasts were too small and her legs were too skinny. She closed her legs and covered herself with her hands.

"Don't. You're beautiful."

"I'm not. I'm skinny and my titties are—"

"Just the right size. Now move your hands and spread your legs for me. And close your eyes."

Gwen obeyed her instructor. Seconds seemed like hours as she waited to see what Ransom would do. Finally, she felt something light and soft on her skin. It was a feather, she realized, as Ransom moved the object over her highly sensitized body. When he rubbed the feather between her legs, she thought she'd die from the pleasure. And when his fingers replaced it, she almost did. He touched her with the precision of a surgeon, and the patience of a painter. He seemed to know just where to touch, and when he placed the tip of his finger on her G-spot, she had as intense an orgasm as she'd ever experienced. It took her a moment to realize the scream she heard was her own voice.

She was still shuddering when Ransom lay down beside her and pulled her into his arms.

"Feel better?" he asked, after a tender kiss.

"I've never experienced anything like that in my life," Gwen admitted. "But what about you? You must be frustrated right about now."

"My time will come," Ransom said. He smoothed Gwen's hair down, and wiped a bead of perspiration from her face. "Right now, it's all about you."

Gwen nestled closer to Ransom and put her arm across his chest. She was happier than she'd ever been, and ready to go against every rule she'd imposed upon herself to be with this man. She decided to call Joe the following day and see if there was any way their court date could be moved forward. Maybe there had been a cancellation, maybe they could talk to someone with connections, pull some strings. Gwen wanted to do whatever she could to be with Ransom, totally and completely. She wanted the whole world, let alone Sienna, to know that this was her man.

"Gwen."

"Hmm?"

"Tell me what Adam did that had you so upset when I arrived."

"Why do you want to hear about that now?"

"So that the next time I see him, I'll know why I'm kicking his ass."

28

Gwen pulled into Kristy's crowded parking lot. She knew she was going to need all the help she could get today, and decided that a large double-Dutch hot chocolate would be the perfect way to begin it.

Or close to perfect anyway. After lying next to Ransom the previous night, she knew that waking up in that same position would be the absolute crème de la crème. She was glad she'd talked with him about Adam too. He was very sensible about the whole thing, his ass-kicking comment not withstanding. But after listening to what had happened at school, he suggested she not make a big deal out of what Adam and Joanna had done.

"It's obvious that Adam wants you, and Joanna wants to *be* you," he'd said while holding her. "Your best move will be to keep it chillin' like Bob Dylan, B-fly. Follow Joanna's changes to the letter and continue being the brilliant teacher you are. Act like what they did doesn't affect you at all. They won't know what to make of your actions and when they realize you're not going to be pulled into their antics, they'll leave you alone."

His advice was so sensible Gwen felt as if Ransom, and not Adam, were the older brother. When Gwen called Chantay late the night before, she had agreed—both with staying calm where Joanna was concerned and with Ransom kicking Adam's behind. She'd also added that if Joanna kept tripping and needed to get jumped, she'd come down and help a sistah out.

Gwen eased into the aromatic coffee shop. There were several people in line, including a group of high school kids. Gwen tried to get Kristy's attention. When Kristy nodded a greeting, Gwen threw up two fingers. Kristy nodded and Gwen moved out of the line. While waiting for her order, she sent a text message to Ransom:

Good morning, teacher. When is my next lesson?

Within moments, her phone beeped with his reply.

We need to talk about that.

Gwen smiled, and texted back.

Hmm, can you give me a hint?

Gwen heard Kristy call her name and motion her over. "What's up, Kristy?"

"You, girlfriend. Barely here a month and shaking things up in this town."

"How's that?" Gwen's phone beeped. She looked

down to read Ransom's message and didn't catch Kristy rolling her eyes.

Two hints: Long. Slow.

"Carol was in here yesterday. Let's just say her conversation was about you and it was nothing nice."

"Carol doesn't know me and she definitely doesn't know my business. So you might as well disregard whatever she said."

"That may be true, but you might want to watch your back regardless. Some people think that girl has a screw loose."

"Well, thanks for the info, Kristy. And for the chocolate." Gwen took a five-dollar bill out of her wallet and laid it on the counter.

"Pick your money up, girlfriend. That 'Monday morning mover' is on me."

"You're the best, Kristy." Gwen put the five dollars in the tip jar, winked at the cheerful coffee shop owner, and answered her phone.

"Good morning."

"Hey, Butterfly."

Gwen still melted when Ransom called her that. It felt especially good hearing it in light of what Kristy had told her. She relayed the conversation to Ransom.

"Carol doesn't have enough business of her own and is always trying to get into everybody else's. I need to talk with her about that."

"Oh, Ransom, don't tell her I said anything."

"I'm not talking about what she told Kristy. I'm talking about what Isis told me. She had quite the conversation with Carol on Monday, where Carol was asking about your being over to our house."

"You mean Friday night? How could she know about that?"

"She may have been fishing for info, or she may have driven over here and seen your car."

Gwen sighed. "Here we go."

"Here goes what? That people know we're seeing each other? We're grown, baby. I don't care if the whole world knows I'm digging you."

"I feel the same way."

Ransom smiled broadly. "You do? And you're admitting it? We're making progress."

"Your lessons are helping, a little," Gwen begrudgingly admitted, her own smile widening. "It's just that . . ."

"Just that what?"

How can I tell him the way I feel? And how Mama used to warn me about being the loose girl on folks' loose lips and making the news. Her mother's paranoia about the town knowing her business was part of what had kept Gwen a virgin until way after she'd left home. "I don't like the small town 'he say she say' mess," she offered finally. "I'm still married."

"Okay, Gwen. But check this out. I'm flying to Chicago with you for the divorce and that night, after your divorce is finalized, we'll have lesson number three."

29

Gwen bypassed the teachers' lounge and went straight to her classroom. She wasn't totally shocked to see Joanna inside, looking at the model city Gwen's class had built for their latest project. Gwen was angry, but was determined not to show it.

"Good morning, Joanna." She walked to her desk, sat down, and began organizing her day.

Joanna was taken aback at the pleasant greeting. "I expected a phone call from you last night."

"Did you?"

"Yes. I asked Adam if you could call me after you'd read the new schedule. I'm sure you heard me."

"I'm sorry. I must have missed that. But I'm here now. What is it I can do for you?"

"Well I, I mean . . ." Joanna stammered and then sputtered into silence. Gwen's poise had obviously unnerved her.

"I read your plan," Gwen continued. "I thought certain components you added, the inclusion of news in age-appropriate translation for instance, were quite good. I should have the one-month overview for my new lesson plans to you by Monday, as Adam requested."

Joanna's chagrin showed up on her face in a bright shade of red. Whatever comeback she'd come up with was interrupted by Gwen's rambunctious student, Patrick, and his mother, Ashley.

"Oh, Gwen, I'm glad you're here," Ashley said, trying to catch her breath. "I have a doctor's appointment before I go to work and hope you don't mind if I drop Patrick off a little early."

"Not at all, Ashley. Hope your appointment is nothing serious."

"I hope so too." Ashley looked as if she wanted to say something else to Gwen, but glancing at Joanna, she simply said, "Thanks. Bye."

"Guess what I've got, Miss Gwen!" Patrick reached into his jeans pocket and pulled out a balled up handkerchief. "A grasshopper!" He ceremoniously unfolded the handkerchief to reveal what was technically called a katydid.

Joanna huffed, rolled her eyes, and stomped out.

"My goodness!" Gwen said to her student, thankful for the timely yet gross interruption. "I sure hope the poor thing wasn't alive when you put it in your pocket!"

Patrick scrunched up his nose. "Of course not, Miss Gwen. I killed it first!"

Mere seconds after her last student left, Gwen received her second uninvited guest of the day. Adam closed her door after walking in.

"We need to talk."

Gwen surreptitiously took a deep breath before responding cheerfully. "About what, Adam?"

"About your reputation, and how sleeping around might not look good for the new first-grade teacher."

Gwen continued to erase the day's lessons from the board. "You know how it is in a small town, Adam. You can't believe everything you hear."

"So you and Ransom aren't hanging out?"

Gwen turned around and crossed her arms. "Who told you this, Carol?"

"Don't matter how I heard it, word got around."

"Well, whoever is spreading this word around should try and get their story straight."

"You weren't over to Ransom's house Friday night? After hours?"

"Adam, I think we've had this conversation before. What I do with my time after hours should be of no concern to either you or the faculty at Sienna. However, let me correct the rumor, for the record. Yes, I was at Ransom's house Friday night. And if whoever brought you this news had bothered to either knock on the door or watch me leave, they would know that I did not spend the night there."

"So you're the fuck 'em and leave 'em type, huh?"

Gwen turned back to the board. "This conversation is over."

"You need to watch yourself, Gwen. The parents in this town are very particular about who teaches their children."

Gwen turned back to face him. "And probably who runs the school as well, I'd imagine."

Adam narrowed his eyes. "Oh, you don't even want to go there."

"Don't start nothing, won't be nothing."

"Does your husband know about these extracurricular activities you're involved in before the ink is even dry on your divorce decree?"

"No," Ransom said from the back of the room. He hadn't made a sound as he'd opened the door and stepped inside. "And you, big brother, have made your last veiled threat to Gwen."

"You have about two seconds to get off the premises before I call security," Adam said to Ransom.

Ransom ignored Adam. "Are you ready to go, Gwen?"

"Did you hear what I just said?" Adam raised his voice and took a step toward Ransom.

"If you're tired of standing upright, just keep coming toward me." Ransom's voice was low, soft, deadly.

"And what if I don't?" Adam asked the question, but stopped walking.

Ransom's smile was menacing. "Gwen's doing her job, and minding her business. Back off her."

Adam took another step toward Ransom. "And just who is going to make me?"

"I am." Ransom grabbed Adam's forearm and swung his leg just below Adam's shins. Adam was on the ground before he knew what hit him. He landed on his stomach, knocking the wind out of himself.

"Oh, that's your ass, punk," he said between gasps. "I'm going to have you arrested for assault!"

"Who assaulted anybody? Gwen, did you see anything?"

"No, Ransom. All I saw was you two talking. Now let's go."

30

Ransom closed Gwen's car door after she got in. He walked over to his Jeep, which was parked next to her Toyota, and got in. He phoned her as soon as they pulled out of the school parking lot.

"I don't know if that was the smartest thing we just did," Gwen said. "I really don't need Adam as an enemy right now."

"Adam was already your enemy. Don't worry about him though. Most of the time he's full of hot air."

"What if now isn't one of those times?"

"He doesn't want to mess with me. I don't make idle threats."

"And I don't want you two brothers fighting over me—although it was quite chivalrous, you coming to my defense back there. Thank you."

Gwen's praise settled around Ransom like a velvet cloak. "Your place or mine?"

"Really, Ransom, maybe we'd better rethink getting together, just until after the divorce is final."

"I need to go get Isis at Carol's. You know that

Burger King just off the Lancaster exit? Meet me there in thirty minutes."

Adam paced his office, contemplating what to do. He was so angry he couldn't see straight. Calling the police was out. After all, what could he tell them? That his little brother knocked him on his butt and then walked out the door with the woman he wanted? He didn't think that would do much for the "Playa' A. J." reputation. Besides, it would just be his word against both Gwen and Ransom. He didn't doubt for a minute that Gwen would side with Ransom, and lie if it would keep his younger brother out of trouble.

Adam picked up a piece of paper, balled it up, and threw it against the wall. Then he picked up another, and another. He wanted to crumple his brother in like fashion, and throw Gwen up against the wall of his bedroom. Her choosing Ransom over him had deflated an already deteriorating ego, and Adam wasn't about to let her get away with making a fool of him.

"I'm going to show that bitch what happens when you mess with The Johnson," he growled as he walked behind his desk and sat down. He reached for the phone with a sneer on his face. "Chicago," he said to the automated system. When it asked what listing, he spoke slowly, clearly: "Joseph Smith."

Carol smiled when she saw Ransom through her peephole. "Hey, handsome," she said when she opened the door.

"Where's Isis?"

"Playing with Kari in her bedroom. Come on in."

"Just tell her I'm out here."

"You're going to wait outside . . . in the hall?"

"That's right."

"Okay, Ransom, what's wrong?"

"You trying to get in my business, that's what."

"What are you talking about?"

"You know what I'm talking about, Carol. Asking Isis about Gwen being at my house. I don't appreciate your pumping my daughter for information that doesn't concern you."

"I didn't pump Isis for information."

"You didn't ask Isis about Gwen being at my house Friday?"

"No," Carol lied.

"Well, that's what she told me, and I believe my daughter. Now go get her."

Carol didn't move, but yelled from the doorway, "Isis!"

Isis came running out of Kari's room, saw the scowl on Ransom's face, and stopped short. "What's the matter, Daddy?"

"Nothing, Princess. Get your backpack. We're leaving."

"Can I stay for dinner? Carol's making tacos."

"No. Get your backpack."

"Look, I don't appreciate your coming over here with an attitude," Carol said. "You're not paying me to pick up your daughter and bring her here after school. I do it as a favor, because she and Kari are friends, and I thought you and I were friends as well. But maybe you should get your new *girlfriend* to be your taxi. See how long Gwen lasts trying to do what I've done for the past two years."

"I never asked for your help with Isis. All of this was your idea. But now that I see it's a problem for you, I'll be glad to make other arrangements. From this moment right here, you no longer have to worry about picking Isis up, either before or after school. Isis, let's go!"

Isis looked at Carol with sad eyes as she walked around her to take Ransom's hand.

"Send me an e-mail of what you think I owe you," Ransom said. He turned to walk away without another word.

"Ransom, wait!" Carol's anger quickly turned to regret as she watched her chances at becoming Ransom's woman fade with every step he took away from her apartment. "Ransom, I didn't mean it!"

Ransom picked up Isis and, bypassing the elevator, quickly disappeared down the steps.

Carol slammed the door, leaned against it, and burst out crying.

"Miss Gwen!" Isis waved frantically as Ransom parked his Jeep next to Gwen's Toyota.

"Hope you haven't been waiting long," he said.

"I just got here. Hello, Isis."

They walked inside the restaurant, placed their orders, and waited for the food.

"Are you okay?"

"I just had it out with Carol."

"Uh-oh."

"It was long overdue, actually. I knew she'd been . . ." Ransom looked down and saw Isis's big brown eyes looking directly at his mouth. "Let's get our food, and then we'll talk."

"Who's going to take me to school?" Isis repeated the question she'd asked on the drive to Burger King.

"I told you that I was."

"But what about after school? And when you go out of town? I like staying at Carol's house, Daddy. Kari's my friend!" Isis's eyes grew bright as tears threatened.

"Do you want a chocolate shake or not?" Ransom offered a threat of his own.

Isis sniffled as she nodded her head yes.

"Well, quit that crying then. You'll still see Kari at school. And you've got other friends."

"But Kari's my best friend!"

Ransom and Gwen looked at each other. Ransom sighed. Gwen offered a sympathetic smile.

Isis thought for a moment and then nudged Gwen. "Miss Gwen, will you be my new babysitter?"

Without looking at Ransom, Gwen answered. "I'll help in whatever way I can."

31

Gwen placed the last item of clothing in her carry-on luggage and zipped it up. She couldn't believe the time had finally come when she'd end her marriage to Joe Smith and officially begin dating Ransom Blake. She marveled at the change that could come in two months: from dreading the end of her marriage to happily anticipating it. And all because of a man almost young enough to be her son.

Except for Sienna Elementary and a couple times at Kristy's, Gwen hadn't seen Ransom for the past two weeks. They'd decided not to get together anymore until after Gwen's divorce was final. Gwen told Ransom it was as a precaution, to make sure there were no last minute snags to the marital dissolution. This was true. But the main reason was because she didn't think she could be alone with him in the same room again and not have sex. It was that simple. Her body was on fire, and Ransom had the equipment to put it out.

As torturous as it was to be away from him, Gwen and Ransom's relationship had actually deepened as a result. Nightly phone calls, most times lasting an hour at least, allowed them to learn more about each other. Gwen opened up to Ransom as she hadn't with any other man, finally coming clean about her sexual inexperience and fear of disappointing him. He let her know in no uncertain terms that he was confident, positive, that she was qualified to satisfy, and he couldn't wait until she got the chance to prove it.

That's probably him, Gwen thought as the phone rang. She wasn't disappointed when her caller ID showed it wasn't him. "Hey, baby brother."

"Hey, big sis. Are you on your way to the airport yet?"

"In about ten minutes. Just double-checking to make sure I've got everything."

"So how does it feel to be a day away from joining the ranks of the divorced?"

"I've never felt better, or been happier."

"Are you sure about that? I know you and Ransom have something going on, but you were with Joe for ten years."

"I'm positive, Robert. But trust me, this outlook didn't happen overnight. I was crushed when Joe said he wanted to end our marriage, you know that. His decision filled me with fear and doubt about myself as a wife, and as a woman. If I'd had a choice at the time, which I didn't, I would have chosen to stay married. Nobody enjoys the feelings of failure that getting a divorce brings on. A part of me will always love Joe, and I wish him well. But being with Ransom has shown me that there are levels to love and intimacy that I had no idea about."

"Okay, sis, this sounds like some grown folks' business I'm not sure I want to hear."

Gwen laughed. "And you won't. Besides, Ransom and I have respected the sanctity of my marriage vows. We haven't, well, we've messed around but we haven't . . ."

"Done the do," Robert said, filling in the silence. "Well, I must tell you, Ransom is sounding more and more impressive every time I talk to you. I can't believe he's only twenty-six."

"He'll be twenty-seven at the end of the month."

"Yeah, and you'll be forty-one in July."

"Who asked you?"

"I'm just happy you're happy. But I have to say this, big sis. Guard your heart. Everything's cool now, but there's a lot of years between you and young blood. I don't want you to get in so deep that you'll drown if things don't go the way you want them to."

Gwen didn't know how to tell Robert that it was already too late for this advice. She was head over heels in love with "young blood."

"Okay, Robert, I need to get moving. I'll call you from Chicago."

Several hours later, Gwen lay across a king-sized bed, freshly showered, and grinning broadly. "You are so bad," she said to Ransom, who'd called moments before.

"What? Just because I said I'm having a really hard time without you?"

"Yeah, and the way you said it. Just like that."

"I'm just sorry I couldn't be there with you, Butterfly."

"Me too. But Isis comes first and I can understand your being leery about who keeps her."

"Yes, Miss Mary is still getting over the flu and didn't want to risk passing on anything. And of all the times for Mom to be going to Vegas . . . I even tried to bribe her into canceling the trip, but she wasn't even trying to hear me. Said she'd had a dream about winning, and her hand had been itching all week."

"Well, just so you know, I'm going to try and change my ticket to come back on Friday, instead of Sunday as we'd originally planned."

"Umm. Definitely let me know about that as soon as possible. Mom will be back by then. The weekend will belong to just the two of us."

"All weekend? Baby, I've got papers to grade, lessons to plan."

"I got your lesson right here. . . ."

"Um-hmm . . . Oh, wait a minute, Ransom. Room service is here with dinner. Hold on."

Gwen hurried to the door, even though the conversation with Ransom had shifted the focus of her appetite. She took a quick peek through the peephole and then opened the door.

"Joe, what do you want? What are you doing here?"

32

Joe looked at Gwen sheepishly. "Hey, Gwen. You look good."

"I never would have told you where I was staying if I had known you would just show up. How did you get my room number? Never mind that . . . What do you want?"

"I need to talk to you before our court date tomorrow. Can I come in?"

A waiter came around the corner, pushing the rolling cart of food Gwen had ordered. Now, both appetites she'd worked up earlier were gone. Still, she stood aside as both the room service and Joe walked into her hotel room. When she turned to get her purse and tip the waiter, she noticed the phone lying on the bed.

"I'll have to call you back," Gwen said to Ransom. Her tone was clipped, businesslike.

"Did I hear you say *Joe*? Is he there?"

"Yes."

"Gwen, is everything okay?"

Gwen took a breath and tried to calm down. There

was no need to get Ransom upset. "Yes, everything's fine. I'll call you back."

"Call me as soon as he leaves."

"Okay."

"Gwen."

"Yes?"

"I love you."

Gwen slowly placed the phone on the receiver and willed her nerves to calm as she turned around. Her first thought was of Adam, that somehow he'd found Joe and the two were in cahoots. To collect herself for a moment, she walked over to the food cart, took the plate containing a hamburger, fries, and a salad, and placed it on the table. She sat down, opened the bottled water, and poured herself a glass. By then, her heartbeat was back to normal and she trusted herself to speak.

"Okay, Joe. You're here. So talk."

"You don't have to be so cold, Gwen. I am still your husband."

Gwen almost spit out the bite she was chewing. "My husband? Have you been drinking?"

Joe walked over to the table and sat down across from Gwen. "No, Gwen. I'm stone-cold sober. You have every right to be bitter toward me and angry with me. I mistreated you terribly. I'm sorry."

Gwen nodded and took another bite of the burger. The choice sirloin was cooked to perfection. The fact that she hadn't eaten since morning was evident as her appetite came back with a vengeance.

"How's Mitzi?" she said once she'd swallowed her food.

Joe squirmed a bit before replying. "That's what I'm here about. That nonsense is over."

"Oh, y'all broke up?" *Umm, these fries are good too.*

Gwen reached for the ketchup and poured some on her plate.

"Baby, that's been done for over a month. I've been back at the house since—"

"Whoa, wait a minute, back at what house? Not the house that we both agreed to vacate in August, to sell in August. Not the house that I've been paying half the note on . . . not *that* house."

"That's why we need to talk, Gwen."

"No, *we* don't need to do anything. *You* need to stop beating around the bush and tell me exactly why you're here, and why you're back living in a condo we're trying to sell."

"That's just it, baby. I'm hoping that after tonight, we decide not to sell it."

While diving into her salad, Gwen looked at Joe as if he had three heads.

"Leaving you for Mitzi is the stupidest thing I've ever done in my life. I screwed up, baby. I know that now. Gwen, what I'm trying to say is . . . I want you back. I don't want to get a divorce."

Gwen sat back and crossed her arms. She reached for a fry and slowly chewed it as she stared at him. "Just like that, huh?" she said finally.

"I know it won't be easy. . . ."

"No, Joe, it won't be *possible*. This relationship is ir-reconcilable. My trust in you is completely gone, my faith in the marriage destroyed, and my love for you now that of a friend I once knew."

"I'll do whatever it takes to save our marriage," Joe continued, as if he hadn't heard her. "Counseling, whatever you want. But just give me another chance, Gwen. We've been together for ten years. Surely that's worth giving me a second chance, giving us a second chance."

"You say that you've been back at the house for over a month. Why are we just now having this conversation? I haven't heard from you in three weeks, and when we talked earlier today, you acted like everything was on for tomorrow with no complications."

"I knew I had to have this conversation in person. And as for the time it took to tell you this . . . I was scared, Gwen, and embarrassed that I had acted like a typical forty-year-old having a midlife crisis. But the closer it got to our going to court and legally ending our marriage, the stronger became my conviction that we had to try again." While all of what Joe said was true, there was something he left out—the telephone conversation he'd had with Adam Johnson. Finding out that his wife had attracted a younger man suddenly made her more attractive to Joe, as did the ten thousand dollars Adam offered if Joe won Gwen back.

Gwen's cell phone rang. She let it go to voice mail, but moments later, the hotel phone followed suit.

"That might be Robert," Gwen said to Joe. "I forgot to call him and tell him I made it. Hello?"

"Is he still there?"

"Yes."

"What does he want? Is he trying to change his mind about divorcing you? Because if he is, tell him that that is not an option. Matter of fact, put him on the phone so I can tell him."

"You know you're psychic."

"So that's it. That fool is trying to get you back."

"You don't have to worry."

"I'd better not. Isis and I will catch a red-eye if we

need to. Woman, there's no way I'll lose you without a fight."

Gwen almost teared up at Ransom's words. He always made her feel special, protected, and loved. No other man had ever made her feel the way he did. When she hung up the phone and turned to Joe, she knew that their conversation was over. And so was their marriage.

"Joe, we're past the point of reconciling. We're getting divorced tomorrow. There is absolutely no chance I'll change my mind."

"There's always a chance. Wait, who was that on the phone? Funny, you didn't mention anybody's name. Not 'what's up, Chantay' or 'hey, little brother.' You've met somebody in Los Angeles, haven't you?" When Gwen wouldn't divulge her relationship with Adam's brother, it made Joe even more determined to win her back, and not just for the money. As was often the case, it took another man being interested to make Joe realize the value of the woman he had and was close to losing.

"What is or isn't happening on the West Coast is neither here nor there. Our marriage ended a long time ago. Tomorrow is just a formality."

"I refuse to believe that." Joe walked over and opened the door. "You're my wife, Gwen. And if I have anything to say about it, you're going to stay my wife." Joe looked at Gwen a long moment, mouthed "I love you," and was gone.

Gwen walked to the door and latched the security bar. Her head was spinning. Had she just had a conversation with her soon-to-be ex saying he didn't want to be her ex? It was too much. Gwen sat on the bed with her head in her hands. Then she shook her head with resolve and picked up the phone. There were a few people she needed to speak to: Chantay, Ransom, Robert, and her lawyer.

33

The next morning, Gwen's attorney met her in the courthouse lobby. They'd barely shaken hands before Gwen fired a barrage of questions. "Is Joe here? Did you talk with his attorney? They can't do anything to stop the proceedings, right?"

"Calm down, Gwen," her attorney, Stephen, suggested. "I haven't seen Joe yet but I have talked to his attorney. Joe has asked him to file a motion delaying the divorce proceeding."

"No!" Gwen yelled. Those in the lobby turned to see what the ruckus was about.

Stephen grabbed Gwen's arm and pulled her down a nearby hallway. "Look, you're going to have to keep it together. I want you fully informed as to what's happening, but I don't want you freaking out. Like I said last night, there are absolutely no grounds for having a continuation granted. Joe had an affair, you've been separated for months, and last night was the first time Joe mentioned the desire to reconcile. Correct?"

Gwen nodded. "Absolutely."

"I do have one last question that I didn't ask last night. Are you having an affair as well? Is there someone back in Los Angeles that I need to know about?"

Gwen's voice rose again. "Is this what Joe is implying?"

"Keep your voice down!"

"Is that what he is telling his attorney?" Gwen hissed. "Because I can assure you that anything happening in Los Angeles has absolutely nothing to do with what is going on here."

"So you have met someone?"

"What business is it of yours?"

Stephen sighed audibly. "Look, Gwen, you can make this easy or difficult. The choice is yours. But in case you've forgotten, I'm your attorney. I'm on your side. I'm asking you because I need to be prepared to defend whatever accusations might be thrown our way."

Gwen crossed her arms and glared in the direction of the courthouse doors. She wanted to see Joe walking through them, so she could give him a piece of her mind as well as a piece of her Coach handbag upside his head.

"Gwen?" Stephen prodded.

Gwen took a deep, cleansing breath and looked at Stephen. "I'm sorry, Stephen. You're absolutely right. Irrational anger isn't going to get me anywhere. I do have a friend in Sienna. We are not having an affair, as Joe might be alleging, but Ransom is very, very special to me."

Gwen told Stephen the background story on Ransom as well as her connection with Adam, and the animosity that existed between the two brothers. She also told him about Carol's infatuation with

Ransom, and Joanna, who she suspected was seeing Adam. Those two had seemed particularly cozy the last time she'd seen them in the teachers' lounge, she explained. Gwen assured Stephen that any information from any of these sources was flimsy at best, and more than likely flat-out lies.

An hour later, Gwen, Joe, and their attorneys sat in the judge's chambers. The judge shuffled through a few papers before beginning the proceedings.

"All parties are aware that a continuation has been requested in these proceedings."

"Yes, your honor, and my client is absolutely and unequivocally against any such continuation occurring. These parties have been separated for months and for at least part of that time, my client's husband was living with another woman."

"Objection!"

"Calm down, George," the obviously overworked judge said wearily. He looked at another paper before addressing Gwen. "Mrs. Smith, your husband wants the chance to reconcile. Why should I not grant him the opportunity to salvage this marriage?"

As Stephen had instructed, Gwen left out emotion and stuck to the facts. "It is my desire to grant Mr. Smith's initial request for a divorce, and his acts of adultery give me more than enough grounds to do so. Your honor, there is absolutely no chance that I will change my mind, or my feelings toward this situation. I've already had several months to think about it. Our vows have been irretrievably broken, and I am clear in my decision to end this union."

"My client denies any such actions," George said.

"*What?*" All of the emotion Gwen had kept in

check during her previous answer was poured into this one word.

Stephen placed a hand on Gwen's arm. "My client is positive of this relationship, your honor."

"She's lying!" Joe yelled.

"You're a liar!" Gwen countered. "And a cheating asshole too!"

"All right, that's enough," the judge said.

"Your honor, we'd like to present this file as evidence." Stephen pulled an envelope from his briefcase, and Gwen thanked God that this astute attorney had suggested they hire a private detective. "Pictures that will conclusively show that Mr. Smith was engaged in illicit activities with another woman while married to my client."

"Your honor," George wailed, "this evidence was not presented at discovery. I have no idea about these photos, whether they've been doctored, where they were taken, or whether the person in the photos is even my client. I demand that this evidence be tossed out, and the continuation of my client be granted so that I can have a chance to view and counter this evidence."

The judge took the pictures out of the envelope and slowly sifted through them. He looked at Joe from time to time, as he examined one picture after another, holding up a photo at one point and looking between it and Joe, who sat in bold defiance. After looking at the last one, he gathered up the stack and handed it to Joe's attorney. "George, your motion is denied."

Gwen was emotionally drained and physically tired. She opened the door to her hotel room, threw her purse on the bed, and walked straight to the shower. She undressed, turned the water to as hot as she could stand it, and stepped under the showerhead.

Her tears mingled with the water. It surprised her, these myriad emotions that did battle in her heart. She wasn't expecting to feel the sense of loss that she did, or the sadness. There was no doubt that divorcing Joe was the right thing to do, but for some inexplicable reason, the finality of the judge granting the divorce decree wrought havoc on her psyche. During the drive from the courthouse to her hotel, all of the good times she'd had with Joe began playing in her head, events she hadn't thought of in years. Gwen soaped her body and let the tears flow.

When she stepped out of the shower, her phone was ringing. Knowing she wouldn't get to it in time, Gwen took her time drying off, putting lotion on, and dressing in a baby blue fleece warm-up. She pulled her wet hair back into a simple ponytail and then went to retrieve the message from the phone.

"You have one new message," the hotel automated service announced.

Gwen pushed the button and immediately recognized Ransom's voice. The tears flowed anew as she heard his succinct message:

"I just want to hear one thing, Butterfly. That it's over, and our time together starts right now."

34

Gwen felt like a schoolgirl going on her first date. All Ransom had told her about where they were headed was to dress nicely, and to only bring toiletries, that he had everything else.

"Even underwear?" she'd asked, regarding his strange request.

"Oh, you won't be needing panties," he'd replied.

Gwen giggled as she held a pair of thongs in her hand. She was sorely tempted to disregard his statement about her needing undergarments, but he'd threatened a heavy penalty if she didn't follow his instructions to the letter. After a few more seconds of thought, she slipped into the panties, put the remaining toiletries into her overnight bag, and zipped it. She looked around the room a final time before grabbing her bag, turning out the bedroom light, and going into the living room to await Ransom's arrival.

After mere seconds, Gwen jumped up from the couch. She was too nervous to sit. She walked to the mirror by the front door and looked at her reflection for the umpteenth time. She'd chosen simple elegance, a form-fitting black sheath dress that hung a couple inches past her thighs. A pair of silver sling-backs with three-inch heels was the perfect complement to the silver jewelry she wore: teardrop earrings, a matching necklace, and at Chantay's near threat of violence, several thin bangles on her right arm. She'd stopped at the beauty shop on the way back from the airport and her freshly straightened hair swung freely, just past her shoulders. The side part and blunt cut the beautician had suggested framed Gwen's face perfectly, the slight wisp of bangs highlighting her arched brows. The perfume she'd sprayed liberally over her body was the final touch of sexy she hoped would drive Ransom wild. Gwen looked at her watch and, seeing she still had ten minutes before Ransom was scheduled to show up, decided to call her mother.

"Hey, Mama."

"Hi, Gwen dear. You children must be on rotation today. I just got off the phone with Robert, and Gerald called earlier."

"That's what happens when you're the most popular person at Sunrise Place. How are you feeling, Mama?"

"Oh, a little tired today, but other than that I'm fine. We stay so busy."

"Well, take care of yourself. Don't overdo."

"Are you still coming by tomorrow?"

Uh-oh. "No, Mama. I'm going out of town with a friend, remember?"

"No, not really," Lorraine responded. "But then again, I don't always remember so well these days. That's why they designed these note boards for us. Guess I didn't put what you told me on there."

Lorraine was grateful for the staff at Sunrise Place, and the new, young, innovative private doctor who was now treating her. His new plan included holistic and alternative measures, along with traditional treatments, to counter her disease, and mental exercises to stimulate and hopefully regenerate cognitive skills. She wasn't healed by any means, but was doing much better than when Gwen arrived in Sienna just three months ago. While she was still forgetful, at least now she was aware of this fact. Before beginning treatments, she was in denial that anything was even wrong with her. "I'll be by on Monday," Gwen said. "But you've got my cell. Is the number up on your board?"

"Oh, yes. All of you children's numbers are there with a bold, red marker. Oh, honey, I have to go. That's Esther knocking at my door. They make us play games all the time, say it's 'mind exercise.'"

"Sounds good, Mama."

"She's teaching me how to play bridge, and you know what, Gwen? I really like it! But don't tell them I told you that," she said, her voice lowered. "Can't have them finding out I'm not the old codger they think I am. I'm coming, Esther," she yelled out. "Bye, darling. You and Chantay have fun."

Gwen smiled, both because her mother remembered Chantay's name, and that she assumed this was the friend she was hanging out with. Gwen looked at the clock and, seeing she still had a few minutes to wait, dialed Chantay.

"I'm surprised to be hearing from you right about now," is how Chantay answered the phone.

"He's supposed to be here in about two minutes. I'm so nervous!"

"Uh-hmm. That coochie knows it's gonna get hit tonight, that's what the deal is."

"Shut up, girl."

"Look, I'm your best friend. Don't even act like you can wait. As long as y'all have been playing around? Girl, you deserve a night of loving."

"Okay, I admit it. I am a little excited about that."

Chantay whooped. "You think?" She cleared her throat. "Has Joe called anymore?"

"No, thank God. It's over, officially. I can't believe that after all these months he was acting as though there's still mad love between us. I just don't get it."

"What about the condo? Is he still there?"

"My attorney is working on that. It's part of the marital property that has to be divided, so Joe either needs to move or buy me out. I don't want this to get dragged out."

"What about the real estate agent you talked to while you were in Chicago?"

"I really like her. She's all about business, so as long as Joe doesn't drag his feet, I think she should be able to sell the condo by the end of the year. With the housing bust, we won't get as much out of the sale as we thought we would, but I'll look at whatever profit as my Christmas present."

"Hmph. Sounds like to me Christmas came in October—first with your divorce being final and now with Ransom getting ready to put the cherry on top of your chocolate sundae." Chantay laughed at her own joke. "So are you wearing panties?"

"I knew I shouldn't have told you anything about that!"

"Well, are you?"

"Of course I am!"

"Gwendolyn Andrews! Didn't I tell you to lose the drawers? The boy already *told* you not to bring any for y'all's little rendezvous. That tells you he'd prefer you without them. When are you going to start listening to a sistah?"

Gwen saw a shiny red Porsche pull up. "Well, it sure won't be right now," she said teasingly to Chantay. "Ransom's here. I'll call you later."

"You better."

Gwen's heartbeat picked up as she watched Ransom come to her front door. It was the first time she'd seen him dressed up, and even in attire best described as simply elegant, he looked amazing. The stark white silk shirt he wore showed off his bronzed skin to perfection. The black slacks fit snugly around his waist, buttocks, and thighs, and the simple silver and turquoise choker he wore accented his strong neck and looked surprisingly masculine. As a further sign that this was indeed a special occasion, Ransom's shiny black hair was out of its usual ponytail, and hung loose and flowing over his broad shoulders.

Gwen met him at the door. "Hey, handsome."

Ransom's teeth seemed to sparkle as he smiled at the compliment. "Come here, Butterfly." He enveloped Gwen's body in a hug, breathed in her scent, and rubbed his hands lovingly over her body. "You look good enough to eat," he said, after searing her with a kiss.

If she could have, Gwen would have blushed. As it were, she flushed warm and was at a loss for words. "Do you want to, I mean, are you ready to . . ."

"Yes," Ransom said as he stepped inside the living room and closed the front door. "I'm ready to . . ." He didn't finish the sentence, but instead leaned back against the front door, crossed his arms, and drank in Gwen with his eyes. Gwen almost began shaking under his intense appraisal, but worked to remain still as he gazed at her. Finally she couldn't take it anymore, and pointed to the large bag he held in his hand.

"What's that?"

After a long pause, Ransom answered. "Presents for my woman." He silently took her hand and walked over to the couch. He sat down beside her and gave her the bag.

Gwen squealed as she pulled out a medium-sized tan and black teddy bear wearing a Chicago White Sox baseball cap. "You remembered I'm a fan," Gwen said, hugging to her the gift that from anyone else would have seemed childish to this forty-year-old. But from Ransom, it was endearing. "Thank you," she said sincerely. "I'll sleep with it every night."

"On the nights you're not sleeping with me. Because on those nights, trust me, there will only be room for you and I in the bed."

Gwen tried to rise from the couch. "Should we go?"

Ransom caught her hand and laughed softly. "Look, B-Fly. You're going to have to get used to being aroused by me. Because after tonight, it's only going to intensify."

Gwen couldn't even think of a comeback. Ransom had read her mind like a New York best seller.

"There's something else in the bag," Ransom said.

Glad for the diversion, Gwen reached into the bag. There was a small box in the bottom, nicely wrapped in glittery iridescent paper and tied with a silver string.

"What's this?"

"Open it and find out."

Gwen untied the string and carefully removed the gift paper wrapping.

"Damn," Ransom said softly. "I can tell Christmas is a long day at your house."

Gwen laughed. "I've always been this way, even as a child. I guess I like to savor the moment of receiving a gift by prolonging the mystery of what's inside."

"Hmm," Ransom said as he rubbed his chin thoughtfully. His deep black eyes bore into Gwen's brown ones. "Powerful words to live by."

Flustered again by his probing stare, Gwen looked down at the box and took off its lid. Inside was another box, covered in black velvet. She slowly took it out of the gift box and opened the lid. She gasped. Inside was a beautifully sculpted silver butterfly, covered in tiny yellow and pink diamonds. It hung on a thin silver chain, and the wings seemed to quiver with the diamonds' sparkle. Tears, unbidden, sprang to her eyes. But unlike the ones she shed for Joe, the emotion accompanying these tears was one of joy, not sorrow.

Gwen scooted close to Ransom and hugged his neck. "It's the most beautiful present I've ever received," she said sincerely. She placed her hand on his face as she stared into his eyes. "You are a very special man."

"Just so long as you know those wings don't mean you can fly away from me, ever. Now that I've caught you, Butterfly, I'll never let you go." Ransom took off the necklace Gwen wore and replaced it with his gift. "Come on, let's get out of here. If we don't go now, I'll have you naked and moaning in less than two minutes."

35

"Ransom, this place is fabulous. How did you find it?" Gwen marveled at the cozy restaurant's elegance. They'd been led to an outdoor patio, shimmering with a backlit waterfall and votive candles placed atop pristine white linen. Their table offered a panoramic view of the mountainous backdrop of Palm Springs, in the California desert.

Ransom shrugged. "I can't be giving away all my secrets, baby." Truth is, one of his wealthiest clients had once gifted him with a weekend stay there after Ransom had finished a job under budget. Ransom had been exhausted, and come alone. At the time he vowed that he'd come back, and that he'd bring someone special.

"Well, this place is beautiful, so intimate and secluded. And the view is fabulous." Gwen's eyes sparkled as she gazed out on a full moon from their corner table, made virtually private thanks to some well-placed potted palms.

"I'm glad you like the view," Ransom murmured, fixing her with his smolderingly familiar gaze.

"Because I'm liking the view myself. It's beautiful . . . fabulous."

The waiter came over, pushing a cart with a silver ice bucket containing a bottle of champagne. He elaborately presented the bottle of Clos du Mesnil, the exclusive 1995 vintage, for Ransom's approval before popping the cork and pouring two bubbling glasses.

Ransom raised his glass to Gwen. "To endings . . . and beginnings."

Gwen raised her glass to Ransom. "To us."

Their eyes locked as both drank from their glasses. "Umm, I'm not much of a drinker, but this is good," Gwen said.

"You'll be drinking more later," Ransom replied casually.

"Probably not," Gwen replied. "Like I said, I don't drink much."

"Believe me, you'll want to," was Ransom's reply. He set down his glass and casually put his arm around the back of her chair. "Come kiss me."

Gwen leaned over and gave him a soft, quick kiss on the lips. Ransom held the back of her head and deepened the exchange. He gently massaged the nape of her neck, placing kisses along her jawline and around to her ear. His breath was warm and moist as he whispered in her ear.

Gwen pulled back to look at him. "What did you say?" she asked, talking barely above a whisper herself.

"You heard me."

"You asked if I was wearing panties?"

"That is correct."

Gwen repeated the answer she'd given Chantay earlier. "Of course."

"Why?"

Gwen took another sip of champagne. "I don't think I understand your question."

"Why are you wearing panties? I told you not to bring any underwear on this trip."

"Exactly. You said not to *bring* any. I am *wearing* these."

"Not for long. Go take them off."

"Excuse me?"

Ransom lowered his voice and enunciated each word. "Go take off your panties, thongs, Spanx, whatever you're wearing. I want them off, now."

Ransom's demand aroused Gwen in a way that surprised her. She felt herself become moist, and her nipples harden. She felt embarrassed and tried to cool down what had become a very hot corner with levity.

"In case you haven't noticed, we're in a public place."

"So?"

"So, I don't go walking around in public with no underwear, that's so."

"Either you can go take them off in the restroom, or I'll take them off right now."

"You will do no such thing."

"Is that a challenge?"

"You wouldn't," Gwen repeated, but the determined look on Ransom's face made her less sure. "Would you?"

"Don't make me ask again, Gwen. Go do as I said." With that, Ransom picked up his champagne glass, sat back casually, and took a long swallow.

Gwen took a swallow from her glass as well.

"Oh, you're still here?" Ransom asked. Before

Gwen could blink, she was on Ransom's lap and his hand was beneath her dress. His movements had been so fluid and precise that the edge of the table-cloth had barely fluttered.

"Ransom, stop!" she hissed. "Okay, all right, I'll go take them off. Please don't do that. Let me go!" Gwen wanted to be angry but the smile on Ransom's face combined with the heat from her now flaming nether folds caused her to simply leap from his lap and hurry from the room, almost knocking over the waitress bringing them appetizers in the process.

"Is everything all right, sir?" the perky Latina asked.

Ransom laughed out loud. "Oh, yeah," he drawled confidently. "Everything's fine."

Gwen felt all eyes were on her as she walked from the restaurant's restroom back to her table. And indeed, many male eyes and several female ones followed her steps, but not for the reason she imagined. Gwen's natural beauty was enhanced by not only her simply elegant outfit but by the glow of love that shone on her face. The scrutiny was unfamiliar, and made her even more nervous than Ransom's penetrating gaze and her now bare goodies. She was thankful to get back to the table and sit down.

"Let me see them," Ransom said as she sat.

"No!" Gwen hissed. "I am not going to pull my panties out at this table!"

"Then pass me your purse."

"What? You don't believe that I took them off?"

Ransom's Cheshire smile widened. "No, I don't. And I'll tell you something else. You're not faring well tonight on your ability to take instruction. Have you forgotten that in matters between us, I'm the teacher?"

Gwen flung her small jeweled bag at Ransom. He laughed out loud as he opened it and proceeded to pull out her lacy black thong.

"Put those away," Gwen demanded through clenched teeth.

Ransom answered her command by putting the sheer fabric up to his nose and inhaling deeply.

"Ransom Blake. Stop that this instant!"

Gwen's tone was that which she would have used on Ransom's daughter. The strident voice didn't work as well on the child's father. But seeing how embarrassed and rattled she had become, Ransom slowly lowered the panties from his nose and placed them in his pocket. His actions left Gwen speechless, and further aroused. Thankfully, the steamy moment was interrupted by the arrival of their dinner.

Later, Gwen would barely be able to recall her perfectly cooked Chateaubriand served with asparagus and potatoes, and Ransom would totally forget how the halibut he ordered fairly melted on his tongue, and how the creamy risotto and winter vegetable medley were a perfect complement to the succulent fish. Because by the time they had finished the last bite of their meal, including the triple-chocolate pudding cake that was to die for, all this couple wanted to taste . . . was each other.

36

No sooner had the door closed to their luxury stand-alone cabin than Gwen was in Ransom's arms. Only this time, she was the initiator. He lifted her off the ground and walked them to the wall, where he pinned Gwen's back against it and plundered her mouth with his tongue. Supporting her with his body and the wall, he took one hand and ran it underneath her hiked-up dress, trailing a stiff finger along the wet folds of her desire before putting the finger to his mouth and licking it sensually.

Gwen was in a sexual frenzy unlike any she'd ever known. She pulled at his shirt, popping one of the buttons off the fabric. She wanted to feel all of him everywhere, and hated that there was cloth between them. But pinned against the wall as she was, Ransom was in total control.

"No," he whispered breathlessly. "We've waited too long to hurry this moment."

"But, Ransom . . ."

"Remember long and slow? That's how this evening is going to be." Ransom walked over to the iPod unit he'd brought with him and turned it on. A melodious, almost haunting voice immediately filled the room, singing about lessons and learning.

Ransom reached for Gwen and began a sensual slow dance. There were no words spoken between the two inevitable lovers, just the encouraging words of jazz singer Al Jarreau: *"teach me tonight."*

The song ended and for a moment, the two simply held each other. Finally Ransom broke the silence. "Come bathe with me," he said.

At most, Gwen was hoping for a two-minute shower. Normally a lover of luxurious baths, tonight she was in no mood for one. Ransom held her hand and led the way to the bathroom. Once there, Gwen's eyes widened. The tub was lined with white votive candles that accented the steam rising from hot, soapy water.

"When did you do this?" she asked.

"I've got connections," he whispered, reaching for the hem of her dress. Ransom pulled the dress over Gwen's head and placed his mouth on her nipple. He trailed a strong finger down the crevice of her backside and pulled her closer. Gwen tried to breathe and slow her heartbeat. But there was no use. This man had her about to hyperventilate!

"Ransom, please . . ."

Ransom quickly took off his clothes. He leaned down and tested the water. "Perfect," he said. He stepped into the large Jacuzzi tub and pulled Gwen along with him. He sat down and leaned back, enfolding Gwen in his arms. He immediately continued his assault, licking a trail around her earlobe, teasing her neck with kisses, fluttering his finger along the folds of her desire.

Gwen tried to turn and kiss him.

"Hmm, just enjoy," he said.

Ransom reached over for a sponge and gel that were positioned on the side of the tub. He lathered the sponge and began to wash Gwen's body. His fingers followed everywhere the sponge went . . . everywhere. At one point, he got out of the tub, but directed Gwen to stay inside. From the side, dripping wet, he continued to wash her legs and feet, all the while staring at her as if she hung the moon. Gwen worked on simply breathing.

Finally, he lifted Gwen out of the tub and enveloped her in a towel. He patted her skin gently, until she was dry, and then quickly dried himself off. Before exiting the bathroom, he reached for a tube on the vanity.

"Edible lotion?" Gwen asked hopefully.

"I love a student who remembers previous instruction," Ransom replied.

Once he'd laid Gwen on the bed, Ransom's focus became more intense. He took the lotion and, starting with her toes, began to lick the skin he'd just dried, causing Gwen to become wet all over again. He caressed each toe, massaged her feet and ankles, calves, and thighs. He spread her legs wide and stared at her for a long moment.

"You're beautiful," he said simply.

Gwen began to tremble. With a look of love boring into her eyes, Ransom took some of the lotion and lightly touched her nub. Gwen thought she would explode. She began to squirm, wanting to feel the pressure of his hand on her, inside her.

"Not so fast," he whispered, as he gently massaged her, ran his fingers along the length of her, until she began to blossom. Soon his tongue replaced his finger, and Gwen thought she'd lose her mind. Still he was light, feathery, licking and then blowing on the wetness. He kissed one thigh, and then the other, ran his tongue up to her navel and back, massaged her breasts with his hands, softly touching . . .

"Ransom!" Gwen cried.

Ransom chuckled. "Okay, Butterfly." With that he plunged his tongue deep into Gwen. She squealed in delight, even as she tried to move away. The pleasure was too much, she couldn't take it. Ransom grabbed her thighs and held her firm, setting her on fire with each nibble, each thrust of his powerful swordlike tongue. Just as quickly as the assault began, it ended.

Ransom calmly got out of bed and walked over to the nightstand.

What is he doing? Gwen thought, but couldn't speak. She lay back on the bed, closed her eyes, and tried to stop shaking. She heard a cork pop, heard the bubbly being poured into glasses. *He wants a drink . . . now?* Gwen opened her eyes, turned onto her side, and her eyes opened wider. Ransom stared at her as he dipped his deliciously formed member into the glass.

His instruction was simple. "Come have a sip."

The rarely imbibing Gwen hurried to his side like an alcoholic at happy hour. She hesitated for just a moment before closing her eyes and trying to take him full into her mouth.

"Slowly, Butterfly, we have all night." Ransom pulled himself away from her, dipped himself into the glass, and nodded slightly.

Gwen tried again, slower this time. She was new at this, but could already tell she liked it. He felt so good, hard and soft at the same time. Instinctively, she ran her tongue around the rim of his circumcised shaft. Ransom hissed. Gwen smiled, and did it again. This time it was she who dunked him in the glass. Ransom had said she'd want more to drink later. He'd been right!

After several moments, Ransom rolled on a colossal condom and climbed back on the bed. He placed Gwen in the very center of it, and once again began his oral assault. He replaced his tongue with his finger and found her G-spot. Gwen climaxed immediately, and while she was still shaking from the ferocity of her release, Ransom spread her folds and entered her. Slowly, at first, he proceeded inch after glorious inch, pulling out to the tip and entering farther, deeper each time. Finally, after allowing her body time to relax and expand to accommodate his size, he pushed himself to the hilt and began the age-old dance of love . . . long, slow movements, as he'd promised. He loved her in a dozen different ways, loved her so good and so thoroughly that Gwen cried. She was experiencing the pleasure of total sexual fulfillment for the first time in her life. And when at last he joined her in release, and Gwen came for the final time, the jolt of pleasure was so intense that her whole body stiffened as if paralyzed . . . and she got a crick in her toe!

37

Ransom bounded up the three steps to Gwen's front door and tapped lightly on the screen. "Anybody home?"

"Daddy!" Isis jumped from the couch and unlocked the door for her father. He came in, lifted her up off the floor, and gave her a big bear hug and kiss.

"How's my princess? Did you have a good day?"

Isis nodded. "We had fun today at school. Miss Gwen has this big map of the United States that covers the floor, like this big." Isis ran in a circle to demonstrate the size of the rug shaped like America. "And it has all the states on it and we played a game to learn where they were."

"Sounds great, baby. Miss Gwen sounds like an excellent teacher."

"Your father's a pretty good teacher too," Gwen said, wiping her hands on her apron as she came from the kitchen into the living room. She walked over to Ransom and gave him a light hug.

"Ooh. Y'all hugging, y'all boyfriend and girlfriend." Isis giggled as she walked around them chanting,

"Miss Gwen likes my daddy, Miss Gwen likes my daddy!"

Gwen and Ransom looked at each other. They had talked about how to discuss their relationship with Isis and had decided that aside from the initial conversation they'd had with her, where they had indeed said they were "friends," they thought it best to just let the situation unfold organically. Gwen keeping Isis after school allowed the three of them to interact daily during the week, and for the past two weekends they had also done activities together. They thought Isis had accepted their friendship as a casual one, much like the one Ransom once had with Carol. But obviously the little cherub was picking up on a different set of vibes.

Gwen looked at Ransom with a "say something" expression. Ransom shrugged, gently grabbed Isis's arm, and said, "Quit running before you hurt yourself."

Isis looked between Gwen and Ransom, her large brown eyes twinkling mischievously. Gwen saw the curiosity in those eyes and knew a more explanatory talk was in order, otherwise Isis might take her little sing-song ditty to the playground tomorrow.

Gwen knelt down to Isis's eye level. "Yes, Isis, I like your father. What do you think that means?"

Isis giggled again. "It means y'all gonna kiss, like this"—Isis made smooching sounds—"and then, and then y'all gonna get married!" She started skipping around the room. "Miss Gwen likes my daddy, Miss Gwen likes my daddy!"

"Princess," Ransom said patiently. "Come here,

Daddy needs to talk to you." He took Isis by the hand and led her to the couch. "Okay, here's the deal. Miss Gwen and I do like each other, but there are some people that aren't too happy about it."

"Like Carol?" Isis asked.

Another look passed between Gwen and Ransom. Gwen marveled at Isis's astuteness and believed that Ransom had passed on the gift of intuition to his daughter.

"Remember how when you and Kari became friends, some of the other kids made fun of you?" Ransom asked. Isis nodded. "What did I tell you about that?"

"You said they were just jealous because they didn't have a best friend."

"That's exactly right. And that's how it is for me and Miss Gwen. Some people are just mad because they don't have"—he nodded toward Gwen—"a best friend."

Isis thought about his answer for a moment, and then asked, "Do best friends get married, Daddy?"

"Sometimes."

"Good, because I would like Miss Gwen to be my new mommy."

Ransom and Gwen were saved by the bell, literally, as little Tianna, a schoolmate who lived on the block, activated the door chime. "Can Isis come play?" she asked through the screen.

Isis jumped off the couch, her interest in Gwen and Ransom's relationship status and the future of said status thankfully diverted. "Ooh, can I go, Daddy?"

"Yes, Princess. But don't leave the front yard."

Isis had barely gotten outside when Ransom grabbed Gwen and walked them back to the privacy of the kitchen where he kissed her, then burst into laughter.

"This isn't funny," Gwen said between giggles.

"Miss Gwen likes my daddy," he mimicked, running his hand across Gwen's bottom and nibbling her neck. "What Isis said about your being her new mommy . . . now there's an idea."

Gwen had always wanted to be a mother. And if she could have a daughter, she'd want a smart, cute, rambunctious one like Isis. But as much as she loved Ransom, and the one-big-happy-family idea, she was fresh out of a ten-year marriage.

Ransom laughed softly, kissed her once more, and then let her go. "Dag, my girl got scared silent. It's okay, Butterfly. I'll wait for your answer."

With Ransom now nibbling on her ear, Gwen tried hard to remember the question.

Ransom delivered another one. "What's for dinner? Something smells good."

Gwen was glad for the change in subject. She had to prepare for a teachers' meeting the following day and couldn't be with Ransom later. "Mini pizzas," she answered. "Can you guys stay for dinner?"

"Baby, I'm ready to eat right now!" He reached again for Gwen but this time she sidestepped him and went to the refrigerator.

"You're so bad," Gwen said.

"Um hmm. And you wouldn't have it any other way."

Ransom and Gwen chatted comfortably as he watched her prepare her pizzas, using English muffins for the crust, a shredded chicken topping, and lots of cheese. In a nod to Isis and the child in Gwen, she topped the creations with happy faces: black olives for eyes, a broccoli floret for the nose, and a slice of red pepper for the mouth. She placed the muffins on a cookie sheet, placed the sheet in the oven, and collected dishes and silverware to set the table.

When she came back into the kitchen and reached for the potato chips in the cabinet, Ransom came up and hugged her from behind.

"Why didn't you and your husband have kids?"

Gwen wriggled out of his embrace and took the soda out of the refrigerator. "It just never happened."

"What, you were using birth control?"

"I was, but not for the last three years of our marriage. We tried, but I never got pregnant."

"Maybe your boy was sterile."

Gwen shrugged, put on an oven mitten, and pulled the pizzas out from under the broiler. "No, I think it's me. Probably just as well, considering what happened to our marriage."

"You'd make an excellent mother," Ransom said sincerely. "You're a natural."

For some reason, Ransom's genuine compliment made Gwen teary. She hid her emotion by busying herself with putting the pizzas on a serving dish and grabbing parmesan cheese from the cabinet. Then she walked to the front door and called to Isis.

"Come on, sweetie, dinner's ready."

Ransom smiled as he heard Gwen call to his daughter and then direct Isis to wash her hands. Isis obeyed, rattling on to Gwen, who walked with her to the bathroom to wash her hands as well. Gwen laughed at something Isis said, their voices less clear as they continued down the hall. Their camaraderie made Ransom happy, and a feeling of contentment bubbled up inside him. Not long ago he'd entertained the idea of a queen for him and his princess. And now, he was sure, he'd found her.

38

Carol got so excited at seeing Ransom's Jeep parked at Kristy's that she almost ran over a little old lady crossing the street.

"Move, you old bird!" she yelled, honking her horn and giving the startled senior citizen the finger. The old woman used her cane to point out the red light that indicated that pedestrians had the right of way. She then shook her head and continued crossing the street.

"I can't believe old Ms. Disney is still alive," Carol mumbled as she tapped her wheel impatiently. "I should have run over the old biddy."

Carol's light turned green and she hurriedly crossed the street and entered the coffee shop parking lot. Just in time, Ransom exited Kristy's and headed to his Jeep the moment Carol parked beside it.

"Hey, stranger," Carol said. She got out of her car and leaned into Ransom's Jeep. He was already inside and had started the engine. "Wait! Ransom, can we talk?"

"About what?"

"Five minutes, please. I thought we were friends."

Ransom hesitated a moment before turning off the car. "Okay."

"Why are you so angry with me?"

"I'm not angry with you, Carol. I'm just done with you. You effectively ended our friendship when you started lying on Gwen, not to mention lying on my child. That was really the last straw, right there."

"How did I lie? You two *aren't* seeing each other? And I would never lie on Isis. I love that little girl, you know that!"

Ransom reached for his keys.

"Okay, maybe I said some things that weren't true," Carol rapidly continued. "But I couldn't help it, Ransom. You know how I feel about you, that I was hoping you and I could have something special together."

"I never gave you reason to think that would happen. I mean we were cool and all, and I didn't mind hanging out because of how our daughters got along but, Carol, I never looked at you like that, as someone to date. Nothing personal, you're just not my type."

"And Gwen Smith is? Good Lord, Ransom, she went to school with Adam, for God's sake! She's ancient!"

Ransom started his car. "Move."

"Just one night, Ransom. I promise the things I can do will make you forget all about—"

"Good-bye, Carol!"

Carol stepped back and watched as Ransom peeled out of the parking lot. She was in a major huff, as a distorted memory of what she and Ransom used to have together played out in her mind. *If it hadn't been for her . . .* Carol fumed, as she got into her car and headed for Joanna's house. *If it hadn't been for that bitch, Ransom would be mine!*

An hour later, Joanna pulled into her apartment complex parking lot and noticed Carol waiting for her, inside her car. Puffy eyes and a red nose told her Carol had been crying.

"What's wrong," Joanna asked as she approached Carol's rolled down window. "Did something happen to Kari? She seemed fine at school today."

"It's not her, it's me. My plan to get Ransom back has backfired. He's really mad that I put his business out there, about him and Gwen."

"Well, it's the truth! He is doing her. Why is he so mad about that?"

Carol's face contorted as crocodile tears ran down her cheeks. "I want him so badly. He's a perfect man for me and father figure for Kari. What am I gonna do?" A loud boohoo punctuated the question.

"Well, you're gonna stop crying for one thing," Joanna said, in a rare moment appearing the older of the two. "Come inside so you can pull yourself together."

Joanna and Carol were silent as they walked up the steps and Joanna unlocked the door to her condo. But as soon as they were inside, Carol started in again. "What about your plan to make her leave the school? And what about Adam?"

"What about Adam?" Joanna retorted quickly.

"I mean, well, isn't he mad at her too?"

Joanna plopped down on the couch and took off her shoes. "Yeah, and I don't know why, to tell you the truth. He's already been with the whore, so why does he care that his brother is doing her now? Unless . . ."

"Unless what?"

"Never mind. Adam doesn't want her. He told me."

"That's what he said. But how can you be so sure that they aren't still screwing? You're the one who saw them coming back from some rendezvous when she first got here, going at it all hot and heavy in the parking lot. And you watched him check her out in the gym that day. That doesn't sound like the behavior of two people who were screwing twenty years ago. It sounds like what people do who are screwing now."

"But why would she want him if she's dating Ransom?"

"I don't know and I don't care, and you shouldn't either. Did you do like we talked about, try to become friends so you can find out what's going on?"

"Really, Carol, Gwen isn't stupid. Why would the very person who couldn't stand her one day be cozying up to her the next? If you're depending on my befriending her for info, I wouldn't count on finding out too much."

Carol angrily wiped the last tears from her eyes, lowered her voice, and looked straight at Joanna. "I will do anything to get Ransom back. Do you hear me? Anything. I ain't never gonna run across anybody like him again." Carol repeated her declaration, this time softly, to herself: "Anything."

39

Ransom looked around quickly before giving Gwen a kiss on the lips.

"Will you stop that?" Gwen looked around too, but satisfied that no one was near her classroom and Isis was enthralled in *Kuchekesha Island*, the children's book Gwen had bought her over the weekend, Gwen continued the kiss, opening her mouth to invite his tongue, before pulling back and wiping her lipstick off his mouth.

"Do you have to go into LA today?"

"I'm going to get you for that," Ransom whispered. He tweaked her nipple through the knit top she wore. "I think so," he said after he'd straightened up and put some much needed distance between him and his woman. Even though they made ardent love almost every night, he couldn't seem to get enough of Gwen. "I was hoping my foreman could handle everything, but these small business owners seem to like having me around."

"That's because you're the man," Gwen said.

"I guess," Ransom responded, while beaming under Gwen's praise.

"I was thinking that maybe I could meet you there," Gwen continued. "In LA. I could bring Isis and maybe we could spend the night there."

"That sounds like a plan, B-fly. I'll call you later and let you know how things are looking on the job."

Ransom walked over and kissed his daughter, then headed toward the door. He almost ran into Joanna, who came in at the same time.

"Oh, sorry," Joanna said to Gwen while staring at Ransom as if he were the Second Coming. *My goodness, I forgot how absolutely gorgeous you are!* "I didn't know you were . . . busy."

"It's okay," Gwen said to Joanna. "See you later, Ransom."

Gwen knew that loving Ransom definitely made it easier to deal with Joanna and Adam, who were still trying to work her last nerve, in and out of the classroom. She looked at her watch and frowned slightly. Some of her other early kids should have arrived by now. Gwen walked to her desk, sat down, and addressed Joanna. "You needed to talk to me?"

"Uh, yeah," Joanna began nervously. She looked over at Isis. "I was hoping we could talk privately."

"Well, that obviously isn't going to happen since we're in my classroom where about twenty other students will be joining the one already here any minute now."

"Yeah, I guess you're right. I'll make a long story short." She walked closer to Gwen's desk and spoke in a low tone. "I've been a total jerk since you've been here, and want to say I'm sorry. We got along so great that first time I saw you, when you came for the interview, remember? It's just that, well, I've been dealing with some financial problems and personal stuff that I'm sure you're not interested in hearing. I just haven't been myself." Joanna's voice dropped even lower. "I didn't want to make you adopt my lesson plans," she lied. "That was Adam's idea." *After I suggested it,* she thought. "You're a great teacher, Gwen. I could learn a thing or two from you."

Of all the things Gwen guessed could have come out of Joanna's mouth, a compliment wasn't one of them. Someone could have knocked her over with a feather. Surprise was her first reaction. Suspicion was her second.

"This sure is a change in tone and attitude," Gwen said. "What brought it on?"

The sound of tiny feet walking into the classroom told Gwen she'd have to wait for the answer.

"I have to get back to my room," Joanna said. "Hopefully we can talk later, maybe at lunch." With that Joanna hurried out.

Gwen's day was so busy that it was late afternoon before she gave the strange conversation with Joanna a second thought. Aside from the regular activities that were more than enough to handle on any given day, little Patrick had gotten food poisoning and thrown up in the classroom, Tianna cut her foot on a piece of glass at recess, and Kari hit a second grader for calling her a butt head.

The mother of the second grader, who in Gwen's opinion was the epitome of an anal cranial, had demanded a meeting with the principal and "those teachers on the playground who'd failed to keep her child safe." Gwen had patiently explained that "children fight," and that the woman's daughter had instigated the situation by name calling. The mother had then threatened a lawsuit, which in California was like ordering a latte—an everyday occurrence. Not even Adam's lick-licking flirtations could calm the woman down, and finally an officer was called in to take affidavits. From a six- and seven-year-old! By the time it was all over, Gwen wanted to hit the mother and give the police a genuine reason to be there.

This drama happened after Ransom called, said he would finish earlier than expected, and for them to meet him in Los Angeles as soon as she could. She decided that there were obviously some forces at work trying to hamper this endeavor. But now, at four-thirty, she was finally going home. Thankfully, Miss Mary had come to the school and picked up Isis, saving the child from a nine-hour school day. Now all Gwen needed to do was go home, take a quick shower, pack an overnight bag, pick up Isis from Miss Mary's, swing by Ransom's house for his and Isis's overnight bag—oh—and get to LA "as soon as she could."

"No problem, Ransom, piece of cake," Gwen said sarcastically, as she listened to the traffic report announce a multicar pile-up on the 14 Freeway. "Just great!" Gwen turned off the radio and put in a CD, thinking that Barry White could help her get in a better mood for the weekend by admonishing her to practice what she preached.

Gwen showered and had her bag packed in twenty minutes. She retrieved Isis from Miss Mary's and they headed over to the Blake residence. It took ten minutes to get to their home and another fifteen minutes to get overnight clothes for Ransom and Isis. The two women had fun going through

Ransom's closet and deciding on the perfect outfit for him to wear to Universal Studios, the outing Isis insisted they take since she hadn't been with them the last time.

"If we hurry," Gwen said as they placed clothes in Isis's Frog Princess backpack, "we can stop and get fries and chocolate shakes to eat on the road."

"Yay!" Isis exclaimed, pushing her sandals into the bag and zipping it with a flourish. "I'll race you to the door!"

Isis grabbed the backpack and was out of the bedroom in a flash. Gwen chased behind her, laughing at Isis's determination to win. "I won, I won," Isis chirped. She fumbled with the key on the deadbolt lock to the front door.

"You sure did," Gwen agreed, as she waited for the door to be unlocked. "You're a fast runner, Isis. Maybe you'll be a sprinter when you grow up."

"What's a splinter?"

Gwen laughed and reached for Isis's hand as she opened the door. "A sprinter," she began, emphasizing the r, "is a person who . . . Oh, excuse me." Gwen was startled by the woman standing on the other side of the door. "May I help you?"

"Yeah, you can help me," the woman replied with a great deal of attitude. "And you can start by taking your hands off my daughter."

40

The venom in Brea's tone surprised Gwen. Of course she knew the woman was Brea. Ransom hadn't lied when he'd said she was drop-dead gorgeous on the outside but that that attribute didn't carry over to her personality. Gwen was prepared to retort in kind until she became aware of Isis, wide-eyed, frightened, and clinging to her hand like a lifeline.

"Hello, Brea," Gwen said calmly. "I'm Gwen."

"I don't care who you are. I came here for my child. Come here, Isis." She spoke to Isis in a softer tone, and even managed a smile. "Come to Mama. I've got a surprise for you in the car. Come on, now."

Isis moved closer to Gwen. "I don't know you," she said softly.

Brea reached into her Monogram Motard Louis Vuitton and pulled out a framed picture. She knelt down and showed it to Isis. "Do you know who this is?"

Isis shook her head no. If she moved any closer to Gwen, she'd be under her legs.

"It's you when you were almost three years old. And that's me. Remember when we took this picture?

Remember this dress? You looked so pretty. But you're even prettier now."

"I don't know you," Isis repeated.

"Well, I'm your mama," a quickly frustrated Brea said. She rose and glared at Gwen, looked her up and down as if she were spoiled meat. "You can consider yourself relieved of your babysitting duties tonight. I'll take my daughter." She reached for Isis.

Gwen shifted her body, becoming a barrier between the child and Brea. "You'll do no such thing. It was inappropriate for you to show up unannounced, and thoughtless of you to think you could just knock on the door and take a child you haven't seen in over three years. I'm sure you don't want to make a scene, especially in front of Isis. So if you'll just give me a number where Ransom can reach you, I'll make sure he gets it. I'm sure he'll call."

"Bitch, I don't need you to get a message to Ransom for me. And I don't need you to tell me what's inappropriate neither. You look old enough to be Ransom's mother, but you sure as hell ain't mine!"

The insult stung, but Gwen was more concerned about protecting Isis than assuaging her hurt and anger. While keeping herself between Isis and Brea, Gwen locked the door, and then stepped around Brea and off the porch to the walkway leading to the sidewalk.

"Go ahead and walk your scrawny ass away if you want to," Brea huffed. "But Brea's back in town, bitch. Your little *mommy/wifey* acting role is about to come to an end . . . believe that."

41

Gwen started her car and pulled away quickly. She wanted to put as much distance between Isis and Brea as possible. Belatedly, she wondered whether it was a good idea to leave Brea at the house. Even though it was locked, the woman seemed the type who wasn't past putting a brick through a plate-glass window. *Maybe I should call the police? No, I need to call Ransom.* Gwen reached into her purse for her cell phone and Bluetooth. She was putting the device on her ear when she looked over at Isis. The child was staring straight ahead, crying silently.

"It's going to be okay, Princess," Gwen said, unconsciously using Ransom's term of endearment. "I'm calling your father now."

"I don't want to go with her," Isis whispered.

"Shh, don't worry about that. Your father will take care of everything." Gwen quickly hit 10 on her speed dial. Ransom's answering machine picked up immediately, meaning hers wasn't the first left message. Gwen hit the pound key to bypass the outgoing message.

"Ransom, this is Gwen. You need to call me as soon as you get this message. It's important." She almost hung up before adding, "Isis is okay, it's just that . . . just call me."

Gwen disconnected the call and sent an emergency text through. If Ransom had his phone on him, which he normally did, it would vibrate. She looked over at Isis, who, while no longer crying, stared wide-eyed out the window. For the first time since Gwen had met Isis, the always-in-motion ball of energy was as still as a statue. She was traumatized, Gwen knew, and experiencing a myriad of emotions right now.

For the second time that day, Gwen wanted to kick a grown woman's ass. How dare that woman waltz into town like she owned it, barge into this child's life, and demand an audience? Gwen's heart physically constricted as she ached for Isis. She'd always been close to her mother and, even in Lorraine's worsening mental state, Gwen didn't know what she'd do without her. She couldn't imagine growing up without a female presence, a role model, a nurturing influence in one's life. In that moment, a protective feeling for Isis came over Gwen as powerful as any birth mother could ever experience. Gwen glimpsed another look at the girl, who looked so much like her father, and knew then that she would do whatever it took, absolutely everything, to protect her.

"That was kinda scary back there, huh?" Gwen asked softly.

Isis nodded.

"You want to talk about it?"

Isis shook her head no.

Gwen waited a beat. "I tell you what. We'll hit the

drive-through for two yummy chocolate shakes and a bag of fries. Chocolate always helps my tummy feel better."

Isis said nothing.

Gwen batted away tears and spoke from her heart. "Isis, I love you. I love you as much as any mommy ever could."

They drove in silence until Gwen took the next exit two miles down. When she looked over at Isis, the merest beginning of a smile was on the child's face.

42

Ransom called while Gwen and Isis were waiting to place their order. "Gwen, what's wrong?"

Gwen kept her tone as casual as possible; she knew a little pitcher with big ears was listening to every syllable. "Someone stopped by your house while Isis and I were there."

"Don't tell me, Carol. What did she say?"

"It was Brea."

Silence. One second. Two seconds, five.

"She didn't stay long," Gwen continued, when Ransom remained quiet. "I asked for her number for you to call her but she . . . prefers to contact you directly."

Ransom's voice was deathly calm. "Where's Isis?"

Again, Gwen worked to sound normal, as if she were discussing the weather, or a Cubs game. "The little princess is right here, about to dig into a cold shake and hot fries in about sixty seconds. Hold on." Gwen paid for the order and took the food from the window. She checked to make sure they had ketchup, salt, and straws, and pulled away.

When Ransom spoke again, there was relief in his voice. "Thank you, Gwen. Whatever happened, I know it went better because you were there. How is my baby?"

"Here, I'm sure she wants to talk to you." Gwen pulled over, took off her earpiece, and helped Isis adjust it over her ear.

"Daddy, I'm scared. I don't want to go with her! She's pretty but she's mean. Is she really my mommy, Daddy? 'Cause I don't like her."

Ransom closed his eyes, so angry at Brea that he could barely breathe. What in the hell was she doing in Sienna, and what right did she think she had to come by his house! *Wait, how does she even know where I live?* Ransom took a breath and tried to concentrate on what Isis was saying. Almost anybody could have given Brea his address. That was beside the point. The point was, she was there now, and she would have to be dealt with.

Isis listened as Ransom talked. Whatever he said must have soothed her, because she visibly relaxed and began eating her fries. She even laughed at something he said, looked over at Gwen, and laughed again. "Uh-huh," Isis said in response to something Ransom said. "Yes!" Isis took a long drink of her chocolate shake and started swinging her right leg. "Okay, I promise," she said. Then she took off the earpiece and gave it to Gwen.

Gwen's brow creased as she listened to the one-sided conversation. What had Ransom said to change that child's attitude so quickly? Then Gwen almost blushed, knowing what he could do to change *her* attitude in a heartbeat. She put on the earpiece and pulled back into traffic.

"What do you want me to do? Should I take Isis back to my place until you get here?"

"Absolutely not, Butterfly. I want you to get your fine self to this hotel room and bring my precious daughter. Coming to LA today was the best suggestion you could have made. Are some of my psychic talents starting to rub off on you?"

"If that were the case, there would have been no meeting, trust."

"Well, I'm not happy there was a confrontation and I'm definitely not happy Brea came to see Isis without contacting me. The same person who gave her my address could have probably given her my number. But I am grateful that you were there, and so is Isis. And just so you know, Gwen Marie Butterfly Andrews, I'm going to have to think up a very special way to say thank you."

43

By the time Gwen and Isis reached the hotel, Isis was back to being her rambunctious self. As soon as Ransom opened the door to his room, Isis jumped in his arms and squeezed his neck tightly. After that endearing moment, she became a chatterbox of questions, all having to do with their trip to the theme park: when they were going (tomorrow, Princess), how long they would stay (as long as you want), what all would they ride (everything), and could they come back and next time bring Tianna?

Ransom looked over at Gwen, who was about to explode with laughter. He turned to his daughter and answered, "We'll see."

"Daddy, is that woman my mommy?"

Isis's abrupt change of subject also changed the mood. The smile faded from Gwen's face. Ransom took a deep, calming breath.

"Why don't I go to my room and freshen up," Gwen suggested. She blew Ransom a kiss and left the room.

"Come here, Princess. Let's have a little powwow on the couch."

Father and daughter walked over to the couch and sat down. Isis turned big, questioning eyes toward her father. Ransom put his arm around her and began to talk.

"Remember two years ago when we went to the park with Carol and Kari? We saw children playing with two parents, remember?"

"Yes."

"And what did you ask me then?"

"I asked you why Kari only had a mommy and I only had a daddy."

Ransom smiled. "And what did I tell you?"

Now it was Isis's turn to smile as she cuddled closer to her father. "You told me that it was so you could have all my love." Isis spread her arms wide and drew out the word "all" for several seconds, as Ransom had done years before.

"That's right, Princess. So I could have all your love. And so I could give you all of mine. And that is the most important thing for you to remember: that I will always protect you, that you will always be my princess, and that I will always give you all my love.

"The woman who came to the house today, her name is Brea. Brea and I were boyfriend and girl-friend when I was a teenager. What are teen ages?"

"Daddy! That's easy. Thirteen, fourteen, fifteen, sixteen . . ."

"All right, all right. That was too easy a question for someone as smart as you. I was nineteen, and she and I dated. We went to movies, out to eat—"

"Like you and Miss Gwen."

"Yes, like me and Miss Gwen."

"So you and Miss Gwen *are* boyfriend and girl-friend!"

"Miss Gwen and I are best friends, like you and Kari."

"Unh-unh. My best friend is Tianna now!"

Ransom laughed as his daughter jumped from one topic to the other, and marveled at how quickly kids could change, adjust, navigate circumstances. For them life was simple, and the only thing constant was change. He trusted this resiliency would help get Isis through the days ahead. He hoped it for himself as well.

"Okay, Princess. Your best friend is Tianna. My best friend is Gwen. And right now, we're talking about Brea. Isis, she is your mother."

Isis frowned and crossed her arms in a huff. "But if she's my mommy, why doesn't she live with us? Why did she leave me with you? Where does she live?"

"Always full of questions, aren't you?" Ransom tugged Isis's braid affectionately. "Brea was very young when you were born. She was a teenager too."

Ransom continued talking to Isis, telling her about how he and Brea modeled together, and that Brea had moved to New York so she could work there. He answered all of Isis's questions as best he could, assured her that she would continue to stay with him, and that he wouldn't let Brea take her away.

After Isis had exhausted her supply of questions, it was Ransom's turn to ask one of her. "Brea probably wishes she hadn't waited so long to come see you, probably wants to know the beautiful girl you now are. If she wants to meet, to talk to you a little bit, do you want to see her?"

Isis pondered the question a long moment. "Will you be there?" she finally asked.

Ransom nodded. "Of course."

"Then maybe I'll talk to her. As long as she isn't mean."

44

Gwen jumped at the sound of tapping on the side door that joined her room with Ransom's.

"That was fast," she said as she opened the door.

Ransom took her into his arms and gave her a long, slow kiss. "I've wanted to do that all day."

Gwen pressed herself against Ransom. He bent down and brushed his tongue across the nipple barely concealed behind thin ribbed cotton, and then sucked it into his mouth.

"What about Isis?" Gwen whispered.

"Sound asleep."

It had been a full day. After Ransom's talk with Isis, the three had gone to dinner and then a movie. Gwen doubted Isis would awake before morning. "Then come to bed," she said.

Ransom's lovemaking was slow and deliberate, each thrust seeming to pierce Gwen's soul. Gwen bit Ransom's shoulder to keep from crying out. Afterward, they lay quiet and satisfied for a long time, Ransom drawing lazy eights across Gwen's flat stomach.

"You asleep?"

Gwen turned her back to Ransom and scooted in so he could spoon her. "No. I'm thinking about Isis, and what a wonderful father she has."

Ransom kissed Gwen's shoulder. "Do you think I should let Brea see her?"

Gwen sighed. "I don't know. I think most would agree that a child benefits from knowing both parents, from being able to identify her roots. But if that parent has been absent, I think one has to look at how reentering the child's life will affect her. But then again, I'm probably not the best one to ask, Ransom. My first impression of Brea was not a good one. So better to ask someone neutral: a therapist, your mother, even Miss Mary. Because I just don't know . . ."

The rest of the weekend passed quickly. Ransom, Gwen, and Isis spent Saturday at Universal Studios and Sunday at the beach. They were all exhausted by the time they went back to the hotel to get Gwen's car and go home.

Ransom and Gwen conversed via their cell phones during almost the entire two-hour trip back to Sienna. Isis busied herself with a new video game her father had bought at Universal City Walk, a maze of stores and eateries adjacent to the theme park. After exiting into Sienna and making plans to drop Isis off at Gwen's the next morning, Ransom ended the call, honked his horn to wave at Gwen, and turned toward home.

As soon as he turned the corner, he saw her. Ransom was stunned. He'd been fully prepared to have a confrontation with Brea, but he'd never once considered that Brea's mother, Pam, would be at his house.

Ransom liked Pam. When he and Brea first started

dating, she still lived at home. Ransom practically lived there too. Pam treated him like a son, and openly approved of their relationship. When Brea became pregnant, Pam wasn't thrilled, but she was supportive. As the relationship became strained, Pam became less friendly toward him, and when he went after full custody of Isis, they stopped speaking.

Ransom glanced at the backseat. Isis was sleeping peacefully. He decided to leave her there while he scoped out the mood of his visitor. Then taking a positive approach, he put a small smile on his face and opened the door.

"Pam, what a surprise."

"Yeah, I'll bet. How are you, Ransom?"

The two hugged.

"Better than I was on Friday," he answered honestly. "Why didn't Brea call me, set things up to see Isis instead of just showing up like she did?"

"You know my child's beautiful but not always bright. I told her she shouldn't have done what she did. But she is Isis's mother, Ransom. She has a right to know her child."

"She signed those rights away, Pam."

"Look, I'm not here to argue with you and I'm not here to discuss legalities. I don't care what Brea signed, or how long she's been gone. A mother has a right to know the baby she brought into the world." Pam looked at Ransom's car. "She in there?"

Ransom nodded. "Asleep," he said, as he walked to the car.

Pam followed. They were both silent as Ransom took Isis out of the car, walked to the door, and let them inside.

"She's adorable," Pam said as Ransom laid Isis on

her bed. "Looks like you. She has Brea's nose though, and look at that chin!" Tears came to Pam's eyes as she continued. "I was so mad at you when you took custody of Isis. I'm not saying you were wrong to do it. Brea acted irresponsibly, and you did what you had to. But I never should have stopped being a part of my granddaughter's life." Pam ran her hand across Isis's hair. "I've missed so much."

Ransom spent the next hour filling Pam in on much of what she'd missed. They flipped through photo albums and Isis's drawings and school papers. They reminisced about old times, the good times, when Pam felt sure Ransom would become her son-in-law. Their easy camaraderie returned, and Ransom remembered why he liked Pam so much. She was warm and down to earth, most of the time. And she had a lot of common sense, something Ransom's father swore was in short supply. Brea's actions seemed to affirm his father's belief.

After finishing the cup of tea Ransom had offered, Pam prepared to leave. "I still don't know what happened to break you and Brea up. I thought y'all were good together. You know I always thought of you as my son-in-law."

Ransom took Pam's cup and rose from the couch. "Yeah, well, life happens. We were young, got caught up. But Isis came out of our relationship so . . . that made everything worth it."

Pam followed Ransom into the kitchen. "Brea tells me there was some old chick taking care of Isis? Someone my age?"

"Isis is well taken care of," Ransom responded, side-stepping Pam's obvious search for information.

"She's her babysitter?"

Ransom turned and put his hands on Pam's shoulders. "It's been good seeing you again, Pam. I was leery when I pulled up and saw you but . . . I'm glad we had this chance to reconnect."

They hugged.

"What about Brea?" Pam asked. "Will she have a chance to reconnect with her child? You know how proud and stubborn she is, Ransom, but she misses her daughter. And whether or not she knows it, Isis misses Brea, too."

"Isis doesn't know Brea, Pam."

"Don't matter. Brea is that child's mother, and not a babysitter, or teacher, or anybody else in the world can take the place of a mother's love."

Ransom hid a frown. Brea had obviously been talking to someone who thought they knew his business, and relayed what she'd heard to Pam. He intended to find out who had talked to her, and why.

Pam reached into her purse and pulled out a piece of paper. "Here's Brea's number. Will you call her?"

Ransom took the paper and studied it for a moment. "We'll see."

45

"When's she coming, Daddy?" Isis asked.

"I don't know, Princess." Ransom looked at his watch. "She's on her way."

Ransom, Isis, and Gwen sat in a large corner booth at IHOP, where they'd agreed to meet Brea. Ransom had insisted Gwen come, more for his support than his daughter's . . . and as a witness in case anything crazy went down.

It was two weeks to the day since Ransom had arrived home and found Pam waiting by the curb. Since then he'd talked to his parents and a therapist, and decided that he would take the chance and let Brea visit Isis. But he was taking it one step at a time. Nothing would be changed legally until he was sure Brea was back in Isis's life to stay. And she had to visit on his terms: in a public place, with him and Gwen present. Take it or leave it. She'd taken it. Or so he thought. The more the minutes ticked by, the more he began to think she'd changed her mind.

* * *

Brea waited for the light to change, eyeing the IHOP in the distance. She knew a lot was riding on this visit—her whole future, in fact. She had succeeded with the first step to getting back with Ransom: showing interest in a relationship with their daughter. As soon as she'd secured Isis's love, she'd begin work on her baby's daddy.

She'd chosen her outfit with this in mind: a light yellow Baby Phat dress that was casual in its design yet accented her in all the right places and looked great against her butterscotch skin. It fell just above her knee, showing off shapely legs further highlighted by flat sandals that laced up midcalf and revealed a fresh pedicure. Her short pixie haircut was flawless, emphasizing her doe eyes, succulent lips, and perfect bone structure. She looked, walked, and acted like a model, and carried herself with a self-assurance tinged with vulnerability that turned heads and melted men's hearts. It had melted Ransom's once, and she was determined it would happen again.

And then there was Gwen, the woman Adam told her was the competition where Ransom was concerned. Brea assumed that's who she'd encountered at Ransom's the other day, and if so, Brea wasn't too worried about her. She had an all right body, but she was no match for Brea James. In fact Adam, whose call to Pam had led to this whole chain of events unfolding, had told Brea that Gwen wasn't the only woman Ransom was seeing. That there was somebody named Carol, and who knew who else. It didn't matter. Brea James was on a mission. And when all was said and done, she intended to be the last female standing.

Brea realized she was frowning and worked to calm

down. She and her mother had discussed a strategy for getting Ransom back, and charm was part of the arsenal Pam advised her to use. "You can catch more flies with honey than vinegar," Pam had said. "Ransom knows you can be a real pain in the ass. Don't remind him."

Brea pulled into the parking lot, took one last look in the mirror, and reached into the backseat for the presents she'd bought. She opened the door and then remembered what she'd forgotten. Closing the door, she reached into her handbag and pulled out a bottle of Vera Wang fragrance. She sprayed her pulse points and between her breasts and legs. *Now, I'm ready. I'm about to make it happen.*

Gwen, Ransom, and Isis were not the only ones who watched Brea enter the dining area and walk across the room. Everyone in the restaurant paused to watch her pass by. A smile lit up her face as she spotted her targets in the corner booth. When she got to the table, she put down her bag, took off her sunglasses, and held out her arms. "Hey, Ran, baby. Don't I get a hug?"

Ransom was surprised at the emotions he experienced as he stood up and gave Brea a brief hug. He'd forgotten how fine this woman was, how she used to take his breath away with her beauty. He stepped back and allowed Brea to scoot into the booth, between him and Isis.

"Hello, Isis," Brea said. "You look nice today."

"Thank you," Isis said softly, and scooted closer to Gwen.

The action sent a flash of anger through Brea, but she played it off with a big smile.

"Gwen, girl, I owe you an apology. I'm sorry for going off on you the other night. It was that time of the month when we met. You got the wrath of day two, cramps and everything!"

Gwen was quiet a moment, not sure of how to respond to this unexpected contriteness. Where was the hellion who appeared on Ransom's doorstep, and who was this charming, cultured woman sitting at the table? "It was a stressful moment," Gwen said finally. "I'm glad you're feeling better."

"Oh, I bought gifts for everybody. Hand me that bag, Ran."

Gwen hated the way Brea called him "Ran." Hated it because it sounded sexy, personal, familiar. It was spoken as a term of endearment, and reminded Gwen of their intimate history as much as Isis ever could. The thoughts unnerved her, as did Brea's poise, good looks, and most of all, youth. The woman didn't look like she'd ever had a pimple or a bad hair day. Men had probably eaten out of her hand her whole life.

Brea reached into the bag and gave a gift box to Ransom. "For you." She reached in again, pulled out a smaller box, and gave it to Gwen. "And you."

"Me?" Now Gwen was truly in shock. "Really, Brea, you didn't have to get me anything."

"Aw, girl, it's nothing," Brea answered, in a tone one would use in conversation with a best friend. "Besides, it looks like you've taken excellent care of Ran and my daughter. We appreciate it, huh, Ran?" The hand she laid on his thigh was placed there so casually, and so naturally, no one knew how to react.

After an awkward moment, Ransom shifted, gently taking her hand and placing it on the cushioned bench. Brea laughed away the gesture; her point had been made.

"And now you, Miss Isis. Mama got you a *few* presents." She winked at Isis as she reached into the bag and pulled out the first box, which contained a toy called Illustory, where the child writes and illustrates her own book. "Mama told me about your drawings," Brea explained. "And how smart you are. I thought you might like it."

The table was silent as Isis examined the gift.

"Well, do you?" The vulnerability in Brea's voice was real, and unmistakable.

Isis nodded.

"Whew, good! I was hoping you would! Now, the next one." Brea's gifts for Isis included a giant word game, a princess mosaic, and two fashionable and age-appropriate outfits.

"I already know these," Isis said with excitement when she opened her last present, a magnetic puzzle map of the United States. "We learned them in Miss Gwen's class."

"Well, that's good, baby. Because your mama sure doesn't know where all those states go on the map."

"You don't?"

Brea shook her head. "But I'd love for you to teach me. Do you think you could?"

Isis nodded her head yes, obviously proud to be granted the teacher role.

"Do you think you could do one more thing for me? Can I have a hug?"

Isis didn't hesitate. She scooted over and placed her arms around Brea's neck. Brea teared up as she hugged her daughter for the first time in such a long time. "Thank you, baby," she whispered when Isis finished. "That was a really good hug."

The waitress came to take their orders and for the next hour and a half, Brea endeared herself to Ransom and Isis with tales of her time in New York, Paris, and Milan. Isis seemed enthralled, particularly when Brea spoke of flying on planes and skating on ice. Even Gwen laughed at Brea's bold antics, after being begrudgingly impressed with the learning gifts she'd bought Isis.

The topic then turned to Ransom, with Brea telling Isis what it was like when her father modeled. The conversation included a lot of "Remember that, Ran?" and underscored his and Brea's shared history. Ransom and Brea went down memory lane: how big Brea got with her pregnancy, the quick labor that almost resulted in a parking lot delivery, Isis's first birthday, and how both of them were there when she took her first step. The longer they shared, the more Gwen felt like the outsider. She noticed Isis stayed closer to Brea now, playing with Brea's fashionably clunky bracelet and watching her talk. And there was one more thing Gwen noticed. After telling a funny story, Brea fell out laughing. Once again, her hand came to rest on Ransom's thigh. This time, he did not move it off.

46

Gwen slapped blindly at the ringing alarm clock. For the second night in a row, she hadn't slept well. It hadn't mattered so much on Saturday night; she made up for it by staying in bed until ten Sunday morning. But today, Monday, duty called.

The reason for Gwen's sleeplessness could be summed up in two words: Brea James. A month had passed since the meeting at IHOP and in that time Brea had seen Isis every week. After the second meeting, when Gwen felt even more like a third leg than she had at the restaurant, she told Ransom it was important that the three of them—Ransom, Isis, and Brea—spend time together. It was one of the hardest suggestions she'd ever made but Gwen knew if she and Ransom continued anything long-term, Brea would be a part of their lives. Gwen would have to trust the strength of the bond she and Ransom shared. The last thing Gwen wanted to be was a paranoid, insecure nag who came between a woman and her child.

For his part, Ransom had been as loving as ever, and

very open and forthcoming with what was transpiring between him and Brea. Isis had warmed up to her mother, he said, and seemed to grow more comfortable around her with every visit. Brea had asked to take her to LA to spend the weekend with her and Pam, but Ransom wasn't ready for that yet. So for the past two weeks, Brea had visited Isis at Ransom's home. Gwen told herself that Brea's visits were the right thing for Isis, and that it didn't matter that these visits took away from the time she and Ransom spent together. She told herself this often, especially on those alone nights when Brea, Ransom, and Isis were creating the family portrait. She told herself . . . but she didn't believe it.

Throwing back the covers, Gwen stumbled out of bed. She walked into the kitchen and put on a rare pot of coffee, then took a quick shower. Thirty minutes later, Gwen was dressed and ready when the doorbell rang.

"Miss Gwen, Miss Gwen! Look what Mommy bought me!" Isis bounded into the room wearing a pair of bright red pants with a matching top that boasted primary colors in geometric designs. Her tennis shoes were made out of a suedelike designer fabric, and lit up with every step. These were the presents Isis excitedly showed her teacher.

"Those are very nice," Gwen said. She walked over to Ransom, who had come into the house behind his bubbly daughter. "Hey, you," she said, and kissed him lightly.

"Guess where we're going?" Isis continued, still bouncing around so her shoes could glow.

"I have no idea."

"Universal Studios! Me, Mommy, Daddy . . . and Tianna's coming too!"

Memories of their trip to the theme park assailed Gwen: the shared laughter on rides, fun meals, steamy nights. . . . Gwen forced away the feeling of melancholy and fixed a smile on her face.

"Well, I know you are going to have a very good time!" She turned to Ransom. "Time for a cup of coffee?"

"Yeah, baby, there's something I want to talk about with you anyway."

Gwen's heart flip-flopped but she kept a calm outward appearance. "Isis, you left your book last time. It's on the dresser in my bedroom. Want to get it?" After Isis ran toward Gwen's bedroom, Gwen walked into the kitchen. Ransom followed behind.

Gwen poured herself a second cup of coffee along with Ransom's. She poured a liberal amount of chocolate caramel creamer in both cups and handed one to Ransom. "What's up?" she asked, after taking a tentative sip.

Ransom sighed and took a sip as well. "It's Brea. She wants to move here."

Later, Gwen would pride herself on how calmly she took this news. She wanted to put her hands on the side of her face and scream like the kid in *Home Alone*. But she didn't. She simply leaned back against the counter, took another sip of coffee, and said, "Really?"

"Yeah, she's planning on looking for a place this weekend, maybe over at Sienna Heights."

"Where Carol lives? Well, that should liven up the neighborhood."

"Tell me about it. But it's not like there are that many apartment choices here. And Isis would have Kari and some of the other kids to play with when she visits Brea." Ransom put his cup down and walked to the door that led to the backyard. He stared out at the early December morning and continued. "She wants us to go back to court and reestablish joint custody."

"How do you feel about that?"

"I don't have a problem with Isis and Brea having a relationship. Isis was always a happy child, but she's blossomed even more since Brea came back."

"But do you think Brea will be happy here? She's used to bright lights, big city. None of that is happening in this town."

"She says it's what she wants. To be near Isis."

Or is it to be near you? "What will she do for work? Drive to Lancaster?"

"She says she's got money saved from the last couple shoots and runway shows she did. That'll last for a minute here. About the only good thing about this small town is the cost of living."

"Well, Ransom, I hope everything works out the way you want, and in the best interest of Isis."

"I think everything will work out all right. Just so long as . . ."

Gwen waited, but when Ransom didn't finish, she prompted. "So long as what?"

"Never mind." Ransom finished his coffee, walked over to the sink and set his cup in it, and then turned to Gwen. "Now, can I get a little more chocolate from those sweet, juicy lips before I leave?"

Ransom kissed Gwen, slowly, lazily. He ran a hand across her shoulders and felt their tenseness.

"Hey, what's this?" he asked, as he kneaded her shoulders and ran strong fingers along her spine and the nape of her neck. "Oh, don't worry, Butterfly.

Brea being here won't change us." He underscored his statement with an intense hug.

Gwen savored being enveloped in Ransom's strong arms. Still, she couldn't help feeling that the relationship ground beneath them, which had felt a tremor with the visits of Isis's mother, was getting ready to experience a straight up earthquake as soon as Brea moved to town.

47

Gwen deposited Isis in the classroom and then went to the teachers' lounge to put her lunch in the refrigerator. The room was more crowded than usual, and when she walked in, she felt an immediate shift in the atmosphere. Several of the teachers either looked away or gave a compassionate smile. Joanna, who had been talking with one of the school's other busybodies, rushed over.

"Oh my gosh, you must be beside yourself!"

Gwen proceeded to the refrigerator without answering. First of all, she wasn't sure what Joanna was talking about. Second, even with the about-face in attitude, Gwen didn't trust Joanna Roxbury as far as she could throw her. Just because the woman apologized, and had been showing a friendly side, did not mean they were friends. Far from it.

"I mean, can you believe it?" Joanna continued. "Brea coming to live here, in Sienna? And she put in an application at Sienna Heights Apartments, did you know that? I sure hope she and Carol don't get too close to each other. That will be a catfight for sure!"

So that's what this is about. Wow, news sure travels fast in this town. "How did you know about Brea?" Gwen asked. Ransom had told her less than an hour ago, and he surely wouldn't have talked to anyone at the school about it.

"Oh, well, I . . ."

Just then, Adam walked into the lounge, and for Gwen, everything suddenly made sense. She'd bet her next month's pay that not only was Adam Joanna's source for information about Brea (and Joanna the reason the rest of the faculty now knew), but also that Adam had something to do with Brea's sudden reemergence into Isis's life. She was determined to get to the bottom of it, but now was not the time. Nor was it the time for folks to be all up in her business, so she put on an armor of nonchalance and looked at Joanna.

"Never mind, I think I know how news is spreading in this town. But don't worry yourself, Joanna, because I'm sure not." With that, Gwen left the room, head held high, and walked back to her classroom.

It was a full, busy day, for which Gwen was grateful. As soon as the last bell rang and the students had exited, Gwen began placing paperwork in her tote bag. She had had enough of Sienna Elementary for one day, and was more than ready to leave. Plus, she was so angry with Adam that she didn't trust herself to be around him. So she was focused on making a quick exit. Two more minutes, and she would have made it. But just as Isis was putting on her backpack, Adam sauntered into the room.

"I hear you're getting ready to have some major competition," Adam said with a smirk on his face. "If you can call it that. Ransom has had a thing for Brea for a long time. I'm sorry, Gwen, but your Stella moment, you know, getting your groove back and all, might be just about over."

"Come on, Isis," Gwen said, ignoring Adam. She began walking toward the door. Adam stepped in to block her.

"Look, I'm here as your friend. And I just want you to know that when Brea and Ransom get back together and you need someone to talk to, a shoulder to cry on—"

"First of all," Gwen snapped, "you need to watch what you're saying in front of this child. You're talking about her parents. Of course, you weren't thinking of her, only yourself, as always. Which is why if yours was the only shoulder left on this continent, I'd rather use a rock. After all, I wouldn't expect a stone to have feelings. And after all these years . . . I don't expect you to either."

Before Adam could form a retort, Gwen and Isis were gone.

48

Gwen waved at Isis and Miss Mary as the two got into Miss Mary's car, on their way to Target, in Lancaster. Gwen was thankful that Miss Mary had been available to watch Isis for a couple hours, until Ransom got off work. She'd held it together for much of the day, but Gwen needed to get a handle on everything that was going on around her. And she needed to talk to someone who could help her navigate the madness. As soon as she got back inside her house, she reached for the phone.

"You know you're in for a beat up *and* a beat down," Chantay said instead of hello. "Why is it harder to reach you than Barack Obama these days? I swear if you hadn't called, I was driving down there this weekend!"

Gwen sighed and flopped on the couch. "I know, Chantay. But things have been crazier than you can imagine. Guess who's moving back to Sienna?"

"Girl, if you tell me it's that bitch baby mama coming back there, I'm gonna lose a shoe in her ass!"

Gwen laughed for the first time all day. "Tay, you'd better be my friend and have my back."

"Girl, I got your back, front, sides, and middle. I haven't had a good fight since Buffy stole my Twinkies back in seventh grade. I told you that girl was trouble the moment she showed up."

"Yeah, and you were right about another thing." Gwen went on to tell Chantay about the run-in with Adam, and the smirk on his face as he delivered the news about Brea's relocation. She talked about her insecurities, her fears, and why the right thing to do might be to back away and give Isis a chance to have a life that included a mother and a father.

"Whoa, wait a minute. What makes you think Ransom wants to get back with Brea? Is that what he told you?"

"No, but, Tay, the writing is on the wall. This is the mother of his child we're talking about: beautiful, young, successful, oh, and did I say beautiful? Wait a minute, did I say young? I can see the things that make her attractive to men. She can be quite charming when she wants to be and sexy without even trying. And the main thing? Isis has gone from not wanting her around to talking about her constantly. Ransom can see a positive change in Isis since Brea came back into her life . . . and so can I."

"Have you talked to Ransom about this . . . what you're thinking, how you feel?"

"I need to."

"Yes, you do. And you need to do it now, today, before you let your emotions and paranoia get the best of you and you start pushing a brothah away who has no intentions of going anywhere."

Gwen knew Chantay was right. So after the two

friends chatted a bit longer and made plans to hang out the following Saturday, Gwen disconnected from Chantay and called Ransom.

Two hours later, Gwen and Ransom cuddled in Ransom's living room. Ransom had fixed dinner, and after cleaning the kitchen and putting Isis to bed, the adults were ready for a little alone time.

"You want to talk about it?" Ransom asked, as he stroked Gwen's back. "You were tense this morning, and you've been quiet most of the night. Talk to me."

Gwen sat up and took a deep breath. "It's about Brea moving here. Don't get me wrong, I'm happy for Isis, that she is getting the chance to know her mother. But I just think . . . I'm concerned that Brea may want to get to know her child's father again too."

"You're probably right," Ransom said, agreeing with Gwen.

Gwen had hoped he wouldn't, that he would tell her she was tripping, and that Brea couldn't possibly be interested in him.

"Have you heard the saying, 'first time, shame on you, second time, shame on me'? I'm happy that Isis is getting to know her mother but, Butterfly, believe me, I don't want to be with Brea again. The person I want to be with is sitting next to me."

"You say that now, Ransom. But feelings can change. Brea is young and beautiful—"

"And immature and full of drama—"

"And the three of you will be spending a lot of time together. It's only natural that you'll grow closer. You'll basically be together all this weekend and . . ."

"Is that what this is about? Us going to Universal? Because, baby, you are more than welcome to come with us. I thought you knew that."

"No, I don't want to go with you, tag along like a chaperone. I want to trust you, and trust our love enough to not feel like I do right now . . . all paranoid and silly and out of control."

Ransom pulled Gwen into his arms and began placing kisses all over her face. "Yeah, that paranoid and silly mess, that's got to go. But, Butterfly . . . right now, I'm going to take off your panties. And I'm going to make it my business for you to lose *all* control."

49

Gwen was in an excellent mood. She'd been with Ransom every night since their talk. His lovemaking had been even more attentive than usual, thorough and deliberate. Her coochie was satisfied but her sleeping had suffered. Last night, Friday, she hadn't left until three A.M.

She'd spent the beautiful Saturday morning that followed with her mother: eating breakfast, shopping, and enjoying a manicure and pedicure at the nail salon. Lorraine still showed signs of her illness from time to time, forgetting names and places, repeating what she'd just said, but more and more, Lorraine was like the mother Gwen used to know. That fact had never been more evident than just before she'd left her mother's apartment.

"Mama, this was fun today, but I really need to be going."

Lorraine had stopped and thought for a moment,

then gave her a blank stare. "Baby, why do you have to leave? This is your home!"

Gwen frowned. "No," she began slowly, "this is *your* home. I live at your old house in Sienna."

Lorraine continued to stare blankly. "Sienna?"

"Yes, Mama." Gwen's happy mood began to dissipate. Her mother hadn't acted this incoherent in quite a while.

"Well, wait. I'm going with you. I need to get some things for Harold. He'll probably want me to cook some beans and . . ."

"Mama!"

"What?"

Gwen tried to control her rising fear. She walked over to her mother and talked softly, as if to a child. "Mama, Daddy's not in Sienna."

"Well, baby, where is he?"

"Mama, Daddy's . . ." That's when Gwen noticed the twinkle in her mother's eye, followed by the tinkling laughter that had filled Gwen's childhood household after one of her father's jokes.

"Gotcha!" Lorraine laughed again, and while Gwen tried hard to keep the frown on her face, soon she was laughing too.

"Mama, don't do that! You scared the living daylights out of me."

"I couldn't help it, baby. Esther did that to her daughter the other day and it was the funniest thing. We're still laughing about it. I hope I didn't scare you too bad."

Gwen hugged her mother. "You must be feeling better if you can joke about your illness. I'm just glad to hear you laughing. As a matter of fact, have you talked to Robert today?"

"No, and he's next. I'm gonna act like I don't know he's married, has a son, and another child on the way. I might even forget he has siblings."

"Mama, you're gonna give Robert a heart attack."

"It's called payback," Lorraine winked. "For all those teenaged years y'all almost gave me one."

Now, Gwen was on her way to Chantay's. She couldn't wait. Gwen hadn't spent quality time with Chantay in months. She didn't count the short time they'd shared drinks with their boyfriends weeks earlier. With Ransom, Isis, and Brea in Los Angeles, Gwen knew that time spent kicking it with her sistah-friend was just the outing she needed. She changed lanes, turned up the music, and added an out-of-tune accompaniment to the day.

"*. . . ain't no particular sign that I'm more compatible with.*" Gwen turned up the volume another notch. "*I just want your extra time and your, dun-dun-dun-dun, kiss.*"

Gwen grooved with the sounds of the eighties all the way into LA. By the time she arrived at Chantay's house, she was ready to party. She reached her friend's door, heard Cameo's thumping bass spilling out from under it, and knew her friend would not disappoint. The party was on! Chantay answered the door singing along with Cameo's lead singer, Larry Blackmon.

After exhausting her eighties supply of Levert, Frankie Beverly and Maze, Freddie Jackson, and Janet Jackson, Chantay and Gwen hit the streets. They shopped at Westfield Mall before heading up Slauson to a nutritionally conscious restaurant called Simply

Wholesome. After healthy meals of vegetarian burritos and lentil burgers with barbeque sauce, the ladies took in a movie at Magic Johnson Theaters, complete with the not-so-healthy yet prerequisite popcorn with butter, nachos, and chocolate-covered raisins. By the time they headed back to Chantay's house, it was early evening. Gwen was not necessarily looking forward to the two-hour drive home, and said as much to Chantay.

"You know you're welcome to stay with me. Sharonna's spending a rare night with her sister."

"Sienna?"

"Yeah, girl, she's got a new apartment and a new man. They're trying to play house. Derek is playing with some band down at the Roosevelt Hotel. If he comes tipping in late tonight, I promise not to scream too loud when we get busy."

"I appreciate it, Tay, but I think I'll head home. I've been doing quite a bit of screaming myself lately, if you know what I mean. But I'm sure Ransom and Isis won't be back until late. It will be good to get a full night's sleep, in my own bed. Oh, and did I thank you?"

"For what?"

"For encouraging me to talk to Ransom. That's the best advice you could have given me."

"I try."

Gwen went into Chantay's house, used the bathroom, borrowed her copy of Luther Vandross's *Greatest Hits*, and hit the road. She'd been on the highway about fifteen minutes when her phone rang.

"Hey, B-Fly."

"Hey you, having fun?"

"Isis and Tianna did. As for me, it was ai'ight. I like seeing Isis happy. What about you, what are you doing?"

Gwen told Ransom about her day, and that she was headed back to Sienna.

"Dang, I wish I'd caught you sooner."

"Why?"

"Because after a long talk with Pam, I let Isis and Tianna spend the night over at her house. I'm at the Universal Sheraton. If I'd known you were up here, I would have had you come over."

Gwen's drowsiness went away in a heartbeat. "I'm not too far to turn around. I could probably be there in about forty-five minutes. That is . . . if you want me to."

"You know you better get that fine ass over here so I can lick it."

Gwen's nana somersaulted as she exited the freeway and reentered on the other side. Luther's smooth sounds were the perfect backdrop for the ride to her young lover.

Brea kneaded cocoa butter into her skin, which was already softer than the butter she applied. She worked hard to keep her body as close to perfection as possible, without blemishes or scars. She remembered how Ransom used to love giving her a tongue bath, loved the feel of her creamy skin. She smiled in anticipation of him doing it again.

The road back to Ransom had been longer than she'd thought but not as long as she feared. In just a little over a month she had him here, right where she wanted him. She knew that getting him out of that hick town and away from Gwen's constant presence was essential. And tonight he was here, in LA, and Gwen was there, in Sienna. Brea reached into the closet and pulled out the dress she'd carefully chosen: a red silk mini with zipper conveniently located down the front. Aside from jewelry, perfume, and shoes, it was the only thing she wore. Brea could hardly wait to knock on Ransom's hotel door.

Ransom pulled into the hotel parking lot and turned off his car engine. Gwen's taste for sweet, sparkling wines had increased following their night in Palm Springs, and he was glad to have found a nearby liquor store with a nice selection. He wanted to recreate that moment, when they'd first come together, and had purchased two crystal wine glasses as well.

Ransom felt women staring at him as he crossed the lobby to the elevator. He was used to it. Women had looked at him with light in their eyes since he was twelve years old. But his heart had finally been captured. And it belonged to Gwen Andrews.

Ransom smiled, remembering the pomp and circumstance with which Gwen had taken back her last name. The week after returning from Chicago, she'd gone to court to have it legally changed back to her maiden name. "I don't want to think of what used to be every time I sign a check," she'd said firmly. "I want all of me back."

Ransom entered his hotel room and called room service. Shortly afterward, a waiter came up with what he'd requested: an ice-filled bucket, fruit, an assortment of crackers, meats, and cheeses, and a large bottle of water. He tipped the employee and pulled the cart inside.

Not long after Ransom placed the sparkling wine into the ice bucket, there was a knock on the door.

He looked at his watch. It had been just over thirty

minutes. "That was fast," he said aloud as he went to the door. He opened it with a flourish, and his smile turned upside down. "Brea, what in the hell are you doing here?"

Brea knew he'd be surprised but she hadn't counted on angry. She got ready to fire a sarcastic retort, and then replaced thoughts of vinegar with honey. She lowered her eyes coyly and added a hint of a smile. "Aren't you going to invite me in?"

Ransom didn't move from in front of the door. "No, Brea, I'm not. What are you doing here? And where is Isis?"

"Isis is with Mama, and I came here to talk. It's very seldom we get time without our daughter around. I was hoping that could happen tonight. Please."

"I can't see what kind of time we need without our daughter around," Ransom retorted angrily. "She's who you need to focus on spending quality time with." Still, he moved away from the door. Brea glided inside.

She took in the scene immediately: chilling wine, food, candles waiting to be lit. *Hmm. Looks like Gwen and I have another bitch to contend with.* But Brea wasn't worried. She was counting on outlasting whoever Ransom had laid out this spread for, Gwen, and anybody else wanting to vie for his affection. Because she had the one trump card that none of these other wenches had . . . his daughter.

Brea walked over to the food cart and plucked a grape from its stem. "Eating for two?"

"I'm obviously expecting company, which is why you can't stay. So say whatever is on your mind and get back to our daughter."

"Isis needs to spend time bonding with her grandmother. Mama is great with kids, you know that. They were getting ready to bake cookies when I left, and then put together a jigsaw puzzle." Brea took off her coat and laid it across the bed. "I can stay for however long you like."

Ransom crossed his arms as he stared at her. Any red-blooded American would be affected by her beauty, and Ransom was no different. He knew the material she wore was soft to the touch, and her skin would be even softer. He remembered how her body felt in his arms, and beneath him.

Brea sat on the bed and leisurely crossed her legs. An expanse of thigh was visible from this angle, and Brea still had some of the prettiest feet Ransom had ever seen. The sparkly sandals showed off her French manicure to perfection. There was no way around it. Brea looked good. But Ransom knew that looks could be deceiving, and he also knew he'd be in trouble if Brea didn't leave—now.

"Brea, you've got to go," he said again.

Brea leaned back and revealed more thigh. "Ransom, I need you. Remember how good it was with us, baby? I've been dreaming about that juicy dick of yours between my legs, pumping into me with that hard, sexy body." Brea began unzipping her dress. Creamy smooth skin was exposed with each pull. "Come get this, Ran. You know you want it."

"That's it. You've got to go!" He angrily strode to the door and yanked it open. "Gwen!"

"Hey, hand—" The scene that greeted Gwen cut off her words, and her breath. She peeped the tableau in an instant: wine, cheese, candles, and an almost naked Brea lounging on the bed. She looked at Ransom with eyes oozing pain. And then, without a word, turned and left.

"Gwen! Wait!" Ransom ran after Gwen and grabbed her arm.

"Get your funky hands off me," Gwen hissed from between clenched teeth, and kept walking.

"Stop, Gwen. Don't do this. She came over here unannounced, Butterfly."

"Don't call me that!" Gwen jabbed the down button on the elevator.

"Gwen, just listen to reason. Why would I call and invite you over if I planned to do something with Brea? She left Isis with her mother and came over here. Obviously that was their plan all along."

"And you just had to let her in."

"She said she had something to talk to me about."

"Yeah, well I saw her *conversation*." The elevator door opened and Gwen stepped inside.

Ransom followed her and pushed the stop button. "Butterfly, how can you not believe me? Please, don't leave."

Gwen rested heavily against the back of the elevator. The look on Ransom's face was sincere, and what he said made sense. But she was no longer in the mood for loving, and the exhaustion she'd felt earlier came back full force. Now she wasn't only physically tired, but mentally and emotionally too.

"Look, Ransom. I believe you. But I'm not going to stay. You've got a situation here that you need to handle. And I need to get some sleep."

"Gwen, I'm going to set things straight with Brea, go pick up Isis, and come home. Will you be there?"

"I'll call you in the morning," Gwen said. She reached past Ransom and disengaged the stop button. "But tonight, I need to sleep at my house, in my bed . . . alone."

50

Gwen and Chantay sat running their toes through the hot, white sand. Neither had ever been to Jamaica, and so far, the friendly, festive island was living up to the hype.

"Gwen, thanks again for inviting me to come with you, girl. This is one helluva way to spend Christmas vacation!"

"Yeah, well, I think we both deserve it. But you're sure your daughters were okay with you not being there?"

"Please, they were helping me pack! Sienna and her dude are talking about getting married. Her ass is pregnant and she actually thinks I, her mother, don't know."

"Oh no, Chantay. You, a grandmother? Are you ready for that?"

"No, but neither was my mother. At least her boyfriend has some sense, plus he graduated college. He's got a pretty good job and seems to be treating her right. She's happy."

"But so young." Gwen was thirty when she got married and wondered even then if she was ready. "How's Sharonna enjoying her time with the paternal grandparents?"

"They're spoiling her, so she's loving it, trying to throw money at all those growing up years they missed with her. But that was mostly my and Tashon's fault though. When I was mad at him, which was often, none of his family saw her."

"Is Tashon spending Christmas in Portland, too?"

"Yes, with his wife and kids. It's good for Sharonna to get to know her half siblings. At the end of the day, it's all good, especially me being here on this beach. I didn't know how much of life I was missing!"

"Well, I wanted to do something special with my part of the profit from the condo sale, so here we are."

"I wonder what Joe is doing with his part."

"For all I care, he can stick it up his—"

"Now, now, Gwendolyn, keep your blood pressure down. He's out your life. You can wish him well now."

She could have gone all day without mentioning that fool. But Gwen knew that Chantay was right. Hard feelings and grudges for things in the past weren't productive for anyone. She repositioned her large, floppy hat and leaned the lounge chair back farther. "I hope Derek wasn't too mad that you decided to spend the holidays without him."

"If he is, he'll get over it. Or knowing his horny ass, he'll get over another pair of legs."

Gwen turned and looked at her friend. "You really think he'd cheat on you?"

Chantay shrugged. "He's a man, ain't he? Most men will screw anything with a hole in it."

Gwen put down her virgin piña colada and frowned out at the impeccable afternoon. She watched as waves lazily beat against the ocean shore, a small boat bobbed up and down in the distant water, and a flock of birds flew overhead. Then laying her head back against the chair, she closed her eyes and thought about Ransom.

Things hadn't been the same since Gwen caught Brea in Ransom's room almost a month ago, and she wouldn't deny the strain in the relationship was largely her fault. For his part, Ransom had worked hard to reestablish their warm camaraderie. He'd called the day after the incident, and they'd met and talked about Brea . . . *again*.

"Baby, this is exactly what she wanted to do . . . come between us," Ransom had pleaded. "Let's not give her the satisfaction of that happening."

Gwen had tried to put that night behind her. But every time she became intimate with Ransom, an image of Brea's perfect, near-bare body swam into her consciousness and brought out every insecurity she ever had. She became reticent in their lovemaking, inhibited, holding back. Having loved raw for some time and not worried about pregnancy, Gwen had even insisted Ransom start using a condom again, just in case. Gwen's feelings were all over the place, and she didn't like how that felt. So when the real estate agent called with the news of the sale, she immediately booked a vacation away from Ransom and the drama of Sienna. Anywhere near his magnetism and she couldn't think straight. And that's exactly what she needed to do—think.

"I guess Ransom could be screwing Brea right about now," she said after a while. "Or somebody . . ."

"Aw, hell, girl. I didn't mean to make you go there. Ransom and Derek are two different men."

"But you just said that men don't care who they screw—"

"Yeah, and sometimes I talk too much. You came here to relax and regroup. Don't ruin your vacation letting your imagination get the best of you. Ransom told you that he explained what's up to that ho: you are his woman and she is his baby mama. End of story. From what you've told me, you don't have a reason to worry."

"Yeah, well that *ho* in Sienna with me in Jamaica is plenty reason," Gwen responded quietly. "Who am I kidding? There is no way I can compete with that girl. She's got everything—"

"Except your man. And if I was fuckin' somebody that fine, you bettah believe *he* would be here instead of you."

"What? You would have chosen Derek over me if given the choice?"

"Baby, ain't that much sistah-girl love in the world where I'd choose a BFF over some good dick."

"Chantay, you are so crass sometimes."

"I'm just keeping it real as a happy meal."

Gwen looked out at the beautiful view in front of her and sighed deeply. It would have been incredible to be here with Ransom. *What was I thinking?* Maybe she wasn't, she decided. "I'm just so *confused* about everything," she said with anguish in her voice. "Ransom is darn near half my age with a young daughter and women after him who put me to shame. What chances do we have of a lasting relationship? What about five years, ten years, twenty years from now. I'll be sixty-one and he'll just be forty-five!"

"No. You'll be dead from worrying too much. Girl, you need to put some alcohol in your next drink, 'cause your sobriety is driving me insane." Chantay sat up. "Either insane or seeing thangs . . . Is that my imagination or are those two fine-ass brothahs heading in our direction?"

Gwen followed Chantay's gaze and saw two handsome men indeed coming their way. One was tall, dark chocolate, with long dreadlocks. The other was a medium-height, butterscotch cutie with a stocky, muscular build and bald head. Both were smiling as they approached.

"Well, it looks like we have two fine creatures here now," the dark-skinned one said in the singsong accent that Jamaicans made famous. "You two lovelies want us to show you around the island?"

Gwen was about to decline when Chantay interrupted. "Baby, you can show me around whatever you want!"

"Oh, so you ladies are looking for a good time?"

Gwen once again began to speak. "Thank you but—"

"We'd love to get the personalized tour," Chantay finished. "And then later you two gentlemen can take us to dinner. Do you think you can do that?"

The tall, dark chocolate man offered a broad smile. His answer was simple: "Yeah, mon."

Gwen sang loudly as she drove down the interstate. She and Chantay had arrived back to the states in one piece, and after dropping her off, Gwen was on her way home. She waited for the next track to begin with a smile on her face. *Man! It feels good to feel good.*

She and Chantay had finished their vacation in grand fashion, a party cruise around the island in a luxury yacht. This courtesy of Johnny, the dark-as-a-raisin-and-twice-as-sweet brothah that Chantay had ended up spending the night with after their introductory dinner, and most of the nights thereafter. Brothah Butterscotch was not so fortunate, and after Gwen rebuffed his initial advances, she never saw him again.

Gwen didn't begrudge Chantay's case of island fever. The time she spent alone was much needed, and allowed her to find clarity in her crazy situation. This was why Gwen felt so good. She finally realized that she didn't have to accept what was happening to her. She didn't have to be a part of the drama that swirled around her: the small-town gossip, the small-school shenanigans, Adam's trippin' and Brea's dippin'. Gwen's mother was still improving and had even made a male friend at the assisted living facility. Gwen had escaped the confines of a small town before; she would do it again. Gwen felt so good because somewhere between the white sand and the blue ocean, the jerk chicken and the fried plantain, the reggae music and the shot of Jamaican rum that had sent her into a coughing frenzy, she had made a decision. She was going to once again take control of her life. Gwen didn't know where she'd be living when the new school year started, but she knew one thing for sure: it wouldn't be in Sienna.

51

It was an unlikely cast of characters: Adam, Joanna, Carol, and Brea. Adam and Joanna sat huddled on Brea's love seat while Carol stood, arms crossed, by the door. Brea sat in the middle of her couch looking regal, beautiful, and in total control—as if she were holding court.

Brea wanted Ransom, bottom line. And after what had transpired over the holidays, she knew she would have him. They'd spent a little time on Christmas together—her, Ransom, and Isis. She'd dressed to impress, definitely sexy. There was no way he hadn't wanted her. That's probably why he ran out of her mother's house so soon. Having learned her lesson with the hotel fiasco, however, Brea had been the epitome of propriety. She knew Gwen had gone on vacation with a girlfriend. Not a good sign when you take another female to paradise instead of your man. Success was within Brea's grasp. She'd decided to step up her game and exhaust all her resources.

The seed for how she'd secure her future with

Ransom was planted a week ago, during a casual conversation with Adam. Brea had voiced how much easier getting back with Ransom would be if Gwen were totally out of the picture. Adam had said he was sick of her too, and wished he hadn't hired her to teach at Sienna. "She's not that good a teacher," he'd said, having become more and more critical of her professional performance with each personal rebuff. "I wish she'd take her ass back to Chicago!" There it was—Brea's answer. Gwen leaving Sienna would take her not only out of Ransom's life, but their daughter's as well.

Involving Joanna and Carol had been Adam's idea. He didn't want whatever scheme they cooked up to be traced back to him. He liked his job as principal of Sienna Elementary. It gave him a sense of power, importance, and a steady supply of willing female teachers to bed. These two, he'd argued, could do the dirty work. Brea had adamantly refused at first, as she trusted few females. But after a conversation with her mother, Brea decided to follow her advice and "keep her enemies closer." War made strange bedfellows indeed. But Brea wanted it understood right up front that she was the general.

"Just so y'all know," she said, looking pointedly between Carol and Joanna, "I don't like either of you bitches. You stabbing Gwen in the back means you'd stab me too. Especially you," she added, fixing Carol with a stare. "But Adam told me y'all want Gwen gone as much as I do, and that four heads working on getting this done might be better than one. Was he right?"

Carol's eyes narrowed. *The feeling is mutual, bitch.* But rather than voice her obvious contempt, she decided to play it cool. "I'm only here because *Adam* asked me." She had absolutely no intention of helping Brea with any kind of scheme. Carol was at this meeting for one reason only: to find out what Brea was up to so she could take the information straight to Ransom and get back in his good graces. Then she'd use concern for her daughter as an excuse to back out of any assistance Adam might expect. *I don't need to run my competition out of town. I can play your hand better than you can.* Carol smiled at the thought. By trying to eliminate Gwen, Brea would effectively eliminate herself.

"I'm only here because of Adam too," Joanna echoed, moving closer to her Svengali. And because Carol had asked for backup. Joanna had spent her entire life in small towns, and had never met anyone as worldly as her new friends. She'd never had a confidante like Carol, and had never been sexed so thoroughly either. She was whipped enough to do whatever Adam asked her. Lastly, it didn't hurt that he was Joanna's boss. Job security was a good thing.

Adam disengaged himself from Joanna and stood. It was time to end the catfight and get this meeting back on track. His first plan to break up Gwen and his brother had failed. Joseph Smith was obviously a wimp, since he couldn't even step up his game enough to collect ten g's. It was time to implement Plan B. "Now that you ladies have emphasized the obvious—that you don't like each other—can we get down to business? We need to work on how to make this happen." He looked around to make sure he had everyone's attention. "Okay, here's what I know. Gwen is very protective of her reputation. She hates a scandal. And believe me, a scandal involving an elementary school teacher would be big news. If we do this right, and keep our own personal animosities in check, we can embarrass Gwen Andrews right out of town."

52

Gwen's fatigue finally came down on her as she rolled her luggage into the bedroom. The blinking light on the answering machine told her she had messages, and reminded her she'd forgotten to turn on her cell phone while driving from LA. After taking a long, hot shower and fixing a cup of hot chocolate, Gwen sat on the bed and pushed Play.

The first message was from Robert, obviously left before he'd called on her cell to wish her a good time in Jamaica and inform her that indeed a daughter, Lorraina, would be joining the Seattle Andrews clan. The next couple messages were from her mother, who'd obviously forgotten Gwen's plans to leave town. It was a good thing, Gwen mused, that she'd phoned her every day from the island. Still, her mother was doing so much better. It was the only reason Gwen had felt free enough to take the vacation, that and the fact that Gerald and his family had spent Christmas with Lorraine. The third and fourth calls were hang-ups. The fifth message was from Miss Mary, asking her to phone when she got in so her neighbor would know she was back safely. The last message was from Ransom:

"Butterfly . . . where are you? You're supposed to be back by now. Call me as soon as you get this."

After placing quick calls to Miss Mary and her mother, letting them know she was back home safely, Gwen fluffed her pillows, hit Ransom's speed dial number, leaned back and waited for him to answer. Having made her decision to change her life one way or the other made her feel more capable of talking to him, and of dealing with whatever had transpired between him and Brea over the holidays.

"Hey, Ransom."

"Damn! I was getting ready to send my boys out on a search party."

"I'm sorry. I forgot to turn my cell phone on when we landed. How are you doing?"

"Missing you," Ransom said, in a voice that stroked her where she hadn't been stroked in ten days.

Gwen felt herself melting, and second-guessing her decision to leave both the town and this man behind. "I missed you too."

"Yeah, tell me anything. With those hot Jamaicans 'down dere,' I'm sure they kept you two beautiful ladies entertained."

Gwen laughed.

"So I'm right."

"You're half right." Gwen shared the highlights of her vacation, including her snorkeling adventure, rum shot, and Chantay and Johnny's affair.

"Uh-huh," Ransom said when she finished. "And just who was keeping you warm at night?"

"The balmy weather," Gwen quickly replied. "And when the air chilled, a blanket. I spent quite a bit of time by myself, but it was what I needed. Time to think, you know?"

"About us?"

"About everything."

"So . . . care to share these thoughts?"

Gwen was quiet a moment. She actually wasn't ready to share her plans with Ransom, or anyone else. They were too new, too sketchy. When she had all her ducks in a row, namely a new teaching assignment, then she felt it would be time to reveal all.

"How was your holiday?" she asked, diverting Ransom's question. "Did Isis like the gift I bought her?"

"Almost more than the ones I got her, especially since it came from you."

"How was Phoenix?"

"Hot. But Mama and Daddy spoiled Isis to death. In fact, she's going to spend a month with them this summer. They couldn't believe how big she's grown, or how fast time flies."

There was a lull in the conversation as Gwen pondered how to ask what she really wanted to know, whether Brea had joined Ransom and Isis in Phoenix. As often happened, Ransom read her mind.

"Isis enjoyed spending time with Brea and Pam, too. We left Phoenix Christmas afternoon, and I dropped Isis off at Pam's so she could spend some time with that side of the family. In fact, that's where she is now, in Los Angeles. I'm going to pick her up on New Year's Day."

"Oh, so that means . . ."

"It means I purposely kept New Year's Eve open to bring in with my butterfly. I'm asking you to spend

New Year's Eve with me. And yes is the only answer allowed."

Gwen didn't hesitate. There was no use trying to deny it. She'd missed her man. "I'd love to spend it with you, Ransom," she breathed.

"Good," he said. "Now get a little rest while I drive over."

"Tonight? Right now?"

"Yes, right now, woman. I haven't seen you for almost two weeks. Do you think I'm going to wait until tomorrow? Now try and catch a catnap because you're going to need it. I've got a special present for you that will probably fit perfectly inside the one that I know you have for me."

53

The second semester at Sienna Elementary started out with a bang and a big announcement: Joanna Roxbury was pregnant. This news trumped everything else on folks' minds: what people got for Christmas, holiday vacation stories, the one-hundred-year-old Methodist church destroyed by arson fire, and even the first snowfall Sienna had seen in fifty years.

Gwen was as surprised by the bearer of this interesting news as she was by the news itself. Mrs. Summers, a rare visitor to Gwen's classroom, came knocking before Gwen had the chance to take off her coat.

Mrs. Summers looked around as if she were trading state secrets. Her blue eyes sparkled with suppressed glee. "You ask me, I think it's Adam Johnson's baby. Everybody knows they were sleeping together most of last semester. But his lips are as tight as a drum these days. I haven't even seen him lick 'em!"

Gwen laughed at this keen observation from the

school's administrative manager, even as she wondered if Ransom knew he might be an uncle in about nine months. "Are you sure?" Gwen asked her.

"Heard it from the horse's mouth just this morning. Joanna is telling everybody, as if she isn't about to give birth to a bastard."

"Well, now, Mrs. Summers, every child is a blessing."

"Folks are supposed to be married before they bring young'uns into the world. Got all these colored kids on welfare now, no offense you understand, 'cause there's more brown than black ones these days. But good Lord! My taxes are helping to feed a slew of children when I've never so much as felt a contraction!"

Gwen tried to have compassion for Mrs. Summers, a childless senior citizen who'd never married. Still, it saddened her that there was still such prejudice and presumption in the world. Gwen knew for a fact that there were more white babies on welfare than black and brown ones put together. But that statistic seemed to get lost in arguments such as the one Mrs. Summers had so self-righteously delivered, which had caused her such discomfort that she'd left shortly thereafter.

But not before revealing the real reason she'd stopped by Gwen's classroom. "Now's your chance," she'd said, her blue eyes sparkling again.

"My chance?" Gwen had repeated.

"Yeah, to get 'em. Sic 'em! For the way they treated you."

"I'm not sure . . ." Gwen began incredulously.

"Oh, pshaw," Mrs. Summers said, waving her hand in a dismissive gesture and using a phrase that saluted

her southern roots. "I may spend my days parked
behind that desk but these peepers don't miss much.
Adam and Joanna have had it out for you since the
beginning, especially Adam. Well, now he'd better
mind his p's and q's. At the end of the day, this is still
a small town. And he's still a black man who's impreg-
nated a white woman. Yes, indeedy. He'd better mind
his manners."

After stunning Gwen for a second time, Mrs.
Summers had swished out of her classroom, as prim
and proper as you please in a floral dress cinched
at the waist and accented with white lace collar and
cuffs. But Gwen had to recover from her shock quickly.
A rambunctious class of mostly six-year-olds kept
her mind occupied for the rest of the day, until the
bell rang.

Gwen was exhausted when she got home, and only
a little disappointed at Ransom's message: that he was
going to stay on the job site in Vegas one more day.
Ransom's mother was staying at his house, watching
Isis. She and Gwen had enjoyed a cordial but brief
conversation when Michelle Blake had picked Isis up
after school. Even in that short time span, Gwen had
seen where Ransom picked up his levelheadedness.

After enjoying her daily conversation with Lorraine, Gwen walked into the kitchen, opened the refrigerator, then decided to head out and get a burger
for dinner. As tired as she was, she didn't feel like
cooking, and as unsettled as she was, she didn't feel
like being home alone. Her mind was filled with
thoughts of Ransom. She remembered their New
Year's celebration and smiled. *He really is romantic,* she

thought, as she went into her room to change from the skirt she wore to a pair of jeans. Her smile grew as she remembered how he'd hired a limo to whisk them away from Sienna to Palm Springs, where their love had officially begun. They'd stayed at the same historic inn, and spent most of the three days there in their suite, and in the bed. Ransom had gifted her with a beautiful pair of ruby earrings, her birthstone. But the gift she most treasured was the small red butterfly he'd had tattooed on his lower back, just above one of the most beautiful sets of buns she'd seen in her life. She'd gotten one as well, a small bag with gold coins spilling out tattooed on her ankle. "The priceless 'ransom' for love," she'd explained to the tattoo artist, and to her man.

Gwen reached for her purse and walked to the door. She was just locking up when her phone rang. She almost didn't answer, but figuring it might be her mother, changed her mind and rushed inside.

"Hello?"

Silence.

Great, I rushed back inside for some foolish kids playing around on the phone! "Hello?" She was about to hang up when she heard her name.

"Gwen?"

"Yes, this is Gwen," she answered impatiently.

"Hi, Gwen, sorry to bother you. This is Brea."

Brea James was the last person Gwen expected on her phone. *What in the heck do you want?* Only one way to find out. "Yes, Brea."

"It sounds like you're in a hurry. Do you have a minute?"

Gwen threw her purse on the couch and sat next to it. "Yes. What do you want?"

Brea cleared her throat. "Well, I, uh, I felt we needed to talk. There are two people that we both love and since we're all going to be in each other's lives, I just wanted to start the year off getting along. I called to wish you a happy New Year."

Gwen was silent. *What does she expect me to say? Thanks, and you too? Come by Friday and let's all have pizza and watch a movie? I don't think so . . .*

"I'm sorry for what went down the last time you saw me. I'm sure Ran told you what happened. He didn't invite me over. I went there on my own, trying to get back with him. But I now know that is not going to happen. So I've moved on. I met someone over the holidays. He's real cool, and I think it could get serious."

Brea sounded sincere. Gwen was leery but polite. "I hope it works out for you, Brea."

"Oh, and there's one more thing. The therapist who's been working with Isis has suggested the three of us spend more regular time together: her, me, and Ran. She said it's important for a child to have happy memories of her parents together. Isis doesn't have too many of those right now. So if it seems like Ran and I start hanging out more, or you see my car at his house or job or whatnot . . . know it's about Isis, nothing more."

"Right, it's about Isis."

"That's right. My daughter is the most important thing in my life."

So important that you left her out of it for almost four years? "I'm glad you are back in Isis's life. Every child needs a mother."

"Okay, Gwen, so we're cool?"

"I'm not sure what you're asking, Brea."

"Ransom and I will be spending more time

together . . . with Isis. I'm coming to you woman to woman so you know what's up, and so you and I can be civil."

"I've never had a problem being civil with you, Brea. I just don't have much conversation for an almost naked woman in the room of the man I'm dating."

"I apologized for that!" Brea was losing her calm facade.

"And you've explained spending more time with Ransom. Is there anything else?"

Yeah, bitch. Your days with Ransom are numbered. "No, that's it, Gwen. You have a nice day."

Brea narrowed her eyes and sneered as she hung up the phone. "That cow really thinks I care about her ass. I'm just getting ready to move it out the way. Ha!"

Gwen walked back to her bedroom. The conversation with Brea had taken her appetite. She changed again, into a comfortable pair of sweat pants and a tank top. On her way to the kitchen for a glass of water, she stopped in the dining room and turned on the computer. *I refuse to let that girl get to me.* Still, the call motivated Gwen to get the ball rolling on the plans she'd begun making in Jamaica. She was going to sit down, brush up her résumé, and then click over to Monster.com and the new job that would lead to a future outside this rinky-dink town.

54

Ransom scowled as he looked out the window. Brea had just pulled into the driveway, the thumping bass of a hip-hop beat almost shaking the sidewalk. But the music's volume wasn't what put the frown on his face. It was the man who occupied the passenger seat in Brea's car who'd done it.

Ransom opened the door before the bell rang. "Hey, Ran. Is Isis ready?" Brea asked breathlessly.

Ransom stared past her to the car. "Who's that?"

Exactly the reaction I hoped for. I knew Ransom was still feelin' me. That's why Brea had worn her skin-tight Gucci pants with a stark white halter, and had bathed in Unforgivable. She knew the outfit showed Ransom everything her boy was hitting and he was missing. She wanted Ransom to rethink his options and his choices. "I told you about him," she purred. "That's Big Jake . . . plays for the Oakland Raiders."

"How long have you been seeing him?"

"What's with the twenty questions?" Brea asked with a smile. She looked beyond him into the house. "Where's my daughter?"

"She's coming. Isis, your mom's here!" Ransom called out, still staring at Brea. "How long have you been seeing this guy? How well do you know him?"

"Well enough to trust him around Isis. He's got a child himself, so he knows how to handle kids."

"Don't leave her alone with him."

"What, Gwen can act like she's Isis's mama but I can't leave her home alone with my man?"

"Gwen *was* practically Isis's mother before you decided to return to the scene," Ransom shot back. "And she's Isis's teacher. Isis knows her and trusts her. So don't try and compare the two."

The door to the passenger side opened. A dark-skinned, bulky brothah around six-foot-two and two-seventy-five got out of the car. "Everything all right, baby?"

"Hey, Mommy!" Isis said, rounding the corner.

"Hi, Isis," Brea said. But her eyes weren't on her daughter. They were on Ransom's receding back as he walked over to where Jake was standing. "Come on baby, let's go."

Ransom looked the massive stranger straight in the eye. "I just want to meet the man who's going to be around my daughter. Ransom Blake," he said, holding out his hand.

Jake twirled a toothpick in his mouth while he sized up Ransom. "Yeah, that's cool," he finally said, taking Ransom's hand in a brother-man handshake. "Jake Moore."

Ransom eyed Jake a little longer, and when he didn't feel any vibes of caution in his spirit, determined it was all right to let his daughter go with them.

"Be good, Princess," he said to Isis, now buckled up and ready to go in the backseat.

"Bye, Daddy."

Brea got in the driver's seat, buckled up, and then shielded her eyes from the sun as she looked up at Ransom. She thought he looked like a warrior standing there—back straight, shoulders broad, straight black hair blowing gently in the breeze. Anything worth having was worth waiting for, is what Pam had told her. Brea had tried the bum-rush tactic with the red dress, and it clearly hadn't worked. So now she was building the road back to Ransom brick by subtle brick. The little "going away party" she'd hatched for Gwen was simply insurance. Everything was coming together just as she'd planned.

"See you Friday?"

"What? Oh yeah, see you Friday."

"What are y'all meeting on Friday for?" Jake asked defensively, after the car had left Ransom's driveway. He'd immediately been intimidated by Ransom but had made sure it didn't show.

"Because of the therapist," Brea answered smoothly. "So Isis can have time with both of us together. Remember, baby, I told you. Kids want to see their parents happy, interacting together, right, Isis?"

"Like when we went to Universal Studios?"

"Uh-huh."

"Yes," Isis said, nodding her head enthusiastically. "I like to see you and Daddy together like that."

Well, you just keep on liking it, Brea thought as she once again turned up the volume on the CD. Because it was only a matter of time before both the therapist and Isis got their wish: to see her and Ransom happy and interacting . . . especially in the bedroom.

Ransom walked back into his house and called

Gwen. He told her about meeting Jake and asked for her opinion on having strange men around his daughter.

"You can never be too careful," Gwen replied. "That said, if this man is going to be in Brea's life . . ."

Ransom snorted. "He's in her life for the moment, but the moment is all Brea lives for. Who's she going to be with next week? I don't want a bunch of fools I don't know around my child!"

"Maybe you should have a talk with her."

"Oh believe me, that's going to happen. As soon as she gets over here on Friday, we're going to get a few things straight."

"She's going over to your place on Friday?"

"Yeah, we're going to start doing things together again . . . for Isis."

"She told me."

"She told you . . . when?"

"Last week when she called me."

There was a slight pause, and then, "Why didn't you tell me she called you?"

"I didn't want to make a big deal of it—one of those woman to woman conversations. She wanted me to know that you two would be getting together, and that she now had a man in her life, so I shouldn't worry."

"Like you were worried, anyway. You know I don't want her. She doesn't need to be calling you. I'll get her straight about that too."

Gwen and Ransom made plans to meet for dinner and then ended the call. As she waited for Ransom to come get her, however, she couldn't help but wonder: was Ransom mad that Jake was with Isis . . . or Brea?

55

"I don't think the baby's mine." Adam leaned against the whiteboard in Gwen's classroom and fiddled with the markers at its base. "That girl was sleeping with some of everybody."

"Well, you'll know the ABCs when you get the DNA," Gwen answered abstractedly. She didn't want to take work home this weekend and was trying to grade papers.

"Besides, there isn't any hard, fast rule against fraternizing in this workplace. Folks better not start tripping."

Gwen's ears perked up and she put down the pen she'd been using. "What exactly is going on?"

Adam started to say something and then caught himself. "Nothing much," he shrugged. "You know how they try and get a brothah down. But if they try and pull anything, I know I can count on you to have my back."

Gwen leaned back and crossed her arms. *So now we're getting to the real reason for this visit.* "Why would you think I need to have your back, and why would you assume I'd support you?"

"Aw, c'mon now, Gwen. You know you're my girl. We go way back."

"Yeah, we go so far back that you let a girl with three years' experience oversee this worker who's put in a decade."

"Oh, baby, you know that was just—"

"You being an asshole—yeah, I know. I wondered why things had changed all of a sudden, why first Joanna and now you suddenly wanted to be friends."

"What's Joanna got to do with this?"

"I don't know, you tell me."

"Far as I know there's nothing to tell."

"I'd say there is, or you wouldn't be standing in here doing the opposite of the Dixie Chicks and trying to make nice."

Adam looked toward Gwen's open classroom door and lowered his voice. "See, it's like this. Even though we're in the twenty-first century, some people still aren't happy when they see a brothah with a white girl. Not saying I'm the daddy or nothing, but me and Joanna kicked it a little bit. And now, there are a few teachers with their eye on my job. Might be trying to move a brothah out the way."

Part of Gwen wanted to rub it in Adam's face, that after months of trying to make her life a living hell, Adam was feeling some heat. But her mama hadn't raised her that way, so she asked the obvious question. "What are you going to do?"

"I don't know. Maybe I'll . . ." Adam's answer was interrupted by the sound of chimes from Gwen's cell phone.

Gwen looked at the ID. "Hey, Ransom, I'm sorry.

I'll be there in an hour, promise. Do you need me to bring anything?" Gwen laughed at Ransom's reply as she hung up the phone.

"I've got to give it to my brother," Adam said. "I didn't think you two would last once the newness wore off, but it's been what . . . six months? Do you think this might get serious? I mean, you know, marriage and whatnot?"

"What I think is that it's time for me to get to these papers and you to get back to your office."

"Okay, Ms. Andrews, I can tell when I'm being dismissed. But I really need to talk to you. Maybe I can come over one evening, *just* to talk." Adam licked his lips as he gave her the once-over. "But my brother better handle his business, 'cause if he lets you get away, I'll be right there to catch you."

Gwen shook her head as she watched Adam saunter out the door. Adam's level of cockiness never ceased to amaze her. Here he was in the middle of a scandal—a baby on the way and about to lose his job—still licking those lips and acting like he was *oh, oh, oh, oh Johnson*!

56

Gwen leaned back and let the wind fly through her hair. It was Valentine's weekend, and she and Ransom were in his Jeep, on the way to their favorite Palm Springs paradise. For this outing, he'd suggested they do casual and laid back, which was fine with Gwen. She'd packed a bag full of jeans, tank tops, and lots of lacy underwear, not that she thought she'd be wearing them long if Ransom had any say in the matter.

Ransom glanced over at her, his lips forming into a slow smile. He took in Gwen's lanky frame, ensconced in a pair of snug black jeans and a T-shirt that had been Isis's Christmas gift. It read: *No. 1 Teacher*. As Ransom continued to glance at her, he realized she was definitely his number one as well.

"What?" Gwen asked, after Ransom had glanced over for the third time without saying anything.

"You are so sexy."

Gwen leaned over and kissed Ransom on the cheek. On second thought, she leaned over again and placed her tongue in his ear.

"Watch out, girl!" Ransom said as the Jeep swerved slightly before he regained control. "You want me to have a wreck out here?"

"No, I want you to have *me* out here." Gwen's eyes widened as she heard her own voice. As God was her witness, she didn't know who had just said something so brazen. But she'd been feeling that way lately . . . brazen and free. Even though Brea's presence still sometimes unnerved her, she was almost back to the confidence she'd felt before the arrival of Miss James. "Wait, what are you doing?"

Ransom had pulled off the road and turned down a narrow pathway partially hidden by overgrown bushes. He turned off the engine and looked toward Gwen. "Get up."

"Why?"

"So I can *have* you . . . with your fine, sexy ass. Get up!"

"So you can . . . Boy, what are you . . . ?"

Ransom sighed, jumped over his car door and reached Gwen's side of the Jeep in four long strides. He opened the door and kissed her passionately. As he did so, he reached for the buttons on her jeans and began undoing them.

"Ransom, wait! I didn't mean what I said back there."

"Too late to take it back, Butterfly." He pushed Gwen back gently, and began working the jeans over her butt, and pulling the pant legs off her.

"Wait, Ransom, what if someone sees us?"

"We'd better give them a damn good show."

The next thing Gwen knew she was out of her seat and nestled between Ransom and the hood of his car.

His erection throbbed against her as he sucked her nipples through the tank top.

"Mmm," he moaned, burying his head in her chest while he held her against him with one arm. With the other, he unzipped his pants and took out his engorged manhood.

Gwen instinctively opened her legs to receive him. Ransom lifted her up and guided his shaft with his hips until he was fully inside her.

Gwen couldn't help the moan that escaped her. They stayed still a few seconds, feeling the wind and fading sun against their skin, the pulse of Ransom's dick throbbing inside her, the feel of Gwen's tongue inside Ransom's ear—the very act that had started it all.

Ransom slowly withdrew to the tip, and then thrust in again. He repeated the slow, torturous act, and then a third time. The words from one of Ransom's lessons wafted into her mind. *Long. Slow.* She was almost in a frenzy with desire, her hips grinding against him, trying to increase the speed. Ransom continued his slow and deliberate thrusts: harder, deeper, resting inside her.

Finally, Gwen could take it no more. "Ransom, please. I want . . . I want it."

Ransom smiled with both pleasure and pride. "You want this, huh, you want this? Well come on, Butterfly. Let's ride."

Two hours later, Gwen stood happy and content underneath the stream of hot water pouring from the powerful showerhead. Ransom had insisted he shower first, so he could then make sure their dinner reservations had been handled. Gwen was so happy, she was almost giddy. She never in a million years dreamed she'd do something so risqué as make love on the side of a highway. It had felt so . . . freaky and . . . sexy! It was something Chantay would do. Gwen couldn't wait to tell her.

Gwen finished her shower and quickly toweled herself dry. She was wearing her hair in its natural curly state, a style Ransom liked. "It suits you," he'd said. She took a band and tied the wild locks away from her face so she could do her makeup. She kept it simple: a light foundation and powder, a hint of blush, mascara, lipstick, and she was done.

Gwen stepped from the bathroom into the bedroom and stopped short. There was a beautiful silver-colored dress lying across the bed, and a jewelry box next to it. Below was an equally beautiful pair of silver shoes, with colorful crystals outlining the straps. Gwen hurried over to the bed and picked up the dress. The fabric was as she'd imagined, silky soft. She rubbed it against her skin and knew it would feel amazing to wear. She picked up one of the shoes. They were her size, eight narrow. She knew they would fit her perfectly. Eyeing the jewelry box, she called out the name of the man behind all this. "Ransom?'

When Ransom stepped around the corner, Gwen almost stopped breathing. She had never seen him look so handsome. He wore a pair of black Calvin Klein slacks, which hugged his hips and flared out to accommodate his muscular thighs. A pale yellow shirt was open at the collar. She admired him, thinking that Ransom should wear colors more often.

Gwen swallowed, and tried to remember the English language. "Uh, baby, what's all this?"

"This," Ransom said as he prowled into the room, "is a special occasion. Do you like the dress?"

"I love it! When did you have time to get this? How did you know my size? Everything is beautiful and so . . . so . . . perfect." Unexpected tears sprang up in Gwen's eyes. She blinked rapidly to hold them back.

"Here, let me help you." Ransom held the silk dress as Gwen stepped into it. The fabric and design hugged her body, emphasizing her long torso and pooch of a booty. The skirt flared with a row of tiny pleats, placing the emphasis on the lower half of the dress, and taking attention away from her small breasts.

Gwen walked over to the full-length mirror. She turned this way and that, and then twirled the way Isis might if she wore a new dress. "I love it!" she gushed. "I feel like Cinderella about to go to the ball."

"You look better than Cinderella could ever dream of looking," Ransom replied. He reached over and picked up the jewelry box. "Because I said we were going casual, I didn't know if you would bring anything that would go with the dress."

Gwen's hand shook slightly as she opened the box. Inside was a double-stranded tennis bracelet, with small yet brilliant diamonds set in platinum. "It's beautiful," she gasped. "But it's too much, Ransom. You've already given me so many things."

"It's just the beginning," he whispered. "Now slip into those pretty slippers, Gwen-derella. Dinner awaits."

Ransom led her past the restaurant where they normally dined, to a set of doors she hadn't noticed before. He opened one of them and stepped back. "After you."

Gwen walked in and indeed felt as if she was

dreaming. Any minute she knew the waiter standing behind the chair would turn into a mouse, and Ransom's Jeep into a pumpkin. A night like this only happened in fairy tales, didn't it?

The private dining room was awash in flowers: roses, irises, lilies, alstroemerias. The table for two had been lavishly set with bone china and Waterford crystal. Ransom pulled out a seat and Gwen sat down. As soon as he'd joined her at the table, the waiter walked over with a bottle of pricey looking champagne. He presented it to Ransom, who nodded. He and Gwen drank of each other with their eyes while the waiter filled their glasses, placed the champagne in an ice bucket, and then disappeared soundlessly.

Once the door closed, Ransom picked up his glass. "To Gwendolyn Marie Andrews, my butterfly."

"To Ransom Blake, wait. What's your middle name? I know this skews the moment a bit but it just hit me that I don't know it. I'm assuming Miss Mary is how you know mine."

"No," Ransom replied. "Your endearing neighbor did not divulge this information. I did some digging around, back when we first met and you were playing hard to get. Turns out somebody who knew somebody had a yearbook with your full name inscribed inside. That's how I know it, Ms. Gwendolyn Marie. And to answer your question, mine is Noel."

"Ah, because of your birthday in December?"

"That's right. This Sag was almost a Capricorn. But my mother always called me her gift." Ransom picked up the glass he'd put down during this exchange. "Now, where were we?"

"Wait a minute. What about Ransom? You know, I've always wondered about your first name, don't know why I haven't asked about it before. It suits you. But how did your parents come up with such an unusual choice?"

"It's simple, really. Somebody used the phrase with my mother once, when she was pregnant. About something being worth a king's ransom. She liked the name. Then she looked it up and liked the meanings: redemption, deliverance, rescue. . . ."

Gwen took a deep breath. "To Ransom Noel Blake, my warrior knight, my . . ." Gwen choked up again. "My everything."

They clinked glasses and as if by magic, the waiter appeared with their first course.

By the time the fifth and final course was set to arrive, Gwen was as bubbly as the champagne. Tonight she'd discarded her two-glass rule. She and Ransom were working on their second bottle.

"Come here," Ransom said, his eyes at half-mast, his voice as silky as the dress Gwen wore.

Gwen rose without hesitation and plumped down in his lap. "Ooh, I think I'm a little tipsy," she giggled.

"It's okay." Ransom eased his hand between her legs and fingered her paradise. Of course, as was the rule, Gwen wore no panties.

Gwen's intake of breath was audible. The alcohol had heightened every one of Gwen's senses. Even though they'd made love just hours before, Gwen felt she could ravish him right there. "Baby, let's take dessert back to our room."

"Hmm," Ransom nibbled Gwen's ear. "We'll enjoy a different type of treat when we get there."

He pulled his hand out from under her dress and took her hand in his. He began examining her nails, her palm.

"Am I going to live a long time?" she asked, as he traced what was known as the lifeline on her left hand.

Ransom looked deep into her eyes. "You're going to live forever." He continued to stare at her and stroke her palm with his thumb. Gwen shivered involuntarily and pushed her thighs together to stop her nub from throbbing.

"Gwen."

"Yes?"

"Why don't you wear any rings?"

Gwen shrugged. "Just never was much of a ring person, jewelry person for that matter."

"Well," Ransom said as he reached into his pocket. "We are getting ready to change that."

Gwen's heart began to beat rapidly. *No, he couldn't be about to do what I think he's about to . . . no!*

But yes, he was about to. Ransom lifted her off him and kneeled before her where she stood.

"There simply are no words for what you mean to me," Ransom said softly. "I've been looking for you a long time, a queen to make my castle complete, with me and my daughter. And now I've found her. So . . . you know the drill, baby. Will you do it?"

"Will I do what?" Gwen whispered. She still couldn't believe Ransom was down on one knee!

He rose and took her in his arms. He cradled her butt with his large hand. "Will you give me this for the rest of our lives? Will you marry me?"

Ransom barely waited for the answer. He swallowed Gwen's *yes* in his kiss.

57

Both Ransom and Gwen were floating on clouds. For the first time in eight years, Gwen called in sick, so that she and Ransom could have an extra day in their self-made paradise. They would have taken yet another day, but after finding out the reason for Ransom's delay—that he and Gwen had gotten engaged over the weekend—Brea had demanded that he come and pick up Isis "right now." And then she'd called Adam.

"Yo, Adam, it's time that we make that little scandal happen so Ransom can see Gwen for the ho she is." Adam and Brea had concocted what they felt was a foolproof scheme to shame Gwen out of California. Only she and Adam were involved. As Brea had anticipated, women could not be trusted. To back out of any involvement, Carol had used some flimsy excuse about Gwen being Kari's teacher, and Joanna couldn't focus on a damn thing past her growing stomach. Their pulling out suited Brea just fine. Why send two girls in to do a woman's job?

"Hold on, now, Brea. What's the rush? There's still

that little rendezvous between me and you that needs to happen."

"I told you I'm gonna let you have some pussy, boy, damn! Is that all anything is ever about for you? Well, peep this. Your girl ain't at school, right?"

"Right, she's home sick."

"Wrong, she's with Ransom. They went to Palm Springs over the weekend and got *engaged*. The only reason she ain't calling in tomorrow is because I demanded that Ransom come get his child."

Adam began pacing his office. Not only had Gwen refused his advances, but she was now straight up lying on top of it. And his brother had actually gone and popped the question? Adam was still pissed from when Ransom floored him in front of the very woman he was trying to impress. Brea was right. It was time to put an end to the nonsense and get both Gwen's and Ransom's heads out of the clouds. Adam smiled. He was getting ready to bring both of them down to earth with a thud. He relished the thought.

"Did you get what I asked you to get?" Adam asked.

"I told you last week that I bought the disposable phone. Now, can you do it tonight?"

"Yeah, I'll pay our sick teacher a little visit, you know, show my concern."

Brea laughed. "That sounds like a very caring thing for a principal to do."

"Oh, I'm gonna care all right."

"Just make sure you get what we need to show Ransom, as well as all the other concerned citizens in this lullaby town."

Now it was Adam's turn to laugh, a sinister, hollow sound. "Make no mistake about it, Brea, I'm going to get it *all*."

* * *

Ransom dropped Gwen off at her house and called Brea to tell her he was on his way. He knew she was pissed at him for being with Gwen, and didn't want to prolong the visit any longer than it took to knock on her door and have Isis walk out. He was still on a high from Palm Springs. Ransom could hardly believe he'd met someone real and loving and compassionate and fine . . . and now that someone was going to be his wife.

Ransom tapped a tune on the steering wheel as he disconnected from Brea's house phone and called her cell. He frowned slightly when that too went to voice mail. "Brea, it's me. I'm on my way to get Isis. Hollah when you get this so I know where you're at." Ransom thought for a second and added, "If I don't hear from you, I'll wait at your house."

Gwen hummed her new favorite song by Al Jarreau as she put the clothes from the weekend, along with a few others, in the washing machine. She turned it on and waited for the cycle to begin so she could add softener. Because of the noise, she hadn't heard anyone knock on the door. Now they were banging.

"All right, all right," she said, coming out of the laundry room located off the kitchen, and around the corner into the living room. She stopped when she saw who was at the door. It was the last person she would have expected.

"Adam," she said through the screen. "What do you want?"

"Well, I can tell you what I don't want," Adam said with a smile. "To talk to you through this datgum screen."

Gwen laughed. "I'm sorry, it's just that I'm surprised to see you. Come on in." She opened the door and stood back while he entered. "What are you doing here?"

"I came to see how you're feeling," Adam said. He stopped in the middle of the living room and looked around. "You know, I think this is the first time I've ever been in your house."

Gwen crossed her arms and tried to gauge what was really going on. She didn't think for one moment that Adam's visit was one of genuine concern, but rather to be nosy. Because Ransom had talked to Brea, Gwen guessed that Adam knew she hadn't been sick at all, but with his brother.

"You want to tell me why you're really here?" she asked directly.

"Dang, girl. A brothah can't come check on you?"

"Check on me or check *up* on me?"

"I'm concerned about the health of one of Sienna's best teachers," Adam said with mock sincerity. "But I must say, you're looking quite healthy, very healthy indeed." He licked his lips, then walked over and sat on the couch. "Can I maybe get something to drink, some water or something?"

Gwen looked at Adam a moment, shrugged, and walked to the kitchen. "I've also got juice or soda if you want."

"Cola is fine."

For once, she didn't feel like fighting with him. After all, like it or not, he was getting ready to be her brother-in-law. Maybe it was a good thing that he'd come over—they could talk away from the workplace. She and Ransom hadn't planned how they'd announce their engagement. Gwen figured that perhaps it was appropriate that Adam be one of the first to know.

Gwen came out of the kitchen with two glasses of cola. She set them down and walked back in the kitchen for a bowl of chips, then sat down in the over-sized armchair next to the couch where Adam sat.

"So who told you I wasn't sick today?" Gwen asked casually.

Adam feigned surprise. "What? I heard you weren't feeling well."

"Cut the bull crap, Adam. Somebody must have told you I was with Ransom this weekend and we just came back today. Was it Brea? Or Carol maybe?"

Adam was surprised at the accuracy of Gwen's assumptions. He hid his sudden discomfort behind a smile. "We never could pull anything over on you," Adam said. "Me and the fellas used to try and get you out of your drawers. We had bets on who would take your cherry. Did you know that?"

Gwen purposely picked up her cola glass with her left hand, the one that was sparkling with a three-carat, emerald-cut diamond. "Nothing you guys did would surprise me," she answered.

"Whoa, what have we here?" Adam sat up and leaned over. "Let me see that."

Gwen couldn't help the smile that spread across her face as she held out her hand. "We're getting ready to be family," she said.

"I see," Adam responded. "Congratulations." He picked up his drink and drained it. "Do you think I could get another one?" he asked Gwen.

"Sure."

Once Gwen was in the kitchen, Adam reached into his pocket. "Hey, Gwen. You got some dip to go with these chips? And some jalapeño peppers?"

"I think I have some French onion. You want jalapeños with that?"

"Yeah, that's cool."

Moments later, Gwen came back into the living room with Adam's dip and peppers. She put them on the coffee table in front of Adam, grabbed a handful of chips, and sat down.

Adam picked up his glass. "To you and Ransom," he said in what sounded like a sincere tone.

"Thank you, Adam." Gwen said. "I really didn't know how you'd take the news. I'm glad it's like this, with no drama. I really do hope we can all get along."

"Ah, no worries, girl. Cheers!"

Once again, Adam drained his glass. So did Gwen. She reached over for more chips and began to engage Adam in small talk, about Sienna Elementary and the news of Joanna's pregnancy. Suddenly, however, her head began to swim.

"Ooh," she said, putting a hand to her head. "I feel woozy."

Adam sprang up from the couch. "Are you okay?"

Gwen frowned and shook her head, trying to clear it of the fuzziness. "No, I'm not. I feel . . . I feel faint."

"Here," Adam said. "Let me help you to the bedroom. Maybe lying down will help you feel better."

Gwen stood on wobbly legs, frowned at the eerie smile that crossed Adam's face, and tried to remove his clammy hands as they grabbed her bare arms. She thought of Ransom. And then she passed out.

58

Ransom looked at his watch for the third time in ten minutes. *Where is Brea?* He'd been sitting for thirty minutes, waiting to see her silver Beamer turn into the lot. He didn't see Carol's car either, but he called her anyway.

"Carol, it's Ransom."

"What? Calling me? Are you sure you've got the right number?"

"Okay, I probably deserve that. But listen, have you talked to Brea by any chance? I'm here at her house to pick up Isis and can't reach her."

"Brea and I are neighbors, Ransom, not friends."

"I know, I just thought that maybe you'd seen them. I didn't see your car but thought you might be home. Okay, I'll catch you later."

"Ransom, wait!" Carol paused before continuing. This was her chance to turn the tide and get back in his good graces. She knew she had to use the moment wisely, and wreck Brea's chances to get back with Ransom.

"I don't know if I should tell you this, but I've heard some things lately."

"What things?'

"Well, for one . . . Brea is leaving town."

"Leaving town?" Ransom immediately thought of Isis and her growing closeness with Brea. How would Isis deal with her mother suddenly disappearing again? "What else?" he asked in the quiet, calm voice that masked his emotions.

"I saw Adam over at her house," Carol continued, figuring he could have only been there for one reason—to plot against Gwen. "Then Joanna told me they were talking about your girlfriend, how Gwen thinks she's better than everybody and how she deserved to be brought down a peg or two. Brea hates that Gwen's with you."

"When was Adam at Brea's?"

"I think it was Saturday."

Two days ago. Before I told Brea about Gwen and my engagement. The more Ransom heard, the less sense everything made. If Brea was so interested in Isis, why was she leaving town? And with Jake in her life, why would Brea care who he was with?

"Are you sure Adam didn't tell you anything, Carol? I know the two of you messed around for a minute."

"I'm telling you what I heard, Ransom. Because I care about you and Isis. And because it sounded like Adam was really pissed at you, said you had a payback coming for something that happened at school, a fight or something?"

Ransom had forgotten about taking Adam down in a jujitsu move he'd learned years ago. Adam had gotten off easy. Ransom could use his body as a weapon if need be, with deadly force. He began feeling a sense of foreboding. Something was not right. "Look, Carol, I've got to go."

"Ransom! I just want you to know that I tried to talk them out of doing anything to her. Told them they should let y'all alone, let y'all be happy. Ransom?" Carol could only hope Ransom heard what she said before he'd hung up the phone. She called his home phone and left the message again, just in case.

Ransom jumped over the door of his Jeep and ran toward Brea's apartment. His heart was beating faster with each step. *Why didn't I feel this earlier?* He got to her door and knocked loudly. He rang the doorbell and then knocked again. "Brea!"

An elderly woman across the hall looked out her window. Then she cracked open her door, but kept the chain in place. "No one's there, young man."

Ransom turned around. "How long ago did she leave?"

"Well, they've been moving stuff all week. But I saw her earlier this morning, her and that sweet little girl."

Ransom turned and tried to look through the blinds. They were closed tightly. He turned back to the woman. "When you say move, do you mean furniture and everything?"

The woman nodded and gave him details that only a nosy older neighbor would remember, including the fact that the "big black guy" she dated had helped her move.

"Thanks," Ransom said before taking the steps two at a time. He dialed Gwen as he sprinted to the car. When he got voice mail on both her home and cell

phones, his anxiety increased. He floored the gas
pedal and sped to her house.

Adam stared at Gwen a long moment. He'd waited
over twenty years to do what he was getting ready to
do. He intended to take his time and enjoy himself.
He'd raided Gwen's kitchen and finally found a
bottle of Tanqueray that looked like it hadn't been
opened in years. He'd drunk straight out of the
bottle, wanting to get a little buzz on, a little celebration for the fact that he was about to fuck Miss Prim
and Perfect. *Hell no, I don't feel guilty,* Adam thought,
as the alcohol began to take effect. *I asked the bitch
nicely. Now I'm getting ready to take what should have been
freely given.*

Adam ran his fingers across the buttons on Gwen's
jeans before he began unbuttoning them, slowly, one
by one. A part of him hated that she was passed out.
He loved to watch a woman's eyes when he was ham-
mering her, how they would usually roll to the back
of her head as he was sexing her real good. Knowing
Gwen, though, she probably wouldn't have screwed
him willingly. She would have probably put up a fight.
Then things might have gotten ugly, Adam sneered. No
need to mess up Miss Lorraine's pretty knickknacks
by brawling. *No, this way will do just fine. Nice and easy.*

Adam took a deep swig of gin before reaching for
the bottom of Gwen's pants and slowly pulling them
down. He smiled at the lacy thong panties Gwen
wore. "Girl, you sure changed from back in the day,"
Adam said aloud. "I bet your butt wore bloomers
then." He ran his hand across Gwen's thigh. His manhood began to grow as he looked at her. A part of

him wanted to ram her right away, but he'd waited too long, and because of his and Brea's plan, he knew he could take his time. Ransom would be looking for Brea and Isis for hours; Gwen probably wouldn't even cross his mind.

"Time to get the party started," Adam said to an unconscious Gwen. He sat on the bed beside her and took off his shoes. Then he stood and took off his pants, shirt, and undershirt. With just his boxers on, he walked into the living room and retrieved the cell phone he'd left on the coffee table. He took a couple pictures of Gwen, then tossed the phone beside her and reached for her top. "Man, you've got little titties."

Adam took a couple pictures of Gwen topless. He spread her legs and positioned her in a way that looked as if she were pleasuring herself with her eyes closed. Then he rolled her over and began taking pictures of her butt, exposed in the pink thong he'd yet to remove. He massaged himself as he stared at her. "Yeah, baby, you're getting ready to meet 'The Johnson.'" Satisfied that he had the pictures he needed to cause Gwen's downfall, the ones he'd doctor with Photoshop before sending to various school board members as well as the *Sienna Sun,* he crawled onto the bed and placed a clumsy hand between Gwen's legs. He began to massage her through the panties, and kiss her unresponsive mouth. It angered him briefly that she was unconscious. He roughly threw her legs apart and got in between them. That's when he heard the sound of Ransom's Jeep.

"Damn!" Adam scrambled off the bed and ran down the hall.

"Adam!" Ransom yanked at the locked door only

once before stepping back and delivering a swift
kick that broke the lock. He charged through the
door and straight through the house, in pursuit of
Adam, who had fled out Gwen's back door in boxers
and socks. Ransom started down the alley behind
him, and then thought about Gwen. *If he's hurt
her . . .* Ransom doubled back to the house, calling
her name.

He stopped short when he saw her, passed out and
nearly naked. He hurried to her side. "Gwen, Butterfly, wake up. Gwen!" When she didn't respond,
Ransom became fearful. *What did Adam do? What's
wrong with her?* He checked for a pulse, and felt one—
faint but steady. Obviously Adam had drugged her.
But with what? Ransom couldn't take a chance on
losing the joy he'd just found. He wrapped Gwen in
the bedspread, picked her up in his arms, and ran to
his Jeep.

Ransom reached the hospital in minutes. He
picked Gwen up and hurried inside. Just as he
reached the information desk, Gwen moaned.

"Gwen! Baby . . ." Ransom kissed her cheek, forehead. "Butterfly, can you hear me?"

Gwen wondered why Ransom sounded so far away
when she could tell she was in his arms. *When had he
come over?* she wondered. She nestled her head into
his chest and went back to sleep.

A doctor rounded the corner. "What's going on
here?"

"This is my fiancée. I found her passed out in her
house. Somebody gave her something. Please, help
her!"

While Ransom explained this to the doctor, two
aides appeared with a stretcher. He laid Gwen on

it, and then started walking with them back to the examining room.

"Wait right here," the doctor said sternly.

"Wait? No, you don't understand."

"You can't come back here. Just wait in the waiting room until we finish examining her. I'll be out as soon as I know something."

Ransom paced in front of the information desk, drowning in worry. He thought about his daughter, dialed Brea, and again got voice mail. *What do I do?* He was torn between staying with Gwen, looking for Isis, and settling the score with Adam. Ransom stopped in midstride. What were the chances that the day's chain of events was coincidence: that Brea would tell him to come back immediately, knowing she'd moved, and that Adam would show up at Gwen's house at the exact same time Ransom was waiting for his daughter? Ransom ran out of the hospital and jumped in his Jeep. He prayed that Gwen would be all right, but he had to find his little girl.

59

Gwen's eyes fluttered as she turned on her side. She gasped and immediately clutched her stomach.

"Careful, Ms. Andrews," the nurse said. "You're okay. Just try to breathe and relax."

Gwen opened her eyes, then squinted as she looked around. "What happened? Where am I?" she asked groggily.

"You're at Bradley Memorial. The doctor will be in shortly," the nurse replied.

A few moments later, the doctor came in. It was Dr. Rolette, the same doctor who'd treated Lorraine when she'd passed out months earlier. "Well," Dr. Rolette said as he checked her pupils and took her pulse. "You're looking a little better than the last time I saw you."

"What happened, doctor? My stomach, it's . . ."

"We pumped your stomach, Gwen."

"Pumped . . . but why?" Gwen closed her eyes and tried to get her bearings. But she was still groggy.

"What's the last thing you remember?" Dr. Rolette asked.

Gwen swallowed, thought hard, and opened her eyes. "I was with Ransom. He was holding me."

Dr. Rolette's eyes narrowed. "Is he the tall guy, long hair?"

Gwen nodded.

"That sounds like the man who brought you here, Gwen. Now I need to ask some tough questions. Were you two using any type of illegal substances prior to his bringing you here?"

Illegal substances? Ransom? And then she remembered. *Adam!* "He was at my house. He asked for something to drink." Fragments of the afternoon began piecing together. She remembered his asking for something to eat, and then for peppers. She was out of the living room for several minutes as she'd searched the cabinets.

"I strongly suspect that Ransom put something in your drink, Gwen."

"No, his brother. Adam. Adam Johnson." Gwen explained the events as she remembered them to her doctor.

The doctor wrote something on his chart. "There were traces of a narcotic in your system. We had to send it out to the lab for specifics. But how well do you know this Adam guy?"

Gwen opened her eyes with clarity for the first time since her hospital arrival. "Enough to know he drugged me."

60

It was a little before midnight when Ransom arrived at Pam's house in the south part of Los Angeles. He didn't hesitate to ring the bell. After what seemed like agonizing minutes but was actually only a few seconds, he rang it again.

"Who is it?" a voice shouted from inside.

"It's me, Pam. Ransom!"

The door opened quickly. "Ransom, what are you doing here?"

Ransom pushed past her and stormed into the house. "Where's Brea?" he asked, looking around.

"Ransom, what's the matter? Brea ain't here!"

Ransom pulled out his cell phone. "Pam, if you don't tell me where she is, I'm calling the police right now!"

Pam rushed over to Ransom and grabbed his hand. "Wait a minute, wait! Let me think for just a minute."

Ransom slowly lowered his arm but kept the cell phone in his hand. He stared hard at Pam. "She's got my daughter, Pam," he said quietly. "Where is she?"

"Okay, Ransom, just calm down a minute. You know Brea wouldn't hurt that girl. . . ."

"I don't know what Brea will do. Because before a few hours ago, I didn't think she'd move out of her apartment and leave town without saying a word!"

"She what? Oh, Lord . . ." Pam walked over to an end table against the wall and picked up her cordless phone. Like Ransom, she got voice mail. "Brea, this is your mom. Ransom is here and he's looking for Isis. If you don't call back in five minutes, he's calling the police. So call me, girl. What's wrong with you?" Pam slammed down the phone and began pacing the room.

"I told her not to do anything foolish," Pam said.

"What do you know, Pam?"

Pam sighed heavily and sat down. "Sit down, Ransom."

"I don't feel like sitting. I want to know where Isis is, that's all I want."

"Brea is so in love with you, Ransom, and she wants desperately for the three of you to be a family. You, her, and Isis. She called me today, crying and screaming about how you had become engaged to that . . . to Gwen. I've never heard her like that before. She just kept going on and on about how if y'all could just give your relationship another chance, she knows it will work. I know that Jake was pressuring her to move in with him, but it's you she wants.

"I know it's hard to hear this, Ransom, but Brea means well. A lot of how she is today is my fault. I spoiled her as a child, tried to make up for the fact she didn't have a father. And then with her looks and everything . . . I encouraged her to depend on that more than her mind, her intelligence. I showed her how her looks could get her places, and they *have*, Ransom! So yeah, she's spoiled and self-centered and a little bratty at times, but you and Brea were great together once.

"Now this is stupid, what Brea did, and I'm not trying to excuse it, not at all. But just try and understand, Ransom. The only reason she did it is to get your attention, and to get you away from Gwen. Just try to see it from her side, Ransom, that's all I ask. And think of your child, think of Isis and how great it would be if instead of rushing into a marriage with Gwen, you slow down, just for a minute, and give you and Brea a chance to make a home for the daughter you both love."

Ransom jumped up and headed for the door. He'd just opened it when the phone rang.

Pam answered it on the first ring. "Brea, where are you?"

Ransom walked over and snatched the phone out of Pam's hand. "Brea, I don't know what kind of games you've been playing, but . . . if you have any thoughts about us being together, then you need to bring my daughter over here, right now."

"Ransom, I'm sorry. I wasn't thinking."

"No, you never do." Ransom rarely raised his voice, but he did so now. "Where are you?"

"Ransom, Isis is fine. We've been having a wonderful time together. She's sleeping now."

Ransom took a deep breath. He felt about ready to explode and he knew such negative energy wasn't good for the situation. He felt with every fiber of his being that Brea was involved with whatever happened to Gwen. But it wasn't time to ask about that now. He had to get Isis back first. "Brea, where are you?" He enunciated each word crisply and clearly, as if he were talking to Isis when she was two.

Brea sighed audibly. "Promise you won't get mad at me?"

You mean more than I am already? I could break your neck right about now! Ransom took another deep breath and staunched the words that threatened to spill out of him. He knew it was imperative to not say anything that would provoke Brea, but to say whatever it took to get Isis back into his arms. "I'm not mad at you, Brea," he said finally. "I'm just worried about Isis. Where are you, baby?"

Brea's heart leapt as she heard him speak the endearment. "I'm with Jake. In Oakland. He's got a big house and Isis has her own room . . . and he's got all these video games. She loves it!"

Ransom clenched his fist, using every form of discipline he knew not to go off. The woman had taken his child to northern California—seven hours away by car, forty-five minutes by plane—without a word to him. *Breathe. One. Two. Release.* He called upon the meditative training he'd learned from the elders to calm him. "I'll take the first flight out in the morning. Give me Jake's address."

"That's okay, Ran. Jake will bring us back there."

"That'll take too long, baby. Just let me fly and pick her up." Ransom almost choked on the kindness he was trying to convey. But after he got back his princess? Then he had a few other choice words to share with Brea James.

61

Ransom left Pam's house and headed for the airport. He called the hospital as soon as he reached his car. Gwen was still there. They connected him to her room. "Hey, baby, sorry to wake you."

"I wasn't asleep. Where are you? The doctor said you were here."

"I was. How are you, Gwen?"

"They said I'll be fine. Adam drugged me, Ransom. He tried to . . ." Gwen couldn't finish the sentence.

"I know what that sorry muthafucka tried to do. Don't worry, baby, I'm gonna handle that business."

Gwen had never heard Ransom curse like that, or sound so angry. "Don't do anything crazy, Ransom. They examined me. He didn't do anything. Something must have scared him and . . . How did you find out about it? And how is it that you were here at the hospital?"

Ransom told Gwen about going to the house, arriving there just before Adam raped her.

"Oh my goodness, Ransom. I can't believe this. If you hadn't come . . ."

"Shh, baby, don't even think about it. Just concentrate on getting better."

"I feel better already. But the doctors want to keep me here overnight, just for observation. Can you come, Ransom? I need to see you right now."

"I can't, Butterfly. I'm on my way to Oakland."

"Oakland?'

"To get Isis."

"What?"

"It's a long story, but she's there with Brea and Jake. Brea left town after . . ." Ransom stopped before telling Gwen his theory, that Brea and Adam were in cahoots regarding what had happened to her.

"After what?"

"Nothing. Just get better . . . And do me a favor? If they release you before I get back, hire a limo and come to LA. Get a hotel room. I'll cover the cost. Just don't go back to your house."

"But, Ransom—"

"No buts, Butterfly. I need you to listen to me right now. There are some things I can't get into, but that you need to know. I'll get on the next plane after picking up Isis and meet you in LA, at the Sheraton. Promise me you'll do this."

"Okay, I promise."

"Good girl. I love you."

62

The first flight out of LAX to Oakland left at five minutes past six. Ransom bought a first-class ticket on the spot and strolled into the cabin. He was wide awake, even though his body hadn't known sleep in almost twenty-four hours. Just under an hour later, they arrived at Oakland International, and thirty minutes after that, he was in a rental car, punching the address Brea had given him into his iPhone's GPS.

The neighborhood was plush and private. Ransom casually took in the mansions as he looked at the numbers painted on the curb. Following the GPS directions, he took a right, then a left, climbing higher and higher into this community called Rio Vista nestled in the California hills.

Jake's mansion was at the very top of the hill. The huge brick home was surrounded by an alarmed wrought iron fence. The landscaping was impeccable, the front yard vast and sweeping, with various types of succulent bushes lining the circular drive. Ransom pulled his rental car up to the speaker and pushed the button.

"Ransom?" Brea asked.

"Yeah."

Seconds later, the heavy gate swung open and Ransom proceeded inside. He parked behind a Mercedes, which was parked behind an Escalade. Ransom thought of his daughter alone with a variety of strangers, football players most likely, and his blood began to boil again.

Brea opened the door timidly. She was wearing a pair of faded jeans and a top with no bra. She was barefoot, and looked as if she hadn't gotten much sleep herself. "I'm sorry," she said by way of greeting.

Ransom nodded. "Where's Isis?"

"She's asleep. Come on in."

Brea opened the door wide and allowed Ransom inside. Even in his anger, he noted the decor was high class and high tech. It had the feel of a bachelor pad, black leather furniture, lots of chrome and glass, and the prerequisite naked woman in the form of a fountain with water spouting from her upturned mouth.

"I'm really sorry, Ransom. I know I should have called you, but so much was happening."

"We can talk later, Brea. Right now, I just want my daughter, and then I have to get back home. I've got some workers waiting on me," he lied.

"You mean it? You're not mad?"

Ransom had never been angrier. But he knew now was not the time for confrontation. He was in another man's house, hours from home, with his daughter in the other room. He knew if Jake got in his face about anything, Ransom would hurt him. And now was not the time to go to jail.

"You shouldn't have done it, Brea."

"I know, baby, but . . . it's complicated. I was going to tell you about the move and then you went out of town and I didn't want to leave Isis in LA with my mother. Then Jake chartered a flight and we had to go. But Isis had a wonderful time, Ransom! Jake brought his son over and we invited a few other kids. They had . . . like a slumber party. Some of the mothers are still here. Those are the cars you see out front." But what Brea didn't tell him was that she was playing both ends against the middle—securing a future with Jake just in case things didn't work out with Ransom. Jake was ready to marry her, he'd practically said as much. Her moving to Oakland was to calm his insecurities where her child's father was concerned. Brea wanted Ransom, but Jake wanted Brea. Pam always told her to keep "an heir and a spare," a term used in royalty, but adopted by Brea's mother to mean a man in your bed and one who can climb in at a moment's notice.

Ransom looked at his watch. "I really have to go."

"Okay." Brea motioned for him to follow her as she walked through the massive living room, up a flight of stairs to what looked like the children's wing of the house. It was painted in bright colors and there was a mini game room at the top of the landing, complete with gumball and candy machines, and even a machine like those in stores and restaurants, where the kid puts in a dollar and tries to lift out a gift using a steel claw. There were a hodge-podge of bean bags scattered around the room, a huge flat-screen TV on the wall, and what looked like a hundred games in an entertainment center that also housed a variety of video games. It was easy for him to see why Isis might have had a good time.

Brea opened the door to a room and Ransom stepped inside. Isis lay sleeping on the bottom portion of a bunk bed shaped like a carriage. Another little girl slept in the top bunk. A sitting room with a couch upholstered in pink polka-dot leather sat off to the side, along with a dollhouse big enough for Isis to run through.

Brea shook Isis gently. "Isis?" Isis was sound asleep and didn't budge.

"That's okay, don't wake her." Ransom gently moved Brea out of the way and took his daughter in his arms. For one brief moment he stood there, hugging her tightly, and thanked the spirits that they had safely returned his child.

Brea didn't miss the emotion of the moment. The magnitude of what she had done began to sink in, as did the thought that the very thing she had done to bring her and Ransom together might take them farther apart. She wanted to ask about Gwen, but didn't dare. Instead, she placed a tentative hand on Ransom's shoulder. "I'm so sorry, baby." She then took her head and rested it on his arm, placing the other hand around their sleeping child.

Ransom immediately moved away, out of the room and down the stairs. He didn't even turn to tell a trailing, still talking Brea good-bye.

Ransom and Isis were almost to the airport when she woke up. She looked around with sleepy eyes. "Where's Mommy, Daddy?"

"She's at home, Princess. How are you?" Ransom had glanced at her often as she sat sleeping in the passenger seat, almost checking to make sure she was really beside him and not just in his imagination.

"I'm fine, Daddy. I had so much fun with Mommy and my new friends!"

"You did? Well, I'm glad, sweetie." Ransom waited a second and then asked, "You weren't scared on the plane, to come all this way with just Mommy?"

Isis shook her head vigorously. "No, Daddy, it was fun! Jake bought me a bunch of toys. And there was a little baby there, only three months old. We all got to hold him. I'm a big girl, huh, Daddy?"

"Yes, Princess. You are a big girl."

Isis continued to rattle on, telling her father everything that had happened that weekend, the games they had played, and how she had spent most of the time with a group of children, a nanny, and, from the sound of it, a chef who worked from Jake's home.

"Where was Jake?" Ransom asked.

"He went out. Mommy stayed with some of the other kids' mommies. They had a party downstairs while we played upstairs."

Ransom became quiet, his emotions roiling. On one hand, he was thankful his child was safe, and understanding of the fact that Brea loved her child. On the other, he could still strangle Brea for what she had done, how she could have potentially placed his daughter in danger. How well did she know all of the people around Jake? They'd only been dating a few months. And how was Brea involved in what happened to Gwen?

"Daddy?"

"Yes, Princess."

"Are you and Mommy going to get married?"

The question shocked Ransom, coming out of the blue as it did. He and Gwen had discussed how to tell

Isis about their engagement. They planned to do so together, on a family outing.

"No, Isis. Brea and I are not getting married. How do you feel about that?"

"But why not, Daddy? Mommy says she still loves you. Don't you love her?"

Ransom knew these were ideas that Brea had planted. The thought of using his child as a bargaining chip got Ransom pissed off all over again. But he kept his voice light.

"There are different ways to love, Princess," he said. "I love Brea because she is your mother, but not enough to live with her. Does that make sense to you?"

Isis placed a finger on the side of her face, thinking the question over in a way that belied her young years. "I guess so," she said at last. "I love Miss Gwen too. Do you love her enough for her to come and live with us?"

Ransom looked over and smiled at his daughter. "Yes, Princess. I love Miss Gwen that much."

63

Gwen was worried sick. Not because she was still in the hospital for the second day, but because she'd tried to reach Ransom and couldn't. She knew he'd returned from Oakland, and that Isis was fine. She also knew that he was livid concerning Adam, and that he felt an obligation to defend his woman and make Adam pay for what he did. She'd pleaded with him to let her file charges, to settle the matter in court. He'd ended the call abruptly, saying he'd talk to her later. That was three hours ago.

Gwen thought about Miss Mary, and was just getting ready to call her when Ransom walked through the door. He looked haggard, but Gwen saw no bumps or bruises and hoped that was a sign that a fight hadn't occurred. He walked over, hugged her, and threw a copy of the *Sienna Sun* on her lap. The headline hit her like a slap in the face: PRINCIPAL OF SIENNA ELEMENTARY ARRESTED.

Gwen's mouth dropped, and she began to read the article:

Adam Johnson, former football standout at Sienna
High and current principal at Sienna Elementary, was
arrested late last night and charged with second degree
burglary. Acting on a tip from a concerned neighbor,
police arrived at a home in the 700 block of Maple
Avenue, and found Mr. Johnson inside the residence,
which had been ransacked. Mr. Johnson was arrested
without incident.

Gwen looked at Ransom, her whole face a question
mark. "Miss Mary," Ransom said simply.

Gwen shook her head, as if to rid it from cobwebs.
She felt she hadn't thought straight since opening
the door to let Adam in on Monday afternoon.

"Miss Mary saw Adam running down the alley,"
Ransom explained. "She stayed by the window to try
and see where he'd go. That's why she didn't see me
take you out of the house. But it's a good thing she
stayed where she was because she saw Adam creep
back into the backyard and into the house. She tried
to call you on the home phone and when you didn't
answer, she called the police."

"That's crazy," Gwen said. "Why would he come
back and ransack the house? Why didn't he just get
his clothes and leave?"

"Who can know the mind of an asshole like my
brother?" Ransom said. "All I know is that jail is about
the safest place he could be right now." Ransom sat
down on the side of the bed and smoothed Gwen's
hair back away from her face. "How's my butterfly?"

"Much better. In fact, I don't know why I'm still
here. I keep telling them I'm fine, but they said Dr.
Rolette wanted to do one final check before they
released me. But there was an accident early this

afternoon and he's been tied up in surgery. The nurse was here right before you came, though. Said he should be here within the hour and then I can go. . . . I guess I'll have to go back there."

"No, you don't. You'll stay with me. I'll go get whatever you need right now and once you've recovered from everything, we'll figure out what to do with the house."

"I need to call Robert and tell him everything."

"And Chantay."

"She's probably ready to kill me. I bet my message box is full of her ranting and raving."

"Yes, and she'll be the first one you call when you get out of here."

"You know it."

A weary-looking Dr. Rolette walked into the room. "Sorry that you had to wait so long, Gwen," he said, looking at her chart. "You heard about the accident."

"Yes, hopefully everyone was all right."

Dr. Rolette looked at Ransom. "You know Carol Connors, right?"

"Yes."

"That's who we operated on. They were broadsided pretty badly when a car ran a red light and plowed into her."

Ransom and Gwen looked at each other. Ransom wasn't too fond of Carol at the moment, but he'd never wish any harm upon her. "Is she going to be okay?"

Dr. Rolette sighed. "We've got her and the little girl stabilized. They're both going to need major surgeries and are being transferred to Cedars-Sinai. As for the outcome? It's in God's hands."

"Kari?" Ransom and Gwen asked at the same time.

Kari was one of Gwen's brightest students, and had once been Isis's best friend. She cared for all of her students and, Kari's mother notwithstanding, she only wanted the best for her child.

"Her daughter was in the car?" Ransom continued. "It looks like they'll make it though, right?"

"Carol's injuries were worse. Such a senseless accident, simply caused by someone not paying attention to where he was going. And wouldn't you know he was the least hurt?" Doctor Rolette shook his head as he reached for Gwen's wrist to take her pulse. "As for you, young lady, I think you're going to be fine." He scanned her chart again. "All of your vitals are normal, your bloodstream is clean. I know you were ready to get out of here this morning, but we can't be too careful with a woman in your condition."

"You mean because of the aftereffects of the drug Adam gave me?"

Dr. Rolette looked from Ransom to Gwen. "No, Ms. Andrews, because of the aftereffects of having sexual intercourse. You're pregnant."

64

Gwen stared at the e-mail from the Pasadena School District. It seemed a lifetime ago that she'd sent them her résumé, the week after she and Chantay returned from Jamaica. After reviewing her information, they were e-mailing to request an interview. When she'd sent the résumé, this was exactly the outcome for which she'd hoped. Now, not only did she not know where she'd be teaching next year, she didn't know if she'd be teaching at all.

It had been three weeks since Adam's attempted rape and receiving the news that at the ripe old age of forty, Gwen was expecting her first child. Life had been a series of transitions and news flashes since then. For starters, Gwen had placed her mother's belongings in storage and moved in with Ransom. Adam had been terminated as principal of Sienna Elementary. Even with this news, Gwen had resigned her teaching position. Everyone knew that Adam had tried to break in to her house, and from the whispers and surreptitious looks she'd received on the few occasions she'd ventured out, they suspected there was more to the story. If Gwen had her way, no one would ever know how much more. What she and Ransom had discovered during what the hospital had thought was a routine release still sent chills down her spine.

"Okay," the nurse had said cheerfully, holding out a bag. "Here are your personal belongings."

"My personal belongings? I don't think I arrived with anything."

"Oh, not much. Just your bedspread and cell phone." With that, the nurse had smiled and left.

Gwen had dumped the bedspread out of the bag and retrieved the cell phone. Right away, she knew it wasn't hers. When Ransom came out of the bathroom, she asked him about it.

"Did you leave this at my house?" Gwen asked. "The night you came over and . . . rescued me?"

Ransom frowned as he took the phone. "No, this isn't mine. Where did you get it?"

"The nurse said it was tangled up in the bedspread."

Ransom and Gwen had a simultaneous lightbulb moment. *Adam.*

"Maybe that's why he ransacked the house," Gwen offered. "He was trying to find his phone."

Ransom flipped open the phone and began scrolling down the text messages. There were intermittent ones between Adam, Brea, Joanna, and Carol, but all of the last ones had been with Brea alone. His suspicions were instantly confirmed—she had known about Adam's twisted revenge plot. Ransom was about to destroy the phone when he noticed the camera button engaged. Instinctively, he pushed it to see what had been taken most recently. His hand shook as he viewed the images. When Gwen tried to look over his shoulder at what was obviously upsetting him, he'd pulled away from her and destroyed the phone with his bare hands. He'd been eerily quiet after that, as Gwen was being checked out of the hospital and during the drive home. Once she and Isis were safe in his home, he'd looked at Gwen somberly, kissed her, and said, "I need to handle something. I love you."

Gwen called his cell phone repeatedly to find out what was wrong with him. After he told her not to worry and ended the first call, her further attempts went directly to voice mail. What had he seen on Adam's cell phone? Then Gwen began to imagine, and became even more frightened for Ransom. She knew she'd arrived at the hospital wearing just her underwear. If Adam had taken pictures . . .

Ransom arrived at the county jail, located in Lancaster, and ran into Carlos. "Where is he?"

Unlike when Officer Carlos Lopez had responded to Gwen's nine-one-one and instead of a burglar, found his friend and ex-classmate looking for squirrels and helping an old lady, his latest call had resulted in arresting the man he'd just transported to jail. Upon seeing Ransom, and hearing the eerie calm in his voice, Carlos immediately became concerned. "Dude," Carlos said. "What's going on?"

"Adam. I need to see him."

Carlos had seen Ransom angry a time or two, and didn't like the vibe emitting from his friend. "He can't have visitors right now," he lied, actually not having any idea about Adam's status regarding visitors. "What's up with you, man?"

Ransom's eyes narrowed as he took in Carlos's countenance. He knew his friend wasn't telling the truth. "He dishonored my woman. Go back in there with me, Carlos. Help me get past the bars, man. I need to see him face to face."

"I can't do that, partner," Carlos said. "Think of your daughter, man. He ain't worth it, dog. Look, I'll do what I can to make sure he's in here for a minute. The sheriff owes me a couple favors, know what I'm sayin'? Go calm down, man. Love your girl, your daughter. Adam is where he belongs. Don't stoop to his level, son."

Ransom took several deep breaths to still his racing heart. He was like a pit bull, ready to tear up anything he got his hands on. But he knew Carlos was right. It would serve no purpose, other than the perverse satisfaction of seeing facial features rearranged, for Ransom to assault Adam right now.

"I'm your boy, right?" Carlos asked softly, as he pulled out his billy club and began tapping it against his hand.

Ransom nodded.

"Then go on home and handle your household. Trust me, partner, we got this."

Unable to concentrate on the e-mails she was reading, Gwen got up and went into the kitchen for a glass of orange juice. Her mind was still replaying the events of the past month, even as Ransom had encouraged her to try and forget the past, to focus on the future.

Gwen despised Adam for what he'd tried to do to her. Ransom refused to tell her what he'd seen on the camera phone, but Gwen wasn't stupid. It had to be shots of her. But why? Any answer that came to her mind was definitely not good. He could have taken the pictures for blackmail purposes, maybe put them on the Internet, who knows? Still, she wasn't happy to hear what happened to him shortly before his release from jail, that he'd been jumped by several inmates and severely beaten. According to Miss Mary, who'd overheard the conversation while waiting for a double vanilla latte at Kristy's, he was holed up somewhere in Los Angeles nursing his injuries, and that once the school year was over, Joanna—now three months pregnant—would join him there. The irony of their similar situations wasn't lost on Gwen, and it was with a tinge of sadness that she realized these babies, first cousins, would likely never know each other. Equally disturbing was Ransom's reaction to the serious assault on his brother. He'd simply shrugged, said "shit happens," and continued slicing vegetables for a stir fry.

The phone rang, and Gwen welcomed the interruption, especially when she saw who it was. "Hey, brother."

"Hey, mother-to-be. How's my favorite big sister?"

"Fool, I'm your only big sister."

"Doesn't make you any less my favorite. How's my little niece or nephew doing?"

"Fine, I guess. I'm only eight weeks, Robert, and since I haven't experienced any morning sickness or other symptoms, I sometimes wonder if I'm really pregnant at all."

"Don't tell me you went out and bought another pregnancy test."

Gwen laughed. Robert was one of only three

people she'd told that since getting the word from the hospital and having her first appointment with her ob-gyn, she'd still taken three at-home pregnancy tests, fearing that this whole episode was just her imagination and that at any moment she was going to wake up from the dream. "I think I almost believe it," Gwen finally answered. "Just one or two more . . ."

"I'll send you a box if you want," Robert said lovingly. "You've waited a long time for this, Gwen. I'm so happy for you. Just think. Our kids will grow up together."

"Wow, so many babies at once. There must be something in the water here in Sienna."

"Are you forgetting we live in Seattle?"

"Are you forgetting that you were here a few months ago checking on Mama?"

"Denise was already pregnant by then."

"Speaking of, how is little Lorraina? And how is Denise holding up?"

"She's good. We had natural childbirth this time. Denise seems to be recovering faster."

"It's only been two weeks. You tell that girl to take it easy," Gwen said.

Robert laughed. "Okay, sis, I'll do that."

"I love you, baby brother."

"I love you, big sis."

Gwen hung up from Robert and dialed her mother. "Hey, Mama."

"Hey, Gwen. You still pregnant?" Lorraine's tittering laughter floated through the phone.

"Last time I checked," Gwen responded, smiling. Lorraine was the third person she'd told about her paranoia, after confiding in Chantay. Ransom already knew—he was the one she sent to buy the at-home tests.

"I'm so happy for you, baby. You can check all you want to, but you're going to be fine. Esther believes in that astrology nonsense, and she said you were going to have a healthy baby boy. I don't believe in it, mind you, but that's what she said.

"We're still on for a girls' day out tomorrow, right?"

"Actually, Mama, someone will be joining us. I want you to meet Ransom."

"I'd love to meet this man who's put pep back in your step. But you'll have to have me home by five. I have a date."

"You what? Mama, have you been taking your medication?"

"Trust me, daughter, I have all my senses about me. Your mother and her man friend are getting serious. Guess you would call it 'going steady.' You'll meet him tomorrow."

"Wow, Mama. This is different. Maybe you can invite your friend along and we'll double date, how's that?"

"Oh, Lord. Now I'm contemplating introducing my sixty-some-year-old boyfriend to my daughter while meeting her twenty-something fiancé. I must be losing my mind!"

"Times they are a'-changing," Gwen agreed.

After another thirty minutes of conversation, Gwen put down the phone in disbelief. Her sixty-three-year-old mother had a boyfriend. No wonder she laughed so much these days. And Gerald, Gwen learned, had just gotten yet another promotion. All in all the Andrews family had a lot to be thankful for, starting with the heartbeat beneath Gwen's still-flat belly.

65

It was the middle of May and the weather couldn't have been more perfect. Neither could the setting. Gwen took in the gardens of The Willows Desert Inn. When she and Ransom had decided to move up their wedding because of the pregnancy, their first thought had been a quickie wedding in Las Vegas. And then Ransom had mentioned Palm Springs, where their love had blossomed, and Gwen immediately knew it was the perfect place.

The ceremony had been short and simple, the wedding party small. Gwen wore a pink chiffon knee-length dress with Lorraine's lucky butterfly brooch prominently displayed on the bodice. Ransom looked stunning in a white tux. Chantay and Carlos were maid of honor and best man, and Isis had served as a "miss of honor" and special witness. Miss Lorraine and Miss Mary were beside themselves with the beauty of their surroundings, and had spent much of the time since the "I do's" walking around the beautiful grounds and catching up on the latest gossip. Lorraine's beau, Frank, was content to sit and watch the festivities while nursing a glass of brandy, a no-no at Sunrise Place, but an indulgence Gwen had over-looked. Robert, Denise, Robert Jr., two-month-old Lorraina, Gerald and his wife, Sandy, Derek (who was back with Chantay following a brief, post-island break-up), Carlos's wife, Lupa, Ransom's parents, and a few employees from Blake Construction rounded out those in attendance. All were happily enjoying a sit-down dinner of Chateaubriand, lobster, roasted potatoes, and spring vegetables.

Gwen and Ransom walked from table to table, per-sonally thanking everyone for sharing their special day. They arrived at the table with Derek, Chantay, Robert, and Denise just as Chantay was being her usual life-of-the-party self.

"I don't mean no disrespect, Denise," she said around a mouthful of lobster. "But that man there was supposed to be *my* baby daddy."

"Chantay," Robert warned.

"Oh no," Denise said, laughing. "Do go on. I want to hear all the old dirt."

"Baby, I got some for you," Chantay said. "Like that time Robert tried to sneak in the girls' locker room and locked his fool self in there. Or what about when you forgot to lotion your legs before that basketball game with the LA Jaguars? Girl, his legs were so ashy that if the scoreboard had gone out, they could have written the numbers on his thighs!"

The table erupted in laughter.

"I'm telling you, the brother was black from the waist up and white from the waist down!"

Ransom and Gwen joined the laughter, made pleas-antries, and moved on. They stopped to chat with

Carlos and Lupa, who were acting like lovebirds in the romantic setting.

"It was a beautiful wedding," Lupa said to Gwen. "Thank you for inviting us."

"I understand Ransom and Carlos went to school together. I'll have you guys over for dinner, as soon as we get settled."

"Do you think you'll like living here in Palm Springs?"

Ransom pulled Gwen to his side and kissed her temple. "We're going to love it!" he replied.

Gwen and Ransom had talked about relocating shortly after the Adam incident. Then, as fate would have it, Ransom's company won a huge bid to build a resort in the area, a project that would take at least three years. The beautiful and laid back community would be perfect for Isis and one where Gwen could find work in a year or so, when she decided to rejoin the workforce. When they toured a brand-new, four-bedroom villa with outdoor pool, Jacuzzi, professional-sized barbeque pit and basketball and tennis courts, they knew they'd found their new home. Finding a plush, private, ten-unit assisted living facility for Lorraine and Frank, located just ten minutes from their subdivision, sealed the deal.

Miss Mary and Miss Lorraine were coming around the walkway just as Ransom and Gwen reached where they'd been sitting.

"Miss Mary, are you still looking for a boyfriend?" Ransom teased.

"Hmph. Gwen better not leave your side for too long," Miss Mary replied as she sidled up to Ransom and placed a brazen arm around his waist. "Or else I'll be done found one!"

Ransom hugged her tightly and kissed her cheek. Miss Mary blushed profusely. "Aw, get on, now," she said, pushing away from him. "You 'bout to start something." Then she lowered her voice. "You heard about Carol, huh?"

"That she's paralyzed from the waist down?" Ransom nodded. "But they think she might walk again. . . ."

"Ms. Disney talked to her parents, who remain optimistic," Miss Mary replied. "Meanwhile, they are left to raise that grandbaby. Not so easy to do when you're nigh onto seventy."

Talking about Kari and her mother made Ransom think about Brea. It was a shame that he couldn't feel safe with her taking his child and spending time on their own. But she was still smarting from the verbal thrashing he gave her once Isis and Gwen were safe, including the command to never take his child *any-where* without his prior permission. Until everything was official through the courts, and he felt he could trust her, it was back to supervised visits only once again.

Isis came up and pulled on Gwen's dress. "I'm getting sleepy, Mommy Too." Gwen smiled down at the little girl she loved like a daughter. On their drive down to Palm Springs, Isis had made up the name "Mommy Too" for her stepmother, and Gwen was still amused by it.

Ransom picked up Isis and hugged her to him. "I think your grandma is about ready to go, too. You're going to have fun in Phoenix. But will you miss me?"

Isis nodded.

"I'll miss you too, Princess. Now, before you go, aren't you forgetting something?"

Isis put her head down on her father's shoulder, then pulled it back up with a jerk. "Oh, yeah!"

She hurried out of her father's arms and took off toward Ransom's mom.

"What's that about?" Gwen asked.

Ransom simply smiled. "You'll see."

"Ransom . . ."

Before Gwen could grill him, the clinking of crystal turned everyone's attention to Carlos.

"A toast if I could," he said, holding up his glass. The other guests found their glasses and held them high. A waiter appeared, handing Ransom and Gwen fresh glasses of champagne. "To the most honorable man I know, and the warmest, most kindhearted woman on the planet. You can buy beauty here in la-la land, beauty on the outside. But these two people have it where it counts most—on the inside. I love you, man," Carlos said to Ransom. "And I wish you, Gwen, Isis, and the baby on the way all the happiness in the world."

"Hear, hear," the crowd responded, amid clinking glasses and murmurs of approval. A few other toasts followed, the cake was cut, and then Isis walked to the front carrying a hatbox.

She took the microphone from Carlos and turned to address the crowd like a seasoned pro. "One day, Daddy asked me if I wanted a queen to come live with us. And I asked him if I would still be the princess."

A spattering of laughter filtered through the garden.

"And then he asked me if I thought Gwen could wear the crown. And I said . . . *yes*! Then he asked me if I could keep it a secret until he was ready to give her the crown. And I said 'I promise.' So now . . ."

Ransom walked over and held the bottom of the box while Isis pulled off the top. "Remember that day when y'all were headed to LA, when Isis was upset and you asked me what I'd said? Well, Butterfly, you just got your answer."

Tears came to Gwen's eyes as a beautiful tiara, encrusted with Swarovski crystals and a row of pink diamonds, was pulled out of the pink velvet box. "For my queen," he said simply. The butterfly became Gwenderella as he gently placed the crown on her head. As if on cue, the sun began setting behind a purple-tinged mountain. It was time for the first dance.

"Mrs. Blake," Ransom said as he reached out a hand to Gwen.

"Mr. Blake," Gwen responded, as she took his hand lightly.

He swept her in his arms and they moved as one, letting the lilting voice of Al Jarreau take them into the bliss of the moment. They were here, together, married, expecting . . . a family. Ransom had found his queen, and Gwen, her king, knight, protector, provider, lover, and redeemer all rolled into one.

"Teach me," Gwen whispered as the song ended. Her heart flip-flopped as she thought of the night ahead, a night in which they would once again recreate the magic of their first coming together, even while they soared to new heights of ecstasy. As she danced around the garden in the arms of her man, there were two things, no, three, that Gwendolyn Marie Blake knew for sure. One, her life had indeed begun at forty. Two, it had begun with some unexpected lessons from a younger lover; and three, when it came to matters of the heart . . . you are never too old to learn.

Want more?

Turn the page for Zuri Day's
Body by Night

Available now wherever books are sold

Turn the page for an excerpt
from *Body by Night* . . .

I

D'Andra Smalls gazed at the entrance to Bally Total Fitness as if the doors led to a gas chamber. Her dread at entering couldn't have been much worse than that of a woman doomed to die, since that's exactly what she thought she'd do the minute she positioned her hefty behind on a treadmill.

With a slight twinge of guilt, she eyed the empty spicy-hot pork rind bag that along with hospital memos, a Bally pamphlet, a workout towel and a bottle of water occupied the tan-colored passenger seat of her recently purchased maroon Suburban. Her favorite snack had tasted good going down, especially with the sixteen-ounce diet soda that accompanied it, but now she wasn't so sure about the wisdom of this hastily eaten pre-workout meal. Her stomach growled its disagreement and called for more, still angry from smelling but not tasting the bacon, eggs and fried potatoes D'Andra had fixed her mother for breakfast. In stark contrast, D'Andra had opted for a single can of Slimfast, just as her co-worker Elaine had suggested. Elaine had recently lost twenty of the fifty pounds she was trying to shed after having two babies in as many years. Seeing how much better her friend looked had been a motivator for D'Andra to lose weight. Not to mention the most literal wake-up call she'd experienced in her twenty-nine years: recently waking up to find herself in Martin Luther King Hospital's emergency room.

Thinking about that brush with death reenergized D'Andra. Picking up the towel and bottled water, she looked again toward what instead of her doom was hopefully a pathway to good health and a noticeable waistline, both of which were currently lacking. Just then two size-fours walked into the gym, laughing, talking and looking fit as fiddles. One, a curvy Latina with thick black hair, could have modeled in a commercial on how to *gain* weight. Her friend, a rail-thin blonde who D'Andra thought could blow away in a two-mile-an-hour wind, looked picture perfect in her tight-fitting top and boy shorts.

D'Andra sighed and dropped the towel back on the seat. She rolled down the window, perched her elbow on the doorframe, and rested her head on her fist. *This is never going to work,* she thought with resignation. Her mother's earlier question, posed as D'Andra prepared to leave the house, echoed in her mind. *What do you look like taking yo fat butt to a gym? People who go there are already in shape.* It looked like her mother was right.

"Maybe I'll come back tomorrow," D'Andra said out loud, pulling the seat belt back over her sizable belly. She should have known that Saturdays would be busy. Especially now, the beginning of the year, when millions of people had undoubtedly made resolutions to lose weight. The Sunday crowd, especially if she came in the morning around church time, should be much lighter. At least this was the rationalization she used for backing out of her workout. "That's it. I'll come back tomorrow with Elaine."

"How can you leave before you even get started?" a male voice asked. The sound was as deep as the ocean and its silkiness matched the flawless onyx skin stretched over the perfectly sculpted six-pack abdomen filling her seated, eye-level view. So far, the only thing D'Andra could find wrong with the man standing next to her car door was his timing, walking by at the exact moment she was blabbering to herself.

"Uh, excuse me?" D'Andra stuttered, shielding her hazel eyes from the sun as she looked up. Granted, she garnered a fair share of testosterone-laced attention but rarely from someone who looked like the man standing here. He was gorgeous.

"Didn't I hear you tell yourself you were leaving? Looks like you haven't been in yet."

"I haven't but—"

"No buts," Six-Pack stated firmly, his hand reaching for the car handle and opening the door. "Come on, doll, I'll walk you inside."

D'Andra was horrified. After seeing America's next top models walk inside the gym, not to mention the ebony Adonis holding her door, she felt inadequately prepared to exercise and inappropriately dressed in her hot pink oversized T-shirt and black leggings. How in the world had she imagined herself cute when she tried the outfit on in Ashley Stewart's dressing room? Now, she thought she looked like the proverbial pink elephant getting ready to walk into the room.

"I like Betty Boop," Six-Pack said, nodding toward

the cartoon character gracing the front of D'Andra's T-shirt. "That color looks good on you."

D'Andra exited the car but made no move toward the gym. "Thanks," she answered, convinced he had said that just to be nice.

Still, she became self-conscious of how Betty rose and fell with her 42DDs every time she took a breath, which was more often than normal since the man in front of her was taking her very breath away. This fine specimen was definitely not good for her blood pressure. D'Andra guessed that if she wasn't careful she'd end up back in emergency before midnight. Yet she risked her health to take another look at the dark chocolate standing next to her. Yes, she quickly deduced, he was still as fine as he was the first time she saw him, a whole sixty seconds ago.

"My name's Night. What's yours?"

"D'Andra."

"D'Andra . . . that's a pretty name."

"Thanks." D'Andra knew her simple, monosyllabic answers were belying her intelligence but any form of smart, casual banter eluded her. A thousand thoughts of things that might impress him ran through her head but not one of them came out. Sometimes it took her a minute or two to warm up to people, but it wasn't like her to act shy. This man had her all discombobulated.

Then she remembered something. She hated men. Something else, or rather someone else, came to mind. Charles, the reason she hated them. What did her friend Elaine call them? *Walking dirt,* in reference to the biblical story of God forming man from the dust of the earth. D'Andra used this analogy to try and temper the flutters in her stomach. But she couldn't lie to herself. If this man beside her was *terra firma* then she'd like nothing better than to get her hands dirty.

But that's exactly what she'd done with Charles, literally, when she spent two grueling weekends—two weekends more than she should have—helping him with his so-called professional cleaning service. The dirt she'd cleaned from the office floors was nothing compared to the mental and emotional filth left behind by the dirty deed she witnessed the night of their breakup. D'Andra stopped the memories abruptly, before pictures from that nightmare night could crystallize. But that wisp of a memory had done the trick: stilled the flutters and renewed her resolve. She hated men. But the least she could do was be polite.

"You said your name is Night?"

"Yeah, that's what they call me."

Ignoring the obvious, she continued. "Why do they call you that?"

Night laughed. "You can't guess?"

"I might guess it's your skin color," she said honestly. "But that could be an offensive assumption."

"It could be," he admitted. "But in this case it would be at least partly accurate. Skin color, scrawny body, big eyes and a small head; my friends back in Texas said I looked like a type of worm, a night crawler, and stuck me with the label when I was around six years old."

D'Andra stifled a laugh. "That's mean," she said while trying to imagine scrawny or small ever describing the man before her.

"It is, but you know how kids are. Then my aunt started calling me Night. But she said it as a term of endearment, saying that the blacker the berry, the sweeter the juice. I started wearing my color like a badge of honor. The final approval came from Sabrina, the prettiest second-grader in all of Dallas. She declared to the playground in the middle of recess that Night was the 'coolest name ever.' That did it. I went from pitiful to popular before the back-to-class bell rang. You might say I grew into my moniker, which now has a whole different meaning."

His voice dropped to a near whisper. "I do some of my best work at night."

D'Andra smiled but remained silent. *Is this brown sugar brotha actually flirting with me?*

"I meant working out, of course, in my home gym." *No, he's not flirting.* "Of course."

"What else could I have meant, right?"

What else indeed! D'Andra felt Night's eyes on her but refused to meet his gaze. She could just about imagine what type of work he was referring to and since it had been a while since a man had gainfully employed any baby-making skills in her bedroom, felt it best not to speculate too long. Besides, the long lashes surrounding those dark brown orbs were bringing back her flutters and making her forget to hate.

"Do you work here?" she asked, nodding toward the gym as she consciously changed the subject.

"I teach a kickboxing class on Wednesday nights, but other than that, their environment is too restrictive for me. I don't like to follow rules." He licked a set of thick, perfectly proportioned lips. "I am a personal trainer though and pretty soon I'll have my own gym. I've got my eye on a prime spot in a strip mall over in Ladera Heights."

"The one with Magic Johnson's Starbucks and T.G.I. Friday's?"

Night nodded. "That's the one. The mall gets good traffic, customers who work out and care about their health. Plus, people who live in that area will more than likely be able to afford my rates. My prices will be slightly higher than some of the chains but I believe my customized workout programs, personal consultations and full-service approach to fitness will make it worth the higher fee."

D'Andra nodded but again remained silent.

"I'm sorry," Night said, realizing he was going on and on about his dream. "Get me started about my business and I can talk all day."

"I don't mind. I like your enthusiasm. I'm really into fitness too. I mean, I'm not fit yet but I'm determined to get there."

Night raised his eyebrows. "Oh, really?"

"What do you mean *oh really*?" she asked with as much attitude as she could muster while looking at an unexpected display of dazzling white teeth against his dark skin. She thought about Night's nickname and concluded that it suited him. Only someone as fine as he was could pull off a name like that though, and not have it sound funny or insulting. On him it was neither; it fit perfectly. But that didn't mean he could talk to her any kind of way!

"What I mean is, you could have fooled me," he said, matching her attitude with his own. He'd seen that façade before, attitude that covered fear, and in her case, fear of working out or worse, of failing. He wasn't known as the motivator for nothing and decided to put his skills to work.

"If you were really serious about getting fit, we'd be in the gym by now. Let's go."

Before D'Andra could react, Night gently grabbed

her elbow and steered her toward the doors. She
didn't know whether to be pissed or impressed. On
one hand, who did this stranger think he was to treat
her like this? On the other hand, he was right. She'd
been in no hurry to go into the gym and while she was
genuinely interested in health and fitness, she'd been
even more interested in delaying her own, happy to
pass the time talking about nicknames. And truth be
told, she liked the firm, authoritative way Night had
taken control of the situation. She'd probably never
let him know it but his actions were a welcome change
from those around her who were content to let her do
everything: family, co-workers, her sorry ass ex-
boyfriend and backstabbing former best friend.

D'Andra shifted her thoughts. She didn't want to
think about any of them right now. While lying hori-
zontal and staring into bright white hospital lights,
D'Andra decided life was too short to pay attention
to or worry about a-holes. She needed to focus on
making herself happy, and that involved flipping the
script on almost every thing in her life. Joining a gym
was the first of many changes she'd vowed would
happen this year, and getting in shape just part of the
plan to turn her life around.

She listened as Night continued to make small talk,
asking what she did for a living, about where she grew
up. *Maybe this man can help it happen,* she thought. But
could she be around him on a regular basis and not
fall in lust? Lost in thought, D'Andra's foot caught in
the door's rubber jamb and she stumbled into the
hard body that was the source of her distraction.

"Careful now. You don't want to hurt yourself
before you even get started."

D'Andra froze against Night's hard frame. Physical

injury was a possibility she hadn't considered. With a strenuous full-time job at a nursing home and physical rehabilitation facility, and an equally demanding mother who mistook her daughter for a personal maid, she couldn't afford to get sidelined.

"I never considered hurting myself," she said, forcing herself away from Night's warm body and taking a step backward, out the door. "Maybe I'd better not . . ."

Night stopped D'Andra's retreat with a firm hand. "Come on now, you'll be fine. I'll take care of you, doll, all right? So stop trippin' and yes, the pun is intended."

Once inside the gym, Night walked a couple steps ahead of her and approached the turnstile. In that instant she took in his close-cropped hair, wide shoulders, strong muscular legs, and a butt that looked as hard as it did round, even encased as it was in baggy pants that rode just below what she later saw was an inward navel. Then and there she determined it his best feature, the best bootylicious she'd ever seen. His tight red T-shirt had been ripped to show off the perfect set of abs that had caught her attention from the start. The arm that had guided her through the door was thick and strong, his Nike shoes long and wide. D'Andra gulped. Nobody had to tell her twice about the meaning of a man with big feet . . .

Night's physique had shifted D'Andra's attention from her body to his, but only for a moment. The sights and sounds inside the gym quickly brought back her purpose for being there, to get in shape, something that now seemed impossible as she looked at all the fit bodies around her. Not one person looked more than ten pounds overweight, twenty tops; there was definitely no one in there big as she was. Her heart sank. She wished Elaine were here. It seemed simple enough

when, at her co-worker's urging, she'd signed up online.
Then it had been easy, fun even. But where was Elaine
now, when she needed her? Home nursing two kids
with the flu. How she'd allowed her friend to talk her
into coming by herself, she'd never know.

Night turned to see D'Andra still standing near the
door. "Where's your card?"

"Card?"

"Your ID to get into the gym." Night held up the
card he'd just scanned.

"I don't have one. I just joined online a couple
days ago."

Night motioned to a young man working behind
the counter, even as he walked over and once again
placed a reassuring hand on D'Andra's elbow. She
stiffened. *Why does he keep touching me?* she thought.
Didn't the man know he was in danger? It had been
almost six months since she'd had sex and her kitty
had been meowing ever since her day turned to Night.

"She needs an ID," Night told the worker.

D'Andra once again forced her mind away from
sensual thoughts. She needed to get ahold of herself,
though truth be told, she'd rather that Night got
ahold of her. But she knew she wasn't ready for another relationship. She couldn't expect someone else
to love her until she learned to love herself. That's
what she'd read in a book on relationships Elaine
had given her. And while she was working on it and
making progress, she wasn't there yet. Until she was,
men were off limits.

"Hey, Night; what's going on, buddy?" A jovial,
handsome man with a tanned face, thick brown hair,
and a hoop hanging from a pierced brow asked as he

joined the worker behind the counter. He and Night did a soul brothers' handshake.

"Nothing to it, Marc. Just here to help my friend D'Andra, uh . . ." Night paused and looked questioningly at D'Andra.

"Smalls. D'Andra Smalls."

"Yes, here to help my friend D'Andra Smalls get her workout on."

D'Andra warmed at Night's words. Her last name had always been a hindrance, like a bad joke fate had played. Her surname was the only thing about her that was little, and ever since she could remember she'd been teased about this fact. But Night breathed her last name like a song; as if it was a promise instead of a lie.

"You ready for your picture?"

D'Andra looked at Night as if he'd cursed. "Oh no, I don't do pictures."

"You have to take one for your ID," Marc interjected. He pointed to a spot at the end of the counter. "Just stand over there."

In that moment, D'Andra wished Night gone. How could she stand there and pose with a man like him staring at her? *This is stupid! Why did I listen to Elaine? Coming here was a big mistake.* These thoughts whirled in D'Andra's head as she walked to the end of the counter and turned around.

"Now, doll, don't stand there looking like you're about to get shot," Night coaxed. "Let me see that pretty smile."

D'Andra willed herself to not be self-conscious. Then, for some unknown reason, she imagined Night's hard bare-naked ass, the one she'd admired as he stood at the counter, being the picture on the back of his ID card. His butt was surely as unique as a fingerprint; God couldn't have sculpted that master-piece twice. She stopped short of laughing out loud, but showed almost all thirty-two pearly whites as the camera flashed.

Look For These Other
Dafina Novels

If I Could
0-7582-0131-1

by Donna Hill
$6.99US/**$9.99**CAN

Thunderland
0-7582-0247-4

by Brandon Massey
$6.99US/**$9.99**CAN

June In Winter
0-7582-0375-6

by Pat Phillips
$6.99US/**$9.99**CAN

Yo Yo Love
0-7582-0239-3

by Daaimah S. Poole
$6.99US/**$9.99**CAN

When Twilight Comes
0-7582-0033-1

by Gwynne Forster
$6.99US/**$9.99**CAN

It's A Thin Line
0-7582-0354-3

by Kimberla Lawson Roby
$6.99US/**$9.99**CAN

Perfect Timing
0-7582-0029-3

by Brenda Jackson
$6.99US/**$9.99**CAN

Never Again Once More
0-7582-0021-8

by Mary B. Morrison
$6.99US/**$8.99**CAN

Available Wherever Books Are Sold!

Check out our website at www.kensingtonbooks.com.